The Psychiatric Novels of Oliver Wendell Holmes

The Psychiatric Novels
of Oliver Wendell Holmes

ABRIDGMENT, INTRODUCTION

AND PSYCHIATRIC ANNOTATIONS BY

CLARENCE P. OBERNDORF, M.D.

CLINICAL PROFESSOR OF PSYCHIATRY

COLUMBIA UNIVERSITY

Second Edition, Revised and Enlarged

GREENWOOD PRESS, PUBLISHERS
WESTPORT, CONNECTICUT

Copyright 1943, 1946, by Columbia University Press

Originally published in 1943
by Columbia University Press, New York

Reprinted with the permission
of Columbia University Press

First Greenwood Reprinting 1971

Library of Congress Catalogue Card Number 72-156193

SBN 8371-6142-8

Printed in the United States of America

FOREWORD TO THE FIRST EDITION

IN PREPARING a paper entitled "Oliver Wendell Holmes—a Precursor of Freud," I found it desirable to read *Elsie Venner, The Guardian Angel,* and *A Mortal Antipathy,* Holmes's three protagonistic "medicated novels." These novels present essentially in fictional form complex psychiatric situations made more vivid by backgrounds reflecting the standards, customs, and ideology of the last half of the nineteenth century. The family relationships portrayed not only helped to produce the neurotic manifestations but at the same time kept them alive.

The study of situations involving medical and psychiatric problems in novels is not uncommon. Some are presented in the form of confessions, as the famous self-revelation of Jean Jacques Rousseau, or in a letter to a psychiatrist, as in Marcel Prevost's *His Mistress and I,* or in deliberate psychoanalytic studies, as the recent phantasy-drama *The Lady in the Dark,* or as a report of personal experiences in an actual psychoanalysis such as "Ghostly Father, I Confess," published in the April, 1942, number of *Harper's Bazaar.*

It is small wonder that the novels of Holmes, especially *The Guardian Angel* and *A Mortal Antipathy,* found little acclaim when they appeared. The average reader discovered in their melodramatic qualities the commonplaces of the second-rate fiction writers of the period—very likely he skipped over the heavier philosophical and psychological paragraphs. If these passages received any of his attention they must have appeared as technical and uninteresting as clinical case reports. Many portions of Holmes's stories make dull reading, with their wordy, stereotyped and old-fashioned dialogue and

the repetition of certain character types almost unchanged
in each of the novels. To add to the monotony, in each story
Holmes has followed a similar plan of treatment and resorted to well-worn models for the introduction of the setting
and the erection of the plots.

Nevertheless these dated novels seemed of sufficient importance as psychiatric and analytic studies of neuroses to
warrant their re-presentation to sociologists and physicians.
So I resorted to a recent device of abridging novels for the
reader who wishes to acquaint himself quickly with the central
theme and the background on which it is developed. John T.
Morse, Jr., in his authoritative biography of Holmes, apolo-
gizing for the shortcomings of Holmes as a novelist, remarks
in connection with *The Guardian Angel:* "Take a pencil,
read carefully and mark on the margin every striking sentence.
You will see how closely the marks follow each other; then
you will have ocular demonstration of what the volume
holds."

In making the condensations, I soon found that my pencil
had a psychiatric point. Thus an intentional emphasis has
been bestowed upon the medical and psychiatric elements
in these stories at the expense of descriptions of the New England scene, prosaic conversation reflecting local opinion, and
the developing details of the banal plots. This has resulted
in a somewhat distorted presentation of the novels but it dis-
closes a new aspect of Holmes, uncovering his psychological
originality and psychiatric insight. On the other hand certain
portions have been retained because of their homely wisdom
and their flavor of Holmes's wit and charm.

Many of the passages which my pencil underscored were
so anticipatory and far-sighted, so cogent and valid in psychiatric thought today that I could not refrain from making
comments upon them here and there. I had thought that the

stories, with the selectivity of their condensation, should speak for themselves but friendly readers to whom I first submitted the manuscript all encouraged, even insisted upon, longer and more frequent notes.

The result has been a disproportion in the amount of space given to annotation. This I think adds interest to the work as a psychiatric study. The notes may also add a value which some of my psychiatric friends actively engaged in teaching medical psychiatry first pointed out to me. It was suggested that this study might serve to introduce undergraduate medical students to the subject of psychiatry and that later in the course of instruction, both in schools of medicine and schools for social work, it could be used as collateral reading to psychiatric textbooks.

Holmes's novels in their original form filled from three hundred pages (A Mortal Antipathy) to five hundred pages (Elsie Venner). The condensations here offered represent approximately one eighth to one tenth of the text. The printing of the book has been so arranged that the condensations which retain Holmes's original wording are above the line of any given page and my annotations are below the line. The summary of those passages in the novels which I have omitted but which are necessary to preserve the continuity of the stories are set in italics.

The liberty I have taken with Holmes's work might have incensed the amiable, fiery autocrat of the "Breakfast-Table," but I hope that any possible detraction from his literary reputation will be compensated by the extension and perpetuation of his fame as a humanitarian and as a psychiatrist.

I wish to express my thanks to Houghton Mifflin and Company of Boston, publisher of all of Holmes's works, for permission to abridge the Riverside Edition of Elsie Venner (1858–59), The Guardian Angel (1867), and A Mortal An-

tipathy (1885), and to W. W. Norton and Company of New York for permission to quote from Ernest Jones, *Nightmare, Witches, and Devils* (1931).

Finally I wish to acknowledge my deep indebtedness for suggestions of arrangement and notes especially to Dr. Phyllis Greenacre, Dr. Leland Hinsie, and Dr. Paul Goolker, and to the late Dr. Isador Coriat, Dr. Iago Galdston, and Dr. Clara Thompson.

C. P. OBERNDORF

New York
March 1, 1943

FOREWORD TO THE SECOND EDITION

THE INTEREST aroused by this book has been as gratifying to me as it was unexpected. It brought forth a great number of letters from persons whose main interest is in literature, medicine, and sociology. The letters called my attention to errors which I have been glad to correct, and also contained welcome suggestions for clarifying certain of the notes and expanding others. I have attempted to meet these ideas in this second edition and take this opportunity of acknowledging a debt for their helpfulness to the readers and friends of the first.

C.P.O.

New York
March 6, 1946

CONTENTS

INTRODUCTION: HOLMES, FREUD, AND DY-
NAMIC PSYCHIATRY   1

ELSIE VENNER: A STORY OF SCHIZOPHRENIA   20

THE GUARDIAN ANGEL: HYSTERIA IN AN ADO-
LESCENT GIRL   112

A MORTAL ANTIPATHY: A YOUNG MAN'S MORBID
FEAR OF WOMEN [GYNOPHOBIA]   200

BIBLIOGRAPHICAL REFERENCES   265

INDEX TO INTRODUCTION AND NOTES   269

INTRODUCTION

HOLMES, FREUD, AND DYNAMIC PSYCHIATRY

OLIVER WENDELL HOLMES was one of the favored few who are born into a setting of maximum privilege and opportunity. His parents were connected with the most influential families of that select group in Cambridge and Boston to which he later gave the name of Brahmins. His education was carefully guided into the best channels, from the time he entered elementary school until he graduated from Harvard Medical School in 1831 and finished the coveted post-graduate medical studies in Europe under the famous masters of Paris. Holmes was one of the fortunate few who are capable of making the most of the rare advantages offered to them.

In 1871 Holmes, just turning sixty, had reached a position of distinction attained by few other physicians, American or European. In the academic Cambridge, then regarded as the fountainhead of American literature and learning, he had become an arbiter whose word of praise sometimes decided the destiny of young authors who flocked to this seat of culture. The brisk, small-statured, "Laughing Doctor," as Holmes was called, had become something more than an arbiter—a liberal, generous, and beloved autocrat.

At this time Holmes was also rounding out a distinguished career as a physician and teacher of medicine. It included some ten years as an active practicing physician in Boston until 1849, the professorship of physiology and anatomy at Harvard from 1847 to 1882, and a long service as dean of the faculty of medicine at this famous university. His lectures had become renowned because of his learning, wit, wisdom, and progressiveness. Already, in 1843, at the age of thirty-four, his fame had become secure. Almost at the outset of his career he made a contribution to science which would have assured him a permanent place among the pioneers of medicine had his lifework ended then, namely, his essay "On the Contagiousness of Puerperal Fever." [1]

The demonstration of the contagious nature of puerperal fever was shared by Holmes and Semmelweis of Austria. The latter has been hailed throughout Europe for this revolutionary discovery, although he published his observations four years after Holmes. Holmes was compelled to face strong opposition to the new theory from reactionary New England colleagues but did not have to meet the bitter antagonism and suffering which Semmelweis endured in Vienna. Ostracism and persecution lent to Semmelweis "the aura of a martyr." On the other hand, in the career of the many-sided Holmes, the observations cencerning puerperal fever assumed the place of an episode in a succession of significant activities. The paradoxical simple normalcy of the genius of Holmes needed no martyrdom or eccentricity for its emphasis and he affected none.

With the theory of puerperal fever accepted in New England because of his vigorous defense and insistence, Holmes threw himself into the investigation and examination of the great mass of knowledge which physics and chemistry were beginning to deliver into the hand of medicine.

To the support of the progressive movements in medical practice and organization which this advance in auxiliary scientific branches now made possible, he added clarifying comment, original amplification, and the weight of his established authority. A particularly significant example of his broad grasp is his enthusiastic activity in the founding of the Harvard Dental School at a time when most physicians considered teeth as detachable bony structures having little to do with the body and continued to regard the dentist as a mechanic who took pleasure in extracting them.

It is rarely recalled that, writing to William T. G. Morton on November 21, 1846, concerning the introduction of sulphuric ether—under the name of Letheon—to produce temporary loss of consciousness, Holmes says, "All I will do is to give you a hint or two as to names, or the name, to be applied—anesthesia." [2] Here, as was so often the case with Holmes's apt and pithy expression, the name anesthesia attained universal adoption.

The period in which Holmes lived and worked (1809–94) saw a tremendous change in medical theories and attitudes. Science was zigzagging forward. But it was also a period when an opposite tendency pervaded New England thought, not sporadically but as a general and sustained movement. The self-frustration and rigid repression long enforced by Calvinistically inclined clergy no longer found a compensatory physical outlet in the struggle for the conquest of stony New England fields and resistive mountainside. As an escape from emotional suppression many an individual and thwarted group in isolated Puritan villages were turning to mysticism. This tendency is regarded by many observers as a serene, unobtrusive substitute for an earlier hysterical reaction, "witchcraft," which two centuries earlier had swept the Massachusetts countryside.

In Austria and later in Paris during the latter half of the eighteenth century, Anton Mesmer was accurately observing and experimenting with some extremely important psychic phenomena. The method he developed bore his name, Mesmerism, and later became known as hypnotism. It was Charcot's method of choice for investigating what are now called unconscious motivations and for treating psychic disorders, when Sigmund Freud, a young physician from Vienna, went to study at the celebrated Paris clinic of the Salpêtrière in 1885. Mesmerism (animal magnetism) and its derivatives had reached the American shore in Holmes's time via England and the work of Dr. James Braid. Here they were not only used therapeutically but became incorporated for the first time with mystical ruminations and religious doctrines.

Thus the era of wide scientific advance in which Harvard and Holmes played such an important role also saw the growth in America of odd cults, most of which, like science of which they were the antithesis, weakened the rigid established ecclesiastic structure. These religiously colored emotional outlets were used to remedy many of the bodily aches and pains for which social, religious, and incidental repressions could be held responsible and which drugs did not touch.

On the bleak Maine coast, Phineas Quimby successfully treated Mary Baker Eddy, among many others, by Mesmerism. Likewise Andrew Jackson Davis and Thomas Lake Harris, combining the power of suggestion with faith in prayer and release in religious ecstasy, performed startling cures in New England and New York. At this time, too, Mrs. Eddy boasted that her poems were printed "side by side with those of Whittier, Holmes and Phoebe Cary and are preserved in the files of the Lynn [Massachusetts] papers." [3] She later succeeded in shrewdly merging conflicting tendencies of fact and falsehood in an illusive paradox under the system she called Christian Science.

Holmes, for all his preferential social background and academic training, could not escape in his home and in his subsequent contacts the impact of repressive environmental influences. Holmes's father was a Calvinist minister; from all account, an exceptionally genial Calvinist. Nevertheless he believed firmly in predestination and preordination. Holmes's reaction to the fatalist religious principles of his father was in an escape, an eminently respectable escape, into science and scholarship. A horror of the depressing damnation theology of his childhood aroused in Holmes a bitter antipathy and lifelong rebellion against its crippling influences and manifestations.

The drive to counteract and correct the hopeless Calvinist philosophy appears time and again in his essays and in his three novels written late in life. A contemporary critic dubbed them "medicated novels." The term is appropriate, for in each the main character presents a psychiatric problem and is under the care of a doctor of skill and experience, who serves as an interpreter of the sickness.

Of course Holmes would not have regarded himself as a psychiatrist because this specialty was not to develop as an extramural practice for another fifty years. The most advanced psychiatrists of his day were concerned almost exclusively with the abolition of forcible restraint and punishment of the insane and the introduction of more humane attitudes and methods in custodial asylums. Even the problems of psychiatric classification and prognosis, which so engrossed the attention and encouraged the debating skill of psychiatrists from approximately 1885 to 1910, had been barely broached. Nevertheless, those tense psychiatric situations which destroy individuals, disrupt families, and disturb social groups were quite as prevalent then as today, and the physician was increasingly displacing the pastor in these cases as the counselor and authority.

To be a truly great physician in any but a purely technical specialty, or even a successful one, the medical practitioner must possess what are sometimes called "intuitive" gifts as a psychiatrist. This quality depends upon his experience as a clinician supplemented by his sympathy and consideration for people whose minds and bodies are distorted by physical pain or disappointments in life. The social import of these psychiatric situations impressed Holmes to such a degree that he assumed the same fighting radicalism in regard to their recognition and treatment as he had toward the control of the contagiousness of childbed fever, the value of scientific dentistry, the folly of overmedication, and the fallacies of homeopathy.

Holmes tried his talents in poetry, essays, and fiction but he continued first, last, and forever, the physician, his thinking dominated by his medical training and his daily scientific work. He was also a theological reformer, a philosopher, and, as indicated above, according to the present concept of this specialty, a psychiatrist many of whose ideas fell in line with the most advanced of this present day. In certain essentials Holmes's theory and philosophy of approach to psychological problems is prophetic of psychoanalysis and anticipated Freud's formulations and the psychoanalytic psychiatry which grew out of it.

Parallelisms between Holmes and Freud

Freud is reported to have replied to a Prussian official, who greeted him as the discoverer of the unconscious, with the words: "The poets and philosophers before me have discovered the unconscious; I have discovered the scientific method with which the unconscious can be studied." [4]

Holmes cannot be regarded as an inspired poet. His poetry followed a conventional manner of metrical expression, popular in his day. It is the philosophic quality of Holmes's mind that led him to the discovery of postulates which Freud, nearly a quarter of a century later, offered to a ridiculing group in the Vienna university where Semmelweis had in 1850 met his discouraging rebuffs.

Holmes's psychological pronouncements and his unremitting fight for liberality and generosity in the estimation of mental aberration encountered relatively mild opposition in a milieu where the abolitionists had long been battling for the physical freedom of all men. It is likely that, into their zeal for the liberation of the Negro, the abolitionists may have displaced and vicariously invested much of the energy unconsciously aimed at self-liberation from their own captivities. It required less personal sacrifice to fight for the freedom of the blacks of the South than to attempt to disturb their own immediate imprisoned selves.

The year 1871 has been selected in our orientation of Holmes because it was the date when he delivered an address entitled "Mechanism in Thought and Morals," before the Phi Beta Kappa Society of Harvard. It was carefully revised, expanded, and annotated before it was printed in *Pages from an Old Volume of Life*.[5] So far as I can determine it has lain there unnoticed. I find no reference to it in accounts of Holmes's contributions to medicine. However, Van Wyck Brooks in *The Flowering of New England, 1815–1865*,[6] an absorbing study of that period of American cultural development, states that this essay of Holmes "was a brilliant anticipation of Dr. Freud." He also writes, "Dr. Holmes, perhaps unwittingly, had played into the hands of Dr. Darwin. He had played into the hands of Dr. Freud, and he had played into the hands of another doctor of whom he had never heard, Dr. Marx."

The Phi Beta Kappa address was considered notable by contemporaries for two reasons; namely, that in the brain there persists a material record of thought; and secondly, that this transmissible record is not at all times available to the

person for the control of his actions. Among the foundation
stones of Freud's psychoanalytic structure one of the most
important is an analogous indestructibility of infantile thought
and impressions. Others are the importance and influence of
unconscious mentation; the value of the contents of dreams
in revealing this unconscious thought; and the effects on behavior of the repression of emotion. The latter force, as we
have seen, was not unknown in the land of the Pilgrims.

Holmes's regular use of the word "unconscious" is of interest. Although William James mentioned the term "unconscious cerebration," he decided that "unconscious" is "better
replaced" by the vaguer term "subconscious" or "subliminal."
Freud, like Holmes, insisted upon the term unconscious,
whereas, in the writings of most of his predecessors and contemporaries, subconscious had been used to signify mental
operations which occurred below the level of consciousness.
Other important pillars in psychoanalysis noted by Holmes
are the free association of ideas, the role of the censor, and, in
the first work of Breuer and Freud,[7] the recognition of the
existence of several personalities in the same individual.

Holmes wrote his earlier psychiatric novels with the direct
purpose of demonstrating that there is no inherited guilt. In
the "Mechanism in Thought and Morals," he has much to
say on processes which might account for personal guilt. He
expounds his ideas clearly, forcefully, and unequivocally. The
object of his thesis is now never in doubt—namely, that such
a thing as absolute freedom of the will cannot exist because
of unconscious processes which are affecting the individual's
conscious activity all the time. If for this reason alone, Holmes
affirms that we must regard with charity and understanding
many deviations in conduct which are asocial and antisocial.
He says: "Do we ever think without knowing that we are
thinking? The question may be disguised so as to look a

little less paradoxical: Are there any mental processes of which we are unconscious at the time, but which we recognize as having taken place by finding certain results in our minds?"

It is worth while to repeat that Holmes's concept of the unconscious is not accidental. He states it unambiguously in such passages as: "Unconscious activity is the rule with the actions most important to life. The lout who lies stretched on the tavern-bench, with just mental activity enough to keep his pipe from going out, is the unconscious tenant of a laboratory where such combinations are being constantly made as never Wohler or Berthelot could put together; where such fabrics are woven, such problems of mechanism solved, such a commerce carried on with the elements and forces of the outer universe, that the industries of all the factories are mere indolence and awkwardness and unproductiveness compared to the miraculous activities of which his lazy bulk is the unheeding centre." [8]

Holmes not only appreciated the constant and restless activity of the unconscious but also that from the unconscious come those urgent drives which ruthlessly thrust aside our more deliberate thoughts and planning, as well as those persistent affect-laden urges that lend conviction and power to our expressed thoughts, choices, and opinions. He says: "And so the orator—I do not mean the poor slave of a manuscript, who takes his thought chilled from its mould, but the impassioned speaker who pours it forth as it flows coruscating from the furnace—the orator only becomes our master at the moment when he himself is taken possession of, by a sudden rush of fresh inspiration. How well we know the flash of the eye, the thrill of the voice, which are the signature and symbol of nascent thought—thought just emerging into consciousness, in which condition, as is the case with the chemist's elements, it has a combining force at other times wholly unknown!"

Therapeutic psychoanalysis is a long and laborious process, with the dramatic episodes described in popular literature few and far between. So the psychoanalyst, listening to the free associations of the recumbent patient, watches with care for all manifestations of affects. They are especially shown in the quality of the voice, the slight movements of the body, the long silences which reveal the inhibition of unconscious urges.

The mechanism of the free association of ideas, a postulate of psychoanalysis and the one upon which the therapeutic process is fundamentally based, did not escape Holmes. In this connection I shall quote paragraphs scattered throughout the essay but here gathered into a sequence to give emphasis to the understanding which Holmes possessed of the value of free association in the mechanism of thought-operation and thought-flow.[9]

"We wish to remember something in the course of conversation. No effort of the will can reach it; but we say, 'Wait a minute, and it will come to me,' and go on talking. Presently, perhaps some minutes later, the idea we are in search of comes all at once into the mind, delivered like a prepaid bundle, laid at the door of consciousness like a foundling in a basket. How it came there we know not. The mind must have been at work groping and feeling for it in the dark; it cannot have come of itself. Yet, all the while, our consciousness, so far as we are conscious of our consciousness, was busy with other thoughts."

This idea of unconscious associative thought-functioning is expressed even more concisely: "The more we examine the mechanism of thought, the more we shall see that the automatic, unconscious action of the mind enters largely into all its processes. Our definite ideas are stepping-stones; how we get from one to the other, we do not know; something carries us; we do not take the step."

Quite in harmony with his philosophy of insisting that society take into account unconscious factors in evaluating human conduct and at the same time holding that this does not necessarily exempt the individual from definite, undeniable responsibility for his acts, he adds: "The flow of thought is, like breathing, essentially mechanical and necessary, but incidentally capable of being modified to a greater or less extent by conscious effort. Our natural instincts and tastes have a basis which can no more be reached by the will than the sense of light a⁻1 darkness, or that of heat and cold."

The scope with which Holmes has covered another of the essential psychoanalytic mechanisms is shown by the following excerpts in regard to dreams and the significant hints of their function of wish fulfillment: "We not rarely find our personality doubled in our dreams, and do battle with ourselves, unconscious that we are our own antagonists. Dr. Johnson dreamed that he had a contest of wit with an opponent, and got the worst of it: of course, he furnished the wit for both. Tartini heard the Devil play a wonderful sonata, and set it down on awaking. Who was the Devil but Tartini himself? I remember, in my youth, reading verses in a dream, written as I thought, by a rival fledgling of the Muse. They were so far beyond my powers, that I despaired of equalling them; yet I must have made them unconsciously as I read them."

In a second comment on dreams Holmes indicated that, in dream life, our problems are solved and we may unconsciously act in obedience to these solutions in waking life. Such a theory was advanced by one of the early Swiss analysts, Alphonse Maeder, and today often appears to be verified by patients under analysis. "The cases are numerous where questions have been answered, or problems solved, in dreams, or during unconscious sleep. Two of our most distinguished professors in this institution have had such an experience, as they tell me. Somnambulism and double-consciousness offer another series of illustrations."

Two further quotations from Holmes's essay are worth while because they concern important topics in two of his stories—namely psychic dualism. The causes for the splitting of personality are baffling and are still under vigorous discussion; in a general way they are attributed to a clash between ego ideals and the ego, between conscience and instinct. This interpretation is at least implied in the following passages:

"We can read aloud, or mentally articulate, and keep up a distinct train of pictured thought—not so easily two currents of worded thought—simultaneously (though this can be done to some extent; as, for instance, one may be reading aloud, and internally articulating some well-known passage)."

"But we are all more or less improvisators. We all have a double, who is wiser and better than we are, and who puts thoughts into our heads, and words into our mouths. Do we not all commune with our own hearts upon our beds? Do we not all divide ourselves, and go to buffets on questions of right or wrong, of wisdom or folly? Who or what is it that resolves the stately parliament of the day, with all its forms and conventionalities and pretences, and the great Me presiding, into the committee of the whole, with Conscience in the chair, that holds its solemn session through the watches of the night?"

In addition, to the significant psychoanalytic dynamisms quoted above, Holmes goes deeply into other problems that are being actively investigated by psychologists and psychiatrists today. Among them we may select the quantity and quality of thought-flow—of the "interval movement" of which we are wholly unconscious, "when one idea brings up another"; the force of childhood memories; the unconscious factors in plagiarism; the function of censorship; the differences in the type of thought in males and females; the effects of sexual frustration in producing physical symptoms and character traits. Also in his novels we find textbook examples of common psychoanalytic mechanisms such as displacement, sublimation, overcompensation, and the like.

Holmes as a Clinical Psychiatrist

All the reflections in "Mechanism in Thought and Morals" constitute a recapitulation of thoughts which Holmes had confirmed in psychopathological conditions during his career as a practicing and consulting physician. But Holmes did not put them in the form of a medical essay. He may have felt that his medical colleagues would be unreceptive and antagonistic, and probably was smarter than he knew. At all events here again he was prophetic of Freud, whose original presentations before the Vienna Medical Society met with a humiliating reception. Discouraged by the hostility of physicians, Freud turned to groups less bound by the factualistic thinking which medical training fosters and produces—to young philosophers, psychologists, and educators. Not until 1910, either abroad or in this country, did psychoanalytic formulations receive any real or wide attention in psychiatric circles.

Holmes at the time his novels appeared was a professor of anatomy, a subject of dry bones and dead bodies, and as an anatomist his opinions on psychiatric disorders would not have been considered important to the practicing physicians and psychiatrists. He therefore deliberately and probably shrewdly chose narrative as a medium through which to bring his views before the public. His three stories are poor fiction when judged by modern criteria or compared with the masters of his time—Poe, Thackeray, Balzac, or even Hawthorne of his own literary group. The novels are *Elsie Venner* (1859), *The Guardian Angel* (1867), and *A Mortal Antipathy* (1884). Their plots are simple, almost juvenile and, in two of them, the reader is not disappointed in the customary thwarting of the villain and the coming of true love to its own.

Although *Elsie Venner* enjoyed something of a popular success, literary critics dealt none too kindly with this or with Holmes's subsequent psychological works of fiction that were "tainted with the physiological." Surely Holmes, far more sensitive concerning his literary reputation both as a poet and novelist than about his clinical ability, would not have been pleased that these studies of abnormal characters should be regarded as case histories. In the light of the development of modern psychiatry they remain as testimony to his medical acuity, his knowledge, and his profound psychiatric understanding.

There can be slight doubt that the doctors who play such a prominent role in these social dramas and employ a similar technique in handling them are none other than a composite picture of Holmes himself. There also should be included in this class the crusty, warm-hearted, old Professor Byles Gridley who plays the part of amateur detective in *Guardian Angel*.

If one were to translate into psychoanalytic parlance the receptive and understanding method of these doctors with their patients it would follow the lines of the "passive technique" generally preferred in psychoanalytic practice today. Certainly it was defiantly at variance with the bad-tasting drug therapy of the time for the treatment of hysteria and other nervous symptoms.

In terms of professional conduct, the doctors' approach

combines those qualities so desirable in every physician but indispensable in a psychiatrist—namely, patience, forbearance, tolerance, equanimity, accurate observation of the patient's actions and utterances, and unremitting consideration for the patient's psychological and environmental handicaps.

These psychiatric and psychoanalytic principles were not merely philosophical musing with Holmes. They rested upon clinical orientation and, because of this fact, his observations have a directness, reality, and cogency which other novelists have been able to portray with greater vividness and emotional appeal. A dozen years intervened between the writing of *Elsie Venner* (which came out under the title of *The Professor's Story* in 1858 and 1859) and "Mechanism in Thought and Morals." During that time Holmes had gathered together his ideas and beliefs supporting the doctrine of limited responsibility and had developed for the treatment of mental disorders principles of theory and practice which are considered modern today.

Holmes saw with unusual clearness the far-reaching effects of mental disorder in the home and in intrafamilial relationships, especially the power of such disorders to restrict and distort the lives of the well—this was the effect of Elsie Venner's illness upon her father, and of the psychically determined invalidism of Mrs. Stoker, the minister's wife, upon her young daughter in *The Guardian Angel*.

Novels must have the element of love. This is not lacking in Holmes's stories. Here it takes the form not of violent, passionate or sensuous love, but of spiritual love, with its vital influence as an agency in molding character and establishing emotional balance. In *Elsie Venner* the love affect had been immobilized and became blocked; in *The Guardian Angel* Myrtle Hazard's capacity to love had been turned into resent-

ment and rebellion; in *A Mortal Antipathy* Maurice Kirkwood's normal tendencies had been held in check by a morbid fear of young women.

All of these characters have one quality in common—they
lost their mothers before the age of two, and during infancy
and childhood had mother substitutes who were deficient in
one way or another. From certain aspects the emotional disorder of each may be regarded as a reaction to a lack of love
and to frustration in their unconscious search for the missing
parent. Elsie Venner made an awkward attempt to free herself by falling in love but was unsuccessful and the rebuff and
denial made her die. In *The Guardian Angel* and *A Mortal
Antipathy* the principal characters achieve love through a
symbolic rebirth (rescue from death by a person of the opposite sex who is an appropriate partner for marriage).

In *Elsie Venner* the circumstance that her mother was bitten by a snake during pregnancy is held responsible for the
reptilian traits which Elsie showed. This is not psychoanalytic
thinking. Yet few would dispute that the case is interpreted
with the insight of analytic psychiatry. Moreover, the interesting question of the influence of very early, even antenatal,
damage on later anxiety has recently been reëxamined in the
light of observations made during the psychoanalysis of patients.

The second novel, *The Guardian Angel*, is a study of hereditary influences on the mind of one individual and on the
development of hysterical symptoms. Written during the
mellowness of Holmes's advancing years it is a final and un-
sparing thrust at meddling by the clergy in situations where
emotional disturbance is threatening the very existence of the
patient.

Holmes maintains that "this body in which we journey
across the isthmus between the oceans is not a private car-

riage but an omnibus." In Myrtle Hazard of *The Guardian Angel*, the traits and experiences of antecedents reappear and produce strange and unaccountable actions (hysteria), seemingly belonging to the personalities of several ancestors. An analogous concept has received wide attention under the term "collective unconscious," as used by the Swiss psychiatrist, Carl Jung, at one time closely associated with Freud. However, in the collective (archaic) unconscious as conceived by Jung, integral figures of remote ancestors as described in Myrtle Hazard are not generally presumed to exist.

The final novel, *A Mortal Antipathy*, is the study, by a fine psychiatrist, of a compulsion type of morbid fear. The preface, like the prefaces of the two previous novels, defends the validity of the actual framework of the story from a medical standpoint. In it Holmes approaches more significantly the psychoanalytic position of Freud—namely, that a personal shock or trauma in very early infancy may cause a conditioning which the individual sometimes does not completely outgrow.

The theory of bisexuality and the importance of bisexual components in influencing the characters of the individuals is more than implied in the description of each one of the abnormal personalities. The masculine traits in childhood of both Elsie Venner, the man-hater, and Myrtle Hazard, something of a tomboy, are unmistakable. The bisexual theme becomes even clearer in *A Mortal Antipathy*, when Holmes repeatedly contrasts the femininity of Euthymia Tower with the masculinity of Lurida Vincent—and it is apparent that he has little sympathy with the latter. The illness of Myrtle Hazard is typical of the hysterias described by the famous French neurologist Charcot, but which are not so often seen today.

The theme of determinism with its variations—whether antenatal, directly inherited, or psychic—is repeated in all the novels. It seems as though Holmes may have been under a compulsion to write off his father's Calvinism and predestination, but never quite succeeded. As he advanced in years, the determinism, as in *A Mortal Antipathy*, assumed individualistic and personal aspects—conditions which fitted a type of causation more in harmony with scientific criteria. But it is not my intention here to interpret these novels psychoanalytically as a reflection of any personal unconscious conflicts which their author may have had. Certainly, whatever these conflicts were and however deep they may have been, they were transformed by him into the highest type of human productivity and helpful coöperation.

⁻ The harsh New England predestinistic morality produced many a dismal domestic drama like those so effectively portrayed by Hawthorne in *The House of the Seven Gables* and by Edith Wharton in *Ethan Frome*. The mystifying physiological manifestations of self-denial and self-restraint Holmes grasped at the bedside. This repressive cultural attitude lingered on after his death. But the scientific spirit continued to grow great and strong in Cambridge and Boston.

Oddly enough Holmes's ideas lay in abeyance for twenty-five years after his death, but the scientific link which Holmes established between Cambridge and Vienna in 1840 appeared again in 1909. A scholarly and distinguished professor of neurology at Harvard, James Jackson Putnam (1846–1918), whose time of medical activity overlapped that of Holmes, became convinced that the theories of a still unacclaimed Viennese investigator were worthy of careful examination. And so Sigmund Freud came to an intellectually alert, but still really conservative, New England. He came at Putnam's instigation and at the invitation of Stanley Hall, President of Clark University at Worcester, Mass. These lectures by Freud have become a milestone in the history of psychoanalysis, but I think that Freud himself could not have conveyed the essence of his theory better and more convincingly to the distinguished yet skeptical and critical audience he faced than do these words: "There are thoughts that never emerge into consciousness, which yet make their influence felt among the perceptible mental currents, just as the unseen planets sway the movements of those which are watched and mapped by the astronomer. Old prejudices, that are ashamed to confess themselves, nudge our talking thought to utter their magisterial veto. In hours of languor, as Mr. Lecky has remarked, the beliefs and fancies of obsolete conditions are apt to take advantage of us. We know very little of the contents of our minds until some sudden jar brings out the old stockings full of gold, and all the hoards that have hid away in holes and crannies." The reader may surmise this was written by Holmes.

One wonders why Holmes's ideas did not receive greater attention when they were written. Probably society at large was far less prepared to entertain them in 1870 than it was to accept Freud reluctantly in 1910. But this does not explain why Holmes's theories were not more critically tested by two truly distinguished scientists of the Boston group who immediately followed him—William James, the philosopher, and Morton Prince, the psychiatrist. This is especially true of Prince, whose painstaking work on multiple personality is an outstanding contribution to twentieth-century psychiatry.

Psychiatry had remained in the sterile stage of description and classification. The social significance of mental deviation, so stressed by Holmes, had not been grasped by science or society. Neither James nor Prince could give heed to dynamism of thought or appreciate its correlation to the masterly clinical descriptions sketched by Holmes and abridged in the pages that follow.

ELSIE VENNER

A STORY OF SCHIZOPHRENIA

HOLMES wrote *Elsie Venner* when he was about fifty. By far the most vigorous and positive of his three novels, it was a novel with many purposes and, like most of those which obviously attempt to teach lessons, it did not please the literary critics. In addition to medical problems it reflected very definite views on education and social customs, philosophies of conduct, especially for the two sexes, and much sharp comment such as made the *Autocrat of the Breakfast-Table* famous.

While the novel serves as a medium permitting Holmes to display his wisdom and learning as a physician and philosopher, it also reveals some of his weaknesses and prejudices. Among the latter is his obstinate eulogy of that "permanent aristocracy," the cultural group of New England into which he had been born—his Brahmin caste. He thinks the difference between the born scholar and the "common country boy" is so marked that any college instructor could upon sight separate his class into the two categories. Most people today, as well as some of his own time, would regard Holmes as a trifle superior about inherited scholarships and smug in the security of his own "privileged order."

In spite of his self-avowed membership in the "better" order, for which he is properly grateful, the theme of *Elsie Venner* was a lifelong favorite of the author, namely that there is no such thing as total depravity. Because of his inherited tendencies no man can be held completely responsible for certain traits of character, certain deficiencies, mental quirks, or even criminal inclinations. The will therefore is never completely free. Later Holmes formulated this lack of complete control of our actions as being due to the continuous operation of unconscious impulses and thought.

The idea that every human being possesses only limited capacity over the direction of his acts and of his aims in life is basic in the Freudian theory of psychic determinism. The doctrine of psychic determinism rests on observations and inductive conclusions similar to those of physical determinism. One of the great contributions of psychoanalysis has been the investigation of determinism in the psychical sphere, where causal relationships are far more difficult to establish conclusively than in the physical.

To be sure, in psychoanalytic theory the influences responsible for our psychic destiny are not directly inherited but depend upon certain determining qualities of experiences which are often quite accidental and occur in early childhood. These circumstances are repressed and we become unconscious of them. Often the determining quality may be so intense and vivid that it impresses the child with all the impact of a shock or trauma. The trauma and the reaction thus experienced is called a primal scene in psychoanalytic literature. The reactions set up at this time are subsequently repeated in situations even remotely suggestive of it and stand in causal relationship to the person's psychic destiny.[1]

The interdetermination of psychic and physical determinants is a field of investigation almost untouched by science. It is striking that, with the evidence of psychic determinism established by psychoanalysis, there has grown an increasing trend to question the existence of the independent and separate functioning of the human organism in a dualistic sense and rather to consider the mind and the body as interdetermined.

Elsie Venner, the heroine of the story, is afflicted with a crippling inherited taint, the venom of a snake's bite, which affected the mother's blood before the birth of the child. Many of the story's implications center about the symbolism of the snake, in the type of Elsie's traits, their significance in her character, and their effect upon people coming in contact with her.

It is extremely doubtful if a purely extraneous element, such as snake venom, introduced into the mother's blood before birth, could have any direct effect upon the character of the child. Good evidence, however, supports the idea that the mother's physical condition and the mental attitudes which she develops toward the offspring even before and during gestation may have their effect on the child. How far this may predispose the child before birth to anxiety is problematic if not merely speculative. Nevertheless much evidence speaks in favor of a continuity of intrauterine with extrauterine life.

Freud originally regarded anxiety as a manifestation of sexual urges which had been denied expression. It was not until some thirty years after he published the *Interpretation of Dreams* that he changed this view and saw in anxiety the mobilization of energy by the organism as a defense reaction in the face of danger. The experiences of the infant during birth are prototypes of the anxiety reaction. Shortly before Freud altered his views regarding the strictly sexual nature of anxiety, Otto Rank had advanced the theory that the shock which an infant receives in being born (the trauma of birth) is the beginning of the neurotic type of reaction formation. To attribute pathological anxiety to an experience upon which all life depends is of highly dubious value.

The relationship of anxiety to antenatal influences has recently been reëxamined in the light of psychoanalytic studies by Dr. Greenacre who states that: "The anxiety response probably manifests itself first in an irritable responsiveness of the organism at a reflex level; this is apparent in intra-uterine life in a set of separate or loosely constellated reflexes which may become organized at birth into the anxiety reaction. Certainly, 'danger' does not begin with birth but may be present earlier and provoke a foetal response which exists at an organic rather than a psychological level. Variations in the birth process may similarly heighten the anxiety potential, causing a more severe reaction to later (psychological) dangers in life." [2]

In addition to the already mentioned accidental handicap of prenatal determinism, Elsie grew up a motherless child. Similarly in the *Guardian Angel* and *A Mortal Antipathy* we have as the principal characters an orphan and a motherless boy. Although Holmes has created exceptional situations in the environment of all of these children, he is inclined to place the emphasis for the scientific determinism of the mental illness of Elsie Venner and of Myrtle Hazard (in the *Guardian Angel*) on heredity. This is done at the apparent neglect of emotional factors and environment so important in shaping growth and character; these are, however, tacitly implied by numerous incidents in the stories.

The type of disorder which Elsie Venner shows would be difficult to classify in any modern psychiatric grouping. A diagnostic label is really not important. The forces contributing to her illness and death are clearly indicated. Her mood-swings at least suggest a cyclothymic disorder. On the other hand the main characteristics of her personality—isolation, introversion, self-indulgence, apparent lack of affect, bizarre conduct, and negativistic tendencies—are fairly constant symptoms in the clinical picture of schizophrenia.

As in so many cases seen in psychiatric practice, the picture of Elsie Venner is complicated by many elements inconsistent with typical descriptions of either manic-depressive disorders, schizophrenia, or neuroses. These atypical reactions appear so often that at one time the term "allied to dementia precox" or "allied to manic-depressive" was in common use in the New York State Mental Hospitals. While a designation of a mental illness is often desirable for quickly conveying a broad conception of its severity and form, it is far more important and valuable that the interplay of those factors responsible for the condition be understood by the physician, the patient, and those persons who come into contact with him day in and day out.

The Story of Elsie Venner

Bernard C. Langdon, a young man attending medical lectures at one of our principal colleges, remained after the lecture to speak with the Professor. There are in every class half a dozen bright faces by the intermediation of whose attention the lecturer seems to hold that of the mass of listeners. Bernard was a young man with such a face; and I found—for you have guessed that I was the "Professor"—that, when I was bringing out some favorite illustration of a nice point, 1 naturally looked in his face and gauged my success by its expression. It was a handsome face, a little too pale, perhaps, and would have borne something more of fullness without becoming heavy.

The student lingered in the lecture room and finally said, "I am going to leave for the present, and keep school."

"Why, that's a pity, and you so near graduating."

"I can't help myself, Sir," the young man answered. "There's trouble at home. I came to ask you for a certificate of my fitness to teach."

A perfectly gentlemanly young man, he means at least as much as he says. There are some people whose rhetoric consists of a slight habitual understatement. This was a self-trusting fellow with family recollections that made him unwilling to accept the kind of aid which many students would have welcomed. I knew him too well to urge him. When a resolute young fellow steps up to the great bully, the World, and takes him boldly by the beard, he is often surprised to find the beard come off in his hand, and that it was only tied on to scare away timid adventurers.

The Reverend Jedediah Langdon, grandfather of our young gentleman, had made an advantageous alliance. Miss Dorothea Wentworth had read one of his sermons which had been printed "by request" and became deeply interested in the author. Out of this circumstance grew a correspondence, a matrimonial alliance, and a family of half a dozen children. Wentworth Langdon, the oldest of these, represented the connecting link between the generation which lived in a kind of state, upon its own resources, and the new brood, which must live mainly by its wits or industry. This "slack-water" period comes before the rapid ebb of prosperity and there are no more inoffensive people than these children of rich families, just above the necessity of active employment.

There is one curious circumstance which is often illustrated in our experience of the slack-water gentry. We shall know a certain person by his looks, familiarly, for years, but never have learned his name. About this person we shall have accumulated no little circumstantial knowledge; his face, gait, his mode of saluting, perhaps even of speaking; yet who he is we know not. In another department of our consciousness, there is a very familiar "name" which we have never found the person to match. We have heard it so often that it has become one of that multitude of permanent shapes which walk the chambers of the brain in velvet slippers in the company of Hamlet and General Washington. But now and then it happens, after years of this independent existence of the name and its shadowy image in the brain on the one part and the person and all his real attributes on the other, that some accident reveals their relation and we find the name we have carried so long in our memory belongs to the person we have known so long as a fellow citizen.*

---

* Even among normal persons there is a frequent tendency to dissociate another person from all reality conceptions of him (that is, from what we customarily think he is like). Generally this is found to be dependent upon a clash between our emotional feeling concerning that person and circumstances associated with him and our intellectual attitude toward him. The reaction of vagueness is akin to that of forgetting things which we know perfectly well. Here, too, the unconscious attitude is in contradiction to the conscious one.

In great national crises, such as the recent war, such conflicts become disconcertingly obvious. Patients, and people who are not patients, at times become very vague in their loyalty to our government's position and policy, of which they consciously believe themselves completely convinced. Unconsciously they may entertain a real sympathy for Nazism, for example, due to a personal identification with Hitler; (this has often appeared in the dreams of sadistic—even Jewish—patients); or to an unconscious identifica-

Now the slack-water gentry are among the persons most likely to be subjects of this curious divorce of title and reality, for the reason that, playing no important part in the community, there is nothing to tie the floating name to the actual individual. To this class belonged Wentworth Langdon, Esq., who had been "dead-headed" into the world and had sat with his hands in his pockets staring at the show ever since.

It was one of the old square palaces of the North, in which Bernard Langdon, the son of Wentworth, was born. If he had had the luck to be an only child, he might have lived as his father had done, letting his meagre competence smoulder on almost without consuming. But after Master Bernard came Miss Dorothea Wentworth Langdon, and others, equally well named. So it happened that our young man found himself stopped short in his studies.

He left, carrying my certificate that his services would be of great value in any academy where young persons of either sex were to be instructed. I wished I had not said "either sex" and brooded over the mischief which might come out of these two words until it seemed they were charged with destiny. What I dreaded most for him was one of those miserable matrimonial misalliances which happen and always must— because a man always loves a woman and a woman a man, unless some good reason exists to the contrary.

I had settled it in my mind that this young fellow had a career marked out for him, by taking care of poor patients in the public charities, and working his way up to a better kind of practice, better, that is, in the vulgar sense. Now if this young man once got into the "wide streets," he would sweep them clear of his rivals. Then I would have him set up a

---

tion of Germans with the idea of coziness (*Gemüthlichkeit*) for which certain lonely people yearn so intensely.

nice little coach instead of coasting about in a shabby one-horse concern and casting anchor opposite his patients' doors like a Cape Ann fishing-smack. By the time he was thirty, he would have knocked the social pawns out of his way and be ready to challenge a wife from the row of great pieces in the background. I would not have a man marry above his level, so as to become the appendage of a powerful family connection; but I would not have him marry until he knew his level—that is, again looking at the matter in a purely worldly point of view.

That is what I thought this young fellow might have come to; and now I have let him go off to teach in a school for either sex! Ten to one he will run like a moth into a candle, right into one of those girls'-nests and there will be the end of him. Oh, yes! country doctor—half a dollar a visit—drive all day—get up at night and harness your own horse—drive again ten miles in a snow-storm—shake powders out of two phials—drive back again, if you don't happen to get stuck in a drift—no home, no peace, no continuous meals, no un-broken sleep, no Sunday, no holiday, no social intercourse, but one eternal jog, jog, jog, in a sulky, until you feel like the mummy of an Indian who had been buried in the sitting posture.

After a brief experience in a district school where young Langdon proved his merit by thrashing the overgrown son of the local butcher, he accepted a position as an instructor of English at the Appollinean Female Institute in Rockland.

Rockland was a town of no inconsiderable pretensions ly-ing at the foot of a mountain and basking in its sunshine as Italy stretches herself before the Alps. One feature of The Mountain that shed the brownest horror on its woods was the terrible Rattlesnake Ledge tenanted by those damnable reptiles which distill a fiercer venom under our cold northern sky than the cobra himself in the land of tropical poisons.

In the year 184–, a melancholy proof was afforded that the brood which infested The Mountain was not extirpated. An interesting married woman, Mrs. Venner, detained at home by the state of her health, was bitten in the entry of her own house by a rattlesnake from The Mountain. Owing to the instant employment of powerful remedies, the bite did not prove immediately fatal but she died within a few months.

*　　*　　*

The Appollinean "Institoot," as it was commonly called, was a "first-class Educational Establishment," to rough out a hundred young lady scholars. Silas Peckham, the Principal, born on the Yankee coast and reared chiefly on salt fish, kept school exactly as he would have kept a hundred head of cattle—for making just as much money in just as few years as could be safely done. The incidental fact, which the public took for the principal one, was the business of instruction.

When Bernard made his appearance in the great schoolroom of the Institute and was introduced by a young assistant, Miss Darley, a general rustle ran all round. The great schoolroom made so pretty a show that Master Langdon might be pardoned for asking Miss Darley questions.

"And who and what is that," he said, "sitting a little apart there—that wild-looking girl?"

The lady teacher's face changed; one would have said she was frightened or troubled. She looked at the girl doubtfully, as if she might hear the master's question and its answer. But the girl did not look up; she was winding a gold chain about her wrist, as if in a kind of reverie.

Miss Darley drew close. "Don't look at her as if we were talking about her," she whispered; "that is Elsie Venner."

*　　*　　*

It was a comfort for Master Langdon to get to a place with something like society, with residences which had pretensions of elegance, and with two or three churches to keep each other alive by wholesome agitation. Rockland was such a place. It had one grand street which was its chief glory, Elm Street, where most of the "mansion-houses" were. It was the correct thing for a Rockland dignitary to have a house in Elm Street.*

---

* Holmes's emphasis on the aristocracy of cultural background and scholarship began to weaken about the time of the Civil War. Until then he identified himself with and approved of the powerful upper class New Englanders who controlled education, social standards, and commerce. Like many an intellectual liberal, Holmes remained conservative and reactionary to the burning question of the abolition of slavery. With the outbreak of the war and the enlistment of his son, Oliver Wendell, Jr., who later became the distinguished Justice of the United States Supreme Court, he threw all the weight of his influence to the preservation of the Union.

To most of the present generation the name Oliver Wendell Holmes would probably mean the late Associate Justice. Perhaps no better corroboration of Holmes's ideas of inherited scholarship could be found than in his own son, who a generation later carried on a similar fight for liberalization in the field of law. Burton Hendrick [3] has said that to the jurist "law was as much an art as a science or department of learning." The remark would have applied equally to his father, the physician. Justice Holmes himself once remarked that "nothing in the course of centuries—unless it is theology—has been so encumbered by fixed ideas and accepted rules of action as the law." Like his father in his efforts to free medicine from theological fetters, the younger Oliver Wendell Holmes, in the hope of reconstructing law, "would substitute intelligence unencumbered by allegiance to solutions that have long outlived their pertinence because they have outlived the circumstances that called them into being."

On this aristocratic thoroughfare two meetinghouses stood on two eminences, facing each other, and looking like a couple of fighting cocks with their necks straight up in the air, as if they would flap their roofs the next thing and crow out of their up-stretched steeples, and peck at each other's glass eyes with their sharp-pointed weathercocks.

The first was a good pattern of the real old-fashioned New England meetinghouse. Here preached the Reverend Pierrepont Honeywood, D.D., who held to the old faith of the Puritans and occasionally delivered a discourse which was considered as a good logical basis laid down for the Millennium. Yet the Reverend Dr. Honeywood was fonder of preaching plain, practical sermons about the duties of life, and showing his Christianity in abundant good works. He exercised his human faculties in the harness of his ancient faith with such freedom that the straps of it got so loose they did not interfere greatly with the circulation of the warm blood through his system.*

However, as it so often the case between father and son, a certain psychological clash seems to have existed between Justice Holmes in his youth and Dr. Holmes, "the Governor," who was "all right . . . but." "Perhaps the Governor was a great man," said the Chief Justice; "but he wished he didn't have so much easy small talk for all occasions. A fellow didn't have a chance." [4] This ever-recurrent rivalry of son and father has been treated at length by Freud under the term Oedipus Complex.

* The Reverend Honeywood is probably a prototype of Holmes's own father, the Reverend Abiel Holmes. The latter was a Calvinist, a firm believer in all its dispiriting theology but a kindly, genial man in his daily contacts. Oliver Wendell seems to have respected and loved his father quite as intensely as he opposed the philosophy of his father's church. A similar paradox of character and theology is carried further in the uncertainty and fearfulness of the timid Mr. Fairweather, the minister of the liberal church in Rockland.

The meetinghouse on the opposite summit was of more modern style, in what may be called the florid shingle-Gothic manner. In this house preached the Reverend Chauncy Fairweather, a divine of the "Liberal" school, bred at a famous college which used to be thought to have the monopoly of training young men in the milder forms of heresy. His ministrations were attended with decency but not followed with enthusiasm. "The beauty of virtue" and "the moral dignity of human nature" ceased to excite a thrill of satisfaction after some hundred repetitions. The minister, unlike his rival, was a down-hearted and timid man. He went on preaching as he had been taught to preach but he had misgivings.

There was a little Roman Catholic church at the foot of the hill which he always had to pass on Sundays. He could never look on the multitudes that crowded its pews without a longing to get in among them and enjoy that luxury of devotional contact. The intellectual isolation of his sect preyed upon him; for of all terrible things to natures like his the most terrible is to belong to a minority.

A mile or two from the centre of Rockland was a pretty little Episcopal church and a trained rector who read the service with such ventral depth of utterance and irreduplication of the irresonant letter that his own mother would not have known him for her son if the good woman had not ironed his surplice with her own hands.

There were two public houses; one dignified with the name of the Mountain House, frequented by city people in the summer months and spreading a "table d'hôte," the other, "Pollard's Tahvern," with a barroom where there was a great smell of hay and boots and pipes, where teamsters came in and middle-aged male gossips, sometimes including the squire of the neighboring law office, gathered to exchange a question or two about the news.

* * *

A commercial establishment like the Appollinean Institute might yet be well carried on if it happened to get good teachers. And Langdon recognized the good genius of the school in Helen Darley. It was the old story. A poor country clergyman dies and leaves a widow and a daughter.

What a miserable thing it is to be poor. Helen Darley was dependent, frail, sensitive, conscientious. She was, in plain English, overworked and an overworked woman is always a sad sight, sadder a great deal than an overworked man because she is so much more fertile in capacities of suffering. She has so many varieties of headache and fits of depression in which she thinks she is nothing and those paroxysms which men speak slightingly of as hysterical. Nobody knows what the weariness of instruction is as soon as the teacher's faculties begin to be overtasked but those who have tried it.

Late one evening Helen sat down with a great bundle of girls' themes. How she dreaded this most forlorn of all a teacher's tasks! But she would insist on reading every sentence. While getting sleepy in spite of herself, she came to one which lifted her drooping lids. It was written in a sharp-pointed long, slender hand. The subject of the paper was The Mountain—a sort of descriptive rhapsody—and the writer must have threaded its wildest solitudes by the stars as well as by day. There was something in its imagery that recalled—Miss Darley could not say what, but it made her frightfully nervous. One passage so agitated her, that the overwearied girl's self-control left her entirely. She sobbed once or twice, then laughed convulsively and flung herself on the bed, where she worked out a set hysteric spasm without anybody to rub her hands. By and by she got quiet, took down a volume of Coleridge and read, and so to sleep and to wake from time to time out of uneasy dreams.

The theme was signed, "E. Venner." The next morning

the teacher looked pale and wearied but she was in her place at the usual hour. "You have been ill, I am afraid," said Mr. Bernard.

"Yesterday I had a kind of fright," she answered. "It is so dreadful to have charge of all these young souls and bodies. Tell me, are there not natures born so out of parallel with the lines of natural law that nothing short of a miracle can bring them right?"

Mr. Bernard had speculated on the innate organic tendencies with which individuals, families, and races are born.

"Why, of course. Each of us is only the footing up of a double column of figures. Every unit tells—some of them are 'plus' and some 'minus.' If the columns don't add up right, it is commonly because we can't make out all the figures. No doubt there are people born with impulses at every possible angle to the parallels of Nature. If they happen to cut these at right angles, of course they are beyond the reach of common influences, and penitentiaries and insane asylums take care of most of them. Obliquities are what we have most to do with in education. Pray, what set you to asking this?"

The meek teacher's blue eyes met the luminous glance that came with the question. She too was of gentle blood—a thousand decencies, amenities, reticences, graces are the traditional right of those who spring from such families. And when two persons of this exceptional breeding meet, they seek each other's company by the natural law of elective affinity. "A gentleman," said Helen Darley to herself, as she read Langdon's expression with a woman's rapid but exhausting glance.

"I am glad you believe in the force of transmitted tendencies, Mr. Langdon," she said, "but it would break my heart if I thought that all faults are beyond the reach of everything but God's special grace. Yet there are mysteries I do not know how to account for." Then in a whisper: "We had a girl that 'Stole' in the school and one who tried to set us on fire—children of good people. And we have a girl now that frightens me so." *

The girls kept coming in until the schoolroom was nearly full. Then a girl of about seventeen entered, tall and slender, but rounded with a peculiar undulation of movement. She was a splendid scowling beauty, black-browed with a flash of white teeth which were always like a surprise when her lips parted. She wore a checkered dress of a curious pattern and a camel's hair scarf twisted a little fantastically about her. She went to her seat and began playing listlessly with her gold chain, coiling it and uncoiling it about her slender wrist and braiding it in with her long, delicate fingers. Presently she looked up—black, piercing eyes, not large, a low forehead, black hair twisted in heavy braids—a face that one could not help looking at for its beauty yet wanted to look away from for something in its expression and nevertheless could not for those diamond eyes. They were fixed on the lady teacher now. Following some ill-defined impulse Miss Darley went to the girl's desk.

"What do you want of me, Elsie Venner?"

"Nothing," she said. "I thought I could make you come." The girl spoke in a kind of half-whisper. She did not lisp yet her articulation of one or two consonants was not absolutely perfect.**

*   *   *

---

* Apparently at that time, as now, the private school had more than its quota of difficult children. Certainly today in the unendowed private schools, one finds a very large percentage of children suffering from the emotional effects of disrupted homes.

** The occurrence of such phenomena as clairvoyance, spiritualism, thought transference, and telepathy has never been proved when

In walking along the main street Mr. Bernard had noticed a large house of some pretensions to architectural display, known as "Colonel Sprowle's villa." Hezekiah Sprowle, the colonel, had made money in trade and had married the daughter and heiress of an old miser. Life became pretty hard work to him as soon as he had nothing particular to do. Country people with money enough not to have to work are in much more danger than city people. They have a feeble curiosity for news perhaps, which they take daily as a man takes his bitters, and then fall silent and think they are thinking. But the mind goes out under this regimen, like a fire without a draught; and it is not very strange if the instinct of mental self-preservation drives them to brandy and water which makes the hoarse whisper of memory musical for a few moments.

As Miss Matilda Sprowle, sole daughter of the Colonel, had reached the age at which young ladies are supposed to "come out," the Sprowles decided to give a party to which "recognized gentility" was invited. This included among others young Langdon,

---

subjected to the control requirements of scientific experimentation. All these supernatural occurrences, it is claimed, demonstrate the transmission of thought from one person to another without the use of the ordinary five senses. Freud [5] in a lecture on "Dream and Occultism" refused to deny the possibility of telepathy and implied that dream interpretation offered a medium for the discovery of telepathic communication. He also pointed out that it may be inexpedient to apply the accepted and customary criteria of scientific proof to the investigation of such phenomena. It is entirely possible that they may operate only under conditions quite at variance with ordinary reality experiences. Very recently extrasensory perception has been subjected to extensive but inconclusive laboratory experimentation at Duke University by Rhine,[6] who is inclined to accept it as a fact.

Elsie Venner, accompanied by her father, Dudley, who rarely appeared socially, and Dr. Kittredge, the Venner's physician.

Dr. Kittredge was the leading physician of Rockland, a shrewd man, sixty-three years old, with a consulting practitioner's mouth—that is, movable round the corners while the case is under examination but both corners well drawn down and kept so when the final opinion is made up. There was some talk about his not being so long-sighted as other folks but his old patients laughed and looked knowing when this was spoken of.

The Doctor knew a good many things besides how to drop tinctures and shake out powders. He could tell at a glance when a nervous woman is in that condition in which a rough word is like a blow to her and the touch of unmagnetized fingers reverses all her nervous currents. It is not everybody that enters into the soul of Mozart's harmonies; and there are vital symphonies in low, sad keys which a doctor may know as little of as a hurdygurdy player of the essence of divine musical mysteries. When the Doctor was listening to common talk, he was in the habit of looking over his spectacles; if he lifted his head so as to look through them at the person talking, he was busier with that person's thoughts than with his words.*

Many eyes at the party were fixed on Elsie when she en-

---

* In every town of ten thousand the bulk of the general practice is usually in the hands of one practitioner. Many times he is not the physician with the best medical background but he possesses qualities equally as valuable as scientific knowledge. He has the capacity to "feel in" (empathy) with his patient, sometimes called sympathy. He will know that many a young girl's indigestion is anxiety concerning her latest beau's intentions, that many a young man's feeling of physical debility is a frustration in a current love affair, or a failure to be elected to a fraternity, or some disappointment which

tered with her father. She was, indeed, an apparition of wild beauty, so unlike the other girls about her that the groups parted to let her pass through them. Her black hair lay in a braided coil with a long gold pin shot through it like a javelin. Round her neck was a golden "torque," a round, cord-like chain such as the Gauls used to wear. Her dress was a grayish watered silk; her collar was pinned with a flashing diamond brooch; her arms were bare and slender, in keeping with her lithe round figure. On her wrists she wore bracelets; one was a circlet of enameled scales; the other looked as if it might have been Cleopatra's asp, with its body turned to gold and its eyes to emeralds.

Her father looked like a man of breeding but one whose life had met some fatal cross. He saluted few persons except his entertainers and the Doctor. Hardly anybody seemed to know Elsie. She drew her arm out of her father's, stood against the wall, and looked with a cold glitter at the crowd.*

The old Doctor came up to her by and by.

"Well, Elsie! Do tell me how you happened to come to such a great party."

"It's been dull at the mansion house," she said, "it's too lonely there—there's nobody to hate since Dick's gone."

The Doctor laughed good-naturedly, as if this were an

---

may seem very trivial to the adult but which is a tragedy at the time.

* Often a solitariness of this type may be the only symptom manifested by a person suffering from pathological introspection at the beginning of mental disorders of the schizoid group. Failure in social adaptation leads to isolation and further solitude and a vicious cycle becomes more and more fixed. Such loneliness may affect not only individuals but couples and families and is only brought to their attention when some striking evidence, as the isolation of Mr. Venner and his daughter, cannot be ignored by them.

amusing bit of pleasantry; but he lifted his head and dropped his eyes a little, so as to see her through his spectacles. She narrowed her lids slightly, as one often sees a sleepy cat narrow hers, so that her eyes looked very small, but bright as the diamonds on her breast. The old Doctor felt very oddly as she looked at him; he did not like the feeling and looked at her "over" his spectacles again.

She continued: "There's nobody left but Dudley and I. I'm tired of it. What kills anybody quickest, Doctor?" Then, in a whisper, "I ran away again the other day, you know—to the old place. Here, I brought this for you," and she handed him a flower of the "Atragene Americana." He knew that there was only one spot where it grew and that not one where a thin-shod woman's foot should venture.

"How long were you gone?" said the Doctor.

"Only one night. Dudley was frightened out of his wits. They hunted all over but I was farther up."

Doctor Kittredge looked worried while she was speaking but forced a professional smile, as he said,

"Have a good dance this evening, Elsie. Where's the young master?"

The girl turned away without answering.

The mansion-house gentry were just beginning to arrive and Bernard came in later than any of them; he had been busy with his new duties. He made his bow to the Colonel, began looking about him for acquaintances and spied sprightly Rosa Milburn.

"What can I do better," he said to himself, "than have a dance with Rosa Milburn?" He was sensible of a strange fascination toward Rosa but remembered that Nature makes every man love all women and trusts the trivial matter of special choice to the commonest accident.

Presently he felt his eyes drawn to a figure he had not dis-

tinctly recognized and felt that Elsie Venner was looking at
him. The diamond eyes affected him strangely and he became
silent and dreamy. The round-limbed Rosa at his side crushed
her gauzy draperies against him but it was no more to him
than if an old nurse had laid her hand on his sleeve. The
girl chafed at his seeming neglect but he appeared unconscious of it.

"There is one of our young ladies I must speak to," he
said. Then went to look for Elsie Venner; she was gone.

*   *   *

During the night Mr. Bernard had been dreaming, as young
men dream, of gliding shapes with bright eyes and burning
cheeks, strangely blended with red planets and hissing me-
teors. The next day after breakfast he found Miss Darley at
work.

It would not have been strictly true to call her beautiful, for
Helen could not in the nature of things have possessed the
kind of beauty which pleases the common taste. Her features
were very still except when her pleasant smile changed them
for a moment.

The young master stood looking at Helen with tender ad-
miration. But her question had asked itself—"Was Elsie
Venner at the party?"

"She was for an hour or so but she was gone when I looked
for her. What does this girl come to this school for?"

Miss Darley answered, "She says very little to anybody and
makes believe to study almost what she likes. I don't know
what she is" (Miss Darley laid her hand, trembling, on the
young master's sleeve), "but I can tell when she is in the
room without seeing or hearing her. I am nervous and no
doubt foolish—but—if there were women now as in the
days of our Saviour, possessed of devils, I should think there

was something not human looking out of Elsie Venner's eyes!"

* * *

"Abel," said Dr. Kittredge, "slip Cassia into the new sulky, and fetch her round."

Abel Stebbins was the Doctor's hired man and had Revolutionary blood in his veins. When he came to live with the Doctor, he made up his mind he would dismiss the old gentleman, if he did not behave according to his notions of propriety. But he soon found that the Doctor was one of the right sort, and so determined to keep him.

The Dudley mansion, where the Doctor was going, was not a mile away but it never occurred to him to think of walking to see any of his patients' families.*

The "Mansion" was near the eastern edge of The Mountain where it rose steepest. Higher up lay the accursed ledge —shunned by all, unless now and then a daring youth or naturalist ventured to its edge in the hope of securing some infantile "Crotalus durissus."

In Colonial times the Hon. Thomas Dudley had built this mansion and after the Revolution it passed by marriage into the hands of the Venners. The house kept its ancient name in spite of the change in line of descent. Its spacious apartments looked dreary and desolate, for here Dudley Venner and his daughter dwelt by themselves, with such servants as their quiet life required. He almost lived in his library on the ground floor. Except this room, the chamber where he slept, and the servants' wing, the rest of the house was all Elsie's. She was always a restless, wandering child from her early years, flitting round as the fancy took her. Sometimes

---

* The advent of the horseless buggy (Ford's Model T) and its glittering successors did not change doctors' indolent habits in this respect.

she would drag a mat into one of the great empty rooms, and coil up and go to sleep in a corner. Nothing frightened her; a "haunted" chamber with the torn hangings that flapped like wings when there was air stirring was one of her favorite retreats.

She had been a hard creature to manage. Her father could influence but not govern her. Old Sophy, born of a slave mother in the house, could do more with her than anybody, knowing her by long instinctive study. Her father had sent for governesses, but none of them ever stayed long; she made them nervous. A young Spanish woman who taught her dancing succeeded best with her for she had a passion for that exercise.

Long before this period she had manifested some extraordinary singularities of taste or instinct. There were stories floating round, some of them even getting into the papers, without name, which were of a kind to excite intense curiosity. Once in a while she had stayed out overnight, in which case men went in search of her but never successfully, so that some said she hid herself in trees or in one of the old Tory caves. Also, it was said she was a crazy girl and ought to be sent to an asylum. But old Dr. Kittredge had told them to let her have her way but to watch her as far as possible without making her suspicious. He visited her now and then, under the pretext of only making a friendly call.*

---

* The tendency in the twentieth century in mental illness has been consistently in the direction of treatment outside of institutions. The psychoanalytic approach has made it possible for many mentally ill persons, who would formerly have been sent to sanitaria and asylums, to continue to live in the community and pursue their work. In the other direction, the old asylum, with its atmosphere of isolation and despair, is gradually being replaced by mental hospitals which stand in closer relationship to the community. One

Now as the Doctor walked up the garden alley, a strange sound jarred upon his ear. It was a sharp prolonged rattle, continuous, but rising and falling as if in rhythmical cadence. He moved softly towards the open window.

Elsie was alone in the room, dancing one of those wild Moorish fandangos. The dancing frenzy must have seized upon her while she was dressing; for she was in her bodice, bare-armed, her hair floating unbound far below the waist of her skirt. She had caught up her castanets and rattled them as she danced with a kind of passionate fierceness, her eyes glittering, her round arms wreathing and unwinding. Some passion seemed to exhaust itself in this dancing paroxysm; for all at once she reeled from the middle of the floor and flung herself in a careless coil upon a great tiger's skin.*

The old Doctor stood motionless, looking at her as she lay panting on the tawny, black-lined robe. In a few moments her

---

of the urgent needs in the care of the mentally ill still remains unfilled—namely, a medically regulated public residence. There persons with mild illnesses might live and still continue to work at their customary occupations while they receive treatment at the psychiatric clinics of hospitals or from private psychiatrists.

* Holmes observed the caution and reticence of his time and polite environment in avoiding direct reference to sex. Nevertheless throughout his novels he indicates that he fully appreciated the conversion of the sexual impulse into indirect manifestations, both physical and mental. A few paragraphs further on the tomboy traits which Elsie early displayed may be interpreted as masculine (homosexual) components. Their existence would conform with psychoanalytic theories concerning the effect of contrary sexual tendencies in causing incomplete social adaptation and lack of friends among one's own sex. Difficulties of this type would eventually lead, as in Elsie's case, to isolation and solitude and these in turn to reaction-formations in temper outbursts, wilfullness and hypersensitivity.

head dropped upon her arm, and she was sleeping. He stood looking at her steadily, thoughtfully, tenderly. Presently he lifted his hand to his forehead as if recalling some fading "remembrance."

"Her poor mother!"

He shook his head, implying that his visit would be in vain today, returned to his sulky and rode away.

As the Doctor rode along he was roused from a revery by the clatter of hoofs and saw a young fellow galloping rapidly towards him.

The rider who passed the Doctor on a wild-looking mustang was Dick Venner, Elsie's first cousin, a dissolute, quick-tempered, unscrupulous youth. He had been raised with Elsie at the mansion until the age of ten and later had spent his youth with his mother's relatives in South America. Recently he had returned to Rockland to avoid arrest in Buenos Aires. Now he had determined to marry Elsie and become his Uncle Dudley's heir. When the Doctor saw him he was just returning from a spree in Boston.

In their early days these two motherless children were as strange a pair as one roof could well cover. Handsome, wild, impetuous, unmanageable, they played and fought together like two young leopards, their lawless instincts showing through all their movements.

Elsie was the wilder of the two. Old Sophy, who used to watch them with those quick, animal-looking eyes of hers—she was said to be the granddaughter of a cannibal chief and inherited the keen senses belonging to all creatures which are hunted as game—seemed to be more afraid for the boy than the girl.

These two wild children loved to ramble and play at boys' rude games as if both were boys. But wherever two natures have a great deal in common, the conditions of a first-rate quarrel are furnished ready-made. Relations are very apt to hate each other just because they are too much alike.* It is so frightful to see all the hereditary uncomeliness or infirmity of body, all the failings of temper, intensified by concentration, so that every fault of our own finds itself multiplied by reflections, like our images in a saloon lined with mirrors! The centrifugal principle which grows out of the antipathy of like to like is only the repetition in character of the arrangement we see expressed materially in certain seed capsules, which burst and throw the seed to all points of the compass. A house is a large pod with a human germ or two in each of its cells or chambers; it opens by dehiscence of the front-door by and by, and projects one of its germs to Kansas, another to San Francisco, and so on; and this that Smith may not be Smithed to death and Brown may not be Browned into a madhouse but mix in with the world again and struggle back to average humanity.

Elsie's father found that it would never do to let these children grow up together. They would either love each other as they got older and pair like wild creatures or take some fierce antipathy which might end nobody could tell where. Master Dick once vexed the girl into a paroxysm of wrath in which she sprang at him and bit his arm. They sent for the old Doctor who had a good deal to say about the danger from

---

* The quarreling in families, such as the rivalry of brothers, often has a deeper basis than reciprocal identification. More often such hatreds originate early in the nursery and home where the children compete for the attention and affection of their parents. The rivalries of children are apt to be intensified where parents give their love unequally and only spasmodically and where the children are compelled to repress their need for love from their parents. Another frequent variation of this process of sibling hatred occurs when a previously favored child is displaced in the parents' affections by a child who is born after an interval of a few years.

the teeth of animals or human beings when enraged and, as he emphasized his remarks by the application of a pencil of lunar caustic to the marks left by sharp teeth, they were like to be remembered by at least one of his hearers.

So Master Dick went off and Elsie was half pleased and half sorry to have him go; at any rate, she was lonely without him. She had more fondness for the old black woman than anybody—as for her father, she had made him afraid of her, not for his sake but for her own. Sometimes she would seem to be fond of him and the parent's heart would yearn within him as she twined her supple arms about him; and then some look she gave him, some half-articulated expression, would make him shiver but he would say, "Now go, Elsie dear," and smile upon her as she went.

Then his forehead would knot itself and drops of anguish stand thick upon it. He would go to the window of his study and look at the solitary mound with its marble headstone. After his grief had had its way, he would pray for his child as one who has no hope save in that special grace which can bring the most rebellious spirit into sweet subjection. All this might seem like weakness, but he had tried authority and tenderness by turns so long without any good effect that he left her in the main to her own guidance.

By the time events made it desirable for Dick to quit South America, he had seen life enough to wear out the earlier sensibilities of adolescence, and began thinking of a far-off village and of the wild girl with whom he used to play and quarrel. He bared his wrist to look for the marks she had left. "That's a filly worth noosing! I wonder if she will bite at eighteen as she did at eight!"

Such was the self-sacrificing disposition with which Richard turned his face in the direction of Rockland. Not long after this, Elsie professed to be pleased with the thought of having the adventurous young stranger an intimate of their quiet family. Under almost any other circumstances, her father would have been unwilling to take a young fellow of whom he knew so little under his roof, but this was his nephew and anything that seemed likely to amuse Elsie was agreeable to him. He felt as if any change in the current of her feelings might save her from some strange paroxysm of dangerous mental exaltation or sullen perversion of disposition.

It had been a curious meeting between the two young persons who had parted so young and after such strange relations with each other. Dick had something of the family beauty which belonged to his cousin but his eye had a fierce passion in it, very unlike the cold glitter of Elsie's. Like many people of strong and imperious temper he was soft-voiced and gentle in his address when he had no special reason for being otherwise. Elsie had a strange attraction for him, quite unlike anything he had known in other women. There was something, too, in early associations: when those who parted as children meet as man and woman, there is always a renewal of that early experience which followed the taste of the forbidden fruit, a natural blush of consciousness not without its charm.*

Nothing could be more becoming than the behavior of "Richard Venner, the guest of Dudley Venner, Esquire, at his noble mansion," as was announced in the "Rockland Weekly Universe." He made himself very agreeable by giving abundant details concerning the South American states and was himself much interested in everything going on. With Elsie he was subdued and almost tender; with the few

---

* Just what "forbidden fruit" might indicate in this connection would depend upon the interpreter. Few would question that it might imply that some early sexual inclination had existed between the two children.

visitors whom they saw, shy and silent. He had tried making downright love to Elsie but the girl was capricious as of old, teasing and malicious. All this, perhaps, made her more interesting to a young man who had tired of easy conquest.

They were sitting alone in the study one day and Elsie had round her neck the golden "torque." Dick was rash enough to put out his hand toward the neck that lay in the golden coil. She threw her head back, her eyes narrowing and her forehead drawing down so that Dick thought her head actually flattened itself. He started involuntarily, for she looked so like the little girl who had struck him with those flashing teeth and he felt the white scars on his wrist begin to sting.

                    *   *   *

When the nervous energy is depressed by any bodily cause or exhausted by overworking, there follow effects which have often been misinterpreted by moralists and especially by theologians. The conscience itself becomes actually inflamed so that the least touch is agony, and, of all liars and false accusers, a sick conscience is the most inventive and indefatigable.

Conscience itself requires a conscience, as nothing can be more unscrupulous than conscience.* It told Saul that he did well in persecuting the Christians and has goaded countless multitudes of various creeds to endless forms of self-torture. Our libraries are crammed with books written by spiritual hypochondriacs who inspected all their moral secretions a dozen times a day. They should be transferred from the shelf of the theologian to that of the medical man who makes a study of insanity.

---

* The extraordinarily strong conscience is usually built up in early childhood through an excessive love of or (and) fear of one parent

This was the state into which too much responsibility was bringing Helen Darley when the new master lifted much of the burden that was crushing her. Many of the noblest women die, worried out of life by the perpetual teasing of this neuralgic conscience. So subtle is the line which separates the almost angelic sensibility of a healthy but exalted nature from the soreness of a soul which is sympathizing with a morbid state of the body that it is no wonder they are often confounded.

As for school, sometimes when Helen Darley thought Elsie was at her desk, she would be on The Mountain, alone always. One day when she had followed the zigzag path a little way up she caught a glimpse of Dick following her. She turned and passed him, giving him a look which again made the scars tingle; then she went to her room. Old Sophy brought her food and set it down, not speaking, but looking into her eyes inquiringly like a dumb beast trying to feel out his master's will in his face.

That evening was clear. As Dick sat at his chamber window, looking at the mountainside, he saw a gray-dressed figure steal along the narrow path which led upward. Elsie's pillow was unpressed that night but she had not been missed by the household. The next morning the young schoolmaster found a flower between the leaves of his Virgil.

The girl got over her angry fit but rather shunned her cousin. She had taken a new interest in her books, which

---

or both. In later life the tenets of the conscience are reinforced by the power for punishment or reward vested in religion, the state, or even social usage. Such rigid consciences attempt to oppress and strangle ego activities and are especially severe with instinctive urges which clash with cultural demands. The type of conscience here described would be called in psychoanalytic writings a "sadistic superego," and is particularly active in causing melancholia and depressions associated with the neuroses.

gave Bernard a good chance to study her ways. The more he saw her, the more the sadness of her beauty wrought upon him. In all her features there was nothing of that human warmth which shows that sympathy has reached the soul beneath the mask of flesh it wears. The look was that of remoteness and in its stony apathy was the pathos which we find in the blind who show no film over the organs of sight; Nature had meant her to be lovely and left out nothing but love. Yet Bernard could not help feeling that some instinct was working in this girl which was leading her to seek his presence. What was the slight peculiarity of her enunciation? Not a lisp, certainly, but the least possible imperfection in articulating some of the lingual sounds, just enough to be noticed.

Not a word about the flower was spoken on either side. Bernard found it was not common and determined to explore the region where the wild girl sought the blossoms of which Nature was so jealous. One day he struck up The Mountain obliquely from the western side of the Dudley house and reached a point many hundred feet above the level of the plain. High up on one of the precipitous walls of rock he saw some tufts of flowers that he had found between the leaves of his Virgil. Not there, surely! No woman would have clung against that steep, rough parapet to gather an idle blossom.

He turned a sharp angle of the rock and found himself at the mouth of a cavern. When he looked into it, his look was met by the glitter of two diamond eyes, small, sharp, cold, shining out of the darkness, but gliding with a smooth, steady motion towards the light. He stood fixed, staring back into them with sudden numbness of fear that cannot move, as in the terror of dreams. The two sparks of light all at once lifted themselves up as if in angry surprise. Then for the first time thrilled in Bernard's ears the long, loud, stinging whirr, as a huge, thick-bodied reptile shook his many-jointed rattle and adjusted his loops for the fatal stroke. His ears rung as in the overture to the swooning dream of chloroform.

Nature was before man with her anaesthetics: the cat's first shake stupefies the mouse; the lion's first shake deadens the man's fear and feeling, and the "crotalus" paralyzes before he strikes. Bernard waited as in a trance, as a man waits for the axe to drop. But while he looked straight into the flaming eyes, it seemed to him that they were growing tame and dull; his numbness was passing away, he could move once more. Half turning, he saw the face of Elsie, also looking motionless into the reptile's eyes which had shrunk and faded under the stronger enchantment of her own.

* * *

The more common version among Rockland folk of the trouble at the mansion house was this: some whispered that at nearly fifteen years, when Elsie was in an irritable state of mind and body, she had become exasperated by the jealous guardianship of her governess and had attempted to get finally rid of her by unlawful means. At any rate, this governess had been taken suddenly ill and the Doctor had been sent for at midnight. Old Sophy said a few words to her master which turned him as white as a sheet. He in turn gave the old Doctor some few hints, on which he acted at once and had the satisfaction of seeing his patient out of danger before he left.

From this time forward her father was never easy. Should he keep her apart or shut her up for fear of risk to others, and so lose every chance of restoring her mind by kindly influences and intercourse with wholesome natures? He took the Doctor as his adviser. The shrewd old man listened to the father's story, his explanations of possibilities, of probabilities.

There was nothing ever heard of like it, explained Mr. Venner. He had had an aunt who was peculiar; he had heard that hysteric girls showed the strangest forms of moral obliquity for a time but came out right at last. Are there not rough buds that open into sweet flowers? In God's good time she would come to her true nature and her eyes would lose that frightful glitter; her lips would not feel so cold when she pressed them against his cheek; and that faint birthmark on her neck—her mother swooned when she first saw it—would fade wholly out; it was less marked, surely, now than it used to be!

There are states of mind which may be shared by two persons in presence of each other, which remain not only unworded but "unthoughted," if such a word may be coined for our special need.* Such a mutually interpenetrative consciousness there was between the father and the old physician. By a common impulse both of them rose in a mechanical

---

* The point at which thought is turned into words often causes great difficulties in persons whose instinctive urges and code of conduct are not in accord. The protection of "unthoughted" feeling is obvious—it does not even allow feeling to come to consciousness as a thought for which the person must assume responsibility. The borderline of conscious and unconscious mentation is probably a wide, shadowy band which exists at that point of human expression where affect turns into thought. Many patients have complained of the great difficulty in finding words which would suitably express their thought. This blocking is due principally to the fact that they wish to find words which would express the affect of their thought yet not reveal their intent. This can seldom be achieved for few such words exist in any language. Sometimes this contradiction may be expressed by intonation—such as "you're *good*," with a sarcastic inflection meaning that you are really quite bad.

way and went to the western window, where each started as he saw the other's look directed towards the white stone in the plot of green turf.

The Doctor stood there looking up at the clouds which were angry and said: "There are a great many more clouds than rains, and more rains than strokes of lightning, and more strokes of lightning. than there are people killed. We must let this girl of ours have her way as far as it is safe. Send away this woman she hates, quietly. Get her a foreigner for a governess if you can—one that can dance and sing and will teach her. In the house old Sophy will watch her best; out of it you must trust her, I am afraid, for she will not be followed round. If she wanders at night, find her if you can. If she will be friendly with any young people, have them to see her—young men, especially. She will not love any one easily, perhaps not at all; yet love would be more like to bring her right than anything else. If any young person seems in danger of falling in love with her, send him to me for counsel."

Dry, hard advice but given in tones which were full of sympathy. This advice was the key to the more than indulgent treatment which the girl received from all about her. The old Doctor came often in the most natural way, got into pleasant relations with Elsie, rarely reminding her that he was a professional adviser.

"Let her go to the girls' school, by all means," said the Doctor. "Anything to interest her. Friendship, love, religion —whatever will set her nature to work. We must have headway or there will be no piloting her. Action first of all and then we will see what to do with it." *

---

* The psychiatrist undertakes a baffling and tedious task when he seeks to reach emotions immobilized and imprisoned beneath the

When Cousin Dick came along, the Doctor, though he did not like his looks any too well, told her father to encourage his staying. If she liked him, it was good; if she only tolerated him, it was better than nothing. Mr. Venner owned that he sometimes thought that this nephew of his might take a serious liking to Elsie. What should he do about it, if it turned out so?

The Doctor thought that Elsie was naturally what they call a man-hater and there was very little danger of any sudden passion springing up between her and Dick.

Although Dick feared Elsie's violence he continued to wish to marry her and succeeded in ingratiating himself with her father but not with the old Negress, Sophy. Meanwhile Bernard had aroused the enmity of Dick, who thought Bernard might also have plans and motives like his own. This was not the case, although Elsie had given unquestionable evidence of her desire to have Bernard love her. The mystery of Elsie's home and conduct perplexed Bernard and he determined to investigate it. He was aware that the relation believed to exist between man and reptiles was held to be so instinctive that the snake had been adopted as the symbol of evil. He also had become acquainted with Braid's work in hypnotism. The latter had found that by "fixing the eyes on a bright object so as to maintain a steady stare there comes in a few seconds a condition characterized by inability to move—a strange exaltation of most senses." He was interested to discover whether it were

surface by patients who remain detached, impersonal. He must attempt gently to probe and pry in the hope that the coiled springs of emotional life may be loosened and brought into action. Often he is able to do this and thinks for a moment that it has been accomplished permanently, only to have the patient again and again close the breach in his protecting wall of impassivity. The approach of Dr. Kittredge is sound, particularly the idea that a "foreigner," not bound by New England traditions of repression might help to achieve a release in Elsie's emotional life.

possible that the snake's eyes served the same purpose as Braid's "bright object" or whether they had any special power of their own. Bernard also learned that certain people could handle rattlers with impunity. He himself procured some reptiles which he placed in a cage for study. He found that he was not the least affected while looking at his reptiles in captivity. Their eyes "with their pitiless indifference were hardly enlivened by the almost imperceptible slit of the pupil through which death seemed looking out."

The first thoughts Langdon's small menagerie suggested to him were the grave though somewhat worn subject of the origin of evil. Look at the "Crotalus," ye who would know what is the tolerance which can suffer such an incarnation of all that is devilish to lie unharmed in the cradle of Nature. Learn, too, that there are many things which we are suffered to slay, but which we must not hate, unless we would hate what God cares for.*

In the meantime Bernard had become curious about several subjects not treated in textbooks, and on a visit to old Dr. Kittredge asked him if he had an extensive medical library.

"Why, no," said he, "and what I have I don't read quite as often as I might. I read when I was in the midst of young men all at work with their books; but it's a mighty hard matter when you go off alone into the country to keep up with all that's going on in the Societies. I'll tell you, though, when

---

* Holmes's scientific interest in snakes may have been dependent upon their symbolism of moral evil rather than upon their typical phallic connotation. This interest, with which he was so concerned, continued until late in his life and was shared by his friend Dr. S. Weir Mitchell, the distinguished Philadelphia neurologist and novelist. Mitchell was an authority on the venoms of serpents and this was the subject of a lively interchange of letters with Holmes as late as 1883.[7]

a man that's once started right lives among sick folks for five
and thirty years, if he hasn't got a library of five and thirty
volumes bound up in his head at the end of that time he'd
better sell his sulky. I know the families that have a way of
living through everything, and I know the other set that have
the trick of dying without any kind of reason for it. I know
the folks that think they're dying as soon as they're sick and
folks that never find out they're sick till they're dead. I don't
want to undervalue science. There are things I never learned
because they came in after my day and I am glad to send my
patients to those that do know them when I am at fault; but
I know these people about here, fathers and mothers, and
children and grandchildren, as well as all the science in the
world can't know them. You can't tell a horse by driving him
once, Mr. Langdon, nor a patient by talking half an hour
with him." *

"Do you know much about the Venner family?" Bernard
finally asked. "I don't know what to make of Elsie. She is
getting a strange influence over my fellow teacher Helen
Darley. Elsie would have been burned for a witch in old
times. I have seen the girl look at Miss Darley when she
had not the least idea of it; I would see Miss Darley move
round uneasily and perhaps get up and go to Elsie, or else
have slight spasmodic movements that looked like hysterics."

"Mr. Langdon," the Doctor said solemnly, "there are

---

* Such close association with families and their characteristics over
a long period of time, now rare in medical practice, helped the intelligent physician to become something of a psychiatrist. Without such firsthand observations and hours spent in intimate talks
with patients, comparable to psychoanalytic sessions, Holmes would
probably never have been able to appreciate the motives and forces
which are determinant in psychiatric conditions. Such experience,
upon which a physician draws, is sometimes called intuition.

strange things about Elsie Venner. Let me advise you all to be very patient with the girl. Her love is not to be desired, and her hate is to be dreaded. Do you think she has any special fancy for anybody else besides Miss Darley?"

Mr. Bernard could not stand the Doctor's spectacled eyes without betraying a little of the feeling natural to a young man to whom a home question is put suddenly.

"Well, Doctor," he said, "I have thought Elsie Venner had rather a fancy for myself."

There was something remote from any shallow vanity in the blush with which the young man made this confession. The old Doctor looked at him admiringly.

"You are a man of nerve, Mr. Langdon?" asked the Doctor.

"I thought so till lately," he replied, "but I don't know whether I might be bewitched or magnetized or whatever it is when one is tied up and cannot move. I think I can find nerve enough, however, if there is any special use you want to put it to."

"Do you find yourself disposed to take a special interest in Elsie, Mr. Langdon—to fall in love with her, in a word?"

"Elsie," said the young man, "has a wild flavor wholly different from that of any human creature. She has marks of genius—poetic or dramatic. She read a passage from Keat's 'Lamia' the other day in such a way that I thought some of the girls would faint. They are afraid of her, and she seems to have either a dislike or a fear of them. Not one of them will look her in the eyes. I pity the poor girl, but I do not love her. There must be something in that creature's blood which has killed the humanity in her."

The Doctor then warned Bernard to beware of Dick and gave him a pistol in case he should need it, for he knew Dick's violence and ruthlessness. Bernard questioned the Doctor concerning the nature of Elsie's peculiarities, but, not quite satisfied with the replies, decided to write to his old professor at Medical School.

Mr. Langdon to the Professor:

MY DEAR PROFESSOR,—You promised me that you would assist me in any scientific investigations in which I might become engaged.

Is there any evidence that human beings can be infected by poisons so that they shall manifest the peculiarities belonging to beings of a lower nature? Can such peculiarities be transmitted by inheritance? Is there anything to countenance the stories about the "evil eye"? Have you any personal experience as to the power of "fascination" said to be exercised by certain animals? What can you make of circumstantial statements of children forming mysterious friendships with ophidians and sharing food with them. Have you read Coleridge's "Christabel" and Keats' "Lamia"? Can you find any physiological foundation for either story? Do you think predispositions, inherited or ingrafted, shall take out certain apparently voluntary determinations from the control of the will and leave them as free from moral responsibility as the instincts of the lower animals? Do you not think that there may be "crime" which is not "sin"?

Your friend and pupil, BERNARD C. LANGDON

The Professor to Mr. Langdon:

MY DEAR MR. LANGDON,—The questions you put belong to that middle region between science and poetry which sensible men, as they are called, are very shy of meddling with. I don't doubt that there is some truth in the phenomena of animal magnetism but when you ask me to cradle for it, I tell you that hysteric girls cheat so and the professionals are such a set of pickpockets that I can do something better than hunt for the grains of truth among their tricks. Do you remember what I used to say in my lectures?—don't begin to pry until you have the long arm of leverage on your side.

To please you I have looked into the old books and I can answer your first question in the affirmative. Cardanus gets a story from Avicenna, of a certain man bit by a serpent, who recovered of his bite, the snake dying therefrom. This man afterwards had a daughter whom venomous serpents could not harm though "she had a fatal power over them."

You may remember the statements of old authors about "lycanthropy," the disease in which men took on the nature of wolves. Actius and Paulus, both men of authority, describe it. "Versipelles" it may be remembered was the Latin name for these "were-wolves." As for the case where rabid persons have barked and bit like dogs, there are plenty of such on record, some of recent date.*

---

* The snake (vampire) is often used as a symbol of sexual danger for men as well as women. In common with other animals, snakes symbolized the devil, danger, and sexuality, and had the power actually to enter the human body. Subsequently in the era of belief in witches, werewolves played a great part as agents of the Devil. A passage from Hertz quoted by Jones [8] throws much light upon this subject: "In the Christian era, when one admitted the existence of heathen gods so as to explain them away as devils . . . there arose with the belief in witches the idea of men who from pure lust of murder used Satan's help to turn themselves into wolves. The Werewolf thus became in sinister poetical symbolism the image of the animal and demoniacal in human nature, of the insatiable egotism that is the enemy of the whole world, which inspired old and modern pessimists to the hard saying: Homo homini lupus." Jones continues: "It was believed that Werewolves gathered together just as witches did, that they travelled through the air, held a Sabbath, . . . and indulged in sexual orgies among themselves. Many of these details were made public at trials . . . in the year

One of the striking alleged facts connected with the mysterious relation existing between the serpent and the human species is the influence which the poison of the "Crotalus," taken internally, seemed to produce over the "moral faculties" in the experiments instituted by Dr. Hering at Surinam. It is natural enough that the evil principle should have been represented in the form of a serpent but it is strange to think of introducing it into a human being like cow-pox by vaccination.*

I am afraid I cannot throw much light on "Christabel" or "Lamia." Geraldine in the former, seems to be simply a malignant witch-woman with the "evil-eye" but with no absolute ophidian relationship. Lamia is a serpent transformed by magic into a woman. The idea of both is mythological and not in any sense physiological. Some women unquestionably suggest the image of serpents; men rarely or never.

Your question about inherited predispositions, as limiting the will and consequently moral accountability, opens a wide range of speculations. Crime and sin, being the "preserves" of two great organized interests, have been guarded against all reforming poachers with as great jealousy as the Royal Forests. It is so much simpler to consign a soul to perdition, or say masses, for money, to save it than to take the blame on ourselves for letting it grow up in neglect and run to ruin. The English law never began to get hold of the idea that a

---

1521. . . . These described how the Devil had transformed the victims into wolves by rubbing them with an ointment. . . . The anointing evidently refers to the well-known witch's ointment."

* Snake venom has been used in recent years in the treatment of epilepsy but with no positive results. The main use of snake venom today is in cases of purpura hemorrhagica and hemophilia where it seems to have the effect of increasing the coagulability of the blood.

crime was not necessarily a sin till Hadfield, who thought he was the Saviour of mankind, was tried for shooting at George the Third.

We recognize all the bodily defects that unfit a man for military service and the intellectual ones that limit his range of thought but always talk at him as if his moral powers were perfect. The limitations of human responsibility have never been properly studied, unless by the phrenologists. You know that I consider phrenology a pseudo-science but, for all that, we owe it an immense debt. If it has failed to demonstrate its system of special correspondences, it has brought out that great doctrine of moral insanity, which has done more to soften legal and theological barbarism than any one doctrine since the message of peace and good will to men.

Automatic action in the moral world, the "reflex movement" which "seems" to be self-determination, has been banged and howled at as such (metaphorically) for nobody knows how many centuries. Until somebody shall study this as Marshall Hall has studied reflex nervous action in the bodily system, I would not give much for men's judgments of each other's characters.*

---

* The idea of charitableness in the judgment of one's fellow man can be traced in more recent times to the influence of such men as Voltaire and Rousseau. Their philosphy and ideals first fostered freedom in religious and liberal thinking and were a powerful force in that awakening which led to the French Revolution. There is evidence that the humane treatment of the mentally ill, which is attributed to Pinel in France about 1795, had its origin in the same wave of liberal thought. Two Viennese physicians, Dr. Francois Gall (1758–1828) who developed phrenology and Dr. Franz Anton Mesmer (1733–1815) who discovered mesmerism, went to Paris because of the intellectual freedom there.

Freud's work is related to Mesmer's discoveries and cures which

I suppose the study of automatic action in the moral world (you see what I mean through the apparent contradiction of terms) may be a dangerous one and is liable to abuse. People are always glad to get hold of anything which limits their responsibility. But remember that our moral estimates come down through ancestors who hanged children for stealing forty shillings' worth and sent their souls to perdition for the sin of being born, and who punished the unfortunate families of suicides.*

I will tell you my rule in life: "Treat bad men exactly as if they were insane." They are "in-sane," out of health morally. Reason, which is food to sound minds, is not tolerated, still less assimilated, and unless administered with the greatest caution, perhaps not at all. Avoid collision with bad men so far as you honorably can; keep your temper if you can, for one angry man is as good as another; restrain them from vio-

---

were based on the procedure later called hypnotism. However, Freud was among the first to investigate those psychologically determined and conditioned reactions which work almost reflexly and which can be set in motion not only by conscious but unconscious motivation. The influence of unconscious mentation is one of Freud's most important discoveries.

* The concept of suicide as a crime had its basis in the age-old idea that it was an offense against both the church and the state, which alone were presumed to have the right to terminate life. As late as 1910, suicide was a crime in New York State, and if a person survived the attempt he was arrested and sent to prison or the prison ward of a hospital. He was presumed to appear before a judge who could then sentence him to a prison term. Many judges at that time were already quite willing to waive the legal procedures calling for the appearance in court of these persons, most of whom were suffering from severe mental illness. Today this practice is almost universally accepted in America.

lence promptly, completely, and with the least possible injury, just as in the case of maniacs. When you have got them so that they can do no mischief, sit down and contemplate them charitably, remembering that nine-tenths of their perversity comes from outside influences, drunken ancestors, abuse in childhood, bad company from which you have happily been preserved and for some of which you, as a member of society, may be fractionally responsible.

Yours very truly,

*   *   *

The Reverend Doctor Honeywood had reached that curious state so common in good ministers, namely, in which they contrive to switch off their logical faculties on the narrow sidetrack of their technical dogmas while the great freight train of their substantial human qualities keeps in the main highway of common sense. Men are tattooed with their special beliefs like so many South Sea Islanders; but a real human heart beats the same glow under all the patterns of all earth's thousand tribes!

At this moment Dr. Honeywood's little granddaughter, Letty, interrupted him. "Do come, grandpapa," said the young girl; "here is a poor black woman who wants to see you!"

The Doctor folded the sermon and, looking at the young girl's face, forgot his logical conclusions and said to himself that she was a little angel, which was in violent contradiction to the leading doctrine of his sermon on Human Nature.

Black women remain at a stationary age (to the eyes of "white" people, at least) for thirty years. Bent up, wrinkled, yellow-eyed, still meek features, large flat hands with uncolored palms and slightly webbed fingers, it was impossible not to see a hint of the gradations with which life climbs up through the lower natures to the highest human developments. Old as she looked, her eye was bright and knowing. She had that touching stillness which belongs to animals that wait to be spoken to and then look up with sad humility.

Old Sophy was a member of Doctor Honeywood's church but there was a heathen flavor in her Christianity.

At last she spoke.

"It is my baby that will do something that will make them kill her or shut her up all her life. Oh, Doctor, save her, pray for her! If they knew all that I know, they wouldn' blame that poor child."

The minister soothed the poor soul and Sophy proceeded to tell her story in the low half-whisper which is the natural voice of grief and fears. She went far back to the time when Dudley Venner left college and fell in love with a young girl left in the world almost alone as he was.

In our pictures of life we must show the flowering-out of terrible growths which have their roots deep, deep underground. Just how far we shall lay bare the unseemly roots themselves is a matter of discretion and taste. The old woman told the whole story of Elsie, of her birth, of her teething, and how, when the woman to whose breast she had clung died suddenly, they had to struggle hard before she would learn feeding with a spoon. And so she came down to this present time. Elsie would hang her head sometimes, and look as if she were dreaming and Sophy had heard her whisper in her sleep as young girls do to themselves when they're thinking about somebody they have a liking for and think nobody knows it.

The minister listened in perfect silence. It was a very awkward matter for him as the Venners had a pew in Mr. Fairweather's meeting house and he would be the natural adviser. Was there enough capital of humanity in Fairweather's somewhat limited nature to furnish unshrinking service in an emergency? or was he too busy with taking account of stock of his own thin-blooded offences to forget himself? Nevertheless, Doctor Honeywood thought the best thing would be to talk over these matters with Brother Fairweather.

When he came to think of it, he did not feel quite so sure "practically" about that matter of the utter natural selfishness of everybody. He had seen young persons naturally unselfish, a family trait in some he had known. But most of all he was exercised about Elsie. If a person receives any injury which impairs the intellect or the moral perceptions is it not monstrous to judge such a person by common working standards of right and wrong?* Certainly it is, where there is a palpable organic change brought about, as when a blow on the head produces insanity. How long will it be before we shall learn that for every wound which betrays itself to the sight by a scar there are a thousand unseen mutilations that cripple, each of them some one or more of our highest faculties? If what Sophy believed was the truth, what tenderness could be deep enough for this blighted child?

The minister thought these matters over, laid by his old

* The type of tolerance for which Holmes pleads has made some progress with the present-day social conscience, but a definite difference and contradiction still exist between the legal and medical definitions of responsibility in cases of crime, ranging from such a relatively mild offense as exhibitionism to murder. Generally all that the law wishes to ascertain in a given instance is whether the accused person knew the nature and purpose of his act at the time of its commission. Such an attitude does not take into consideration the innumerable forces, conscious as well as unconscious, social as well as ethical, entering into the commission of any crime, especially those in which the defective intelligence or the weak moral inhibitions of the criminal play a determining part.

sermon and began to write one, afterwards so famous, "On the Obligations of an Infinite Creator to a Finite Creature." It astonished the good people to hear their minister insisting on what was reasonable and fair to his fellow creatures was really much more respectful to his Maker and a great deal manlier than if he had pretended that man had not rights as well as duties. The same logic carried him so far that he put his foot into several heresies, for which men had been burned so often. He argued that if a person inherited a perfect mind, body, and disposition and had perfect teaching from infancy, that person could do nothing more than keep the moral law perfectly.

This was the dangerous vein of speculation in which the Reverend Honeywood found himself involved, as a consequence of old Sophy's communication. Hence he was in a seemingly self-contradictory state of mind when he went forth to call on his heretical brother.

The old minister took it for granted that Mr. Fairweather knew the private history of his parishioner's family. He did not reflect that there are griefs men "never" put into words, that there are fears which must not be spoken, intimate matters of consciousness which must be carried as bullets which have been driven deep into the living tissues are sometimes carried for a whole life time, "encysted" griefs, if we may borrow the chirurgeon's term, never to be reached, never to be thrown out but to go into the dust with the frame that bore them during long years of anguish, known only to the sufferer and his Maker.*

---

* In the earlier days of psychoanalysis, unconscious mental trends were known as "hidden complexes." In this connection I should like to relate an amusing prank which was played on each new interne coming to the Manhattan State (mental) Hospital about 1909. An older doctor would ask the novitiate if he had brought his gum

Dudley Venner had talked with his minister but there was something about Mr. Fairweather which repressed all attempts at confidential intercourse. It sealed Dudley Venner's lips. The minister could not help discovering, however, that Elsie had manifested tendencies from an early age at variance with the theoretical opinions he was in the habit of holding for truth.

About this terrible fact of congenital obliquity his new beliefs began to take form. He might have struggled against them, had it not been for the little Roman Catholic Chapel with its worshippers running over at the door like berries heaped too full in the measure. Oh, could he have felt that he was in the great ark which holds the better half of the Christian world while all around it are wretched creatures, some struggling against the waves in leaky boats, some on ill-connected rafts, and some with their heads just above water, thinking to ride out, upon their own private, life-preservers, the flood which is to sweep the earth clean of sinners! His people and he were clearly in a minority and his deep inward longing was to be with the majority.

If a man wishes to get rid of his liberty, if he is really bent upon becoming a slave, nothing can stop him and the temptation is to some natures a very great one. Liberty is often a heavy burden on a man. It involves that necessity for perpetual choice which is the kind of labor men have always dreaded.* In common life we shirk it by forming "habits,"

---

shoes. When the newcomer credulously replied, "What for?" the answer would be, "You've got to have them if you want to stay on the staff now-a-days to sneak up on those 'hidden complexes.'"

* In unconscious longings of this type the desire is retained by the adult to continue dependent upon replicas of the authorities of childhood rather than to assume the responsibility for and consequences of his own actions. They are partially accountable for such

which take the place of self-determination. In politics, party organization saves us the pains of much thinking before deciding how to cast our vote. In religious matters there are great multitudes watching us perpetually, each propagandist ready with his bundle of finalities, which having accepted we may be at peace. The more absolute the submission demanded, the stronger the temptation becomes to those who have been long tossed among doubts and conflicts.

So it is that in all the quiet bays which indent the shores of the great ocean of thought, at every sinking wharf we see moored the hulks and the razees of enslaved or half-enslaved intelligences. They rock peacefully as children in their cradles on the subdued swell which comes feebly in over the bar at the harbor's mouth, slowly crusting with barnacles, pulling at their iron cables as if they really wanted to be free but better contented to remain bound as they are. For these no more the round unwalled horizon of the open sea, the joyous breeze aloft, the foam, the sparkle that track the rushing keel! Happiest of souls, if lethargy is bliss and palsy the chief beatitude!

We are liable to be intolerant and forget that weakness is not in itself a sin; that even cowardice may call for lenient judgment, if it spring from innate infirmity. The boldest thinker may have his moments of languor and discouragement, when he feels that if he could drop all coherent thought, and lie in the flowery meadow with the brown-eyed, solemnly unthinking cattle—no individual mind-movement

---

emotional upheavals as Naziism in Germany with an almost absolute subordination to a leader. The need for dependency may be rationalized in many ways. In Germany, particularly, the ideal of strict training of children has prevailed for many centuries and this childhood training may partially account for the readiness with which the Germans submitted to a dictatorship.

such as men are teased with, but the great calm cattle-sense of all places that know the milky smell of herds—if he could be like these, he would be content to be driven home by the cow-boy. Let us be very generous, then, in our judgment of those who leave the front ranks of thought for the company of the meek noncombatants who follow with the baggage and provisions. Age, illness, too much wear and tear, a half-formed paralysis may bring any of us to this pass. But while we can think and maintain the rights of our own individuality against every human combination, let us not forget to caution all who are disposed to waver that there is a cowardice which is criminal, and a longing for rest which it is baseness to indulge.

The Reverend Honeywood did go to visit the Reverend Fairweather, a querulous, dissatisfied man, to talk with him about Elsie. The interview was not too happy. Mr. Fairweather knew little about Elsie but thought her self-willed and unamenable to good influences. He held it as a personal grievance that she had once thrown a book he had given her from the Sunday school library out of the window. In fact, Elsie had proved to be precisely the type of child who was driving the liberal minister to believe in the doctrine of original sin. He was mystified when the Calvinist Dr. Honeywood disagreed with him and tried to convince him that "perversion itself may often be disease."* However, he was not very successful.

---

* Such a contradiction between theory and practice often surprises children as well as adults. It is illustrated by the following incident in the life of a young male patient. He had been brought up by his mother, a strict and severe woman, an Episcopalian. When he was about eight years old his mother took him to visit two cousins about his age, children of a Quaker family in Pennsylvania. The children in their play had rummaged about in an old garret and had come upon some Revolutionary muskets, with which they began to parade around the front yard. A Quaker uncle, seeing them,

There were particular times when Elsie was in such a mood that it must have been a bold person who would have intruded upon her with reproof or counsel. A strange, paroxysmal kind of life belonged to her, which seemed to come and go with the sunlight. All winter long she would be easy to manage, listless, slow in her motions, and her eye would lose something of its lustre. As the spring came on Elsie would have her tiger-skin spread in the southern chamber and lie there basking for hours in the sunshine. The light would kindle afresh in her eyes and Sophy knew that there was no trusting her impulses or movements.

At last, when the veins of the summer were hot and swollen, and the juices of all the poison plants and the blood of all the creatures that feed upon them had grown thick and strong, the life of Elsie seemed fullest of its malign instincts. She was never so much given to roaming over The Mountain as at this season and to take the night as the day for her rambles. All her peculiar tastes in dress came out in a more striking way and never was she so threatening in her scowling beauty.

* * *

Dudley Venner had been so long in the habit of looking at Elsie as exceptional in the law of her nature that it was

---

remarked to the Quaker children's mother, "Dost thee not think it wrong for the children to act thus? It will give them bellicose ideas." But the Quakeress knowing full well the Quakers' ideas about war replied, "They are only children, let them play." However, the Episcopalian mother, whose faith included no such tenets about war and fighting, immediately cried to her son, "William, put that musket down at once," which seemed to the boy "very funny and incongruous," and did not increase his respect or love for his mother.

difficult for him to think of her as a girl to be fallen in love with. Many persons are surprised when others court their female relatives; they know them as good, young or old women but never think of anybody's falling in love with them. But in this case there were special reasons; who would "dare" to marry Elsie? He talked about it with Dr. Kittredge.

"Let her have the pleasure at any rate of the wholesome excitement of companionship," said the Doctor; "it might save her from lapsing into melancholy or a worse form of madness." *

Dudley Venner had a kind of superstition that, if Elsie could only outlive twenty-one years, so that, according to the prevalent idea, her whole frame would have been thrice made over, she would revert to health of mind and feelings. The thought of any other motive than love being sufficient to induce her cousin Richard to become her suitor had not occurred to him. Dudley had married early, and his single idea of marriage was that it was the union of persons naturally drawn towards each other by some mutual attraction. Very simple, perhaps; but he had lived lonely for many years since his wife's death and judged the hearts of others by his own.

---

* Apparently Holmes appreciated that melancholy was not the worst form of "madness," perhaps that people usually recovered from it, whereas they rarely did from another form which so frequently afflicted young people—a form now called dementia precox or schizophrenia. The differentiation between these two types of mental disease, manic-depressive and dementia precox, the former recoverable, the latter often chronic, was first clearly made by Emil Kraepelin at Heidelberg about 1890. It is possible that Holmes suspected that the mental disease which he described in Elsie approached the incurable type. The symptoms in the early stages of schizophrenia and the manic-depressive group of psychoses may be quite similar and a diagnosis may be difficult to establish.

It is easy to criticize other people's modes of dealing with their children. Outside observers see results; parents see processes. They notice the trivial movements and accents which betray the blood of this or that ancestor. To be a parent is almost to be a fatalist. This boy's grandfathers both died before he was born but the boy had the movement of the eyebrows of one of them and the gusty temper of the other.

These are things parents can see and must take account of in education but which few except parents can be expected to really understand. Here and there a sagacious person who has observations from the several standing places of three different generations can tell pretty nearly the range of possibilities and the limitations of a child, actual or potential, of a given stock. Errors must be excepted always, because children of the same stock are never bred the same and because each human being has, after all, a small fraction of individuality about him which occasionally makes a genius or a saint or a criminal of him.

There were not wanting people who accused Dudley of the great mistake of not "breaking her will" when Elsie was a little child. She'd got the upper hand now but if he'd only taken hold of her in season! * Still, so soon as Elsie's father found that he could not govern his child, he gave his life up to pro-

---

* One of the great advances in social practice in America has been the increasingly early attention paid to deviations in conduct in young children and the utilization of psychiatrists and psychiatric social workers in schools and colleges to investigate such departures properly. The neglected child often becomes overaggressive or too recessive. The courts today are inclined to regard a child detected in stealing, destructiveness, arson, and so on, as neglected rather than delinquent. The responsibility for the antisocial conduct has thus been shifted from the child to its parents, its guardians, and

tecting her as far as he could. It was a stern and terrible trial for a man of acute sensibility, not without force of intellect and the manly ambition for his family name. Passive endurance is the hardest trial to such persons. What made it still more martyrdom was the necessity for bearing his cross in utter loneliness.

In the dawn of his manhood Dudley Venner had found that second consciousness for which young men and young women go about looking into each other's faces. He had found his other self early, before he had grown weary in the search and wasted his freshness in vain longings. The life he had led for a brief space, that delicious process of the tuning of two souls to each other, string by string, not without little half-pleasing discords now and then when some chord in one or the other proves to be overstrained or overlax, but always approaching nearer to harmony until they become at last as two instruments with a single voice. Something more than a year of this blissful consciousness had passed over him when he found himself alone save for the diamond-eyed child lying in the black woman's arms.

He would not die by his own act. There may have been other, perhaps better, reasons but this was enough; he did not come of suicidal stock. He must live for this child's sake, at any rate. Sometimes her little features would look placid, but all at once her eyes would narrow and she would throw her head back and a shudder would seize him. He could not

---

finally to society and to the social state which the people construct and uphold.

Such changes in legal positions must come gradually, for they depend on popular support. If the social ideals of advanced thought are too far ahead of the general ethical level of the average man, they cannot succeed. Even the Court of Appeals depends for its authority on the standards of the common people, in the last analysis.

look upon her—nay, there would sometimes come into his soul such frightful suggestions that he would hurry from the room lest the hinted thought should become a momentary madness and he should lift his hand against the hapless infant.

He loved to dwell upon the chances that an overhanging cliff, which frowned upon his home beneath in a very menacing way, might crash down on the roofs below. He thought of such a catastrophe with a feeling almost like pleasure. It would be such a swift solution of this problem he was working out in ever-recurring daily anguish. Danger is often the best "counter-irritant" in cases of mental suffering; he found a solace in careless exposure of his life.*

Time, the great consoler, helped and he gradually fell into

---

* This statement concerning danger is true at least to a limited extent. It involves the concepts of fear and anxiety. Danger which is actual and real arouses fear which provokes the organism to take measures for its own preservation. Threats which are imaginary or actual dangers which are regarded in an exaggerated degree give rise to anxiety. Generally the person is conscious of the close relationship between the danger and the fear. Often the fundamental threat which gives rise to anxiety may be unconscious and the anxiety is referred to (displaced upon) some more tangible, "real" danger.

In anxiety there is usually some indecision as to the method of meeting the threat, often due to an uncertainty as to whether to yield to the threat because of a feeling of guilt or to struggle against it for self-advantage or self-preservation. For this reason when an imminent danger arises concerning which the person has no doubts as to his immediate course of action, he is likely to take action which will replace the vacillation of anxiety.

The following excerpt from the dream of a married man, aged thirty-four, the father of three children, will illustrate that this reaction takes place even in dreams. He suffered, among other symp-

more easy habits of life. By an infinite effort, he forced himself
to become the companion of this child for whom he had such

---

toms, from chronic anxiety and a phobia that in a frenzied moment
he might kill his family.

His dream was that he was riding with his wife and children on
an elevated train. They came to a station where his family got out
but he remained on the train. When he realized this he became
much disturbed and developed an acute anxiety in his dream. He
could not decide whether at the next station he would stop and take
a train back to rejoin his family or walk back. When the train arrived at the next station people got off and began to jump directly
from the station to the street. He realized that it was a danger
he had to face. Possibly some one pushed him off the platform.
(He is not sure.) However in the dream, when the actual danger
confronted him, all the anxiety, feeling of weakness and doubt disappeared and he felt much relieved.

Often the anxiety is associated with the threat of punishment
for unsanctioned sexual indulgences (infidelity, masturbation)
which might include insanity or castration for the offender. This
mechanism based on infidelity existed in the mind of the above
dreamer.

Edgar Allan Poe, the tormented poet, who has been the subject
of several psychiatric analyses, has reported his own reactions on
this question of anxiety and decision. In a letter he describes his
own suffering at several intervals when his beloved wife was threatened with death from hemorrhages from the throat. "Each time
I felt all the agonies of her death. I am constitutionally sensitive—
nervous in a very unusual degree. I became insane, with long intervals of horrible sanity. During these fits of absolute unconsciousness
I drank, God only knows how often or how much.

"As a matter of course, my enemies referred the insanity to the
drink rather than the drink to the insanity. I had, indeed, nearly
abandoned all hope of a permanent cure when I found one in the
death of my wife. This I can & do endure as becomes a man—it
was the horrible never-ending oscillation between hope & despair

a mingled feeling, and Elsie grew up with a kind of filial feeling for him, such as her nature was capable of.* She never would obey him; that was not to be looked for. The mere physical effects of crossing her will betrayed themselves in such changes of expression and manner that it would have been senseless to attempt to govern her in any such way. Leaving her mainly to herself, she could be to some extent indirectly influenced.

Dudley Venner had grown gentle under this discipline and his expression was that of habitual sadness and anxiety, yet he disguised no misery to himself with the lying delusion of wine and sought no sleep from narcotics, though he lay with

---

which I could not longer have endured, without total loss of reason. In the death of what was my life, then, I received a new, but—oh God! how melancholy an existence!"

* The psychiatrist would necessarily be compelled to ignore any antenatal influences, such as a toxemia of pregnancy, in his plan for the rehabilitation of a patient like Elsie Venner. On the other hand, he would consider the mixed (ambivalent) feelings of the father (even hatred to the point of killing her, for all his sense of duty) as being actively responsible for much of her conduct, especially for the child's withdrawal from him and her rebellion. In effect Elsie had become a child rejected or never fully accepted by her father. No matter how conscientiously a rejecting parent attempts to disguise or compensate negative feelings, nevertheless through lack of sympathy and understanding they become manifest to the child at critical moments. This in turn may produce in the child some form of exaggerated resentment or a tendency to solitude and isolation. Sometimes there may develop an alternation between outbursts of temper and sullenness or seclusiveness, which are apparently contradictory but are nevertheless rooted alike in the feeling of not being really wanted or loved. An interesting sequence of this early feeling is the unconscious desire of the child not to mature. He lives in the hope that as long as he remains young he may still achieve the love which he feels he has missed.

·

throbbing, wide-open eyes through the weary hours of the night.

It was understood between Dudley and Doctor Kittredge that Elsie was a subject for occasional medical observation, on account of peculiarities which might end in a permanent affection of her reason. Beyond this nothing was said, whatever may have been in the mind of either. But Dudley had studied Elsie's case in the light of all the books he could find. As in all cases where men meddle with medical science for a special purpose, having no previous acquaintance with it, his imagination found what it wanted in the books and adjusted it to the facts before him. So he held vague hopes for her recovery. Not for the world would he have questioned his sagacious old medical friend as to the probability or possibility of their being true. We are very shy of asking questions of those who know enough to destroy with one word the hopes we live on.

Dudley Venner was tenderer in soul when he entered that period of forty to fifty years, which marks the decline of men who have ceased growing in knowledge and strength, than he had been in his younger years. The traces of that ineffaceable calamity of his life were softened and partially hidden by new growths of thought and feeling, as the wreck left by a mountain slide is covered over by the gentle intrusion of the soft-stemmed herbs which will prepare it for the stronger vegetation that will bring it once more into harmony with the peaceful slopes around it.

If Dudley Venner did not know just what he wanted, many people in Rockland thought they did: "Why shouldn't he make up to the Jedge's daughter? She was genteel enough for him, and—seven-n' twenty." But he said to himself that the Judge's daughter was a good specimen of the grand style of woman; and then the image came back to him of his wife, a woman not quite so judicial in her opinions but with two or three more joints in her frame and two or three soft inflections in her voice, so that he told her half his secrets in less time that it would have taken him to discuss the champion paper of the last Quarterly with the admirable "Portia." *

The woman a man loves is always his own daughter.** It is not the outside woman who takes his name that he loves: before her image has reached the centre of his consciousness, it has passed through fifty many-layered nerve strainers, been churned over by ten thousand pulse beats, and reacted upon by millions of lateral impulses which bandy it about through the mental space as a reflection is sent back and forward in a saloon lined with mirrors. With this altered image of the woman before him, his preëxisting ideal becomes blended. The object of his love is in part the offspring of her legal

---

* Holmes had little use for aggressive, formidable women, especially disliking those who were too intellectual. Apparently he appreciated that a disproportion of characteristics considered masculine in women and feminine in men led to difficulties in the adjustment of such persons both to themselves and to their environment. Freud shared these views emphatically as a personal reaction. He also believed that there were no factors which prepared the way for the development of a neurosis in a boy as surely as a strong, masculine mother and a weak father. In many case reports in psychoanalysis the compulsive symptoms are attributed to latent or unconscious bisexual conflicts which the patient has been unable to resolve because of a strong identification with the anomalous parent.

** Here again is a hint of the incest fantasy. The loss through death of Venner's wife may have unconsciously overdetermined his interest in the odd child she left with him. He not only loved her but also wished she were not there, and may have regarded his daughter as an obstacle to remarriage because unconsciously she was "the woman a man loves" but who is forbidden to him.

parents but more of her lover's brain. The difference between the real and the ideal objects of love must not exceed a fixed maximum. The heart's vision cannot unite them stereoscopically into a single image, if the divergence passes certain limits. A formidable analogy, much in the nature of a proof, with very serious consequences, which moralists and matchmakers would do well to remember! Double vision with the eyes of the heart is a dangerous physiological state, and may lead to missteps and serious falls.

Whether Dudley Venner would ever find a breathing image near enough to his ideal one was very doubtful. Some gracious and gentle woman, gliding into his consciousness without hurting its old griefs, might call him back to the world of happiness. He could never forget the bride of his youth whose image hovered over him like a dream while waking and like a reality in dreams. It was a deep wound that Fate had inflicted on him but the weapon was clean. Such wounds must heal with time in healthy natures, whatever a false sentiment may say.* The recollection of a deep and

---

* The distinction between depression and grief, between melancholy and mourning, according to Freud, lies in just this quality. When the object lost through death is loved fully and completely, the bereaved one reacts to such a deprivation with grief which usually disappears gradually. It is a normal feeling. When, however, the lost object is hated as well as loved, when the feelings in regard to the deceased are mixed, a person may react with depression, worry, and self-recrimination rather than with mourning and grief. This is an abnormal reaction and the unconscious hostility borne by the melancholic toward the dead person is now turned in a punitive way against himself. It takes the form of feelings of unworthiness, self-accusation, worry over past shortcomings, neglect, and the like.

true affection is rather a divine nourishment for a life to grow strong upon than a poison to destroy it.

Dudley Venner's habitual sadness could not be laid wholly to his early bereavement. It was partly the result of the long struggle between natural affection and duty, on one side, and the involuntary tendencies these had to overcome, on the other—between hope and fear, so long in conflict that despair itself would have been like an anodyne and he would have slept upon some final catastrophe with the heavy sleep of a bankrupt after his failure is proclaimed.

Encouraged by the town's opinion on Dudley's remarriage, a recent widow, who "in widow's weeds was in the full bloom of ornamental sorrow," invited the Venners to "tea." Dudley accepted only because Elsie wished it—she suspected that Bernard might be there. So he was, as were all the other important characters of the story including Dr. Honeywood, Dr. Kittredge, Helen Darley, Dick and an attractive young city girl, Letty, as a dinner partner for Bernard. In the course of the evening it became apparent that Dudley Venner's attention went not to the Widow but to modest Helen Darley and that Bernard was greatly attracted by Letty.

During the entire dinner Elsie had been silent, with her singular look. Her head just a little inclined on one side, perfectly motionless for whole minutes, her eyes seeming to grow small and bright, as always when she was under her evil influence, she was looking obliquely at Letty, the young girl next to Bernard Langdon. Sometimes her eyes would wander off to Mr. Bernard, and their expression, as old Dr. Kittredge noticed, would change perceptibly. One would have said that she looked with a kind of dull hatred at the girl, but with a half-relenting reproachful anger at Mr. Bernard.

Letty, at whom Elsie had been looking from time to time in this fixed way, was conscious meanwhile of some unusual influence. First it was a feeling of constraint, then a diminished power over the muscles, as if an invisible elastic cobweb were spinning around her, then a tendency to turn away from Mr. Bernard and to look straight into those eyes which seemed to be drawing her towards them, while they chilled the blood in her veins.

All at once Bernard noticed that some little points of moisture began to glisten on Letty's forehead. But she did not grow pale perceptibly; she had no involuntary or hysteric movements; she still listened to him and smiled naturally enough. Mr. Bernard turned toward Elsie in such a way as to draw her eyes upon him and looked steadily and calmly into them. It was a great effort for some inexplicable reason. But he was determined to look her down and believed he could do it. All this took not minutes but seconds. Presently Elsie changed color, shut and opened her eyes two or three times, as if they had been pained or wearied, and turned away baffled, and shorn for the time of her evil-natured power of swaying the impulses of those around her.

Her cousin Richard had sat quietly through this short pantomime. Of course he thought that the schoolmaster had been trying to make Elsie jealous and had succeeded. Dick involuntarily moved his chair a little away from her. Somehow this girl had taken strange hold of this dare-devil fellow's imagination and he swore to himself that when he married her, he would carry a loaded revolver to his bridal chamber.

The company soon after this left the tea table and began to converse. Before long Dr. Kittredge and Dr. Honeywood had "squared off" in a spirited controversy about the scientific and theological attitudes in regard to moral and physical ills. Holmes makes this the occasion for summarizing in a formal way what Dr. Kittredge has to say on the subject. This presentation ends as follows:

"As for our getting any quarter at the hands of theologians, we don't expect it. You don't give each other any quarter. I have had two religous books within a week or two. One is Mr. Brownson's; he is a real, honest thinker and has tried all sorts of religions. He tells us that the Roman Catholic Church is the one 'through which alone we can hope for heaven.' The other is by a worthy Episcopal rector who talks about the 'Satanic scheme' of that very Church 'through which alone,' as Mr. Brownson tells us, 'we can hope for heaven'! What's the use in our caring about hard words after this— 'atheists,' heretics, and the like? They're, after all, only the cinders picked up out of those heaps of ashes round the stumps of the old stakes where they used to burn men, women, and children for not thinking just like other folks.

"Doctors are the best-natured people in the world, except when they get fighting with each other. And they have some advantages over you. You inherit your notion from a set of priests that had no wives and no children, or none to speak of, and so let their humanity die out of them. It didn't seem much to them to condemn a few thousand millions of people to purgatory or worse, for a mistake of judgment. They didn't know what it was to have a child look up in their faces and say 'Father'! It will take you a hundred or two more years to get decently humanized, after so many centuries of dehumanizing celibacy.

"Besides, though our libraries are, perhaps, not commonly quite so big as yours, God opens one book to physicians that a good many of you don't know much about—the Book of Life. That is none of your dusty folios with black letters between pasteboard and leather, but it is printed in bright red type, and the binding of it is warm and tender to every touch. They reverence that book as one of the Almighty's infallible revelations. They will insist on reading you lessons out of it, whether you call them names or not. These will always be lessons of charity. No doubt, nothing can be more provoking to listen to."

The Reverend Honeywood was on the point of expressing himself very frankly to Doctor Kittredge regarding the latter's honest opinions, but he saw that the physician's attention had been arrested by Elsie. He looked and could not help being struck by her expression. There was something singularly graceful in the curves of her neck, but she was so perfectly still that it seemed as if she were hardly breathing. Her eyes were fixed on the young girl with whom Mr. Bernard was talking. Now they appeared dull and the look on her features was as of some passion which had missed its stroke.

The Doctor presently went up to Elsie, determined to get her out of her thoughts, which he saw were dangerous. At ten o'clock the Reverend called Miss Letty, who had no idea it was so late; the Doctor gave Elsie a cautioning look and went off alone, thoughtful; Dudley and his daughter got into their carriage and were whirled away.

* * *

After the tea party Elsie became more fitful and moody than ever. She fed on her grief until it ran with every drop of blood in her veins and, except in some paroxysm of rage or in some deadly vengeance wrought secretly, she had no outlet for her dangerous, smouldering passions.

Beware of the woman who cannot find free utterance for all her stormy inner life either in words or song! So long as a woman can talk, there is nothing she cannot bear. If she can sing or play,* all her wickedness will run off through her

---

* During a psychoanalysis one of the most important factors, not only for women but equally for men, is such a verbal catharsis of

throat or the tips of her fingers. How many murders are executed in double-quick time upon the keys which stab the air with their dagger strokes of sound!

Elsie never sang nor played. She never shaped her inner life in words; such utterance was as much denied to her nature as common articulate speech to the deaf mute. Her only language must be in action.

*   *   *

The Doctor rode down to the Dudley mansion solely for the sake of seeing old Sophy. He began talking with her as a physician—how her rheumatism had been. The shrewd woman saw through all that and spoke presently in an awed tone, as if telling a vision.

---

repressed thoughts and a living through of emotions which have been repressed by the patient as dangerous or unworthy. Stammering is often due to inhibitions in connection with thoughts expressed in words beginning with certain letters and syllables. It is interesting to note that stammerers can usually sing with ease and fluency words over which they stumble in speaking.

In modern occupational therapy for mental cases, attention is, or rather should be, focused on the selection of that type of occupation which permits the liberation of repressed affects. Inasmuch as aggression is one of the emotions which it is necessary to repress most frequently in our social structure, games with a destructive element, as bowling, or occupations like brass hammering are valuable in many cases where the shyness of the individual would seem contradictory. On the other hand, a robust and rough longshoreman may at times spontaneously show interest in some such occupation as knitting or painting, thus indicating that this individual, because of his life's situation, had for some reason been compelled to repress gentle and tender interests.[9] Solitary, almost orgastic, dancing served now and then as such a release for the inhibitions of the usually impassive Elsie.

"We shall be havin' trouble. They's somethin' comin' from the Lord. I've had dreams, Doctor. Three times I've dreamed one thing, Doctor!"

She had a kind of faith that the Doctor was a mighty conjuror who could bewitch any of them. But she had only one real object of affection in the world—this child that she had tended from infancy.

"Doctor," she said, "there's strange things goin' on here. I don' like that Dick."

Her eyes sparkled with the old savage light, as if her ill-will to Richard might perhaps go a little farther than the Christian limit.

"Dick wan's to marry our Elsie, 'n' he hates her, Doctor, as bad as I hate him! But, Doctor, oh Doctor, Elsie mus'n' never marry nobody. If she do, he die, certain! She's no like any other creatur' th't ever drawed the bref o' life. If she ca'n' marry one man 'cos she love him, she marry another man 'cos she hate him."

"Marry a man because she hates him, Sophy? No woman ever did such a thing as that."

"Who tol' you Elsie was a woman," said Sophy, with a flash of strange intelligence in her eyes. "She don't cry 'n' laught like other women. An' she ha'n' got the same kind o' feelin's as other women.* Do you know that young gen'l'm'm up at the school, Doctor?"

---

* In this situation Holmes again infers that the patient is not fully feminine. It is likely that many psychoanalysts would interpret the snake's venom introduced into Elsie's body as a symbol of a masculine component and part of her difficulty as being dependent upon an unconscious homosexual identification with her father.

A similar idea of strongly sexually tinged interplay between parent and child is indicated in *The Guardian Angel* in the devout attendance of the Reverend Mr. Stoker's daughter upon her mother.

"Yes. Tell me, Sophy, what do you think would happen, if he should chance to fall in love with Elsie and marry her?"

She whispered a little to the Doctor, then added aloud, "He die, that's all."

"But surely, Sophy, you a'n't afraid to have Dick marry her? He can take care of himself."

"I should like to hab her see that pooty gen'l'm'n up at the schoolhouse, Doctor. 'N' jes' think a little how it would ha' been, if the Lord hadn' been so hard on Elsie. Doctor, Elsie lets ol' Sophy take off that necklace for her but 'f anybody else tech it she strike 'em—not with her han's, Doctor!" The old woman's significant pantomime must be guessed at.

"But you haven't told me what Mr. Venner thinks of his nephew."

"Massa Venner, he good man but he no more idee 'f any mischief 'bout Dick than he has 'bout you or me. The fus' year after young Madam die he do nothin' but come up 'n' look at the baby's neck 'n' say, 'It's fadin', Sophy, a'n't it?' 'N' 't las' he got 's quiet 's a lamb."

The Doctor assured the old woman that he was thinking a great deal about them all and that there were other eyes on Dick besides her own.

* * *

Dick had two sides in his nature, almost as distinct as we sometimes observe in subjects of the condition known as "double consciousness." * On his New England side he was

The daughter's assumption of her father's position and obligations toward her mother had gone so far that the latter states that the daughter had so replaced her neglectful husband that she would think of her as a lover if she were not her own daughter.

* The term "double consciousness" has been used to designate widely differing concepts, but rarely in exactly the sense implied

calculating, always cautious, measuring his distances before he risked his stroke, but he was liable to intercurrent fits of rage and blinding paroxysms of passion such as the light-hued races are hardly capable of conceiving. They for the time overmastered him and, if they found no ready outlet, transformed themselves into the more dangerous forces that worked through the instrumentality of his cool craftiness.

He failed in getting evidence that there was any relation between Elsie and the schoolmaster. In the meanwhile he followed Elsie's tastes as closely as he could, determined to make some impression upon her. To humor one of her tastes he said to her one morning, "Come, Elsie, take your castanets and let us have a dance."

He had struck the right vein in the girl's fancy. This particular kind of dance excited her and she became almost fearful in the vehemence of her passion. The sound of the castanets seemed to make her alive all over. Dick was almost afraid of her at these moments, for it was like the dancing

---

above. Sometimes it is considered as synonymous with "double conscience." Generally "double consciousness" means a condition of the mind where two independent, unrelated currents of thought involuntarily become conscious to the person at the same time. In instances of this type which I have analyzed, the "psychic dualism" or co-conscious mentation consisted of the constant presence in consciousness of a criticizing, corrective element. This critical element in the second thought current was necessary if the patient's normal conscious currents of thought were to be permitted to operate. Without the presence of commentating thoughts he would feel uncertain or even guilty in thinking at all but he would be assured of his right to think by the very presence, and also the punishing, censorious quality, of the comments of his secondary consciousness.[10]

mania of Eastern devotees more than the light amusement of joyous youth—a convulsion of the body and the mind.

Elsie rattled out the triple measure of a saraband. Her eyes began to glitter more brilliantly and her shape to undulate in freer curves. Presently she noticed that Dick's look was fixed upon her necklace. The chain of mosaics she had on at that moment displaced itself at every step and he was peering with malignant eagerness to see if an unsunned ring of fairer hue or any less easily explained peculiarity were hidden by her ornaments.

She stopped suddenly, settled the chain hastily in its place, flung down her castanets and stood looking at him, with her eyes narrowing in the way he had known so well.

"What is the matter?" he said. "You wouldn't act so, if you were dancing with Mr. Langdon, would you, Elsie?"

Elsie "colored," not much, but still perceptibly.* Dick could not remember that he had ever seen her show this mark of emotion before, in all his experience of her fitful changes of mood. Blushing means nothing in some persons; in others

---

* Blushing is an autonomic reaction which occurs most often when a person's sincerity is questioned and is usually associated with incidents related to honesty or sexuality. Often it concerns honesty in sexual life. On the one hand the blushing person, by his blush, protests that he wishes to have nothing to do with the topic but on the other hand the blush betrays the person's repressed interest in (concern with) those very topics of which he is ashamed. Because of this latter function, blushing may become the equivalent of unconscious exhibitionism. The fear of blushing (erythrophobia) is a fairly common symptom in neuroses and in such cases is considered psychoanalytically to be the expression of repressed sexual impulses (a flush of blood), displaced from the normal organs to the face.

it betrays a profound 'perturbation of the feelings far more trying than the passions which with many easily moved persons break forth in tears. All who have observed much are aware that some men, who have seen a good deal of life in its less chastened aspects, will blush easily, while there are delicate and sensitive women who can faint or go into fits if necessary, but rarely betray their feelings in their cheeks even when their expression shows that their inmost soul is blushing scarlet.

Presently she answered, abruptly and scornfully, "Mr. Langdon is a gentleman and would not vex me as you do."

Elsie's bosom was heaving, the faint flush on her cheek was becoming a vivid glow. Whether it were shame or wrath, he saw that he had reached some deep-lying centre of emotion which was decisive and final. Elsie loved Bernard.

She glided out of the room to her own apartment, bolted the door and drew her curtains close. Then she threw herself on the floor and fell into a dull, slow ache of passion, without tears, without words, almost without thoughts. So she remained, perhaps for a half-hour, at the end of which time it seemed that her passion had become a sullen purpose. She arose and went to the hearth, which was ornamented with old Dutch tiles and pictures of Scripture subjects. One of these represented the lifting of the brazen serpent. She took a hairpin from one of her braids and insinuating its points under the edge of the tile raised it from its place. A small leaden box lay under the tile which she opened and, taking from it a little white powder in a scrap of paper she replaced the box.

Dick suspected that he had loosened the murder impulse (through poison) in Elsie and became thoroughly alarmed. But he was equally convinced of her love for Bernard and decided to kill him. His attempt did not succeed and he himself was injured, captured, and finally saved from being hanged by the irate townspeople through the intervention of humane Dr. Kittredge.

The morning after Dick's assault on Bernard, Elsie came and took her place at school. Her expression was somewhat peculiar and was attributed to the shock her feelings had undergone on hearing of the crime attempted by her cousin. As Helen Darley said, "there was something not human about Elsie."

Bernard's professional training made him slow to accept forms of superstition. Yet, he well knew that just on the verge of the demonstrable facts of physics and physiology there is a nebulous borderland which what is called "common sense" perhaps does wisely not to enter, but which uncommon sense may cautiously explore. In so doing it finds itself behind the scenes which make up for the gazing world the show which is called Nature.

It was with something of this finer perception that he set himself to solving the problem of Elsie's influence to attract and repel those around her. Here was a magnificent organization, yet through this rich nature ran some alien current of influence, as when a clouded streak seams the white marble of a perfect statue.

Was she from birth one of those frightful children who form unnatural friendships with cold, writhing ophidians? That the girl had something of the feral nature, her wild, lawless rambles proved clearly enough. But the more he thought of her strange modes of being, the more he became convinced that whatever alien impulse swayed her will or displaced her affections came from some impression that reached far back before faithful Sophy had rocked her in the cradle.

When school was over, Helen lingered to speak with him.

"Did you remark Elsie's ways this forenoon?" she said. "Bernard, her liking for you is growing into a passion. But

Elsie is infinitely dangerous to herself and others, for this poor girl does not know what to do with a passion."

"Why don't they take her away from the school, if she is in such a strange state?" said Bernard.

"I believe they are afraid of her," Helen answered. "It is just one of those cases that are ten thousand times worse than insanity—these peculiar children for whom parents go on hoping every morning and despairing every night! The worst of all diseases of the moral sense are those which all the Bedlams turn away from their doors as not being cases of insanity!" *

* * *

The Saturday evening after the scenes just described the Reverend Chauncy Fairweather received a note. Its words were these:

---

* These borderline states of mental disorder not definitely insane yet obviously abnormal still present great difficulties for the patient, his family, and the psychiatrist. It becomes particularly apparent in the case of obsessive homosexuality or when the patient, torn by conflict and dissatisfaction, takes refuge in periodic indulgence in alcohol. During the intervals he may be so competent, productive, and affable that it would seem cruel and costly to have him confined behind lock and key. Many mental hospitals close their doors not only to patients of this kind but to that group of badly adjusted young and older people suffering from what is called constitutional psychopathic inferiority.

This type of situation was well summed up by a nineteen-year-old girl who came to see her seventeen-year-old brother Benny, committed to a State Hospital because he had stolen a coal wagon. Said she to me, "Doctor, what's the matter with Benny? He ain't crazy, he ain't no dope, and he ain't no fool, but there is something the matter with him." In psychiatric nomenclature these designations would correspond very grossly to manic-depressive psychosis (crazy), dementia precox (dope) and feeblemindedness (fool).

"One who is in distress of mind requests the prayers of this congregation that God would be pleased to look in mercy upon the soul that he has afflicted."

There was nothing to show from whom the note came and he could think of nothing better than to step into old Doctor Kittredge's and see what he had to say about it.

The old Doctor received Mr. Fairweather pleasantly, expecting as a matter of course, that he would begin with some new grievance—dyspeptic, neuralgic, or other. The minister, however, began with questioning the old Doctor about the sequel of the adventure of Dick and thought that the Doctor had been too charitable in the way he had allowed Dick to escape punishment.

"I can't judge men's souls," the Doctor said. "What if you or I had inherited the tendencies that were born with Dick's cousin Elsie?"

"Oh, that reminds me," the minister said, in a sudden way; "I have received this note and wish you would have the kindness to look at it."

The Doctor examined it carefully. It was just possible Elsie might have sent that note. Nobody could foretell her actions.

The Reverend Mr. Fairweather folded the note and put it into his pocket.

"I have been a good deal exercised lately, myself," he said. "You do not know the mental trials I have been going through for the last few months."

"I think I do," the old Doctor said. "You want to get out of the new church into the old one, don't you?"

The minister blushed deeply; he thought that nobody suspected his secret. He began, after an awkward pause, "You would not have me stay in a communion which I feel to be alien to the true church, would you?"

"Have you stay?" said the Doctor, with a friendly look,

"not a day, if I could help it. You have got into the wrong pulpit and I'm very glad you don't mean to stop half-way. Don't you know you've always come to me when you've been dyspeptic or sick anyhow and wanted to put yourself wholly into my hands, so that I might order you like a child just what to do and what to take? That's exactly what you want in religion. You never liked to take the responsibility of your own body; I don't see why you should want to have the charge of your own soul."

The Doctor saw into the minister's soul through those awful spectacles—into it and beyond it, as one sees through a thin fog. Many a time, when he had come desponding, the Doctor had listened patiently while he told his ailments and then, in the large parental way, had given him a few words of wholesome advice and cheered him up so that he went off with a light heart, thinking that the heaven he was so much afraid of was not so very near, after all.

Now the minister felt as feeble natures do in the presence of strong ones—circumscribed, humbled; yet it seemed as if the Doctor did not despise him any more for what he considered weakness of mind than when he complained of his nerves or digestion. A film of gratitude came over the poor man's uncertain eye. He was gravitating to the majority, where he hoped to find "rest" but he was dreadfully sensitive to the opinions of the minority he was on the point of leaving.

The old Doctor saw what was going on in his mind.

"I sha'n't quarrel with you," he said, "but you musn't quarrel with me if I talk honestly with you; it isn't everybody that will take the trouble. You flatter yourself that you will make a good many enemies by leaving your old communion. Not so many as you think. This is the way people will talk: 'You have got your ticket to the feast of life, as much as any other man that ever lived.' Protestantism says, 'Help yourself; here's a clean plate and a knife and fork of your own and plenty of fresh dishes to choose from.' The Old Mother says, 'Give me your ticket, my dear, and I'll feed you with my gold spoon off these beautiful old wooden trenchers—such nice bits as those good old gentlemen have left for you!' *

"There is just the same difference in spiritual patients that there is in bodily ones. One set believes in wholesome ways of living and another must have a great list of specifics for all the soul's complaints. You belong with the last, and got accidentally shuffled in with the others."

The minister smiled faintly but considered that way of talking as the result of the Doctor's professional training. It would not have been worth while to take offense for he might wish to consult him the next day for his dyspepsia. Yet he left the Doctor with a hollow feeling at the bottom of his soul. His hollow aching did not explain itself in words but it grumbled and worried down among the unshaped thoughts which lie beneath them.**

---

* A patient, Protestant, much worried by a sense of guilt and in a severe religious conflict, once expressed this idea similarly. He protested that he could not accept salvation "a la carte," that is by the confession to a priest of sins selected from his own long list or the list already made by the Church, in order to obtain absolution. Nor did he relish the idea of "table d' hote," offered by the Protestant Church, which promised salvation to him if he would "accept the Blood of the Lamb."

** Expressions in many languages convey the idea that mental and emotional attitudes are responsible for and are replaced by physical counterparts. Some of these, such as "not being able to stomach it" or being "scared stiff," require no explanation. One of my patients who suffered in both these directions remarked that I was not the first person who had thought his digestive disorders to be psycho-

The Reverend Fairweather, however, was too much taken up with his own condition to be deeply mindful of others. He carried the note requesting the prayers of the congregation in his pocket all day and the soul in distress, which a single tender petition might have soothed, found no voice in the temple to plead for it before the Throne of Mercy!

Mr. Fairweather's congregation was not large but select. It is expected of persons of a certain breeding, in some parts of New England, that they shall be either Episcopalians or Unitarians. Among the latter Dudley Venner worshipped, when he attended service anywhere—which depended very much on the caprice of Elsie. But she was uncertain about going to church and loved rather to stroll over The Mountain on Sundays. There was a story that she had her own wild way of worshipping the God whom she sought in the chasms of the cliffs.

On the Sunday morning after the talk recorded, Elsie made herself ready to go to meeting. She was dressed much as usual, excepting that she wore a thick veil. She sat quietly

---

genic. A previous diagnosis had been made by an orderly in the hospital where the patient's appendix had been removed. The orderly one night remarked to the complaining patient, "The trouble with you, Mr. Smith, is not with your guts—it's that you haven't got any."

In general we may say that a hysterical conversion symptom is a symbolic body representation of a repressed emotional reaction. This may be fairly obvious, as vomiting at the sight of certain objects or situations, or less apparent, as an asthmatic attack representing a cry for the mother. Where an actual organic change is produced, as in gastric ulcer, it is assumed to be the end result of body tensions; gradual changes occur in the blood supply which eventually affect the tissues themselves.

through the first part of the service but her father knew her state of feeling. The hymn had been sung, the Bible read and the long prayer was about to begin. This was the time at which the "notes" of any who were in affliction from loss of friends, the sick who were doubtful of recovery, those who had cause to be grateful for some signal blessing, were wont to be read. Just then Dudley noticed that his daughter was trembling, a thing so rare, that he began to fear some nervous paroxysm.

The minister had in his pocket two notes. One from a member of this congregation returning thanks for his preservation through great peril, the other was the anonymous one. He forgot them both but he prayed through all the frozen petitions of his expurgated form of supplication. The people sat down as if relieved when the dreary prayer was finished. Elsie alone remained standing until her father touched her. Then she sat down and looked at him with a blank, sad look. She remained ominously still as if she had been frozen where she sat.*

Can a man love his own soul too well? This grave question must suggest itself to those who know profoundly selfish persons who are perpetually occupied with their own future, while there are others who are perfectly ready to sacrifice themselves for any worthy object but are really too little oc-

---

* The frozen posture suggests what is known as catatonia, a condition encountered in schizophrenia. The patient appears as if in a stupor and has rigidity of the muscles. If the extremities are placed in one position, the patient does not change them, but allows them to stay as if they were frozen. One patient, whom I shall mention again, presented a clinical picture closely resembling Elsie's. When badly rebuffed, she lapsed into a stuporous state. Another of her symptoms was a feeling which she described as "a frozen mind."

cupied with their exclusive personality in this world to think much what is to become of them in another. Mr. Fairweather did not, most certainly, belong to this latter class.

The services were over at last and Dudley and his daughter walked home together in silence. He saw that some inward trouble was weighing upon her but there was nothing to be said for Elsie could never talk of her griefs. An hour, a day or a week of brooding, with perhaps a sudden flash of violence: this was the way in which impressions which make other women weep showed their effects in her mind and acts.

She wandered up into The Mountain that day after the service and late at night when Sophy bound up her long hair for sleep it was damp with the cold dews.

Suddenly Elsie turned to Sophy.

"You want to know what there is troubling me," she said. "Nobody loves me. I cannot love anybody. What is love, Sophy?"

"It's what poor Ol' Sophy's got for her Elsie," the old woman answered. "Tell me, don' you love somebody? Darlin', don' you love to see the gen'l'man at the school? Don' be 'fraid of poor Ol' Sophy, darlin', she loved a man once!"

Elsie looked her in the face. What strange intelligence passed between them through the diamond eyes and the little beady black ones—penetrating so much deeper than articulate speech? This was the nearest approach to sympathetic relations that Elsie ever had: a kind of dumb intercourse of feeling, such as one sees in the eyes of brute mothers looking on their young. But, subtle as it was, it was narrow and individual; whereas an emotion which can shape itself in language opens the gate for itself into the great community of human affections, for every word we speak is the medal of a dead thought or feeling, struck in the die of some human experience, worn smooth by innumerable contacts and always transferred warm from one to another. By words we share the common consciousness of the race, which has shaped itself in these symbols. By music we reach those special states of consciousness which, being without "form," cannot be shaped with the mosaics of the vocabulary. The language of the eyes runs deeper into the personal nature, but it is purely individual and perishes in the expression. If we consider them all as growing out of consciousness as their root, language is the leaf and music is the flower, but when the eyes meet and search each other, it is the uncovering of the blanched stem through which the whole life runs but has never taken color or form from the sunlight.

For three days Elsie did not return to the school and lingered in her old haunts. Some internal conflict was going on that must have its own way and work itself out as it best could. As much as looks could tell Elsie had told her old nurse. Something warped and thwarted the emotion which would have been love in another, but that such an emotion was striving in her against all malign influences which interfered with it Sophy had a perfect certainty.

Everybody who has observed the working of emotions in persons of various temperaments knows well enough that they have periods of "incubation" which differ with the individual and yet evidently go through a strictly self-limited series of evolutions, at the end of which, their result—an act of violence, a paroxysm of tears, a gradual subsidence into repose or whatever it may be—declares itself, like the last stage of an attack of fever. At the end of three days, Elsie dressed herself with more than usual care and came down superb in her stormy beauty. The brooding paroxysm had changed its phase. Her father saw it with great relief for he had many fears for her in her hours of gloom.

Now Elsie went off at the accustomed hour to school where

the girls all said that the beautiful cold girl meant to dazzle the handsome young gentleman but that he would be afraid to love her.

Elsie had none of the wicked light in her eyes, she looked gentle but dreamy.

The school hours were over. Elsie came up to Mr. Bernard.

"Will you walk towards my home with me?" she said in little more than a whisper.

So they walked together toward the Dudley mansion.

"I have no friend," Elsie said all at once. "Nothing loves me but one old woman. I cannot love anybody. They tell me there is something in my eyes that draws people to me and makes them faint. Look into them, will you?" *

She turned her face towards him. It was very pale and the diamond eyes were glittering with a film, such as beneath other lids would have rounded into a tear.

"Love me!" said Elsie abruptly.

Mr. Bernard trembled almost as if he had been a woman listening to her lover's declaration.

"Elsie," he said presently, "I do love you—as one whom I

---

* The inability to give love and, through not giving, the failure to receive it are fundamental factors in many types of severe neuroses and especially in schizophrenia. The infant has an absolute, essentially a biological, need for warmth and attention, in the spiritual as well as the physical sense, and also for affection and love. Denied these, one solution remaining to the child for satisfying the instinctive need is to find it within himself and to love himself excessively. During adolescent years this self-love may lead to self-indulgence in the form of masturbation, and a vicious circle is begun which fosters shyness, asocial tendencies, and sullenness from which the person may not emerge.

In passing I may add that masturbation does not "cause insanity." However, because of its ease and convenience it does tend to unfit the person for the competition and demands of normal love-making.

would save at the risk of my happiness and life. You have been through trouble lately and it has made you feel such a need for love more than ever. Give me your hand, dear Elsie, and trust me as if we were children of the same mother."

Elsie gave him her hand mechanically. He pressed it gently, looked at her with a face full of grave kindness, then softly relinquished it.

It was all over with poor Elsie. They walked almost in silence the rest of the way and Elsie went at once to her own room and did not come from it at the usual hour. At last Sophy entered cautiously and found Elsie lying on her bed, her brows strongly contracted, her eyes dull, her whole look that of great suffering. Sophy's first thought was that Elsie had been doing herself a harm by some deadly means or other. But Elsie reassured her.

"No," she said, "there is nothing wrong such as you are thinking of; I am not dying. You may send for the Doctor; perhaps he can take the pain from my head."

The old Doctor always came into the sickroom as if he had a consciousness that he was bringing sure relief. The way a patient snatches his first look at his doctor's face to see whether he is doomed or reprieved is only to be met by an imperturbable mask of serenity, proof against anything and everything in a patient's aspect.

"Sick, my child?" he said to Elsie in a soft voice.

She nodded without speaking.

The Doctor sat a few minutes, looking at her with a kind of fatherly interest, but noting how she lay, how she breathed, her expression, all that teaches the practised eye so much without a single question being asked. He said presently, "You have pain somewhere?"

She put her hand to her head. As she was not disposed to talk, he questioned Sophy a few minutes and made up his mind as to the probable cause of disturbance. Some silly people thought the old Doctor did not believe in medicine because he hated to give anything loathesome to those who were uncomfortable enough already, unless he was sure it would do good.

The next day came and the next and still Elsie was on her bed—feverish, restless, wakeful, silent. There was a settled attack, something like what they called, formerly, a "nervous fever." On the fourth day she asked for Helen Darley.

The old Doctor told them they must indulge this fancy of hers. The caprices of sick people were never to be despised, least of all of such persons as Elsie, when rendered irritable and exacting by pain and weakness.

As a result of this request Helen Darley found herself installed in the Dudley mansion as a companion to Elsie. Even in such intimate contact the gentle Helen found herself unable to enter into the confidence of the stricken girl. Through Sophy she learned of the antenatal influence which had affected Elsie, her lisping, silence, soberness and solitude as a child. By this understanding Helen began to look leniently on the contradictions of Elsie's moral nature. One tendency made her a woman, the other "infused into her soul something watchful and dangerous which waited its opportunity and then shot out of the coil of brooding premeditation." Helen made no headway in breaking through Elsie Venner's barriers, but it became apparent that Dudley Venner had fallen deeply in love with her.

After several days of Elsie's illness the old Doctor was beginning to look graver, in spite of himself. The fever, if such it was, went gently forward, wasting the young girl's powers of resistance from day to day; yet she showed no disposition to take nourishment and seemed literally to be living on air.*

---

* The refusal of food is characteristic of stupors and catatonic states. Unwillingness to eat is often due to the resentment of the patient

It was remarkable that with all this her look was almost natural and her features were hardly sharpened so as to suggest that her life was burning away. The Doctor did not like this nor various other unobtrusive signs of danger.

Little tokens of good-will were constantly coming to her and several of the schoolgirls wished to make her a basket of autumnal flowers. Mr. Bernard found out their project accidentally, and, wishing to have his share in it, brought some boughs of variously tinted leaves and the already fallen leaflets of the white ash, remarkable for their olive-purple color and forming a beautiful contrast with lighter-hued leaves. The girls covered the floor of their basket with the purple ash leaflets and filled it with late flowers.

Elsie was sitting up in her bed when the basket came, languid but tranquil. She began looking at the flowers and taking them from the basket, that she might see the leaves. All at once she appeared to be agitated as if there were some fearful presence about her. She took out the flowers, one by one, her breathing growing hurried, her eyes staring, her hands trembling, till, as she came near the bottom of the basket, she flung out all the rest with a hasty movement, looked upon the olive-purple leaflets as if paralyzed for a moment, shrunk up into herself in a curdling terror, dashed the basket from her and fell back senseless, with a faint cry which chilled the blood of those at her bedside.

"Take it away!—quick!" said Sophy. "It's the leaves of the

toward his environment and may denote defiance to a disliked parent. It may also be an unconscious demonstration of the extremity of the patient's plight and a plea that he be helped to live, in other words it may be a silent begging for food. Such patients will often eat mechanically when they are coaxed or spoon-fed like little children. Sometimes they will secretly eat food which they have steadfastly refused from an anxious husband or mother.

tree that was always death to her! She can't live wi' it in the room!"

The old woman began chafing Elsie's hands and tried to rouse her with hartshorn. She came to herself after a time, but exhausted and wandering. In her delirium she talked constantly as if she were in a cave, with such exactness that Helen could not doubt that she had some such retreat among the rocks of The Mountain.

All this passed away and left her weaker than before. But this was not the only influence the unexplained paroxysm had left behind it. From this time forward there was a change in her whole expression and her manner. The shadows ceased flitting over her features and the old woman, who watched her as a mother watches her child, saw the likeness she bore to her mother coming forth more and more, as the glitter died out of her eyes.

With all the kindness and indulgence her father had bestowed upon her, Elsie had never felt that he loved her. The reader knows what fatal recollections and associations had frozen up the springs of natural affection in his breast. There was nothing in the world he would not do for Elsie but his very seeming carelessness about restraining her was all calculated; he knew that restraint would produce nothing but utter alienation. Just so far as she allowed him, he shared her few pleasures. No person could judge him, because his task was not merely difficult, but simply impracticable to human powers. A nature like Elsie's had necessarily to be studied by itself, and to be followed in its laws where it could not be led.*

---

* The successful treatment of any mental disorder usually depends upon such a study and appreciation of the patient's individual needs. Generalization is impractical in mental cases, no two of which are alike, nor have the same demands or setting. For this reason, the

Every day during his daughter's illness, Dudley had sat by her, doing all he could to soothe and please her—always the same thin film of some emotional non-conductor between them; always that kind of habitual family interest mingled with the deepest pity on one side and a sort of respect on the other, which never warmed into outward evidences of affection.

It was after she had been profoundly agitated by a seemingly insignificant cause that her father and Sophy were sitting at her bed. She had fallen into a light slumber. As they were looking at her, the same thought came to both. Old Sophy spoke:

"It's her mother's own face right over again—she never look' so before—the Lord's hand is on her!"

When Elsie woke and lifted her languid eyes upon her father's face, she saw in it a depth of affection seen at rare moments of her childhood, when she had won him to her by some unusual gleam of sunshine in her fitful temper.

"Elsie, dear," he said, "we were thinking how much your expression was like that of your sweet mother."

The yearning of the daughter's heart for the mother she had never seen, perhaps the under-thought that she might soon rejoin her in another state of being, all came upon her with a sudden overflow of feeling which broke through all the barriers and Elsie wept. It seemed to her father as if the malign influence had at last been driven forth or exorcised and these tears were the pledge of her redeemed nature.

---

physician who understands and fulfills the needs of one patient often fails signally with another. This is so even in a presumably impersonal system as psychoanalysis, where I have seen symptoms disappear before interpretation has been made by the physician—so-called "transference cures"—because of confidence (faith) in him and the parent type he represented.

After her tears she slept again and her look was peaceful as never before.

Old Sophy told the Doctor all the circumstances connected with Elsie's extraordinary attack. It was the purple leaves, she said, and remembered that Dick once brought home a branch with the same leaves, Elsie had screamed and almost fainted. Sophy had asked her what it was in the leaves that made her feel so bad. Elsie couldn't tell but shuddered whenever Sophy mentioned it.

This did not sound so strangely to the Doctor. He had known some curious examples of antipathies and remembered reading of others still more singular—a stout soldier who would turn and run at the sight or smell of rue; that even olive-oil had produced deadly faintings in certain individuals—in short, that almost everything has seemed to be a poison to somebody.*

"These purple leaves are from the white ash," said the Doctor. "You don't know the notion that people commonly have about that tree, Sophy?"

"I know they say the Ugly Things never go where the white ash grows," Sophy answered. "Oh, Doctor, dear, what I'm thinkin' of a'n't true, is it?"

The Doctor smiled sadly. Nobody would have known by

---

* Holmes points out that the traumatically determined antipathies and phobias of neurotic patients, which he subsequently used as the theme for A *Mortal Antipathy*, may also be operative in and complicate such extremely profound disturbances as existed in the case of Elsie Venner. In one of my cases the fear of her mother's violent outbursts produced an almost complete blocking of affect, beginning at the age of eight. In an affectless, toneless voice and with a bland, immobile face the patient remarked, "Mother was held in great esteem by the community—with whom she rarely came in contact."

his manner that he saw any special change in his patient. He spoke with her as usual, made some slight alteration in his prescriptions and left the room with a cheerful look. He met her father on the stairs.

"There is," the Doctor said, "not much to hope."

"What is the meaning of this change which has come over her whole being?" her father asked. "Tell me, can it be that the curse is passing away and my daughter is to be restored to me such as her mother was?"

"Walk out into the garden," the Doctor said, "and I will tell you all I think about this mystery."

"She has lived a double being, as it were, the consequence of the blight in the dim period before consciousness. You can see what she might have been but for this. For these eighteen years her whole existence has taken its character from that influence which we need not name. But few of the lower forms of life last as human beings do and thus it might have been hoped, as I have always suspected you trusted perhaps more confidently than myself, that the lower nature would die out and leave the real woman's life she inherited to out-live this accidental principle which poisoned her childhood. I believe it is dying out; but I am afraid—yes, I must say it —it has involved the centres of life in its own decay. It looks as if life were slowly retreating inwards, so that by-and-by she will sleep as those who lie down in the snow and never wake."

Her father heard all this not without deep sorrow but with resignation. Dear as his daughter might become to him, all he dared to ask of Heaven was that she might be restored to that truer self which lay beneath her adventitious being.

There was little change in Elsie the next day, until all at once she said in a clear voice that she should like to see Mr. Langdon. It seemed as if Elsie had forgotten the last scene with him. Might it be that she had sent for him only to show

how superior she had grown to the weakness which had betrayed her into that request, so contrary to the instincts and usages of her sex? Or was it that the change which had come over her had involved her passionate fancy for him?

She welcomed Mr. Bernard with perfect tranquillity. She did not speak of any apprehension but he saw that she looked upon herself as doomed. So friendly did she seem that Bernard could only look back upon her manifestation of feeling towards him as the vagary of a mind wholly at variance with the true character of Elsie. He looked with almost scientific closeness of observation into the diamond eyes but that peculiar light was not there. Something of tenderness there was in her tone towards him but through his visit she never lost her self-possession.

Weak and suffering as she was, she had never parted with one particular ornament. The golden cord which she wore round her neck at the great party was still there. A bracelet was lying by her pillow and before Mr. Bernard left she said, "I shall never see you again. Some time or other, perhaps, you will mention my name to one whom you love. Give her this. Good-bye and thank you for coming."

She followed him with her eyes as he passed through the door and when it closed sobbed tremulously once or twice. Then she asked for Helen.

"I have had a very pleasant visit from Mr. Langdon. Sit by me, Helen; I should like to sleep—and to dream."

* * *

The Reverend Fairweather, hearing that his parishioner's daughter was very ill, could do nothing less than tender consolations. It was rather remarkable that the old Doctor did not exactly disapprove of his visit. He knew by sad experience that it is a dreadful mistake to overlook the desire for spiritual advice which patients sometimes feel and with the frightful "mauvaise honte" peculiar to Protestantism are ashamed to tell. As a part of medical treatment, it is the physician's business to detect the hidden longing for the food of the soul as much as for any form of bodily nourishment. Especially in the higher walks of society, where this unutterably false shame of Protestantism acts in proportion to the general acuteness of the cultivated sensibilities, let no unwillingness of the sick person to suggest the need suffer him to languish between his want and his morbid sensitiveness. What an infinite advantage the Mussulmans and the Catholics have over many of our more exclusively spiritual sects in the way they keep their religion always by them and never blush for it!

The reader must pardon this digression, which introduces the visit of Mr. Fairweather to Elsie. He came and worked the conversation round to religion and confused her with his hybrid notions.

When he had gone, Elsie called Sophy.

"Sophy," she said, "don't let them send that cold-hearted man to me any more. If I should die one of these days, I should like to have that old minister say whatever there is to be said over me. It would comfort Dudley more—for some of you will be sorry when I'm gone—won't you, Sophy?"

The old black woman could not stand this question.

"Don't talk so, darlin'!" she cried passionately. "When you go, Ol' Sophy 'll go; 'n' where you go, Ol' Sophy 'll go."

The Reverend Doctor did come and sit by her and spoke such soothing words of peace that she was tranquil as never before. He found a bruised and languishing soul and bound up its wounds—a blessed office, one which is confined to no sect or creed but which good men in all times, under various names and with varying ministries have come forward to discharge.*

After this there was little change in Elsie, except that her heart beat more feebly every day. Even the old Doctor, with all his experience, could see nothing to account for the gradual failing of the powers of life and could find no remedy to arrest its progress.

"Be very careful," he said, "when a person is so enfeebled any effort may stop the heart in a moment."

Her father came in to sit with her in the evening. He had never talked so freely with her as during the hour he had passed telling her little circumstances of her mother's life, living over with her all that was pleasant in the past.

"Good-night, my dear child," he said and stooping down, kissed her cheek.

Elsie rose by a sudden effort, threw her arms round his neck, kissed him and said, "Good-night, my dear father!"

Her arms slid away from him like lifeless weights, a long sigh breathed through her lips and she lay dead.

Dudley Venner prayed that night that he might be forgiven, if he had failed in any act of duty or kindness to this unfortunate child.

Old Sophy said almost nothing but sat day and night by her dead darling. Sometimes her anguish would find an outlet in strange sounds, something between a cry and a musical

---

* One of the shortcomings of the modern hospital system is its lack of provision for the spiritual needs of patients. The introduction of more psychiatric care might help to remedy this defect if only the psychiatrist himself did not become too scientific. When the psychiatrist approaches the patient with too searching a manner, the patient is apt to regard the whole procedure as merely another test; what he needs most is reassurance and kindly understanding.

note such as none had ever heard her utter before. These were old remembrances surging up from her childish days, death-wails, such as they sing in the mountains of Western Africa when they see the fires on distant hillsides and know that their own wives and children are undergoing the fate of captives.

At the last moment, when all the preparations were completed, Old Sophy stooped over her and with trembling hand loosed the golden cord. She looked intently: there was no shade nor blemish where the ring of gold had encircled her throat.

Comments

The illness and death of Elsie Venner corresponds in many aspects with that of a woman whom I observed and treated intermittently for over ten years. I have referred to her in a previous note as the woman with a "frozen mind." The patient, an immature woman with a girlish body, was referred to me because of insomnia and depression, shortly after her marriage at the age of twenty-four. Before long it developed that even more distressing than these two symptoms were two others: an irresistible compulsion to act sweetly toward all people even when she had the conscious desire to do otherwise; and the feeling that her mind was frozen and numb.

The patient's father had been a patient in a mental hospital from the time she was six years old and she saw him very seldom before his death in an institution when she was twelve. Her mother, a worldly, selfish and not too intelligent woman, had little sympathy and no love for the patient, who from childhood had been scrawny, homely, and timid—certainly not a child about whom a parent could boast. As a young lady she found herself excluded from the social set which she would have been expected to join and instead she drifted into a small group which she termed "dubs" and where she met her husband, a similar social misfit. Her marriage to him was arranged and underwritten by an officious, wealthy aunt. It proved from the start to be an unsuccessful living together of two awkward, unhappy, rejected young people, both thoroughly enslaved and tyrannized by the forceful mother of the patient.

Her husband, concerned with his own neuroses and deeply immersed in his own autoerotism, could not love her. The patient, handicapped since childhood by fear which blocked all emotional expression, tried to love her husband in a way that a timid child in an attempt to reëstablish contact might touch a parent who had scolded her.

The patient's compulsion to act sweetly constituted an attempt to avoid rebuke. As soon as she was offended or rebuffed in the slightest degree, the defense of immobility began to assert itself and made it possible for her to exist in society by acting as an automaton. She almost never had any outbursts of temper but at times her green-gray eyes would flash anger and fight. Often when she became hopeless over her predicament, she would attempt suicide or lapse into a depressed stuporous state, or both. At such times her husband, stricken with a guilt-laden sense of obligation, would sit by her bedside for days, feeding her orange juice and milk with a spoon. Then she would gradually recover.

It so happened that the patient eventually went abroad for psychiatric treatment and would write me from time to time that she was "feeling very well." This meant that she was not improving, as she confessed in one letter, for when her mind was "frozen hard" to protect her sensitivity against the emotionally intolerable thrusts and the impact of the outside world, she felt and appeared to be much better. When the defense of freezing weakened and contact with persons became real, she became anxious and uneasy and felt "rotten"; but it was just at such times that she was on the path toward health.

One day her husband received a long cable from the European physician saying that the patient had fallen into a state of depression and refused food. He described the symptoms of an attack such as her husband and I had observed so often. A week later she died. A subsequent talk with the physician convinced me that the attack had been identical with those we had seen in New York but now there was no one to show her through attention and feeding that some vestige of love still remained for her in the world and she, like Elsie, wasted away.

Probably very few persons die quickly or suddenly from a lack of love, given or received, but many become dry and brittle and shriveled. On the other hand, some few persons seem to thrive fairly well on a free liberation of hate and the chastisement of everybody but themselves. Perhaps it is not the type of emotion repressed but the abnormal repression of any primary instinct-component which plays the greatest havoc with our contentment and emotional growth.

All doctors take into account the will of the patient to get well in their prognosis of any serious case and this will for health is often dependent upon unconscious as well as conscious factors. Unconscious, often guilt-laden, elements seem to constitute the forces which indirectly drive to self-destruction certain persons who have everything in the world to live for. The term "psychic suicide" has been applied to situations of the kind described above, where the wish to die seems to facilitate, if not actually cause, death. Instances of this successful will to die have been observed by anthropologists among primitive peoples when they have violated some important tribal taboo, as well as in mentally afflicted persons.[11]

THE GUARDIAN ANGEL
HYSTERIA IN AN ADOLESCENT GIRL

The Guardian Angel is psychiatrically by far the most significant of Holmes's three novels, as it introduces specifically many factors which are today considered of essential importance in the production of mental disorders. Among these may be mentioned such questions as the pernicious influence of austerity upon a child, the power and effect of unconscious forces, the elements entering into personality formation, and the role of faith and religion as curative agents.

Particularly unexpected is the fine understanding of the nature of transference, often regarded as an entirely modern contribution as a guide to the interpretation and treatment of psychiatric reactions. Furthermore, we come upon the concept of regeneration through rebirth, and finally, the rehabilitating and integrating effect of the liberation of repressed love impulses. Where Elsie Venner succumbed to the denial of love, the heroine in this story is rescued from herself through it.

The Guardian Angel appeared in 1867. Like its predecessor, Elsie Venner, it depicts the plight of a girl disturbed by many conflicts, especially social and religious ones. In Elsie Venner these influences are held due to the accidental introduction of a noxious element before birth, and this circumstance is utilized by Holmes to oppose the doctrine of original sin. In The Guardian Angel Holmes delineates the effect of inherited moral and mental qualities on the character of an orphan, Myrtle Hazard. One of her ancestors, Ann Holyoake, is portrayed as continuing her existence in Myrtle almost as if she were a separate entity within the personality of her young descendant. She acts as a guide and mentor, symbolically in lieu of the dead mother, ready to guard and guide Myrtle in situations where danger threatens her.

The central thesis of the novel is thus indicated; namely, that characteristics of persons long dead "may enjoy a kind of second- ary and imperfect, yet self-conscious life"—a "co-tenancy" in our bodies. The emphasis centers upon dissonant traits inherited by the young girl from ancestors with widely diverging characteristics. These include masculine as well as feminine forebears.

As mentioned in the introduction of this book, the assumption of a collective unconscious forms the basis for Carl Jung's theory of the origin of neurotic symptoms in adult life and also for his interpretation of dreams. In Jung's theory, in addition to the per- sonal unconscious, which consists of forgotten repressed material— personal experiences—there exist "other contents which do not originate in personal acquisitions but . . . those motives and images which can spring anew in every age and clime without tra- dition or migration. I term this the collective unconscious." [1] Thus, in the psychology of Jung emphasis is shifted from sex and infantile sexual conflict to a conflict of the living individual with the proces- sion of unconscious cultural impressions which he carries with him at birth.

In this latter sense it seems to me Holmes postulates the exist- ence in the unconscious mind of Myrtle Hazard certain traits and experiences of her varied collection of ancestors, remote and re- cent, from India and Elizabethan England to early America. These have been preserved intact in her unconscious, to reappear as images or as definite fears in times of stress. As we know, in periods of emo- tional disturbance material long repressed and possibly even un- conscious may come to the surface much as it does in dreams.

The archaic unconscious of Jung postulates a very far distant heritage which nevertheless persists in every person as a vital influ- ence—the racial unconscious. Eugene O'Neill has relied upon this theory for the fears which grip a pursued Negro in his drama Em- peror Jones. Here the threats to which his successive ancestors were subjected from the primitive jungle in Africa to slave days in America rise up before the terrified Negro as he gropes his way through the darkness of a tropical jungle night.

Aside from the clash of antagonistic inherited forces, Myrtle's adjustment to life has been aggravated by the attitude of a repressive, gloomy, unsympathetic household and by specific terrifying experiences in early childhood. Holmes relies on such inherited and environmental circumstances to support his crusade against judging the actions of our fellow men without taking into consideration all the factors entering into their personalities.

This position renews the old controversy between theology and science, religion and medicine, which has already been discussed in *Elsie Venner*. Now in the illness of Myrtle Hazard the question no longer remains theoretical but becomes a practical issue, even as it often does under similar circumstances today. Only recently I was in consultation in a case of typical manic excitement in a young Jewish girl, where to my surprise, the mother asked if Christian Science might not cure the patient more quickly than the able care her physician was giving her. The search for some mysterious, magical force, which shall operate over and beyond realistic procedures, remains strong and recurrent in mankind. Most religions, in one form or another, imply such power and propose such hopes for sufferers from physical disability or emotional disappointments. This need for and belief in the miraculous remains the basis for many cures.

One evening on the Main Street of a Kansas village bustling with Saturday night activity, I watched a medicine man peddle his wares. Tall, gaunt, and glib, from a soap box he held the group about him interested and spellbound. He told of the virtues of his remedy, mentioning by name people who had been benefited, how the medicine would cure headache, rheumatism, pains in back, indigestion, and so on and on. Finally holding up the bottle he ended his harangue with this astonishing sentence: "And folks, I won't fool you. In this wonderful medicine, this magic medicine, there's nothing but God's crystal pure water and God's pure earth from Idaho." And many of his listeners came forward and paid their fifty cents per bottle.

The medicine man's words were well chosen to impress the credulous. Firstly, the water is that of God to whom we all appeal when illness is regarded as a punishment. No substance is more commonly accepted than water as a symbol for washing away our sins. Purity is an antidote to the sin and evil which are responsible for illness and this water is divinely pure. The faith in the unknown is emphasized to the people of Kansas by the earth which comes from Idaho, just remote enough to be a bit mysterious.

Religious healing has been practiced by priests since primitive times, and the separation of medical from religious healing did not occur until about the fourth century before Christ. Various religious cults and movements still flourish widely, even in countries where science and medicine have advanced furthest and are most firmly established, especially in those disorders which are not manifestly due to some physical cause.

The fact that many diseases are self-limited, that spiritual aches are converted into bodily expression, that diagnosis in many instances is difficult to establish, and that mistakes are often made by physicians has tended to keep alive religious healing. No honest physician would deny that psychically determined symptoms can simulate the gravest types of physical illness and vice versa, and that he has been fooled both ways. Aside from this, it is certain that a subtle, intangible force aids the physician in his healing, so that the same drug works wonders, "like magic," when administered by one doctor but proves useless when prescribed by another. Psychoanalysts call this intangible element transference. Sometimes, also, faith heals where medicines have failed. Possibly faith relieves the patient's anxiety and allows nature's healing processes to work undisturbed.

The most extensive and the best-organized cult in the United States devoted to spiritual healing is Christian Science, whose founder, Mrs. Eddy, was cured of a paralysis in 1862 by Phineas Quimby. The latter, as already noted, based his mind cure on the hypnotic practices of the French followers of Mesmer and of the Englishman James Braid.

The Catholic churches had always retained certain shrines, many of them famous and fabulous such as Lourdes, where cure through prayer was practiced. When Christian Science began to make inroads upon established Protestant churches, they too sought to regain an imperiled prestige through the establishment of clinics for spiritual healing. Among these early in the present century were the Emanuel Movement of Boston, where the minister acted for a while in close coöperation with medical men; the Nazarene Movement; and many miscellaneous individual religious efforts. In addition may be mentioned numerous cults, such as the prosperous New Thought Movement (which aims to put its followers "in tune with the Infinite"), spiritualism, divine science, and the like—all dependent upon that elusive force called faith. And persons in dire need of help are ready to place their hopes in numberless forms of agents or even to change them readily. In *The Guardian Angel* the great need of Myrtle Hazard for a guiding father allows her to displace her faith without effort from her doctor to her minister.

The comfort derived by their adherents from all these types of religious, semireligious or metaphysical thought and ceremonial must be considerable. Many of them are self-sustaining and profitable. While the benefit of religious comfort in disease situations cannot be measured, most of the persons who testify to their cures have had previous unsatisfactory contact with physicians. Occasionally there may have been an indirect and unconscious tendency on the part of the doctor to admit and permit chronic invalidism.

The search for some miracle that will painlessly and quickly relieve the ills which afflict man goes on and on. The growth of scientific knowledge with its specifics for the cure of many diseases and problems of health does not alter the unconscious yearning for miracles, but rather leads to the presentation in new formulations, wearing a pseudo-scientific guise and based upon prayer and faith. The tendency is reflected in the perennial publication of many new books on the topic. One of the latest, a collaboration between a psychoanalyst-psychiatrist and a pastor, is characteristically entitled *Faith Is the Answer*.[2] It is surprising to find the psychiatrist saying: "In both spheres the problem is essentially the same."

Finally a word in regard to multiple personality. I have never encountered a case of double personality of the Dr. Jekyll and Mr. Hyde type, where two integrated personalities alternate completely and regularly, and those reports which I have read in psychiatric literature are far from convincing. Very numerous, however, are the cases of alternating personality—in which there is more or less complete forgetfulness by the active personality of the behavior of the inactive one—and of co-conscious personalities, in which two or more personalities co-exist and one becomes periodically and transiently dominant, although never entirely free from the influence of the other.

In Myrtle Hazard the latter picture is the one presented. Psychoanalytic investigators attribute such co-existent personalities to multiple and unintegrated identifications. In cases of double consciousness which I have studied, the force of the dissociation tendency seemed to rest in two or more fairly distinctly formed strivings for antagonistic ideals (Freud's superego). Such two opposing ideals seem to have the power to regard each other vigilantly, intensively, and critically, now one, now the other gaining the upper hand but without being able to retain it permanently or establish it completely.

The Story of The Guardian Angel

On Saturday, the 18th day of June, 1859, the "State Banner and Delphian Oracle," published weekly at Oxbow Village, a thriving rivertown of New England, contained an advertisement which startled the small community.

MYRTLE HAZARD has been missing since Thursday morning, June 16th. She is fifteen years old, tall and womanly for her age, has dark hair and eyes, pleasant smile, but shy with strangers. Her common dress was a black and white gingham check. It is feared she may be wandering in a state of temporary mental alienation. Any information will be properly rewarded by her afflicted aunt, MISS SILENCE WITHERS, residing at "The Poplars."

The advertisement brought the village fever of the last two

days to its height for now it was clear that the gravest apprehensions were justified.

The Withers Homestead was naturally the chief centre of interest. Nurse Byloe, a voluminous woman, who had known the girl when she was a little bright-eyed child, went straight up to The Poplars. Mistress Fagan, the Irish house servant led her into the best parlor, where Silence Withers' cousin, Cynthia Badlam, was rocking back and forward.

"Nuss Byloe? Well, I'm glad to see you, though we're all in trouble."

The two women looked each other in the eyes with subtle interchange of intelligence, such as belongs to their sex. Talk without words is half their conversation, only the dull senses of men are dead to it. Their minds travelled along, as if yoked together, through fields of suggestive speculation, until the dumb growths of thought ripened into speech—consentingly, as the movement after the long stillness of a Quaker meeting.

"They needn't go beating the woods," said Cynthia. "It's that dreadful will of hers never was broke. I've always been afraid that she would turn out a child of wrath. Men are so wicked, and young girls are so ready to listen to all sorts of artful creatures." She wept.

"Dear Suz," said the nurse, "I won't believe no sech thing as wickedness about Myrtle Hazard. You mean she's gone an' run off with some good-for-nothin' man? If she was five-an'-thirty or more and never'd had a chance to be married and if one o' them artful creatures you was talkin' of got hold of her, then—dear me—law, I never thought, Miss Badlam."

A sort of hysteric twitching went through the frame of Cynthia. There was not a more knowing pair of eyes than those kindly, tranquil orbs that Nurse Byloe fixed on Cynthia.

It took not so long as it takes to describe it but it was an analysis of imponderables.

At this moment Silence Withers entered, followed by Bathsheba, a daughter of Rev. Joseph Stoker and a friend of Myrtle, who had come to comfort Miss Silence. Silence was something more than forty years old, a bloodless woman, with the habitual look of the people in the funeral carriage which follows next to the hearse.

Bathsheba was not called handsome but she had her mother's youthful smile, which was so full of sweetness that she seemed like a beauty while she was speaking or listening. She had been trying consolation on Miss Silence. "It was a sudden freak" of Myrtle's. "Besides, she would take care of herself; for she was afraid of nothing and nimbler than any boy of her age." To all this Miss Silence answered only by sighing. Bathsheba had said all she could and hastened back to her mother's bedside, which she hardly left except for the briefest of visits.

"Cousin Silence," said Miss Cynthia, "it isn't your fault. If going to meeting three times every Sabbath day and all needful discipline could have corrected her sinful nature. It's that Indian blood. What can you expect of children that come from heathens and savages?"

"The Lord will lay it to me," she moaned.

Nurse Byloe was getting very red in the face. "Miss Badlam, Myrtle was as pretty a child as ever I see, and the handsomest young woman, too, sence Judith Pride that was—the Pride of the County they used to call her. I tell y', she's got a soul that's as clean and sweet—well, as a pond-lily when it fust opens of a mornin'." A half-suppressed utterance implied that there was a good deal more which might be said.

Friends and neighbors were coming in and out, among

them the old minister, the Rev. Eliphalet Pemberton, a man of noble presence. His creed was one of the sternest: he was looked up to as a bulwark against all the laxities which threatened New England theology. However, he had a good deal in him of what he used to call the "Old Man," meaning certain qualities belonging to humanity, as much as the natural gifts of dumb creatures belong to them.*

The Rev. Joseph Bellamy Stoker had become the colleague of Father Pemberton. Good Father Pemberton could not love Mr. Stoker but never complained to him or of him. It would have been of no use if he had: the women of the parish had taken up the Rev. Stoker and when the women run after a minister or a doctor, what do the men signify? Why the women ran after him, some thought it not hard to guess. He was not ill-looking and was considered eloquent. But he also was fond of listening to their spiritual experiences and had a sickly wife. This is what Master Byles Gridley said but he was apt to be caustic.

Gridley was a bachelor, who had been a college tutor and professor, a man of whims and crotchets, such as are hardly to be found except in old, unmarried students—the double flowers of college culture, their stamina all turned to petals, their stock in the life of the race all funded in the individual.

Father Pemberton's presence had a wonderful effect on restoring despondent Silence Withers to her equanimity; for not all the hard divinity he had preached for half a century had spoiled his kindly nature.

The Withers Homestead was the oldest mansion in town. The Hon. Seleah Withers, Esq., built it for his own residence in the early part of the last century. Long afterwards, a bay

---

* As we have seen, this type of kindly minister in a church with a severe creed has been well depicted in the study of Dr. Honeywood in *Elsie Venner*.

window, almost a little room of itself, had been thrown out of the second story so that it looked directly down on the river running beneath it. The chamber had been for years the apartment of Myrtle, and the boys paddling about on the river would catch glimpses through the window of the little girl dressed in the scarlet jacket. Cyperian Eveleth had given it a name which furnished to young Gifted Hopkins the subject of one of his earliest poems, "The Fire-hang-bird's Nest."

If we would know anything about the persons now living at the Withers Homestead we must take inventory of some of their vital antecedents. It is by no means certain that our individual personality is the single inhabitant of these our corporeal frames. Nay there is recorded an experience of one of the living persons mentioned in this narrative which tends to show that some, at least, who have long been dead, may enjoy a kind of secondary and imperfect, yet self-conscious life in these bodily tenements which we are in the habit of considering exclusively our own.* There are many circumstances which favor this belief. Thus, at one moment we de-

---

* Henri Bergson, the philosopher, later framed this theory similarly in his *Creative Evolution:* that each person regards his own experiences as new and original and acts as though life's broad movements "stopped with him instead of passing through him. Each species thinks only for itself—it lives only for itself. Hence the numberless struggles that we behold in Nature." Bergson's *élan vital*, the driving force in life, corresponds in many ways to Freud's libido. Under a philosophy such as Bergson's, the neurotic conflict would depend principally on the clash between the individual as a unit and the impact of the accumulated experiences of the human species to which he belongs. One of the most recent adaptations of psychoanalytic theory regards man as moving in a hostile world and the immediate production of neurotic symptoms as due to this clash.

tect the look, at another the tone of voice, at another some characteristic movement of this or that ancestor in our relations.

There are times when our friends do not act like themselves but apparently in obedience to some other law than that of their own proper nature. We all do things both awake and asleep which surprise us—perhaps we have co-tenants in this house we live in. No less than eight distinct personalities are said to have co-existed in a single female mentioned by an ancient physician of unimpeachable authority. In this light we may perhaps see the meaning of a sentence, from a work which will be referred to in this narrative, viz.: "This body in which we journey across the isthmus between the two oceans is not a private carriage, but an omnibus."

The ancestry of the Withers family had counted a martyr to their faith before they were known as Puritans. A portrait, marked "Ann Holyoake, burned by ye bloudy Papists, ano 15 . ." was still hanging over the fireplace at The Poplars. The following words were yet legible on the canvas:—

"Thou hast made a covenant O Lord with me and my Children forever."

The story had come down that Ann Holyoake spoke these words in a prayer she offered up at the stake, after the fagots were kindled. There had always been a secret feeling in the family that none of her descendants could finally fall from grace in virtue of this solemn "covenant" and that the martyred woman's spirit exercised a kind of supervision over her descendants; that she either manifested herself to them or in some way impressed them from time to time.

There was a remarkable resemblance between Ann Holyoake, as shown in the portrait, and the miniature likeness of Myrtle's mother. Myrtle adopted the nearly obsolete superstition more readily on this account and loved to cherish the fancy that the guardian spirit was often near her and would be with her in time of need.

The wife of Seleah Withers had been accused of sorcery in the evil days of that delusion. A careless expression in one of her letters, that "ye Parson was as lyke to bee in league with ye Devill as anie of em," had given great offense to godly people. There was no doubt some odd "manifestations" had taken place in the household when she was a girl and that she presented many conditions belonging to what are at the present day called mediums.

Major Gideon Withers,* her son, was of the common type of hearty, loud, portly men, who like to hear themselves declaim patriotic sentiments at town meetings. If he had married a wife like himself, there might probably enough have sprung from the alliance a family of moon-faced children,

---

* The names chosen by Holmes for his characters, such as Gideon (the hewer), Silence Withers, Cynthia Badlam, reflect their qualities. There is a theory that the name a person bears unconsciously exerts a considerable influence as a stimulus to act in accordance with the name—"the names that have become famous are those which have a sonorous and stately ring," as Arturo Toscanini. But one also finds famous John Smiths, Abe Lincolns, and John Browns. Many persons experience an unpleasant reaction to their own names. This results from a conscious or an unconscious feeling that the name may reveal some inherent weakness or unfavorable characteristic which they wish to conceal. Being named bad-lamb would be extremely distasteful to such a person as Miss Cynthia Badlam. Likewise in view of the withering significance of her family name, her given name of Silence would very likely annoy the somber Miss Withers. Even when the name from a family source represents an occupation, such as Butcher, or is descriptive, such as White, the person may react to it with an identification which is very pleasing to him or, because of an unconscious rejection of the identification, with a reaction-formation in the opposite direction.*

who would have dropped into their places like posts into their holes, asking no questions of life, contented with the part of supernumeraries in the drama of being, their wardrobes of flesh and bones being furnished them gratis and nothing to do but to walk across the stage wearing it. But Major Withers, for some reason or other, married a slender, sensitive, nervous, romantic woman, which accounted for the fact that his son David, "King David," as he was called, had a different set of tastes from his father, showing a turn for literature and sentiment in his youth.

King David Withers, who got his royal prefix partly because he was rich and partly because he wrote hymns, occasionally, when he grew too old to write love poems, married the famous beauty Miss Judith Pride, and the race came up again in vigor.

Their son Jeremy took for his first wife a delicate, melancholic girl, who bore him two children, Malachi and Silence. When his wife died, he mourned for her bitterly almost a year and then went across the river to tell his grief to Miss Virginia Wild. This lady was said to have a few drops of genuine aboriginal blood in her veins and it is certain that her cheek had a little of the russet tinge which a Seckel pear shows on its warmest cheek. Love shuts itself up in sympathy like a knife blade in its handle and opens as easily. All the rest followed in due order according to Nature's kindly programme.

Captain Charles Hazard, of the ship Orient Pearl, fell desperately in love with the daughter of this second wife, married her, and carried her to India. Here their only child was born and received the name of Myrtle, as fitting her cradle in the tropics. So her earliest impressions, besides the smiles of her father and mother, were of dusky faces, of loose white raiment with the sweet exhalations of sandalwood, all the languid luxury of the East. Pestilence took her father and mother away and the child was sent back, while a mere infant, to her relatives at the old homestead. During the long voyage, the strange mystery of the ocean was wrought into her consciousness so deeply that it seemed to have become a part of her being. The waves rocked her as if the sea had been her mother; and, looking over the vessel's side from the arms that held her, she used to watch the play of the waters until the rhythm of their movement became a part of her, almost as much as her own pulse and breath.

The instincts and qualities belonging to the ancestral traits which predominated in the conflict of mingled lives lay in this child in embryo, waiting to come to maturity. It was as when several grafts, bearing fruit that ripens at different times, are growing upon the same stock. All came uppermost in their time, before their several forces had found equilibrium in the character by which she was to be known as an individual.* The World, the Flesh, and the Devil held mortgages on her life before its deed was put in her hands, but sweet and gracious influences were also born with her and the battle of life was to be fought between them, God helping her in her need and her own free choice siding with one or the other.

This was the child delivered into the hands of Silence Withers, her mother's half-sister, keeping house with her brother Malachi, a bachelor, already called Old Malachi. Both these persons had inherited the predominant traits of their sad-eyed mother. Malachi, chief heir of the family property, was rich but felt very poor. He had money in the bank

---

* This is reminiscent of the theory of the collective unconscious of Jung. In Freudian psychology the difficulty in establishing a unified personality is dependent upon the weak and uncertain integration of contradictory early identifications in the individual.

and a large tract of Western land, the subject of a lawsuit which it seemed would never be settled and kept him always uneasy. Some said he hoarded gold about the old house and, in spite of his abundant means, he kept the household on the narrowest footing of economy.

The "little Indian," as Malachi called Myrtle, was an awkward accession to the family. Silence Withers knew no more about children and their ways and wants than if she had been a female ostrich. Thus she found it necessary to send for a woman well known as the first friend of little people.

Thirty years of practice had taught Nurse Byloe the art of handling the young with the soft firmness which one may notice in cats with their kittens. Myrtle did not know she was held; she only felt she was borne up, as a cherub may fall upon a white-woolly cloud, and smiled accordingly at the nurse.

"As fine a child as ever breathed. But where did them black eyes come from? Born in Injy?—No, it's her poor mother's eyes to be sure. Doesn't it seem as if there was a kind of Injin look to 'em? She'll be a lively one to manage." This was when Miss Silence came near and brought her severe countenance close to the child for inspection of its features.

It was not a great while before Miss Silence and Myrtle, the two parties in that wearing conflict of alien lives which is often called education, began to measure their strength. The child was bright, observing, of restless activity, inquisitively curious, very hard to frighten and had a will which seemed made for mastery, not submission.* The stern spinster

---

* The idea of breaking a child's will as a preparation for its moral salvation has disappeared today except in isolated cases. Nevertheless, an ever-increasing necessity continues for directing and curb-

was disposed to discharge her duty to the girl faithfully and conscientiously, for she was one of those beings whose one single engrossing thought is their own welfare, in the next world, it is true, but still their personal welfare.

The Roman Church recognizes this class and provides every form of a specific to meet their spiritual condition. But in so far as Protestantism has thrown out works as a means of insuring future safety, these unfortunates are as badly off as nervous patients who have no drops, pills, no doctors' rules to follow. Only tell a poor creature what to do and he or she will do it and be made easy, were it a pilgrimage of a thousand miles with shoes full of split peas; but if once assured that doing does no good, the drooping Little Faiths are left to worry about their souls as the other weaklings worry about their bodies.

The practical difficulty was that Miss Silence attempted to

ing instinctive tendencies to enable the child to conform to social customs and benefit from socially advantageous opportunities. This involves some form of discipline which will eventually lead to self-restraint.

The home still remains the cradle of culture where parents or their substitutes implant their own patterns upon the young, and must do so if their offspring are to survive. Generally speaking the manner in which such ideas and ideals are impressed upon children is more important than their content, so far as the training affects the child's emotional growth. Many a parent today feels it necessary to break the child's "will," not to save his soul but because the parent loves the sense of his own authority. Of course if too great freedom is allowed a child, too much individual expression and almost no discipline—as advocated by some of the progressive schools—the child fails to acquire the self-control and organization needed for his own happiness and for a good social adaptation to preëstablished standards.

Certain current cultures, such as totalitarianism and perhaps com-

carry out a theory which developed a mighty spirit of antagonism in Myrtle and which threatened to end in utter lawlessness. Silence started from the approved doctrine that all children are radically and utterly wrong in all their feelings, thoughts, and deeds, so long as they remain subject to their natural instincts. It was by the eradication and not the education of these instincts that the character of the child she was moulding was to be determined. The first great preliminary process, so soon as the child manifested any evidence of intelligent and persistent self-determination was to break her will. No doubt this was a legitimate conclusion from the teaching of Priest Pemberton, but he wrought in the pure mathematics, so to speak, of the theology and left the working rules to the good sense of his people.

Miss Silence had been waiting to apply the great doctrine and it came in a trivial way.

---

munism, make a point of insisting with firm discipline that most of the thinking and feeling of all children be of an identical pattern, thereby hoping to ensure greater strength and power for the group, nation, state. The study of deviant children by psychiatric and psychoanalytic methods has shown at what great cost and suffering to the individual the suppression required by state ideology is often attained. Such mass ideology represents parental discipline greatly intensified but not softened by the normal parental love which may come to a child at times and in some acceptable form from the harshest father or mother.

Most Americans would agree that the aim of education should be, as Frederick Allen, Director of the Philadelphia Child Guidance Clinic,[4] puts it, not merely to "bring up" children but to regard the child "as an individual who could be helped to grow and to become a person in his own right." Through such full maturation the family and also the adult, nonpaternalistic state must profit and become truly strong, secure, and responsible in the end.

"Myrtle doesn't want brown bread. Myrtle won't have brown bread. Myrtle will have white bread."

"Myrtle is a wicked child. She will have what Aunt Silence says she shall have."

Thereupon the bright red lip protruded, the hot blood mounted to her face, the child got down from the table, took up her one forlorn, featureless doll and went to bed without her supper. The next morning the worthy woman thought that hunger and reflection would have subdued the rebellious spirit. So there stood yesterday's untouched supper waiting for her breakfast. She would not taste it. Miss Silence, in obedience to what she felt to be a painful duty, without any passion but filled with high, inexorable purpose, carried the child to the garret and fastening her so that she could not wander about and hurt herself, left her to repentant thoughts, awaiting the moment when a plaintive entreaty for liberty and food should announce that the evil nature had yielded and the obdurate will was broken.

The garret was an awful place. All the skeletonlike ribs of the roof showed in the dim light, naked overhead. It looked like a horrible cell to put criminals into. The whole place was festooned with cobwebs, the home of old hairy spiders. Here this little criminal was imprisoned eighteen dreadful hours, hungry until she was ready to gnaw her hands, a prey to all childish imaginations, and here at her stern guardian's last visit she sat, pallid, chilled, almost fainting but sullen and unsubdued. Miss Silence recognized her defeat. Then the Irish maid, Kitty, who had no theory of human nature, rushed to Myrtle with a cry of maternal tenderness and bore her off to her own humble realm, where the little victorious martyr was fed until there was as much danger from repletion as there had been from famine. How the experiment might have ended but for this most unphilosophical interference, there is no saying but it settled the point that Myrtle's rebellious nature was not to be subjugated in a brief conflict.

The untamed disposition manifested itself in greater enormities as she grew older. At four years she was detected making a cat's-cradle during sermon-time and on being reprimanded for so doing, laughed out loud.*

At eight years old she fell in love with a high-colored picture of Major Gideon Withers in a crimson sash. Then her Aunt Silence remarked a resemblance between the child and the portrait. Up to this time, Myrtle had always been dressed in sad colors, as was fitting, doubtless, for a forlorn orphan, but happening one day to see a small Negro girl in a flaming

---

* From their chronological order one would assume that Myrtle's experience in the garret preceded this transgression in church at the age of four. Incidents such as are recorded here would often be forgotten by an individual. Nevertheless they exert a tremendous influence in the establishment of the sense of guilt in the unconscious or in the formation of hostility as a reaction to the person or forces responsible for the punishments or prohibitions.

Holmes was well aware of the irresistible power of some of these unconscious forces, as he has repeatedly referred to them in his sociologic essays. Investigation of these influences subsequently became the basis of psychoanalytic therapy not only for the neuroses and borderline psychoses but for personality and character defects without definite neurotic traits. Such character analyses might be undertaken by people who feel that they are habitually too mean or too hard, too yielding or too indifferent in their usual manner of meeting life; also by those who regularly show too marked inconsistencies or who startle their friends by some sudden action which seems to be entirely out of harmony with their personality. Unconscious forces explain why "there are times when our friends do not act like themselves."

scarlet petticoat, she struck for bright colors and carried her point at last.

When she was ten years old she had one of those great experiences which give new meaning to the life of a child. Her Uncle Malachi had seemed to have a strong liking for her at one time but of late years his delusions of poverty had gained upon him and he seemed to regard her as an encumbrance and extravagance. One dreary Friday in November, Myrtle was alone in the house. Her uncle had been gone since the day before and the two women were away at the village. At such times the child took a delight in exploring the hiding places of the old mansion. She groped her way up to the garret, the scene of her memorable punishment. A rusty hook projected from one of the joists and something was hanging from it. She went bravely up and touched —a cold hand. She did what most children of that age would do—uttered a cry and ran downstairs with all her might. What could be done was done, but it was too late. Uncle Malachi had made away with himself. He had money enough, and yet he had hanged himself, for fear of starving to death.*

---

* Infantile shocks, albeit usually those having a sexual connotation, are stressed in psychoanalysis as a starting point not only of children's neuroses but of adult neuroses as well. They occur in two of Holmes's narratives. In the case of Myrtle Hazard one of the psychic traumas is this discovery at ten of the suicide of her pathologically miserly uncle. It possibly epitomized to her the futility of selfishness and overcaution. It may also have originated the idea of her subsequent attempt to escape from a barren existence through floating down a swift, unknown river, where great peril of death lurked (suggestion of suicide).

In A Mortal Antipathy the victim's shock consisted of a fall at the age of two from the arms of a young woman into a thorn bush.

He was found to have left a will leaving his property to his sister Silence, with the exception of a certain legacy to be paid to Myrtle when she should arrive at twenty years. The household seemed more chilly than ever after this tragical event. Its depressing influence followed the child to school and to the Sabbath-day catechisings. The dreary discipline of the household had sunk into her soul and she had been shaping an internal life for herself, which it was hard for friendship to penetrate.

Myrtle was now fast growing into a large dower of hereditary beauty. Always handsome, her color grew richer, her figure promised a perfect womanly development. She could not long escape the notice of the lovers of beauty and the time of danger was drawing near.

At this period of her life she made two discoveries which changed the whole course of her thoughts and opened for her a new world of possibilities. Ever since the dreadful event of November, 1854, stories that the house was haunted gained in frequency. But Myrtle was bold and inquisitive and explored its recesses at such times as she could creep among them undisturbed. She found an old trunk covered with dust and cobwebs, containing papers which her great-grandmother, the famous beauty, had left behind her. They were a strange collection, which, as so often happens with such deposits in old families, nobody had cared to meddle with and nobody had been willing to destroy, until they waited for a new generation to bring them into light again.

The other discovery, under one of the boards, was an old leather mitten, having a fat fist of silver dollars, and a thumb of gold half-eagles. Thus knowledge and power found their way to the secluded maiden.

*   *   *

Byles Gridley, the old college tutor, was a notable man. His strong, squared features, his solid-looking head, his iron-grey hair, his positive stride, his slow, precise way of putting a statement, the strange union of trampling radicalism in some directions and high-stepping conservatism in others made it impossible to calculate on his unexpressed opinions. His testy ways and his generous impulses were characteristics that gave him a very decided individuality.

The people about the village did not know what to make of such a phenomenon. He did not preach, christen, or bury like the ministers nor jog around with medicines for sick folks nor carry cases into court for quarrelsome neighbors. But he had more wisdom also than they gave him credit for, even those who thought most of his abilities.

Master Gridley considered himself, as he said a little despondently, like an old horse unharnessed and turned out to pasture. He felt that he had separated himself from human interest, and was henceforth to live in his books with the dead.* He owed something of his sadness, perhaps, to a cause which many would hold of small significance. Though he had

---

* As Ann Holyoake symbolizes the spirit of the phantom, watchful mother in the life of Myrtle, so Gridley subsequently assumed the role of the realistic, protecting father (grandfather).

In a case which I analyzed, the patient, like Myrtle Hazard, had lost her mother very early in life—at the age of two. Nevertheless she had fabricated a phantom mother to whom she constantly referred her actions. She would give as the reason for her conduct that her mother, whom she had really never known, would or would not have approved: she would wear a certain dress to a dance because her mother "wished it." Until she came for analysis it had never entered her mind that the actual mother to whose image she was so obedient might have been of a type quite different from the one she had constructed in fantasy.

mourned for no lost love, he too had his private urn filled with the ashes of extinguished hopes—he was the father of a dead book.

Why "Thoughts on the Universe," by Byles Gridley, A.M., had not met with an eager welcome, it would take us too long to inquire. He had a copy of his work, sumptuously bound, and loved to read in this, as people read over the letters of friends who have long been dead. In his more sanguine moods he looked forward to the time when the world would acknowledge its merits.

It followed from the way he lived that he must have had some means of support and his money matters led him to have occasional dealings with the legal firm of Penhallow and Bradshaw. He had entire confidence in the senior partner but not so much in the young man who had been recently associated in the business.

William Bradshaw was about twenty-five years old, by common consent good-looking, with a sharp-cut mouth which smiled at his bidding without the slightest reference to the real condition of his feeling. This was a great convenience, for it gave him an appearance of good-nature at the small expense of a slight muscular movement which was as easy as winking and deceived everybody but those who had studied him. A favorite with the other sex, he had one great advantage in the sweepstakes of life: he was not handicapped with burdensome ideals and he accepted the standard of the street as a fact for to-day, like the broker's list of prices. All the young girls were on his list of possible availabilities in the matrimonial line.

Master Gridley could not help admiring him. Indeed, of late, the master had shown a certain degree of relenting in his attitude toward his landlady's, Mrs. Hopkins', son Gifted, and had become unexpectedly amiable with the little twins who had been adopted by the good woman. His liking for the twins may have been an illustration of that law which old Dr. Hurlbut used to lay down, namely, that at a certain period of life, say from fifty to sixty and upward, the grand-paternal instinct awakens in bachelors, the rhythms of Nature reaching them in spite of her defeated intentions, so that when men marry late they love their autumn child with a twofold affection, father's and grandfather's both in one.

Certainly Master Gridley was beginning to take a part in his neighbors' welfare and, among others, Myrtle Hazard's. He had been taken with her beauty and her apparent unconsciousness of it. But there was something about Myrtle —dignity, pride, reserve or the mere habit of holding back, brought about by the system of repression under which she had been educated—which kept even the old Master at his distance.*

He noticed that her name was apt to come up in his conversations with Bradshaw; and as he himself never introduced it, of course the young man must have forced it.

"It was a demonish hard case," said William one day, "that

---

* The critics of Holmes's day were not in the least prepared to accept the idea of an unconscious force represented symbolically by a "Guardian Angel." W. S. Kennedy [5] in his biography of Holmes misses the theme of the story to the extent that he remarks: "Every young girl ought to walk locked close arm in arm between two guardian angels. Myrtle Hazard, however, has but one, the old bachelor, Byles Gridley whom it seems slightly absurd to dub with the title of Angel."

The idea of a force such as the "Guardian Angel" is embodied in the Freudian concept of a superego. The superego, in Freud's sense, not only possesses ideals to which the person (the ego) looks for guidance and safety, but also has the power to enforce them upon the ego.

old Malachi had left his money as he did. Myrtle Hazard ought to have it. If old Silence Withers gets the land claim it would be an even chance whether she marries Stoker after his wife's dead or gives it to him."

"You don't seem to think well of the Rev. Stoker?" said Mr. Gridley, smiling.

"Too fond of using the Devil's pitchfork. Besides, he has a weakness for pretty saints and sinners. No, sir, he belongs to the class I have seen described somewhere: 'There are those who hold that truth is only safe when diluted—about one fifth truth to four fifths lies—as the oxygen of the air is with its nitrogen, else it would burn us all up.' "

Gridley started a little. This was one of his own sayings in "Thoughts on the Universe," but the young man quoted it without seeming to suspect its authorship.

"Where did you pick up that saying, Mr. Bradshaw?"

"I don't remember—sounds like Coleridge."

"That's what I call a compliment worth having," said Gridley to himself.

Not long after this, happening to call in at the lawyer's office, Byles Gridley quite by chance confirmed his suspicion that Bradshaw had read "Thoughts on the Universe." A short time before Myrtle Hazard's disappearance he also learned that Bradshaw, who was like the scheming villain of a nineteenth-century melodrama, had knowledge of a secret will of old Malachi Withers. The fact that Bradshaw had kept this knowledge to himself made Master Gridley all the more suspicious.

Myrtle left a letter, written before she fled from home, for her friend Olive Eveleth. It read as follows:

MY DEAREST OLIVE: Think no evil of me for what I have done. The Fire-hang-bird's nest is empty. I can live as I have lived no longer and must find another home. You will not hear from me again until I am there.

You know where I was born—under a hot sun and in the midst of strange scenes that I seem still to remember. I must visit them again: my heart always yearns for them. I must cross the sea to get there—the beautiful great sea that I have always longed for and that my river has been whispering about to me ever so many years. My life is pinched. I feel as old as aunt Silence. I hate to leave you all, but my way of life is killing me and I am too young to die.

I have had a strange warning to leave, Olive. Do you remember how the angel of the Lord appeared to Joseph and told him to flee into Egypt? I have had a dream like that. There is an old belief in our family that the spirit of one who died many generations ago watches over some of her descendants. They say it led our first ancestor to come over here when it was a wilderness. I have had a strange dream at any rate, and the figure I saw told me to leave this place.

Keep my secret. Never think hardly of me, for you have grown up in a happy home and do not know how much misery can be crowded into fifteen years of a girl's life.

MYRTLE HAZARD

Olive could not restrain her tears, as she handed the letter to her brother Cyprian. "But this is madness, Cyprian. What she means to do is to get to Boston and sail for India."

*   *   *

Look at the flower of a morning-glory the evening before the dawn which is to see it unfold. The delicate petals are twisted into a spiral, which at the appointed hour, when the sunlight touches the hidden springs of its life, will uncoil itself and let the day into the chamber of its virgin heart. But the spiral must unwind by its own law and the hand that shall try to hasten the process will only spoil the blossom which would have expanded in symmetrical beauty under the rosy fingers of morning.

We may take a hint from Nature's handling of the flower in dealing with young souls and especially souls of young girls, which, from their organization, require more careful treatment than those of their tougher-fibred brothers. Many parents reproach themselves for not having enforced their own convictions on their children in the face of every inborn antagonism they encountered. Let them not be too severe in their self-condemnation. A want of judgment in this matter has sent many a young person to Bedlam whose nature would have opened kindly enough if it had only been trusted to the sweet influences of morning sunshine.*

In such cases it may be that the state we call insanity is not always an unalloyed evil. It may take the place of something worse—the wretchedness of a mind not yet dethroned, but subject to the perpetual interference of another mind

---

* During this adolescent period in a girl's life, certain mental and emotional problems associated with social and sexual adaptation appear which are peculiar to her and perhaps are only fully appreciated by her own sex. For this reason it seems that such problems are likely to be more sympathetically and understandingly treated by female rather than by male psychiatrists. Therefore the increasing number of women physicians now entering the field of psychiatry is especially desirable for they are greatly needed to assist young women over such critical periods as adolescence.

The sex of the woman physician facilitates an identification with the woman ideal, which is so necessary at this time for the average young girl. It is especially important with those girls who, because of mixed feelings toward their own mothers, become uncertain in the process of maturation. They hesitate in growing up because they cannot accept fully the woman ideal as seen in their mother, yet cannot abandon it and remain childish until a period far beyond the average.

governed by laws alien and hostile to its own. Insanity may perhaps be the only palliative left to Nature in this extremity.* But the mind does not know what diet it can feed on until it has been brought to the starvation point. Its experience is like that of those who have been long drifting about on rafts. There is nothing out of which it will not contrive to get some

---

* Such a conception of the defensive, compensatory function of insanity as a means of survival in the face of a desperate reality would be unusual even in the psychiatric literature of Holmes's time. Since the advent in the twentieth century of psychoanalysis and dynamic mechanisms in psychiatric thought, much attention has been devoted to the investigation of the protective function of symptoms, especially in their relation to repression. Often through the development of such symptoms certain desired objects are attained by the sick person—such as the retaliation against and domination of parents by an unmarried daughter who develops a pathological fear to go out alone. She is compelled by her illness to stay at home, often to plague her parents, and enforces their attention by requiring their presence when she goes out.

I have seen such a case of agoraphobia where a mother became virtually chained to her daughter as an attendant because of the daughter's neurosis and mother's sense of guilt in regard to it. The daughter's punishment of the mother might have taken an even more drastic turn had her death wishes found actual expression. The neurosis protected the daughter not only from the inclination to murder her mother but possibly from becoming insane through complete suppression of her violent hatred.

When pressure from without becomes too strong for a patient to bear or when he feels himself unable to continue the struggle against threatening forces from within himself or from without, the defense symptoms may take the form of mutism, negativism, refusal to take food or to associate with other people. If these symptoms become sufficiently severe and incapacitating they are considered insanity. Nevertheless their protective nature is often correctly interpreted by the layman.

sustenance. A person of note, long held captive for a political offense, is said to have owed the preservation of his reason to a pin by throwing it carelessly on the dark floor of his dungeon, and then hunting for it in a series of systematic explorations.

Perhaps the most natural thing Myrtle Hazard could have done would have been to go crazy and be sent to the nearest asylum, if Providence, which in its wisdom makes use of the most unexpected agencies, had not made a special provision for her mental welfare. She was in that arid household as the prophet in the land where there was no dew nor rain for long years. But as he had the brook Cherith and the bread and flesh in the morning and in the evening which the ravens brought him, so she had the river and her secret store of books.

The river was light and life and music and companionship to her. But there was more than that—it was infinitely sympathetic. A river is strangely like a human soul. It has its dark and bright days, its troubles from within and its disturbances from without. It often runs with a smooth surface over ragged rocks and is vexed with ripples as it slides over sands that are level as a floor. It betrays its various moods by aspects which are the commonplace of poetry, as smiles and dimples and wrinkles and frowns. It talks too, in its own simple dialect, murmuring as it were with busy lips all the way to the ocean, as children seeking the mother's breast and impatient of delay.* Of late the river appeared all at once as a Deliverer. Did

---

* Here, as later in A Mortal Antipathy, Holmes implies the symbolism of water in the fantasy of return to the mother's womb and rebirth. An original turn in the application of this symbolism is that of the River representing a connection (silver cord) leading back to the nourishing maternal (intrauterine) situation (the ocean). This symbolism of the water is earlier indicated in the

not its waters lead to the great highway of the world? So she began to follow down the stream the airy shallop that held her bright fancies.

The literature furnished for Myrtle's improvement had not been chosen with regard to its fitness for her special conditions. Of what use was it to offer books like the "Saint's Rest" to a child whose idea of happiness was in perpetual activity?

But the very first book she got hold of out of the forbidden treasury was the story of a youth who ran away and lived on an island—one Crusoe—evidently true, though full of remarkable adventures. There too was the history, coming much nearer home, of Deborah Sampson, who served as a soldier in the Revolutionary War, with a portrait of her in man's attire, looking intrepid rather than lovely. A virtuous young female she was and married well and raised a family with as good a name as wife and mother as the best of them.*
But perhaps not one of these books took such hold of her imagination as Rasselas. The prince's discontent in the Happy

---

description of Myrtle's ocean voyage as a baby, when the "waves rocked her as if the sea had been her mother." It has often been pointed out that many heroes and mythical figures, such as Venus and Moses, were born from or found in the water (of Mother Earth).

* Deborah Sampson was one of those unusual cases in which a woman has successfully assumed the role of a man without any evidence of overt homosexuality apparent in her action. Masquerading as a man, she enlisted in the Revolutionary Army in May, 1782, and participated in raids against the Tories in the Hudson Valley. Her sex was finally disclosed when she became ill with fever. Shortly after the end of the war she married; her husband was apparently a man of weaker character than her own and somewhat beneath her socially. Three children were born of the marriage, which apparently was a happy one despite Deborah's one-time masculine activity.[6]

Valley haunted her sleeping and waking for she too was a prisoner.

In the weary spring before her disappearance, a dangerous chord was struck which added to her growing restlessness. In an old closet were some sea shells and coral fans and dried starfishes and sea horses. The dim sea odors which still clung to them penetrated to the very inmost haunts of memory and called up that longing for the ocean breeze which those who have once breathed and salted their blood with it never get over.

"You are getting to look like your father," Aunt Silence said one day; "well, I hope you won't come to an early grave like poor Charles—or at any rate that you may be prepared."

She looked Miss Silence in the face very seriously, and said, "Why not an early grave, aunt, if this world is such a bad place as you say it is?"

Between Cynthia and Silence, Myrtle found no rest for her soul. Each of them was for untwisting the morning-glory without waiting for the sunshine to do it. Ever since Aunt Silence's failure in that moral coup d'état by which the sinful dynasty of the natural self-determining power was to be dethroned, her attempts in the way of education had been a series of feeble efforts followed by plaintive wails over their utter want of success.

Both these lone women were gifted with a thin vein of music. They gave it expression in psalmody, in which Myrtle, who was a natural singer, was expected to bear her part. There is a fondness for wailing cadences common to the monotonous chants of cannibals and savages generally, to such war songs as the wild, implacable "Marseillaise" and to the favorite tunes of low-spirited Christian pessimists.

A fortnight before her disappearance Myrtle came home with her hands full of leaves and blossoms. Aunt Silence

looked at them as if they were a kind of melancholy manifestation of frivolity of the part of the wicked old earth. Cynthia had formed the habit of crushing everything for its moral,
until it lost its sweetness and grew almost odious. "There's a
worm in that leaf, Myrtle; there is a worm in every young
soul."

"But there is not a worm in every leaf. Are there never any
worms in the leaves after they get old and yellow, Miss Cynthia?" That was a pretty fair hit for a simple creature of
fifteen.

The sweet season of summer was opening, calling on all
creatures to join the universal chorus of praise that was going
up around them.

"What shall we sing this evening?" said Miss Silence.

"It is Saturday evening, let us prepare our minds for the
solemnities of the Sabbath," said Miss Cynthia.

She took the hymnal, one well known to the schools and
churches of this nineteenth century and said:

"Book Second. Hymn 44. Long metre. I guess 'Putney'
will be as good a tune as any to sing it to."

> Far in the deep where darkness dwells,
> The land of horror and despair,
> Justice has built a dismal hell,
> And laid her stores of vengeance there.

"I won't sing such words," Myrtle said, "and I won't stay
here to hear them sung. You can't scare me into being good
with your cruel hymnbook."

She could not swear: she felt obdurate, scornful, outraged.
All these images, borrowed from the Holy Inquisition meant
to frighten her, had simply irritated her.

Without heeding the cries of the two women, she sprang
upstairs to her hanging chamber and looked down into the

stream. For one moment her head swam with the overwhelming, almost maddening, impulse to fling herself into those running waters and dare the worst these dreadful women had threatened her with. Something—she often thought afterwards an invisible hand—held her back and the paroxysm passed away. She remained looking, in a misty dream, into the water far below. Its murmur recalled the whisper of the ocean waves. And through the depths it seemed as if she saw into that half-remembered world of palm trees and amidst them lighting upon her with ineffable love until all else faded, the face of a fair woman. Was it Ann Holyoake's or that dear young mother's who was to her less a recollection than a dream?

*   *   *

On the 15th of June, Myrtle was wandering by the river when a boat came drifting along. She paddled it into a cove, where it could lie hid among the thick alders. That night the household was asleep at the usual early hour. Myrtle severed her beautiful dark hair with a pair of scissors and stood so changed that she felt as if she had lost herself and found a brother she had never seen before. "Good-bye, Myrtle," she said.* Then she dressed herself in the character of

---

* From a remark concerning Myrtle's resemblance to her father and from her assumption of boy's attire in the flight from home, we gather an indication that Holmes may have considered these evidences of masculinity as due to characteristics directly inherited from her adventuresome male ancestors. It is more likely, however, that Myrtle had identified herself with boys and this may have been reinforced by a subsequent identification with Deborah Sampson, the Revolutionary patriot.

Wearing boy's clothes in the case of Myrtle could hardly be regarded as a compulsion to adopt the apparel of the opposite sex.

her imaginary brother, let herself out of a window, reached the boat she had concealed and pulled herself into the swollen stream.

Not till the last straggling house had been long past did she give way to the sense of wild exultation which was coming fast over her. No living thing moved in all the wide level circle which lay about her. She had passed the Red Sea and was alone in the Desert. She lifted her hands like a priestess and her strong, sweet voice burst into song—the song of the Jewish maiden when she went out before the chorus of women and sang that grand solo:

> Sound the loud timbrel o'er Egypt's dark sea.
> Jehovah hath triumphed, his people are free.

The tumult in her blood was calmed, yet every sense was awake to the manifold mysterious impressions of that wonderful June night. Sweet odors from dewy flowers, from spicy leaves stole out of the tangled thickets and made the whole scene more dreamlike with their faint, mingled suggestions. By and by the banks of the river grew lower and marshy and in place of larger forest trees stood slender tamaracks, looking as if they had been moonstruck. The country people called this region the "Witches' Hollow." There were many legends connected with this spot and no superstitious or highly imaginative person would have cared to pass through it alone in the dead of night.

Such a compulsion is sometimes the presenting symptom in certain mental aberrations. It is called transvestitism and affects both sexes. In the case of Myrtle the disguise may be considered as an easy way to avoid detection. Nevertheless the fact that she cut her hair and chose to wear boy's apparel would indicate that she felt a dissatisfaction with her own role in life. Possibly this was a reaction-formation to the cold and austere women of her household.

The boat was floating quietly along and now there stole upon her ear a low, gentle, distant murmur, so steady, so uniform, that it soothed her to sleep, as if it were the old cradle song the ocean used to sing or the lullaby of her young mother.

So she glided along slowly, slowly, down the course. The gentle murmur grew louder and louder but still she slept, dreaming of the murmuring ocean.

To amplify her experiences during the night of her escape, Holmes introduces an account which Myrtle, aged 15, wrote at the request of a friend—in all probability Byles Gridley. The account is called a "vision" by Myrtle.

"The place where I saw these sights is called Witches' Hollow. The first strange thing that I noticed was on coming near a kind of hill or mound that rose out of the low meadows. I saw a burning cross lying on the slope of that mound. I know that I was awake while I was looking at this cross. I think my eyes were open when I saw these other appearances but I felt just as if I were dreaming while awake.

"I heard a faint rustling sound and on looking up I saw many figures moving around me and seemed to see myself moving among them as if I were outside of myself.* The

---

* The mental state of Myrtle is one between waking and sleeping —a semiconscious or a twilight state of the mind. The feeling that she was observing herself as if she were another person is a frequent symptom in a condition known as depersonalization. Myrtle, in her new role as a boy, was certainly "not herself."

My own studies support the theory that unconscious homosexuality is an important factor in the production of conflicts and cross-identifications eventually leading to feelings of estrangement and depersonalization.[7] The homosexual component of personality usually has been very thoroughly repressed and has assumed the

figures slid or glided with an even movement, as if without any effort. They made many gestures, and seemed to speak, but I cannot tell whether I heard what they said or knew its meaning in some other way.

"The faces of some of these figures were the same as I have seen in portraits. I saw my father and my mother as they look in the two small pictures; also my grandmother and her father and mother and grandfather and one other person, who lived a great while ago. The longer they had been dead the less like substance they looked, so that the oldest was like one's breath of a frosty morning but shaped like the living figure.

"There was no motion of their breasts but their lips seemed to be moving as if they were saying, Breath; Breath, Breath. I thought they wanted to breathe the air of this world again in my shape, which I seemed to see, as it were, empty of myself and of these other selves, like a sponge that has water pressed out of it.

"Presently it seemed to me that I returned to myself. My father and mother came up, hand in hand, looking more real than any of the rest. Their figures vanished and they seemed to have become part of me; for I felt all at once the longing to live over the life they had led, on the sea and in strange countries.

"Another figure was just like the Major, who is said to have drank hard sometimes, though there is nothing about it on

---

form of an unconscious identification with the parent of the opposite sex. For instance, the longing of a girl to be able to attain the intellectual brilliance and distinction of her father may be so far removed from any conscious thought that it appears strange when first brought to her attention. Nevertheless in fantasies, dreams, and slips of the tongue, the wish to possess physical and mental qualities of the man often appears in girls and women.

his tombstone. It seemed to me that there was something about his life that I did not want to make a part of mine but that there was some right he had in me through my being of his blood, and so his health and his strength went all through me and I was always to have what was left of his life in that shadowlike shape.

"So in the same way was the shape answering to the famous beauty who was the wife of my great-grandfather and the face of that portrait marked Ruth Bradford, who was before the court in the witchcraft trials.

"There was with the rest a dark, wild-looking woman with a headdress of feathers. She kept as it were in shadow but I saw something of my own features in her face. Also the shape of that woman who was burned long ago by the Papists came very close to me and was in some way made one with mine. I feel her presence in me since, but not always, only at times, and then I feel borne up as if I could do anything in the world. I had a feeling as if she were my guardian and protector.

"It seems to me that these, and more, whom I have not mentioned, do really live over some part of their past lives in my life. I do not understand it all but I write it down as nearly as I can from memory by request."

MYRTLE HAZARD

This statement must be accounted for in some way, or pass into the category of the supernatural. Probably it was one of those intuitions with the objective projection which sometimes come to young persons, especially girls, in certain exalted nervous conditions.* The study of the portraits, with the

* The adolescent period, as is well known, with its physiological changes and demands for new psychological adaptations is a particularly difficult one for many people. At this time some of the conflicts of adolescents which have been latent or cannot be adequately

knowledge of some parts of the history of the persons they represent and the consciousness of instincts inherited in all probability from these same ancestors, formed the basis of Myrtle's "Vision." It might seem that those whose blood flows in our veins struggle for mastery and, by and by, one or more get the predominance, so that we grow to be like father or mother; or two or more remote ancestors are blended, not to the exclusion, however, of a special personality of our own, about which these others are grouped. Independently of any possible scientific value, this "Vision" serves to illustrate the above-mentioned fact of common experience, not sufficiently weighed by most moralists.*

One statement of the narrative admits of a simple natural

---

handled by them may cause a psychopathological disturbance to become evident. The experience of Myrtle Hazard seems in the nature of a semi-hallucinatory episode in an hysterical young girl rather than the more serious form of mental disorder, schizophrenia, which so often begins between the ages of sixteen and nineteen. This latter disease was first described by Professor Emil Kraepelin of Heidelberg about 1890 under the name of Dementia Precox, and usually affected boys and girls who are of the introspective, withdrawing type. Elsie Venner more nearly resembles this type than Myrtle Hazard. The former's failure in adptation was intra-psychic, the latter more the result of the pressure of an unsympathetic environment.

* The whole vision may be interpreted as a kind of rebirth fantasy and a yearning for an adequate ideal-identification—a search for phantoms such as exist in the depths of all minds. Visions of this kind often contain an element of wish fulfillment, are induced by repression, and have compensatory value. The same may be said of hallucinations where the person actually has false sense perceptions of sight, hearing, or smell, instead of seeming to have them in the semiconscious state as described above. The fiery cross, as Myrtle described and explained it, would be an illusion, that is, a faulty interpretation of an object actually observed.

explanation—decaying wood is often phosphorescent. Country people are familiar with it in wild timberland and have given it the name of "Fox-fire." Two trunks of trees in this state, lying across each other, will account for the fact observed and vindicate the truth of the young girl's story without requiring any exceptional occurrence outside of natural laws.

*   *   *

It was morning when Clement Lindsay, who lived in Alderbank, after thinking the unutterable thoughts that nineteen years of life bring to the sleeping and waking dreams of young people, took from his desk a long letter written in a hardly formed female hand.

The letter was from Susie Posey in Oxbow Village and was addressed to Clement, "a stately youth of high purpose and fastidious taste." In it she reproached him for his neglect and wondered whether he still cared for her. His interest in her had in fact died out but he felt a sense of obligation for an earlier love avowal. He had outgrown "simple, trusting" Susie, but determined to remain true to his word. He was in the midst of replying when he heard a cry for help coming from the river which flowed past his home.

HELP, HELP, HELP!

A cry of a young person's voice was heard faintly, coming from the direction of the river. He ran straight to the bank just above the beautiful falls which break the course of the river. A skiff was lying close to a rock between it and the brink of the fall. In it was a youth of fourteen or fifteen years, holding on by slender twigs. The boat was threatening to tear away and go over the fall.

Clement seized the boat and with a desperate effort clambered over its side and found himself its second doomed passenger. He caught up the single oar and with a few sharp paddle-strokes brought the skiff into the blackest centre of the current, where it would plunge them into the deepest pool. Down they went together into the whirling waters; a choking flood hammered them down into the black depths.

A cap rose to the surface—it was the one the unknown "boy" had on. And then—after how many seconds by the watch cannot be known—Clement Lindsay felt the blessed air against his face and taking a great breath, came to his full consciousness. The arms of the boy were locked around him as in the embrace of death. A few strokes brought him to shore, dragging his senseless burden with him.*

He loosed the ribbon that was round the neck, and tore open the checked shirt—the story of Myrtle Hazard's sex was told.

He placed his lips to hers and filled her breast with the air from his chest. At last, when he had almost ceased to hope, she gasped and rolled her eyes wildly around her—she was born again into this mortal life.*

He bore her to the house, laid her on a sofa and having spent his strength in this last effort, reeled and lay in a faint.

The first thing Clement Lindsay did when he was fairly himself again, was to finish his letter to Susan. However, it contained far

---

* This episode of the skiff floating down a river, the falls, the drowning and the rescue is symbolically a pretty example of rebirth. The tender care which Myrtle received in the home of the motherly Mrs. Lindsay would be a reassuring factor to the distressed girl in beginning life anew, and would aid her in the reaffirmation of her sex. It stands in strong contrast to the continual rejection she had met in the Withers' household. Gridley soon appears on the scene to assume the function of a solicitous father, or more accurately, of a grandfather.

too much about the adventure and too little of love for the senti-
mental girl. For consolation she rushed to her understanding old
friend, Mr. Gridley. The latter immediately surmised a connec-
tion between the disappearance of Myrtle and the rescue and de-
cided to drive some thirty miles to Alderbank, where he easily
located the Lindsay home.

"Is there a stranger here?" he asked. "A young friend of
mine is missing."

The matron came nearer to Gridley. "There is. This person
is a young woman disguised as a boy. She was rescued by my
nephew and has been delirious ever since. Is the person you
are seeking a niece of yours?" (Why did she not ask if the
girl was his daughter? What is that look of paternity and of
maternity which observing mothers and old nurses know so
well in men and women?)

"No, she is not a relative. But I am acting for those who
are."

Gridley moved gently to the bed and looked upon the pallid, still features of Myrtle. Her face, so marked with the recent traces of acute suffering, was even now showing that she
was struggling in some fearful dream.

She started with a slight convulsive movement and the cry
escaped—how heart-breaking when there is none to answer it
—"Mother." Gone back again through the chilling years of
her childhood to that hardly remembered morning of life
when the cry she uttered was answered by the embrace of
caressing arms.

Myrtle opened her eyes but they were vacant as yet.

"Are we dead?" she said. "Where am I? This isn't heaven
—there are no angels— Oh, no, no, no; don't send me to the
other place—fifteen years, no father, no mother—nobody
loved me. Was it wicked in me to live?" Her whole theological training was condensed in that brief question.

"Wicked to live, my dear? No indeed. Look at me, my child. Don't you know your old friend Byles Gridley?" *

She stretched her arms and looked round—this was a sign that she was coming right.

"Has this adventure been told about in the village, Mrs. Lindsay?" asked Mr. Gridley.

"Not one word has been or will be told by any one of us," she replied.

"And now I want to see the young man that rescued my friend."

Now Master Gridley saw well enough that Clement was of the right kind—fellows with lime enough in their bones and iron enough in their blood to begin with, shapely, large-nerved, firm-fibred, with well-spread bases to their heads for the ground floor of the faculties and well-vaulted arches for the upper range of apprehensions and combinations. "Plenty of basements," Gridley used to say, "without attics and sky-lights. Plenty of skylights without rooms enough and space enough below." But here was "a three-story brain." **

---

* This rebirth situation gives Holmes his chance to affirm again his faith in the worth and dignity of human beings as such and to protest against the Calvinist doctrine of the damnation of babies at, or even in, birth.

** In this concept of the three-story brain there is something suggestive of the three categories of the mind—the superego, the ego, and the id—eventually adopted by Freud in 1925 as a basis for personality study. Freud's three levels may be roughly interpreted as follows: the superego on top, as a skylight for ideal formation; the ego, "the living room" in constant contact with the tasks and demands of the minute; and the id, the basement of the unconscious, in which the instinctive urges roam freely and in which all sorts of relics of the individual's experiences, and possibly also those of the race, are housed.

It was agreed that the young girl should not know the name of her deliverer; it might have awkward complications.

The effect of the violent shock she had experienced was to change the whole nature of Myrtle for the time. Her mind was unsettled, she could hardly recall anything except the plunge over the fall. She was perfectly docile and plastic and at half-past four o'clock on Sunday morning the shepherd brought the stray lamb into the paved yard at The Poplars.

Kitty Fagan looked for a moment to assure herself that it was the girl she loved. What crying and kissing and blessings were poured forth, those who know the vocabulary and the enthusiasm of her eloquent race may imagine better than we could describe it. The welcome of the two other women was far less demonstrative. There were awful questions to be answered before the kind of reception she was to have could be settled. While Miss Silence was weeping with joy that her "responsibility" was removed, Cynthia Badlam waited for an explanation before giving way to her feelings.

Mr. Gridley repeated in the most precise manner where and how he had found her. It was agreed that nothing more was to be told to anyone.

*　　*　　*

The Rev. Mr. Stoker had a remarkable gift in prayer, an endowment by no means confined to profoundly spiritual persons. But there is no gift more dangerous to the humility and sincerity of a minister. While his spirit ought to be on its knees it is too apt to be on tiptoe, following with admiring look the flight of its own rhetoric.

The minister gave out his text from the Book of Esther: "For she had neither father nor mother, and the maid was fair and beautiful." The reverend gentleman availed himself of the excitable state of his audience to sweep the keyboard of their emotions, while all the stops were drawn out. The sermon, with its hinted application to the event of the past week, was over at last. The shoulders of the various women were twitching with sobs and old men were crying in their vacant way.

As the sermon was finished, the sexton handed a note to Father Pemberton, who rose in the beauty of his tranquil old age.

"Sisters and Brethren,—Rejoice with us. This our daughter was dead and is alive again. Let us return our thanks to our God and Father, who hath wrought this great deliverance."

*   *   *

It was necessary to summon a physician to advise as to the treatment of Myrtle, who had received a shock, bodily and mental. Her very tranquility was suspicious and the reaction must sooner or later set in.

Dr. Lemuel Hurlbut, ninety-two, very deaf, nearly blind, liable to odd lapses of memory, was yet a wise counsellor in difficult cases and Miss Silence Withers went herself to see him.

"Miss Withers, father, wants to talk with you about her niece, Miss Hazard," said young Dr. Fordyce Hurlbut.

Old Dr. Hurlbut had to wait a minute before his thoughts would come to order; with a little time, the proper answer would be evolved by the slow automatic movement of the rusted mental machinery.

"Myrtle Hazard, Myrtle Hazard, to be sure. The old Withers' stock—good constitutions—a little apt to be nervous. I've given 'em a good deal of valerian and asafoetida—there isn't the change in folks people think. I've seen six fingers on a child that had a six-fingered great-uncle, and I've seen that child's grandchild born with six fingers. Does this girl like to have her own way like the rest of the family?"

"A little too well I suspect, father. Her aunt wants you to see her; they think there's nobody like 'old Doctor.'"

He was not too old to be pleased with this preference and said he was willing to go.

There was too much color in Myrtle's cheeks and a lustre in her eyes as the old man looked at her long and curiously. Then he felt her pulse with his shrivelled fingers, and asked her various questions about herself, which she answered with a tone not quite so calm as natural, but willingly and intelligently. The younger Dr. Hurlbut was disposed to think she was suffering from a temporary excitement that would soon pass off.

Father and son left the room to talk it over.

"It does not amount to much, I suppose, father," said Fordyce Hurlbut. "Rest and low diet and all will be right, won't it?" *

Was it the feeling of sympathy or the pride of superior

---

* Not long after this story was written Dr. S. Weir Mitchell introduced the "rest cure" for the treatment of neurasthenia, a name which covered a great variety of nervous disorders. In this rest cure the patient was isolated and kept on a diet of high caloric value, the idea being to build up the body energy. Psychologically the rest cure contained elements of punishment (confinement) and threw much of the patient's self-love back on himself. Eventually he tired of both elements, being babied and at the same time restricted, and was ready to return, temporarily at least, to face his duties and problems in life.

The rest cure for a while became a much abused cure-all and vogue in medicine but with the better understanding of nervous troubles today is used principally in acute emotional disturbances.

sagacity that changed the look of the old man's wrinkled features? "Not so fast, Fordyce," he said. "I've seen that look on another face of the same blood—dead before you were born, my boy. It meant trouble then and I'm afraid it means trouble now. Cut her hair close and keep her temples cool and put some drawing plasters to the soles of her feet and give her some of my Pilulae compositae. Live folks are only dead folks warmed over. I can see 'em all in that girl's face—that queer woman, the Deacon's mother—there's where she gets that hysterical look."

He paused again until the thoughts came slowly straggling up.

"Four generations—man and wife—before this Hazard child I've looked on with these old eyes. When Myrtle speaks, I've heard that same voice before—yes, as long ago as when I was first married; my first wife Rachel used to think I praised Handsome Judith's voice more than it deserved."

The old Doctor's sagacity was not in fault about the threatening aspect of Myrtle's condition. With the exception of sluggishness rather than loss of memory, his mind was almost as trustworthy as in his best days. At any rate the first danger was averted but the hysteric stage began to manifest itself by the usual signs, if anything can be called usual in a condition the natural order of which is disorder and anomaly.

The mental excitement so long sustained, followed by a violent shock to the system, coming just at the period of rapid development, gave rise to that morbid condition, hysteria, accompanied with a series of mental and moral perversions which in ignorant ages and communities is attributed to the influence of evil spirits.* Few households have ripened

---

* The struggle between science and religion has no more far reaching triumph than that which it has almost completely achieved over the concept of demoniacal obsession. Both Luther and Calvin

a growth of womanhood without witnessing some of its manifestations, and its phenomena are largely traded in by scientific pretenders and religious fanatics. Into this cloud, with all
its risks and all its humiliations, Myrtle Hazard is about to
enter.

After the ancient physician had settled the general plan
of treatment, its practical applications were left to the care
of his son. Dr. Fordyce Hurlbut was a vigorous nature and a
favorite with his female patients; many of them would have
said because he was good-looking and pleasant, but some
thought it in virtue of a magnetic power to which certain
temperaments were impressible. He himself never attempted
any of the exploits which some thought were in his power.
At once he saw that neither of the two women about Myrtle
exercised a quieting influence, so he got her old friend, Nurse
Byloe.

The old nurse looked calm enough at his first visits but one
morning her face showed that something had been going
wrong.

"She's been attacked, Doctor, sence you been here, dreadful," said Nurse Byloe. "It's them high stirricks, Doctor, 'n'

---

accepted the idea that the entrance of a personalized devil into the
body caused many illnesses, but particularly mental illnesses. All
sorts of weirdly assembled, foul smelling and bad tasting concoctions
were given to patients with the notion that the devil himself could
not withstand them and would leave the body of the sufferer thus
freeing him of illness caused by the devil's presence. Even today
two extremely nauseating drugs, relics of this practice, are occasionally used by physicians in treating nervous disorders, especially hysteria. They are asafoetida and valerian which have no scientifically
demonstrated sedative value. Old Dr. Hurlbut mentioned that he
has used them many a time on certain members of the high-strung
Withers family.

I never see 'em higher. Cryin' 'n' sech spassums. And ketchin' at her throat, 'n' sayin' there was a great ball a risin' into it from her stomach."

"Where is your uneasiness, Myrtle?" he asked.

She moved her hand very slowly and pressed it on her left temple. He laid his hand upon the same spot, kept it there a moment and then removed it. As he sat watching her, he saw that her features were growing easier and in a short time her deep, even breathing showed that she was asleep.*

---

* Treatment by hypnosis of many forms of physical and mental disease spread from France and Britain to the United States about 1850. In England it had gained the approval of some competent physicians, including Dr. John Elliottson, who ranked with the best and who was expelled from the College of Physicians for his opinions. It attracted wide notice in America through the successful results of Dr. Quimby about 1860. The medical profession has never adopted hypnosis extensively as a curative method, but apparently in Holmes's day, as today, legitimate practitioners were tempted to resort to it for transient results in cases of hysteria. Now, even as then, the nature of hypnotic phenomena remains somewhat obscure. In the case of Myrtle, an exceptionally susceptible girl, the procedure of Dr. Hurlbut produced a hypnotic state very rapidly and by extremely simple suggestion.

One of the important contributions concerning the forces operative in the production of the hypnotic states has come from the psychoanalytic school, especially from the work of Ferenczi. It has been able to point out that the hypnotic subject who responds to the "command" hypnotic suggestion identifies the hypnotist with a powerful father image. Where the patient is persuasively lulled into a hypnotic sleep he identifies the hypnotist and his sing-song method with the mother and her soothing crooning.

In the past few years interest of psychiatrists has returned to the study of hypnotic phenomena, using the postulate of the transference element in hypnosis and the psycho-dynamics of Freudian

"It beats all," the old nurse said. "It's jes' like them magnetizers, Dr. Hurlbut."

"I can't say, Nurse, I never thought of its quieting her so quickly."

The Doctor became thoughtful. Did he possess a hitherto unexercised personal power which put the key of this young girl's nervous system into his hands?

At the next visit it did seem as if some of Nurse Byloe's "seventy devils" had possession of the girl. All the spasmodic movements, the laughing and crying were in full blast. As the remedies ordered seemed to have been of no avail, the Doctor placed the tips of his fingers on her forehead. The storm was soon calmed and she fell into a quiet sleep.

Here was an awkward affair. The physician held this power in his hands, which no remedy and no other person seemed

psychology in the management and interpretation of the productions of the hypnotic subject. The latter no longer remains submissive and passive in the hypnotic state, but discusses his problems and reënacts them. Sometimes he may relive very early anxiety-laden incidents, like falling from a crib. In this type of psychoanalytic treatment under hypnosis, great care is used in the language addressed to the subject, and efforts are directed toward the integration of the personality in the pattern indicated by the conflicts expressed in the transference situation.

In other words, transference phenomena are the forces which stimulate the induction of the hypnotic state. Freud first employed the term transference in connection with the patient-physician relationship, but its scope has been extended. Today it is used to designate the unconscious endowing of persons with qualities which the patient desires to find in them. Most of the emotions thus shifted were originally experienced in early childhood in relation to parents, nurses, and siblings.

Neurotic persons, because of early denial or repression, are almost insatiable in their need to be loved and to hate. Before long

to possess. What would be the consequence of the mysterious relation which must necessarily spring up between a man like him and a young girl organized for victory over the calmest blood and the steadiest resistance?

Every day after this made matters worse. His "Peace, be still" was obeyed by the stormy elements of this young soul as if it had been a supernatural command. How could he resist the dictate of humanity which called him to make his visits more frequent that her intervals of rest might be more numerous? *

---

they begin to throw their positive love feelings upon the physician and establish what is known as a positive transference. At times it is difficult to differentiate these feelings for the physician, a stranger to them, from the true love that comes as a result of the interplay of emotion between two persons who have had mutual experiences and close associations.

Some physicians seem more frequently to establish with their patients what is called a negative transference. In this situation all the patient's hostile and aggressive feelings are expressed in the analysis in the form of dissatisfaction, quarreling, and hatred of the physician, who becomes a sort of whipping post. Of course the existence of positive or negative transference from the patient to the physician is not dependent entirely upon the method or personality of the physician. This is evident from the fact that, during the analysis, the same patient may undergo wide fluctuations of friendly and hostile attitudes toward the same physician, as reactions are brought to light which he believes the physician approves or condemns.

* The development of psychoanalysis began with the study of a case of Dr. Joseph Breuer of Vienna, who noted that certain disturbing hysterical symptoms in a young girl disappeared after the emotional release of feelings against her father which she had kept pent up. When Freud later joined his older colleague, Dr. Breuer in the study of hysterical conditions, they hypnotized the patient and al-

The Doctor was a man of refined feeling as well as of principle. It was the common belief in the village that his only love was buried in the grave of his wife, and it did not occur to him to suspect himself of any weakness with regard to this patient, little more than a child. It did not at once suggest itself to him that she, in her excited condition, might fasten her wandering thoughts upon him, too far removed by his age to strike the fancy of a young girl under any conceivable conditions.

Thus it was that many evenings found him sitting by his patient, the river rippling and singing beneath them. Every time they were thus together, the subtle influence which bound them to each other brought them more and more into inexplicable harmonies and almost spiritual identity.*

---

lowed memories and repressed feelings to come to the surface under hypnosis. This method was popularly known as mental catharsis.

A situation not dissimilar to the one arising between Myrtle and Dr. Hurlbut occurred in an early case of Breuer and Freud. A young girl established to Breuer a transference so strong and sexually colored that Breuer became perturbed and decided to discontinue his investigation of these states so laden with complications for the physician. Freud, bolder than his colleague, directed his attention to the study of the mechanisms producing this reaction and thereby established the subtle, unconscious, emotional nature of transference.

* The physician in the psychoanalytic method should remain objective and detached from the patient as a person—not always too easy in practice. Holmes gives here a vivid picture of the phenomenon known in psychoanalysis as counter-transference; that is, when the physician's own emotions become mingled with his patient's, either as love or as dislike.

When the physician becomes emotionally involved either way, he may fail to appreciate that his own interest in the patient, male or female, is personal and excessive. This in turn may lead him to a misinterpretation of symptoms in the disease picture evident to an

All this did not hinder the development of new conditions in Myrtle. Her will was losing its power. "I cannot help it" —the hysteric's motto—was her constant reply and she was rapidly undergoing a singular change of her moral nature. She feigned all sorts of odd symptoms and it became next to impossible to tell what was real and what simulated. At one time she would squint, would be half paralyzed, and again would pretend to fast for days, while living on food she had concealed.

The nurse was getting worn out and the two spinsters were beginning to get nervous themselves. Mr. Stoker said in confidence to Miss Silence, that there was reason to fear Myrtle might have been given over for a time to the buffetings of Satan and that perhaps his (Mr. Stoker's) personal attention might be useful.* It appeared that "young doctor" was

---

outsider, physician or layman, who is not emotionally concerned. For this reason the analyst should keep constantly on guard against counter-transference. Freud some years ago recommended that every analyst be himself reanalyzed every five years so that he might become aware of his own counter-attachments and psychological blind spots. Recently I suggested that where a patient has been analyzed for roughly over three hundred hours, the situation should be reviewed by an impartial psychoanalyst or psychiatrist with the idea of determining if such emotional factors were interfering with progress toward cure.

* Occasionally this question as to whether a person is ill or sinful —that is, a subject for the doctor or the minister—may be an obsessively prominent symptom in cases of compulsion neurosis. One of my patients, an unmarried woman of fifty, Protestant, with a strict religious background, suffered from a stubborn fear of contagion. She would repeatedly seek reassurance during the analysis because of an overwhelming sense of guilt involving death wishes against her family with an agonized plea: "Doctor, am I wicked, or am I sick?"

the only being left with whom she had any complete relations. She had become so passive in his hands that it seemed as if her only healthy life was, as it were, transmitted through him. Except when the physician's will was exerted upon her, she was drifting without any self-directing power. Eventually this became known to some persons in the village, among them William Bradshaw. That gentleman was far from being pleased with the look of things. What if the doctor should get a hold on this young woman?

So he concluded to be ill with dyspepsia, and picked up a medical book, read ten minutes or more, and was an accomplished dyspeptic: for lawyers half learn a thing quicker than the members of any other profession.

He presented himself with a somewhat forlorn countenance to Dr. Fordyce Hurlbut, and got into a conversation about nervous feelings which accompanied his dyspeptic attack, thence to nervous complaints in general and to the case of the young lady at The Poplars. The Doctor talked with a reserve, but it was plain enough to Bradshaw that if this kind of intercourse went on much longer there was no saying how it would at last turn out.

Bradshaw was afraid to meddle directly. He therefore artfully hinted his fears to Byles Gridley and left his hint to work itself out. However suspicious Master Gridley was of him, he thought it worthwhile to inquire of nurse Byloe what was this new relation.

She imparted her opinion to him with great freedom. "Sech doin's. The gal's jest as much bewitched as ever any gal was sence them that was possessed in Scriptur'. Ef that Doctor don't stop comin', she won't breathe without his helpin' her to before long. And, Mr. Gridley, I can't help thinkin' he's gettin' a little bewitched too. I'll tell ye what, Mr. Gridley; you get old Dr. Hurlbut to come and see her once a day for a week and the young doctor to stay away. She'll have some dreadful tantrums fust, but she'll come to in two or three days." *

---

* The dilemma which young Dr. Hurlbut faced—namely, the breaking of the transference—was not peculiar to him, his case, or his time. The handling of transference remains one of the most intricate—some say the crucial—problem of psychoanalysis and also the most dependable gauge in estimating progress. Theoretically the transference to the physician is supposed to disappear when its nature and its unconscious value become known to the patient. However, this is not always so and some of the major tragedies in psychoanalytic cases may be traced to the fact that the patient, male or female, becomes desperate because he feels he no longer has the attention of his doctor. This is particularly likely to be true when the patient has suffered severe, early, and long-standing deprivations of love, as was the case with Myrtle.

Likewise the attitude of family and friends toward the doctor and his patient in the confidential relationship and long-continued treatment of psychoanalysis is often identical with that described above. The transference situation acts as a bridge which allows the patient a free pathway of affects and the analyst becomes the recipient of them. He accepts them, good or bad, friendly or antagonistic, without a decided personal reaction. Here and there he may say a few words which make the patient realize that he can express himself with complete impunity. The most the analyst wishes to know is why the patient feels this way or that—and again "why." As a result of this reëxamination, gradually the patient may become less bold, less meek, or less rebellious in his character.

The change in the patient's attitude toward those with whom he is associated or dependent upon may become very apparent to them. Often they appreciate and approve it but often, too, as in Myrtle's case, they do not like it or the process which brings it about.

The family may and often does prefer to have a wife, husband, or child sick, but subservient to them, than one well but independent

Master Gridley decided to ask young Dr. Hurlbut to call and treated him to a cup of such tea as bachelors sometimes keep hidden away. He presently began asking certain questions about the grand climacteric, which eventful period he was fast approaching. He said he had a few old medical books which he should like to show Dr. Hurlbut.

"There, now. What do you say to this copy of Jannes de Ketam, Venice, 1522? Look at these woodcuts—see this scene of the plague patient—a very curious book, Doctor, and has the first phrenological picture ever made. Take a look, too, at my Vesalius, with the grand old original figures—so good that they laid them to Titian. Brave old fellows; put their lives into their books as you gentlemen don't pretend to do nowadays. And good fellows, Doctor, scrupulous, conscientious. Did you ever read the oldest of medical documents, the Oath of Hippocrates?"

The Doctor thought he had but did not remember much about it. "Doctor, it is just as good to-day as when it was laid down as a rule of conduct four hundred years before the Sermon on the Mount. Let me read it to you, Dr. Hurlbut."

Master Gridley turned so as to face the Doctor and read the famous Oath aloud. When he came to these words, he pronounced them with special emphasis.

"Into whatever house I enter, I will go for the good of the patient: I will abstain from inflicting any voluntary injury and from leading away any, whether man or woman, bond or free."

---

and mature and competent to decide for himself. For that reason the family or friends of the patient may openly or secretly attempt to interrupt an analysis, giving plausible reasons for their action— the expense, too little or sufficient progress, questioning the psychic origin of the illness, and the like.

The Doctor changed color as he listened and moisture broke out on his forehead.

Then Master Gridley spoke at length, for the plain honest words had touched the right spring of consciousness; not too early, for young Dr. Hurlbut saw now whither he was tending, not too late, for he was not yet in the inner spirals of the passion which whirls men and women to their doom in ever-narrowing coils, that will not unwind at the command of God or man. He spoke as one who is humbled by self-accusation, yet in a manly way.

"Master Gridley," he said, "it is true, I cannot continue my attendance on Myrtle without peril to both of us. She is not herself; God forbid that I should cease to be myself. I will leave this patient in my father's hands."

Doctor Fordyce went off the next morning without a word to Myrtle. That night the spirit tore her and so the second night. But there was no help for it: her doctor was gone and the old physician came instead, spoke kindly to her, left wise directions and assured the family that if they would have a little patience, they would see all this storm blow over.

On the third night after his visit, the spirit rent her sore and came out of her, or, in the phrase of to-day, she had a fierce paroxysm, after which the conflict ceased. Her impressible and excitable condition was just the state to invite the spiritual manipulations of one of those theological practitioners who consider that the treatment of all morbid states of mind short of raving madness belongs to them. If Myrtle Hazard was in charge of any angelic guardian, the time was at hand when she would need all celestial influences, for the Rev. Stoker was about to take a deep interest in her spiritual welfare.

Mr. Stoker had the art of sliding into easy intimacy with women. The gossips maintained that many of the younger women would have been willing to lift for him that other end of his yoke under which poor Mrs. Stoker was fainting, unequal to the burden.

That lady had long passed the prime in which he was still flourishing.* She had borne him five children, and cried her eyes hollow over the graves of three of them. Household cares had dragged upon her and her thoughts had fed too much on death and sin—good bitter tonics to increase the appetite for virtue but not good as food and drink for the spirit. Another grief, deeper than all the rest, was a feeling which had hardly risen into the region of inwardly articulated thought but lay unshaped beneath all the syllabled trains of sleeping and waking consciousness.

The minister was often consulted upon spiritual matters and was in the habit of receiving such visitors in his study; poor Mrs. Stoker thought she noticed that the good man had more leisure for the blooming sister than for the more discreet matron or spinster. More than once the faded wife had made an errand to the study, and, after a look at the bright cheeks flushed with the excitement of spiritual communion, had gone back to her chamber with the bitterness of death in her soul.

The end of all these trials was that the minister's wife had fallen into a state of habitual invalidism,** such as only women

---

* One of the important factors in marital unhappiness is the uneven aging of couples, psychologically as well as physically. The disparity may affect either the husband or the wife. In the case of the husband, for instance, a man alert and active at the time of marriage may gradually restrict his interests to his score at golf and "keeping a job." The wife, after a brief period of child-rearing, may continue to grow intellectually and may find little congeniality in the deadening habits of her husband.

** A chronic illness of this type tends to foster an overinvestment of the person's own body with emotion, which sours through being

can experience. Her bed had become her home as if it belonged to her organism, and there she lay, a not unpleasing invalid to contemplate, always looking resigned except when the one deeper grief was stirred. She did not know how steadily this artificial life was draining her daughter Bathsheba, one of the every-day air-breathing angels without nimbus who belong to the story of quite a few households. The Rev. Stoker's

---

turned back upon itself or lodged in unsuitable places. The illness may also serve as a face-saving device by allowing the patient to escape humiliation before the world, with its unwelcome commiseration and pity. Often the symptoms of such patients baffle physicians.

I have seen one such case of protracted illness where a lady in her late fifties had not left her bed for eight years. She was brought to New York from a small Ohio town on a stretcher at the suggestion of a registered nurse, who suspected that the chronic weakness, "fallen stomach," astasia abasia, and a host of other complaints might be of psychic origin. Significantly the patient became ill after her older daughter had borne an illegitimate child. Also she was proud of the fact that although flat on her back she could take a complete bed bath "without spilling a drop of water." After three or four talks with me, during which I suggested mildly that her illness might be a defense and self-indulgence, the patient left her bed, regained the power of her legs and soon became and remained symptom free. A dramatic cure had been affected for which I got credit.

As a matter of fact, I happened in just at the right moment and the timing of a fact explained or suggestion offered a patient is one of the most important factors determining its effect in cure. Just prior to her trip to see me her younger daughter, aged twenty-three, who had nursed her with dutiful sacrifice all through the long illness, finally married and moved to New York. With the patient it was a case of getting well and continuing to see this daughter frequently or staying sick and practically giving up any contact with her. At this critical moment she became particularly susceptible to

duties did not allow much time for his suffering wife. Thus the intimacy of mother and daughter was so complete that Bathsheba came at last so to fill with tenderness the space left empty in the neglected heart that her mother only spoke her habitual feeling when she said: "I should think you were in love with me, my darling, if you were not my daughter." *

This was a dangerous state of things for the minister. Unsafe speculations began to mingle with his dreams and reveries, for the thought that another's life is becoming superfluous feeds like a ravenous vulture on the soul. Woe to the man or woman whose days are passed in watching the hourglass through which the sands run too slowly for longings that are like a skulking procession of bloodless murders. It would not

---

my comments and remarks and made an unconscious choice to recover. I, the physician, merely served as a timely vehicle on which her new determination could safely travel.

In this instance, the favorable timing depended primarily upon external circumstances. However, in the frequent visits of psychoanalytic treatment much of the value of the analyst's remarks depends upon the moment at which he reveals or affirms interpretations which the patient may have already sensed but not formulated.

* Here Holmes indicates one phase of parental-filial attachments which often have a dominant effect in weakening the capacity for a normal love life in a son or daughter of the same sex. If the attachment is especially strong, the child may feel a sense of guilt because he believes that his excessive feeling may have had some part in depriving one parent of the love of the other. When the emotional interplay is reciprocal as in the above situation, it may become a strong force in the development and maintenance of unconscious homosexuality in later adult life. In such cases the homosexual traits would be likely to develop as a result of identification with the parent (or surrogate) of the opposite sex, and not because of an inherited tendency as implied in the case of Myrtle Hazard.

be libelous to say that Mr. Stoker was ready to yield to temptation; he would even court it, but he did not shape out any plan as a more desperate sinner would have done. There is a borderland where one can stand on the territory of legitimate instincts and affections and yet be so near the garden of the Adversary, that his dangerous fruits and flowers are within easy reach. And Stoker was fond of this borderland.

In tracing the history of a human soul through its commonplace nervous perturbations, still more through its spiritual humiliations, there is danger that we shall feel a certain contempt for the subject of such weaknesses. It is easy to laugh at the erring impulse of a young girl; but you who remember when ——, only fifteen years old, untouched by passion, unsullied in name, was found in the shallow brook where she had sternly and surely sought her death * (a generation had passed since then), you will not smile so scornfully.

*   *   *

* Suicidal attempts and suicide in adolescence and even in childhood are not unknown (there are about .5 actual suicides per 100,000 deaths between the ages of ten and fourteen). Various immediate reasons are assigned for the act—fears of many types, bad records at school, failure of promotion, and so on. Especially in those cases where failure in study is reported or no cause can be ascribed, the act often stands in close relation to the child's feeling of hopelessness concerning sexual matters and problems of puberty.

The case of a Harvard freshman, aged seventeen, who first attempted suicide shortly after his admission by drinking iodine will illustrate such a displacement of cause. He had entered college as a Pulitzer scholar but immediately began to fail in his work. To this fact he and his family attributed this first and subsequent attempts at self-destruction, one of which finally succeeded several years later. Investigation showed that the primary worry concerned not his scholastic failure but masturbation and its attendant sense of guilt.

Myrtle Hazard's mind had good balance of its faculties. She was of a good natural constitution, but, though happening to have been born in another land, she was of American descent.

Now, it has long been noticed that there is something in the influence, climatic or other, prevailing in New England, which predisposes to morbid religious excitement. The graver reader will not object to seeing the exact statement of a competent witness belonging to a bygone century, confirmed as it is by all that we see about us.

"There is no Experienced Minister of the Gospel who hath not in the Cases of Tempted Souls often had this Experience, that the ill Cases of their distempered Bodies are the frequent Occasion and Original of their Temptations. . . . The Vitiated Humours in many Persons, yield the Steams whereinto Satan does insinuate himself, till he has gained a sort of Possession in them, or at least an Opportunity to shoot into the Mind as many Fiery Darts as may cause a sad Life unto them; yea, 't is well if Self-Murder * be not the sad end into

---

The masturbation had become excessive when he went away from home to Harvard and was accompanied by fantasies involving a younger sister to whom he was much attracted. It was the emotionally tinged sexual conflict that interfered with his studies, not the failure in studies which induced his despondency and suicidal impulses.

* The term Self-Murder, as used here, has a connotation which coincides with a psychoanalytic interpretation of depression and suicide. Often, in suicide an unconscious hostility in the form of a murder impulse has existed for many years toward a person, especially a parent or sibling, whom one is supposed to love. This impulse is suppressed, eventually also repressed, and instead of the violence finally being expressed openly in attacking the hated relative, it is turned against the person harboring it, as an attack against the self.

which these hurried People are thus precipitated. New England, a country where splenetic Maladies are prevailing and pernicious, perhaps above any other, hath afforded Numberless Instances, of even pious People, who have contracted these Melancholy Indispositions which have unhinged them from all Service or Comfort; yea, not a few Persons have been hurried thereby to lay Violent Hands upon themselves at the last. These are among the unsearchable Judgments of God."

Such are the words of the Rev. Cotton Mather.*

*   *   *

Rev. Stoker had hardly recovered from a vexatious defeat where the Widow Hopkins had won her point that Susan Posey should visit his study only in her company, when he received a note from Miss Silence, which contained a request that he would see Myrtle. She seemed to be in a very excitable condition and might perhaps be easily brought under those influences which she had resisted from her early years. Mr. Stoker drew a long breath and presently a flush tingled up to his cheek, where it remained a fixed burning glow.

To know whether a minister is in safe or dangerous paths, there are two psychometers: the first is the black broadcloth

---

* The frequency of suicide in the New England colonies mentioned by Cotton Mather is a little-known fact. His explanation of this frequency leaves much to be desired. The Reverend Mather is remembered principally because of his relentless and merciless persecution of heretics and witches in Salem about 1692; for his sermons attacking as Devil's agents anyone who ventured to propose that kindliness and beauty had their place in the scheme of life. To such austere suppression which denied all human emotions and fostered hatred—rather than to the climate of Boston Bay—can these suicides be more plausibly attributed.

forming the knees of his pantaloons; the second, the patch of
carpet before his mirror. If the first is unworn and the second
is frayed and threadbare, pray for him. If the first is worn and
shiny, while the second keeps its pattern and texture, get him
to pray for you. Mr. Stoker should have gone down on his
knees then and there, but he stood up before his looking-
glass and parted his hair as carefully as if he had been sepa-
rating the saints of his congregation from the sinners. For
Myrtle Hazard was, he thought, the handsomest girl he had
ever seen. He felt sure that he could establish intimate spiritual relations with her by drawing out her repressed sympathies, by exercising all those lesser arts of fascination so
familiar to Don Giovannis and not always unknown to San
Giovannis.

The Rev. Stoker loved to feel his heart beat; he loved all
the forms of non-alcoholic drunkenness,* which are so much
better than the vinous because they taste themselves so

---

* Indulgence in alcohol, especially when excessive, is a flight from
difficulties, conscious or repressed. The person becomes intoxi-
cated not only from the effects of the alcohol but also partially
from his own released urges of boisterousness, sensuality, temper,
and the like, as in the so-called "dry jag." There are many forms of
nonalcoholic, non-drug indulgences which become a species of intoxication or narcosis, such as chess habituation or book wormish-
ness. A. A. Brill has reported cases of the gorging of food which
replaced alcoholic intoxications. To one excess of this kind which
consisted of huge meals of red meats the habitue applied the term
"roast beef jag." [8] A few of my patients, especially young women,
would indulge in eating orgies of such foods as chocolates and pea-
nuts, when confronted with severe difficulties which they felt unable to solve. Said one of them, "When I am desperate about my
husband, I just gulp food and am relieved of my troubles for a
while."

keenly, whereas the other (according to the statement of experts who are familiar with this curious phenomenon) has a certain sense of unreality connected with it. He delighted in the reflex stimulus of the excitement he produced in others by working on their feelings and was noted for the vividness of his three sermons on the future, known as the sweating sermon, the fainting sermon, and the convulsion-fit sermon.

Myrtle's excitability, which had been showing itself in strange paroxysms, was concerned in the emotional movements of the religious nature. In the old communion, some priest might have wrought upon her while in this condition and we might have had at this very moment among us another Saint Theresa. She found a dangerous substitute in the spiritual companionship of a saint like Stoker.

People think the confessional is unknown in our Protestant churches. It is a great mistake. The principal change is that there is no screen between the penitent and the father confessor. The minister knew his rights and very soon asserted them. He gave Aunt Silence to understand that he could talk more at ease if he and his disciple were left alone together and he assured her that Myrtle was in a state of mind which promised a complete transformation of her character.

As to his rougher formulae, he knew better than to apply them to a creature of Myrtle's fine texture. How could he talk to her as if she must be under the wrath of God for the mere fact of her existence? As he knew that the merest child, so soon as it begins to think at all, works out for itself something like a theory of human nature, he said he would be pleased to know about her natural condition as one born of a sinful race and her inherited liabilities on that account?

Myrtle smiled like a little heathen. That kind of talk used to worry her when she was a child, sometimes. Yes, she remembered its coming back to her in a dream she had, when

—when— Did he think she hated every kind of goodness and loved every kind of evil?

The minister looked straight into her eyes, and answered, "Nothing could help loving you, Myrtle."

Did he suppose, she asked, that any persons could be Christians, who could not tell the year of their change from children of darkness to children of light?

The shrewd clergyman had provided himself with authorities of all kinds to meet these awkward questions in casuistical divinity. He had hunted up recipes for spiritual neuralgia, indigestions, and hypochondriasis, just as doctors do for their bodily counterparts.

"To be sure they could." Why, didn't President Wheelock say to a young man who consulted him, that some persons might be true Christians without suspecting it? All this was so very different from the uncompromising way in which he used to present religious doctrines from the pulpit. The minister found it impossible to think of her in connection with those denunciations of sinners for which his discourses had been noted. The truth was, he was preaching for Myrtle Hazard. He was getting bewitched by the intoxication of his relations with her. All this time she was utterly unconscious of any charm that she was exercising on the minister, but the time also came when the words he uttered were treasured as from something more than a common mortal.

In the woods on one of the loveliest days of the Indian summer, Cynthia Badlam discovered the minister preparing to make love to Myrtle. She talked it over with Mrs. Hopkins, who suggested she ask Mr. Gridley to intervene. The latter, with a few telling remarks, persuaded Myrtle not to see Mr. Stoker alone again, even though this decision came close to upsetting her emotionally.

It is not the words that others say to us but in those other words which these make us say to ourselves that we find our gravest lessons and our sharpest rebukes. The hint another gives us finds whole trains of thought which have been getting themselves ready to be shaped in inwardly articulated words and only awaited the touch of a burning syllable, as the mottoes of a pyrotechnist only wait for a spark to become letters of fire. In some such way the grave warnings of Byles Gridley had called up a fully shaped but hitherto unworded train of thought in the consciousness of Myrtle. She saw its truth, but how hard it is to tear away a cherished illusion, to cast out an unworthy intimate.*

---

* This type of fixed dependency upon some infallible support, be it something actual which has served the patient well in the past or an illusory, fictitious trust, is characteristic of compulsive persons. The patient has become so accustomed to relying on some particular thought or mode of action for reassurance in a given type of situation that he cannot conceive that some other simpler, easier, and more advantageous method of approach might be available to him. During the long process of psychoanalysis, especially as a result of transference phenomena, the unconscious sources upon which the patient has drawn in order to continue in methods and positions on which he has relied and which he has retained at great suffering and with little benefit to himself are carefully traced and examined.

Psychoanalytic treatment has never for its aim the denial of the authority of the parent or the state. It does often find a necessity for freeing a child or adult from a dependence on authority from which he may be attempting to liberate himself because such authority is not compatible with his chronological development. When made independent, he should be in position to coöperate with leadership or even assume it himself in a new group or in the family he establishes.

It often happens that what the analyst may remark concerning a situation cannot be accepted by the patient until his psychological attitude has been gradually changed by this procedure. The final awakening and conviction of the patient frequently comes not from

After her talk with Mr. Gridley, the night was far gone when Myrtle awoke. The starlight dimly illuminated her chamber and the darkness seemed alive with fearful presences. She lighted another lamp, which she held up to the picture of Judith Pride and then turned it upon the pale face of the martyr-portrait.

In those dead hours of the night two women, Judith and Ann Holyoake, had been with her, as real as any that breathed the breath of life, yet both had long been what is called, in our poor language, dead. One came full-dressed by nature in that splendid animal equipment which had captivated lusty lovers. The other, how aerial she seemed, yet real and true to the lineaments of her whom the girl looked upon as her hereditary protector.

The beautiful woman, with a face full of loathing, pointed to one of the reptiles beneath the feet of a chair. The flattened and half-crushed creature seemed to swell and spread. A shadow of disgust ran through Myrtle and she shrieked. She felt herself lifted from the floor and then a cold, thin hand seemed to take hers. The warm life went out of her and she was to herself as a dimly conscious shadow that glided with passive acquiescence wherever it was led. Presently a great serpent seemed to arch his neck and bring his head close down to Myrtle's face; and it hissed out words she had read that day in a note: "Come to my study tomorrow and we will read hymns together."

Again the two women were looking into her eyes with strange meaning in their own. Something in them seemed to plead with her to yield to their influences and her choice

the analyst but from the comment of some outsider who more nearly corresponds to the childhood conceptions of reliability and who happens to make his remark when the patient has become psychologically prepared to accept it.

wavered which to follow. It was the contest of two lives for the mastery of her soul. The might of beauty conquered. Myrtle resigned herself to the guidance of the lovely phantom, which seemed so much fuller of the unextinguished fire of life.

Then came a confused sense of eager search for something hidden which she was to find for her talisman. In the midst of this she awoke.

The impression was so strong that with all her fears she could not resist the desire to find what meaning there was in this frightfully real dream. She determined to follow the hint of her nightmare.

In one of the upper chambers stood a tall, upright desk of the ancient pattern. "That desk is yours, Myrtle," Uncle Malachi had once said to her; "and there is a trick about it that it will pay you to study."

She stole from her chamber and glided along the narrow entries as she had seemed to move in her dream. In her newborn passion of search, she held her light so as to illuminate all the deeper spaces and thought she saw marks of a finger. She pressed her own finger on this place and a small mahogany pilaster sprang forward, revealing a deep, narrow drawer. There was a golden bracelet which she recognized as the ornament of Judith. She clasped it upon her wrist and from that moment she felt as if she were the captive of the lovely phantom who had been in her dream.

It seems probable enough that Myrtle's whole spiritual adventure was an unconscious dramatization of a few simple facts which her imagination tangled together into a kind of vital coherence. The philosopher will remark that all the elements of her fantastic melodrama had been furnished her while waking, but he might not find it so easy to account for the change which came over Myrtle when she clasped the bracelet of Judith upon her wrist and felt a sudden loathing of the man whom she had idealized as a saint. The natural instincts of girlhood with returning health? Perhaps so. An impression produced by her dream? An effect of an influx from another sphere of being?

As we have to tell not what Myrtle ought to have done and why she should have done it, but what she did do, our task is a simpler one than it would be to lay bare all the springs of her action.* Until this period nothing could be soberer

---

* It is the function of modern psychiatry, particularly psychoanalysis, "to lay bare all the springs" of action, specifically the unconscious ones, as a means of interpreting the patient to himself. The patient gradually comes to realize that certain of his tendencies and characteristics which he had not accepted or even thought to exist in himself may long have been very evident to others.

This may occur among physicians as well as among others. Thus a physician who is extremely devoted to his patients may regard his conscientious attention as entirely altruistic. Yet it may be apparent to outsiders that his devotion satisfies a need for power over life and death. The observant secretary of such a physician once remarked of her employer, whom she respected highly, "Dr. X loves all the world, and not a soul in it." No one could have been more astonished than the good doctor himself when he reflected and admitted that "it might be so."

Holmes has well stated how changes in attitude are brought about by modern psychiatry when he said, "It is not the words that others say to us but in those other words which these make us say to ourselves, that we find our gravest lessons and our sharpest rebukes."

In the dream the conflict between the growing feeling of womanhood in Myrtle (symbolized in Judith Pride) gains ascendancy, but she rejects sexuality, symbolized in the snake and personalized in the minister. The golden bracelet may be regarded as a symbol of chastity and unity. At all events here again the function of the dream appears to be the unconscious working through of a problem and subsequently acting in response to it.

than the dresses which the severe household had established as her costume. But the girl was no sooner out of bed than a passion came over her to see herself in that less jealous arrangement of drapery which the Beauty had insisted on. She turned down the prim collar of her dress and glanced from her glass to the portrait. The same finely shaped arms and hands and something very like the same features startled her by their identity. The world was hers. Who was this middle-aged minister that had been talking to her about heaven when there was not a single joy of earth that she had tested? The revulsion was a very sudden one.

Thus Rev. Stoker was pacing the room with feverish impatience when at last Myrtle appeared by an envoy who delivered the following missive:

REVEREND SIR,—I shall not come to your study this day. I hope we shall sing hymns together in heaven some time, but I want to wait for that awhile. I want to see more of young people and I have a friend, Mr. Gridley, who I think is older than you are, that takes an interest in me.

Respectfully yours, M.H.

The Rev. Stoker uttered a cry of rage. It would hardly do to stab Myrtle Hazard, shoot Byles Gridley, and strangle Mrs. Hopkins. His savage mediaeval theology came to his relief and he clutched out his well-worn "convulsion-fit" sermon which he preached the next day as if it did his heart good.*

Gradually Myrtle recovered from her emotional illness, perhaps as a result of living through many repressed experiences and also of

---

* The mechanisms known as displacement and overcompensation are frequently noted in psychoanalysis and interpreted to the patient. This is a fine illustration. Anger is converted into vehemence, personal resentment into railing against the devil, and the whole feeling of rage overcompensated into a virtuous tirade intended to save man from mortal sin.

finding a tangible support in Mr. Gridley. Two young men of the village, beside William Bradshaw, began showing her attention, one Gifted Hopkins who wrote poems, son of Mr. Gridley's landlady, and the other Cyprian Eveleth, brother of her friend Olive. This introduces an element of mild love suspense into the story.

Cyprian was sensitive, contemplative, a lover of lonely walks, one who listened for the whispers of Nature and was alive to the symbolisms she writes over everything. Thus Nature took him into her confidence. She loves the men of science well and tells them all her family secrets—who is the father of this or that member of the group, who is cousin and so on. But there are others to whom she tells her dreams; not what species or genus her lily belongs to but what vague thought it has when it dresses in white or what memory of its birthplace is that which we call its fragrance.

A short time after this Clement Lindsay went to Oxbow to see Susan. He felt obligated to carry out his promise to marry her, although he had become an artist and felt he had completely outgrown simple Susan.

Clement was by nature an artist and had given himself up to his art with a kind of heroic devotion, because he thought his country wanted a race of builders to clothe the new forms of religious, social and national life afresh from the forest and the quarry. The young American of any freshness of intellect is stimulated to dangerous excess by the conditions of life into which he is born. There is a double proportion of oxygen in the New World air. The chemists have not found it out yet but human brains and breathing organs have long since made the discovery.

Clement felt that there was a certain grandeur in the recompense of working out his defeated instincts through the medium of his noble art. Had not Pharaohs chosen it to proclaim their longings for immortality and priests to symbolize their conceptions of the heavenly mansions? In the region of his art alone he hoped always to find freedom and a companionship which his home life could never give him.*

On arriving in Oxbow, Clement walked in the direction of Mrs. Hopkins' house thinking of the pleasant surprise his visit would bring. As he drew near he saw rosy Susan with a youth walking at her side. There was an undefined feeling on Clement's side that if he had happened to have drowned when he went down with the young girl, that Susan would in time have listened to consolation. Easy-crying widows take new husbands soonest; there is nothing like wet weather for transplanting, as Master Gridley used to say.

As a poet, his thoughts were gloomy, running a good deal on the more picturesque methods of bidding a voluntary farewell to a world with visions of beauty. His mother hid her late husband's razors—an unnecessary precaution, for self-

---

* This conception of the transformation of defeated (inhibited) instincts into activities agreeable and acceptable to the ego is one which Freud subsequently described under the term sublimation. In such transformations, according to psychoanalysis, there is an unconscious exchange of aim-inhibited, infantile sexual impulses for activities and interests on a higher cultural plane.

This process of sublimation has far reaching effects on the activities of the individual and society. It determines art, etiquette, science, careers. The choice of an individual's life work is more often the result of sublimation than he ever suspects; it depends upon the exchange of sexual drives into socially useful work. Thus the surgeon who skillfully saves a patient's life may be deriving from the cutting and sight of blood incidental to his humane work a certain degree of sadism, although he is quite unaware of this as one of the impulses which leads to interest in his art and even skill in its execution.

elimination by those who have the natural outlet of verse to relieve them is rarely followed by a casualty. Those who meditate an imposing finish naturally save themselves for it and this is apt to be indefinitely postponed so long as there is a poem to write or a proof to be corrected.

As a visitor to Oxbow Village, Clement was invited to a small party at the Eveleths. There for the first time since the rescue he met Myrtle, who was gradually yielding to the designing Bradshaw.

It was a strange meeting. The young artist had begun a bust of Innocence, but after his memorable adventure the image of the girl he had rescued so haunted him that the pale ideal which was to have worked itself out in the bust faded away in its perpetual presence. Now the original was before him.

Myrtle's bosom was heaving and presently she became giddy and was on the point of going into an hysteric spasm but came to herself after a time without anything like a regular paroxysm.*

---

* At this meeting Myrtle had no memory of having seen Clement before, although she experienced an intense emotional reaction— violent feelings which did not register as thought or recognition. The memory of her rescue and all its immediate sequences had been lost. Such losses of memory (amnesia) for events during and immediately preceding a shock which initiates an hysterical attack are common. I have observed a case where a competent girl, a stenographer, aged eighteen, was thrown back to the age level of five following a scolding by her mother which the patient felt showed great ingratitude. The mother had been holding her in virtual slavery to support the family, which consisted of the widowed mother, an older sister, and the patient. Following the rebuke, the patient reverted to baby talk and to the lisping of a little girl. All memory of the rebuke and of knowledge acquired after the age of five vanished from her mind. She recovered her memory under

"I—I—have seen that young lady before," Clement said.

"Where did you meet her?" Bradshaw asked, with eager interest.

"I met her in the Valley of the Shadow of Death," Clement answered, very solemnly.

The next day he returned to the city in a state of mental agitation. He had seen for the second time a girl who, for the peace of his own mind, he should never again have looked upon.

If the person in mental conflict is a young man, he can take to the philosophic meerschaum and nicotinize himself until he begins to "color" like the bowl of his own pipe. Or he can have recourse to stimulants, which will dress his future up in possibilities that glitter like Masonic regalia until the waking headache reveals his illusion. Some kind of spiritual anaesthetic he must have if he holds his grief fast tied to his heartstrings. But as grief must be fed with thought or starve to death, it is the best plan to keep the mind busy in other ways.

Clement determined to stun his sensibilities by work, but passion still wrought within him. If he drove it from his waking thoughts, it haunted his sleep until he could endure it no longer. So he uncovered the bust which he had but half shaped, and struck the first flake from the glittering marble. The toil, once begun, fascinated him and in a few days he had finished the bust. His hours were again vacant to his thick-coming fancies and he could not disguise from himself their source, which was Myrtle. Like the story of the ancient sculptor, the image in which he had fixed his recollection of

---

treatment by mild hypnosis, suggestion, and reëducation, and the memory for the void between the ages of five and eighteen returned completely.

its original served only to keep her living presence before him.

It was a singular impression which the sight of him had produced upon her. How could she but have listened to him who was, as it were, a second creator to her.* He had recalled the dread moments they had passed in each other's arms, with death not love in all their thoughts.

Clement was sitting one afternoon before the fatal bust which had whispered away his peace, when the postman brought him a letter from Susan. Something had grieved her and she gave free expression to her feelings.

Clement dropped the letter from his hand and sat looking at the exquisitely wrought features of her who had come between him and his plighted word. Then he took a heavy hammer and shattered his lovely idol into shapeless fragments. The strife was over.

Old Byles Gridley watched the development of Myrtle into young womanhood with warm affection and noted with alarm her interest in Bradshaw and the latter's obvious intention to marry her. Gridley therefore decided that he would pay for her attendance at a fashionable "finishing school" in Boston. While there she was selected to play the part of Pocahontas in tableaux representing the "Rescue of John Smith." **

---

* Clement has now become an unconscious father substitute. Implicit in the whole situation is the unconscious fulfillment of the almost universal incest fantasy on which Freud and Jung built up the concept of the "Oedipus Complex."

** In tableaux and masquerades, as on the stage, the individual identifies himself with the character he plays. In the roles where a performer is more than merely "being himself" on the stage, the effectiveness of his acting is due largely to the extent and intensity with which unconscious affects are allowed to come to the surface. When talk of psychoanalysis became something of a rage in America about 1920, "suppressed desire" parties became a passing fad.

Myrtle had sufficient reason to believe that there was Indian blood in her veins. It was one of those family legends which some members are a little proud of and others are willing to leave uninvestigated. It had almost frightened her sometimes to find how like a wild creature she felt when alone in the woods. She often thought she could follow the trail as unerringly as a Mohegan.*

As they dressed her for the part of Pocahontas she felt herself carried into the dim ages of the American wilderness. If this belief had lasted, it is plain enough where it would have carried her. But it came into her imagination and vivifying consciousness with the unwonted costume and might well leave her when she put it off. It is not for us to solve these mysteries of the seeming admission of unhoused souls into the fleshly tenements belonging to air-breathing personalities. A

Everyone was supposed to come in the costume of his "suppressed" desire. The number of pirates, Merry Widows and clowns who appeared was amusing—it was also a revelation of the number of persons who unconsciously long for these roles with their implication of violence, sexual liberty, and unrestraint. Psychiatry has not neglected the therapeutic value of dramatics, both as a medium of releasing repressed affects and of studying the personality of patients. Called psycho-dramatics, it has been used extensively by psychiatrists dealing with children, groups of adults, and individual patients, who may be uncommunicative when directly approached.

* Old Sophy, the Negress not far removed from her cannibalistic ancestors, is used by Holmes in *Elsie Venner* as a symbol for primitive impulses. Now again he represents the untrammeled wild urges of our unconscious by the Indian in Myrtle Hazard. Each might be considered symbolic of that category of the mind called by Freud the id, where violent, primitive, and unacceptable urges remain and only appear at moments of excitement and stress when the barriers of the ego and superego are lowered.

very little more and from that evening forward the question would have been treated in full in works on medical jurisprudence.

Tableau I: Captain John Smith (Miss deLacy) bound, ready for execution; Powhatan (Miss Smythe) sitting upon a log; savages with clubs (Misses Van Boodle, Booster, etc.), standing around; Pocahontas (Miss Hazard) holding the knife in her hand, ready to cut the cords.

Tableau II: Captain Smith kneeling before Pocahontas, whose hand is extended in the act of presenting him to her father. Savages in various attitudes of surprise.

The programme went off with wonderful éclat and there were loud cries for Pocahontas. Bouquets were flung to her and a wreath, which one of the young ladies had expected for herself, was tossed upon the stage just as the curtain fell upon the second scene.

"Put the wreath on Myrtle for the next tableau," some of the girls whispered.

The disappointed young lady could not endure this and in a jealous passion snatched it from Myrtle's head and trampled it under her feet at the very instant the curtain was rising. With a cry which had the blood-chilling tone of an Indian's battle shriek, Myrtle caught the knife up and raised her arm against the girl. The girl sank to the ground covering her eyes in terror. Myrtle, with the blade glistening in her hand, stood over her rigid as if she had been changed to stone. Many thought all this a part of the show and were thrilled with the wonderful acting. Before those immediately around her had had time to recover from their fright Myrtle had flung the knife away and was kneeling with her head bowed. The audience went into a rapture of applause, but Myrtle was oblivious to all but the dread peril she had just passed and was thanking God that his angel—her own protecting spirit—had stayed a passion such as she believed was alien to her truest self but which had lifted her arm with deadliest purpose. Myrtle tore the eagle's feathers from her hair. The metempsychosis was far too real to let her wear the semblance of the savage from whom had come her lawless impulse.

While at school in Boston in the spring of 1861, Myrtle was invited to a great party at the luxurious home of Mrs. Clymer Ketchum. Many of her friends were there, including Mr. Gridley, Clement, and Bradshaw, who was an intimate friend of the hostess.

On the morning of the great party Mr. Bradshaw received a brief telegram regarding Malachi Withers' will, which caused him to make up his mind that very evening to propose to Myrtle. He had been watching the opportunity for carrying out his intentions and Master Gridley, looking unconcerned, had been watching him. Bradshaw was a lawyer, in love as in business, and considered himself as pleading a cause before a jury of Myrtle's conflicting motives. In accordance with this plan he proceeded on the evening of the party to propose to Myrtle.

"There is but one word more to add," he murmured softly, as he bent towards her—

A grave voice interrupted him. "Excuse me, Mr. Bradshaw," said Byles Gridley, "I wish to present a young gentleman to my friend here. Miss Hazard, I have the pleasure of introducing Mr. Clement Lindsay."

For the third time these two young persons stood face to face. Myrtle was no longer liable to those nervous seizures which any sudden impression was apt to produce when she was in her half-hysteric state. She was conscious at once of the existence of some peculiar relation between them and it broke the charm which had been weaving between her and Bradshaw.

Gridley had something of the detective's sagacity and a certain cunning. He would be apt to take pleasure in matching his wits against another crafty person's, as Mr. Macchiavelli Bradshaw. Now Mr. Gridley realized that the time had come to act promptly. By patience, ingenuity and finally firmness, he obtained a confession from Cynthia that she was conspiring with Bradshaw even though she did not "choose to be catechized about Mr. Bradshaw's business." * *They had plotted to conceal a will which might eventually provide a fortune for Myrtle. This constituted one of the main motives for Bradshaw's desire to marry her. Finally Cynthia broke down completely, crying out:*

"Have pity on me, Mr. Gridley—I am a lost woman. I am in the power of a dreadful man—William Bradshaw. But don't prosecute him, Mr. Gridley," she pleaded. "He isn't every way bad. The wicked in him lies very deep and won't ever come out, perhaps, if the world goes right with him."

Master Gridley's thoughts wandered a moment from the business before him; he had just got a new study of human nature, which in spite of himself would be shaping itself into an axiom for an imagined new edition of "Thoughts on the Universe," "The greatest saint may be a sinner that never got down to 'hard pan.'"

*　　　*　　　*

The spring of 1861 arrived, that eventful spring which was to show the first scene in the mighty drama which fixed the eyes of mankind during four bloody years. The little schemes

---

* When President Calvin Coolidge of Massachusetts in 1928 announced that he "did not choose" to run for a third term, the use of the New England colloquialism "choose" in the above sense had become obsolete. A long discussion arose concerning his intentions in regard to reëlection. This reflects how quickly change overtakes our fluid language which is, in a certain sense, the symbol of thought.

of little people were going on without thought of the fearful convulsion which was soon coming to shatter the hopes and cloud the prospects of millions. Oxbow Village was the scene of its own commotions, as intense to those concerned as if the destiny of the nation had been involved in them.

Clement appeared there suddenly and Gifted Hopkins, walking home, all at once saw him coming straight towards him. Gifted put his hand out, smiling with all his native amiability, and Clement greeted the young poet in the most cordial manner. Gifted then told Clement that he was ready to offer Susan the devotion of a poet's heart.

Clement had come to Oxbow with a single purpose—to trust himself in the presence of Myrtle. Should he tell her that she owed her life to him? No, he could not try to win her affections by showing that he had paid for them beforehand. She seemed to be utterly unconscious that it was he who had been with her in the abyss of waters.

Clement found the three ladies sitting in the chill parlor at The Poplars, with Myrtle reading aloud the last news from Charleston Harbor. The impression this young man produced upon her was not through the common channels of the intelligence but was something which seemed to reach her through an inexplicable mechanism. He passed an evening of perplexed delight and inward conflict. He had found his marble once more turned to flesh and blood.

In the meantime, the first gun of the four years' cannonade hurled its ball against Fort Sumter. There was no hamlet in the land which its reverberations did not reach and no loyal heart in the North that did not answer the call which went forth two days later. The contagion of war-like patriotism reached the most peacefully inclined young persons.

"My country calls me," Gifted said to Susan Posey, "and if I can pass the medical examination, though I fear my constitution may be thought too weak, I think of marching in the ranks of the Oxbow Invincibles." *

Susan forgot all the rules of reserves to which she had been trained. "Never, never," she said, mingling her tears with his, which were flowing freely. "Your country does not need your

---

* The gifted "Hopkinses" furnished the same problem for the medical staff of the induction centers for soldiers in the second World War. A very distinct difference, however, existed. In the beginning of the Civil War and the beginning of the first World War, the "slacker" could decide for himself whether or not he would fight. The universal draft removed this choice. As a result of the experience in the first World War, not only was the initial medical examination more rigid in the second, but the psychiatric examination in many parts of this country became thorough and adequate. Persons with severe psychoneurotic tendencies and those who had shown previous signs of inadequate adaptation to the ordinary demands of society or who were emotionally immature were excluded.

Cases of simulation of mental or physical disease in order to evade service were infrequent in the late war. Most of those who failed to appear for physical examination were, by and large, poor military material. The disheartening feature, especially to psychiatrists at induction boards, was that they had to reject the feeble-minded, the alcoholics, the habitual criminals, the homosexuals, who remained behind to preserve society. The healthy in mind and body were sent forth to face death so that the weak ones might live.

One day at the induction board when I had been compelled to reject a particularly large number of such inadequate men, I became heartsick at the whole situation. I let my impatience out—as, of course, I should not have done—on an effete, unctuous morphine addict, with the remark that it was too bad that men like him were excused, while others had to go. He replied, "Don't blame us, doctor. It's not our fault that there's a war. Wars must be blamed on society which agrees to them." I turned my head aside, for I had no rejoinder.

sword. Your poems will inspire . . . our soldiers. . . . The Invincibles will march to victory, singing your songs."

"My own Susan," he said, "I yield to your wishes. Yes, my voice shall encourage my brave countrymen. I will give my dearest breath to stimulate their ardor."

It was not in this way that the gentle emotion awakening in the breast of Myrtle Hazard betrayed itself. As the thought dawned in her consciousness that she was loved, a change came over her such as the spirit that protected her might have wept for joy to behold. She forgot herself and her ambitions.

Myrtle and Clement were sitting together and Clement alluded to Susan, speaking kindly of her. "You know how simplehearted she is; her image will always be a pleasant one —second to but one other." In another moment Clement was pressing his lips to hers, after the manner of accepted lovers.

"Our lips have met today for the second time," he said presently. She looked at him in wonder.

"I have a singular story to tell you. On the morning of the 16th of June, now nearly two years ago . . ."

When it came to the "boy" in the old boat, Myrtle's cheeks flamed and she covered her face with both hands. But Clement told his story calmly through to the end.

*   *   *

One morning shortly after this Master Gridley received a letter which made him forget almost everything. It was from the publisher to this effect: That Our Firm propose to print the work originally published under the title of "Thoughts on the Universe"; said work to be remodelled according to the plan suggested by the Author, etc., etc.

At last book-hunters, some keener-eyed than the rest, had seen a virtue in this unsuccessful book, for which there was a new audience educated since it had tried to breathe before its time. His heart swelled with joy.*

He took down his own particular copy and began reading. The reader may like a few specimens from this edition, now a rarity. He shall have them, with Master Gridley's verbal comments.

"The best thought, like the most perfect digestion, is done unconsciously—Develop that." Ideas at compound interest in the mind—while you're sleeping they'll be growing. Seed of a thought today, flower tomorrow—next week—ten years from now, etc.

"Idols and dogmas in place of character; pills and theories in place of wholesome living. See the histories of theology and medicine passim."—Hits 'em.

"Flying is a lost art among men and reptiles. Bats fly and men ought to. Try a light turbine. Rise a mile straight, fall half a mile slanting, rise half a mile straight, fall half a mile slanting, and so on. Or slant up and slant down." Pooh, you ain't such a fool as to think that is new, are you?

"Poets to be sure. Sausage-makers. Empty skins of old phrases, stuff 'em with odds and ends of old thoughts that

---

* Possibly here Holmes may be thinking of his own essay, "The Mechanism in Thought and Morals" and his interpretation of mental disease which he felt "had not been properly appreciated at this time." Dr. Reginald Fitz of Harvard in an address before the New York Academy of Medicine in February, 1943, on the occasion of Holmes's centenary of the discovery of the contagiousness of childbirth fever remarked that Holmes was a man one hundred years ahead of his time. Perhaps it is a little prophetic that now after seventy years the annotator has seen the merit in Holmes's unsuccessful books, for which "a new audience has been educated" through the contributions of many social and physical sciences that have made for a new social and psychological approach.

never were good for anything. Bah; what a fine old style of genius common-sense is.*

"Where there is one man who squints with his eyes, there are a dozen who squint with their brains. It is an infirmity in one of the eyes, making the two unequal in power, that makes men squint. Just so it is an inequality in the two halves of the brain that makes some men idiots and others rascals. I know a fellow whose right half is a genius but his other hemisphere belongs to a fool and I had a friend perfectly honest on one side but who was sent to jail because the other had an inveterate tendency in the direction of picking pockets."

Then he fell into a revery. He saw men of a new race, alien to all that had ever lived, excavating with strange vast engines the old ocean bed now become habitable land. And as the great scoops turned out the earth they had fetched up, from the unexplored depth, relics of a former simple civilization that revealed the fact that here a tribe of human beings had lived and perished.

A knock interrupted his revery.

Mr. Penhallow presented himself in a high state of excitement.

"You have heard the news, Mr. Gridley? First, my partner

---

* Too often the fine merit of unusual common sense and of normality in an individual does not receive recognition and due appreciation merely because that person is so nicely balanced and so dependable that no one questions that he may fail or fall. He has none of the spectacular fluctuations which make people stop, gaze, and gasp, wondering when, if, and how the erratic performer will regain his balance. Thus the person with the "genius of common sense" is apt to miss the plaudits of more colorful personalities and is apt not to be noticed or fully appreciated until he is no longer there and we find his place difficult to fill.

has left unexpectedly to enlist in a regiment. Second, the land case is decided in favor of the heirs of Malachi Withers and as you know the land was willed to Myrtle alone."

*   *   *

What change was this which Myrtle had undergone since love had touched her heart? One would have said her features had lost something of that look of imperious beauty. If it could be that, after so many generations, the blood of her who had died for her faith could show in a descendant's veins and the soul of that elect lady look out from her far-removed offspring's dark eyes, such a transfusion of the martyr's life and spiritual being might well seem to manifest itself in Myrtle.

Her lover had left her almost as soon as he had told her the story of his passion, quitting all—his newborn happiness, his art, his prospects of success—to obey the higher command of duty. War was to him, as to so many who went forth, only organized barbarism, hateful but for the sacred cause which alone redeemed it from the curse that blasted the first murderer.

How brief Myrtle's dream had been. She almost doubted whether she would not awake from it, as from her other visions, and find it all unreal. There was no need of fearing any undue excitement of her mind after the alternations of feeling she had experienced. Nothing seemed of moment to her which could come from without—her real world was within and the light of its day came from her love, made holy by self-forgetfulness on both sides.

The day of Myrtle's accession to fortune, the secret was told that she had promised herself in marriage to Clement. But her friends hardly knew how to congratulate her for her lover was gone, not improbably to come home a wreck, crippled by wounds or worn out with disease. Some wondered to see her so cheerful, for they could not know how the manly strength of Clement's determination had nerved her for womanly endurance. They had not learned that a great cause makes great souls or reveals them to themselves.

Clement—now Captain Lindsay—returned at the end of his first campaign. Later he came again with the eagle on his shoulder and then asked Myrtle if she would return with him as his wife.

The ceremony was performed in the presence of a few witnesses at The Poplars. One witness looked on with unmoved features yet Myrtle thought there was a more heavenly smile on her faded lips than she had ever seen before beaming from the canvas—it was Ann Holyoake, the guardian spirit of Myrtle's vision, who seemed to breathe a holier benediction than any words—even Reverend Pemberton's—could convey.

They went back together to the camp. In the offices of mercy which Myrtle performed for the wounded and dying, the dross of her nature seemed to be burned away. The conflict of mingled lives in her blood had ceased. No lawless impulses usurped the place of that serene resolve which had grown strong by every exercise of its high prerogative. If she had been called now to die for any worthy cause, her race would have been ennobled by a second martyr, true to the blood of her who was burned by "Ye bloudy Paptist" Ano 15 . ."

Comments

The principal incidents in this story are concerned with the elements of emotional suppression and social prohibitions more or less sanctified by the authority of religion. Their effect in distorting the character and thwarting the development of the natural impulses of a young girl are related with dramatic force, especially in the earlier chapters. This may be safely said notwithstanding Holmes's intention to demonstrate the unconscious influence in the formation of personality through the direct though remote inheritance of multiple traits. The characteristics of these ancestors have been deliberately portrayed as heterogeneous, dissimilar, conflicting and contradictory.

Holmes has been much more successful in supplying the factors and determinant impressions responsible for the mental disturbances of Myrtle Hazard, than he had been in tracing the method by which the synthesis and reconstruction of her personality took place. In this he shared a difficulty frequently encountered by the psychotherapist who sees his patient three to five hours a week and is well acquainted with the significant episodes which have changed the direction or blocked the development of the patient's personality.

Synthesis of previously discordant elements occurs spontaneously with and sometimes without analysis. In analysis prohibitions, repressions and inhibitions are interpreted and revalued. Through this the troubled person finds himself. However, especially in young people, the need of support, the assurance of being wanted if not actually needed, must be supplied by the environment. Thus Holmes is psychiatrically sound when he provides a more receptive world for Myrtle after her rescue from drowning and regaining consciousness, in such forces as the dependable Byles Gridley and a sincere lover, Clement Lindsay.

Aids such as these would be valuable to the physician in readjusting any case of neurosis. But it must be admitted that in the process of liberating a patient from the psychological fetters of his personal and hereditary past the physician sometimes is at a loss to know just why and when his efforts have become effective. Often it has appeared to me that this receptivity is a matter of the appropriate timing of his comments or suggestions of which neither the patient nor the physician may be fully conscious at the moment.

No neurosis of this kind is very satisfactorily solved until the patient is psychologically prepared for heterosexuality and is sufficiently free of his attachments, parental and sibling, so that he is enabled to fall in love. In the case of Myrtle Hazard, her bitterness against the world as represented by the austere environment offered her by her aunts turned, during the course of transference, into something akin to love for the physician who treated her. Once awakened, this emotional attachment could readily be transferred to the minister and then to a mate more suitable to her young womanhood, in the person of Clement.

Through the release of Myrtle's potentialities to love, a regeneration of her character occurred, and she and Clement were "married and lived happily ever after." It is obvious that marriage does not of itself always relieve difficulties like Myrtle Hazard's; much of the psychiatrist's work is with persons in whom the emotional upsets first come to the surface under the stress of adaptation to the intimate demands of the marriage relationship.

A MORTAL ANTIPATHY

A YOUNG MAN'S MORBID FEAR OF WOMEN
[GYNOPHOBIA]

A *Mortal Antipathy* is from a psychiatric standpoint the simplest and most direct of the novels. Perhaps it is oversimplified for it represents Maurice Kirkwood, the sufferer from a phobia, as perfectly normal except in respect to his fear of women. It is extremely rare to find such obsessive fears unaccompanied by a more or less generalized anxiety or other nervous disturbances.

Holmes was over seventy-five when he wrote the story in 1885. It presents theories far in advance of that time concerning the structure of neuroses and the understanding and management of such cases. One may consider it as a summary of observation and theories with which Holmes had occupied himself over the last three decades of his life. He was fully aware of the scepticism and incredulity which his story was likely to evoke, and for that reason thought "it would have to be wrapped in some tissue of circumstance or would lose half its effectiveness."

In the preface to the book he refers to the case of "a middle-aged man who could never pass a tall hall clock without an indefinable terror. While an infant in arms the heavy weight of one of these tall clocks had fallen with a loud crash and produced an impression which he had never got over." This incident is recorded in the story as a personal experience of Dr. Butts, the physician treating Kirkwood's neurosis. Because of the repetition we may infer that it is an experience of Holmes himself.

An atmospheric impression of falling, women, and injury had associated itself with the shock experienced by the subject of the neurosis. The idea seemed far too improbable and fantastic for Holmes's biographer, John T. Morse, Jr.,[1] who in 1896 writes, "From 'Elsie Venner' with her mysteriously envenomed nature to that absurd young man, Maurice Kirkwood, who could not bear the sight of a young girl because his pretty cousin had caused him to fall from a balcony in his boyhood, the downward step was indeed a long one."

However, one of my patients in commenting on the feeling of repression which pervaded her home throughout her childhood described it very neatly as being "atmospheric rather than incidental." What the patient meant was that neither her father nor her mother specifically prohibited this or that, but the aura of the cold, grim household was sufficiently forbidding not to allow one even to think of unconventional conduct. In the hushed and limpid atmosphere of a convent, one does not think of lighting a cigar even though one might feel a strong desire to disrupt the perfect formality of one of the irreproachable rooms.

Holmes states that such impressions could not be outgrown, but might possibly be broken up by some sudden change in the nervous system affected by a cause as potent as the one which had produced the disordered condition. This theory is being actively revived today in shock therapy in its various forms for the alteration of the mental states found in depressions, schizophrenia, and borderline cases.

The suspicion of Holmes that he would be misunderstood was valid. The leading neurologists at that time, who treated most of the fears, obsessions, and compulsions, had, nevertheless, little knowledge of their structure. Often the physician's approach and advice were most discouraging to the patient, for the medical man was apt to dismiss a sufferer with agoraphobia with an irritable assurance that he had nothing to fear on the street. To which the patient might reply with equal dissatisfaction and scorn, "But, Doctor, I know that."

Of particular interest is the emphasis in this story on the origin of the neurosis in a traumatic scene associated with a physical injury and having a certain analogy to what in psychoanalytic theory is called a primal scene. These primal scenes in psychoanalysis are always associated with the witnessing or participation in some occurrence of a sexual nature, early in childhood. The mystification or fright which the child experiences at the time subsequently becomes unconscious but can be reactivated by situations of similar psychoanalytic import.

The physical injury associated with fear of women in *A Mortal Antipathy* brings up complicated problems involved in the disease picture known as traumatic neurosis. The degree to which sexual components may accentuate a physical shock sustained in adult life and may cause a regression of the person's psychosexual organization to earlier fixations is still a matter of debate. Whether the accent is placed on the sexual or on the ego elements often seems to depend on the personal bias of the physician in regard to the importance of sex or self. According to Freud [2] it is of value to us to seek the origin of hysterical symptoms in a traumatically determined episode or scene "only if the scene in question fulfills two conditions—if it possess the required determining quality and if we can credit it with the necessary traumatic power."

The situation as described in this story meets both these requirements. However, it is not clear that the cause and effect ever became unconscious to the patient. Apparently he had been told that the fear and the accident stood in close relationship, but this knowledge did not enable him to overcome his phobia. In psychoanalysis we frequently have the same experience, namely, that the uncovering of the probable starting point of the neurosis, even of a primal scene, does not cause any change in the patient's attitude toward the obsession. Only a further painstaking investigation of all the sources which helped to keep the neurosis alive may eventually succeed in weakening it.

In *A Mortal Antipathy*, as in *Elsie Venner*, Holmes focuses the reader's attention upon a single infantile shock; in the former, he neglects, relatively, the important subsequent motivations of the neurotic hero's search for a mother, his fear of masculinity in women, and, inferentially, a fear of breaking his attachment to his father. These inferential motives, however, carry us rather deeply into psychoanalytic dynamics beyond the scope of this study.

The Story of A Mortal Antipathy

*Holmes chose for the locale of his narrative Arrowhead Village,
situated on a New England Lake, at one end of which is a men's
college and at the other a young woman's finishing school. It may
surprise present-day readers that the story begins with a handicap
race between eight-oared crews from these two institutions. This
gives Holmes an opportunity to introduce two contrasting types of
young womanhood: Miss Lurida Vincent, The Terror, the coxswain
of the crew, who was the leader of the "advocates of virile womanhood"—one of Holmes's pet aversions; and Euthymia Tower, well
beloved by her fellow-students, thoroughly feminine in body and
attitudes but withal not lacking in intelligence and good sense. The
race was won by the girls' crew through a ruse on the part of Miss
Vincent—an adaptation of the Atlantis myth (the judgment of
Paris reversed). The race also serves to introduce the main character of the novel, a mysterious stranger, Maurice Kirkwood, who
watched the race from a birchbark canoe at some distance. One of
his outstanding peculiarities was his apparent indifference to the
young women at the finishing school. No one knew his history, although he had been summering in the village with his Italian
servant, Paolo.*

Mr. Paolo had that wholesome, happy look so uncommon
in our arid countrymen, a look hardly to be found except
where figs and oranges ripen in the open air. It seemed as
if it would be a very simple matter to get the history of his
master out of this guileless being but the leading gossip of
the village tried her skill—all in vain.

It so happened that Paolo took a severe cold and asked the
baker, when he called, to send the village physician. In the
course of his visit Doctor Butts inquired about the health of
Paolo's master. "He always so," replied Paolo. "Una antipatia." That was all the doctor learned, but the more he re-

flected the more he was puzzled. What could the antipathy
be that made a young man a recluse.*

Dr. Butts carried this question home with him to his wife.
She buried the information in the grave of her memory, where
it lay for nearly a week. At the end of that time it emerged
in a confidential whisper to her favorite sister-in-law, a perfectly sane person. Twenty-four hours later the story was all
over the village that Maurice Kirkwood was the subject of a
mysterious, unheard-of antipathy to something.

There was nothing strange that Maurice Kirkwood should
have his special antipathy; a great many other people have
odd likes and dislikes. One story was that Maurice had a great
fear of dogs. A fright in childhood from a rabid mongrel was
said to have given him such a sensitiveness to dogs that he
was liable to convulsions. But one of the village people had a
large Newfoundland dog and when the animal walked up to
the stranger in a very sociable fashion, Maurice patted him
in a friendly way.

A much more common antipathy is with regard to cats, but
it could in no manner account for Maurice Kirkwood's isolation. He might shun the fireside of old women whose tabbies

---

* A differentiation exists between a morbid fear, such as is the
theme of this story, and a dislike which may be quite violent—an
antipathy as the term is usually used. In a morbid aversion the person is unaware of the unconscious motives upon which the dislike
is founded and he is unable to control it. In an ordinary antipathy
the person is aware of at least some reasons for his attitude and
can modify it by a conscious effort of the will should he so desire.
In the case of Kirkwood, the patient's conduct has all the characteristics of a morbid fear, although he is willing to assign the reasons for its existence solely to the accident and scene of which he
had been told. The unconscious elements which nourished the
fear are implied throughout the story and the picture is that of a
phobia rather than an antipathy.

were purring by their footstools, but these worthy dames do not make up the whole population.

These two antipathies having been disposed of, a new suggestion was started. This was that Maurice was endowed with the unenviable gift of the evil eye. It can blight and destroy whatever it falls upon. If Kirkwood carried that destructive influence, so that his clear blue eyes were more to be feared than the fascinations of the deadliest serpent, it could easily be understood why he kept his look away from all around him whom he feared he might harm. This story just suited the more flighty persons in the village, who had meddled more or less with Spiritualism and were ready for any new fancy, if it were only wild enough.

A student of Stoughton, whose sailboat had capsized in the lake, had been rescued by Maurice. He was one of the few people who had spoken with Kirkwood. His impression follows.

"I judge him to be perhaps a New Englander—a good-looking fellow, with nothing to excite special remark unless it be a certain look of anxiety or apprehension.

"If you ask what my opinion is, I think Kirkwood is not what they call a 'crank' exactly—has nothing more than the dread of human society or dislike for it, which under the name of religion used to drive men into caves and deserts."

* * *

Every private book-owner, who has grown into his library, finds he has a bunch of nerves going to every bookcase, a branch to every shelf, and a twig to every book. They come to feel at last that the books are outlying portions of their own mental organization.*

---

* This process by which objects belonging to the outer world become very closely a part of the personality of the individual has

Although Maurice had a good many volumes of his own, he frequently sent Paolo to the Public Library for books. Not much was to be made out of the books he drew beyond the fact of his wide scholarship.

Both the local clergyman and the physician took a very natural interest in the young man. The rector would have been glad to see him at church and the doctor kept wishing that he could gain the young man's confidence.

Dr. Butts was the leading medical practitioner of all the surrounding region. He was an excellent specimen of the

---

been renamed appersonation in psychoanalysis.[8] In appersonation the ego enlarges itself, but its character and behavior do not change because the person merely ascribes the qualities of objects about him to himself. Through such an emotionally tinged extension of his scope and self-esteem without encountering opposition or attack from the outside world. The attempt has been made to differentiate appersonation from identification, in that in the latter the individual's ego becomes altered and his character changed through the fact that he unconsciously adopts the qualities of another person with whom he wishes to have something in common.

In this mechanism of appersonation through which the individual extends the boundaries of his personality, he reveals many of his unconscious longings through the choice of the objects he makes. We sometimes find this shown in the library of a scholar, where among scientific tomes one may discover rows of detective novels. The latter may indicate a strong unconscious interest in murder apparently far removed from dry investigation into science. Perhaps one of the most striking examples of this unconscious extension of characteristics is in the type of dog chosen by the master. In more ways than one there is truth in the adage "love me, love my dog," because the dog is so often an appersonation of his master. The tenacious, pugnacious man frequently has a bulldog for his companion, the lady of leisure a silky Pekinese.

country doctor, self-reliant, self-sacrificing; he had that sagacity without which learning is a mere incumbrance. He well knew that oftentimes innocent sounding words mean grave disorders; that "run down" may stand for a fatigue of mind or body from which a week or a month of rest will completely restore the overworked patient, or may represent an advanced stage of a mortal illness; that "seedy" may signify the morning's state of feeling which calls for a glass of soda water and a cup of coffee, or a dangerous malady which will pack off the subject of it to the south of France. When, therefore, Dr. Butts heard the word "antipatia" he was prepared to believe in some anomalous sensibility.

In thinking the whole matter over, Dr. Butts felt convinced that, with patience and watching his opportunity, he should get at the secret. The first thing was to study systematically the whole subject of antipathies and the doctor began with those referable to taste, which are among the most common. In any collection of a hundred persons there will be found individuals who cannot venture on honey, cheese or veal with impunity. There is a whole family connection in New England, to many of whose members, in different generations, all the products of the dairy are the subjects of a congenital antipathy.*

---

* Today food idiosyncrasies are usually classified as allergies but their relationship to psychologic conditioning is still undetermined. Skin tests for specific substances often vary in value. In a case suffering from asthmatic attacks which I observed for a long period of time, the patient gave strongly positive skin reactions to cat's fur, dog's fur, corn, cabbage, chicken. These provocative agents were held accountable for her asthmatic attacks and she had attempted rigorously to avoid contact with these animals and foods. Yet when the patient's repressed hostility to her mother became lessened under analytic treatment, she could be freely exposed to

Montaigne says there are persons who dread the smell of apples more than they would dread being exposed to a fire of musketry. The smell of roses, of peonies, of lilies, has been known to cause faintness, and stranger still is a case where the subject fainted at the sight of red color. There are also obnoxious noises, as the crumpling of silk stuffs, the croaking of frogs, the effects of which have been spasms, a sense of strangling, profuse sweating—profound disturbance of the nervous system.

A very singular case, the doctor himself had recorded: At the head of the doctor's front stairs stood a tall clock. He could not go near one of those stately timepieces without a profound agitation, which he dreaded to undergo. This idiosyncrasy he attributed to a fright when he was an infant in the arms of his nurse.* She was standing near one of those tall clocks when the cord which supported one of its leaden weights broke, and the weight came crashing down to the bottom of the case. Some effect must have been produced upon the pulpy nerve centres from which they never recovered.

The doctor also remembered that the records of our asylums could furnish many cases where insanity was caused by

---

the presence of cats and dogs and was able to eat corn, cabbage, and chicken without developing any attacks.[4]

* The theory of infantile impressions as a cause for neuroses, here expressed by Holmes, was first stressed in psychiatric investigation by Freud. He insisted that all adult neuroses have their origin in infancy and that the determinant occurrences were usually in some way connected with sexual experiences. In actual practice at times it is difficult to establish definitely whether such significant shocks actually occurred to the neurotic or are fantasies reconstructed from knowledge later acquired through other children.

a sudden fright, and that hardly a year passes that we do not read of some person, a child, commonly, killed outright by terror, scared to death literally.*

This point was settled in the mind of Dr. Butts, namely, that as a violent emotion caused by a sudden shock can kill or craze a human being, there is no perversion of the faculties, no prejudice, no change of taste or temper, no eccentricity, no antipathy, which such a cause may not rationally account for.

The doctor soon discovered that the story of Maurice's "antipathy" had got about. He would be a little more careful the next time, for he had to concede that it was among the possibilities that his worthy lady had forgotten the rule that a doctor's patients must put their tongues out and a doctor's wife must keep her tongue in.

* * *

The Secretary of the Pansophian Society in Arrowhead Village was getting somewhat tired of the office and the office was getting somewhat tired of him. The woman suffragists

---

* Such cases are actually rare and, when they do occur, further investigation usually reveals that the individual had suffered severe emotional disturbance for some time previous to the fright. The relationship of terror to the development of such partly constitutional mental disorders as schizophrenia and manic-depressive is still a debated point. The question of such a relationship arises repeatedly in situations where these illnesses follow fright or accidents and where compensation or liability is involved. The best psychiatric observation indicates that the direct association between trauma and manic-depressive psychosis or schizophrenia is so infrequent that the burden of proof rests upon the party maintaining that such a connection exists.

saw no reason why the place of Secretary need as a matter of course be filled by a male, so they agitated, and finally their candidate Lurida Vincent "The Terror" was elected.

Among the anonymous papers the new Secretary received was one of which she felt Maurice, "the Night-Hawk," must be the author. Here is the paper:

MY THREE COMPANIONS

"I have been from my youth upwards a wanderer. From time to time I have put down in a notebook the impressions made upon me. I have long hesitated to let my notes appear before the public.

"I have lived on the shore of the great ocean where its waves broke wildest and its voice rose loudest. I have passed whole seasons on the banks of mighty and famous rivers and I have dwelt on the margin of a tranquil lake, and floated through many a long, long summer day on its clear waters.

"I have learned the 'various language' of Nature, of which poetry has spoken.

"The Ocean says to the dweller on its shores: 'you are neither welcome nor unwelcome.

" 'I have my own people, of an older race than yours; more numerous than all the swarms that fill the air or move over the thin crust of the earth. This horseshoe crab I fling at your feet is of older lineage than your Adam—perhaps, indeed, you count your Adam as one of his descendants. What feeling have I for you? Blank indifference to you and your affairs. Oh yes, I will cool you in the hot summer days, I will rock you on my rolling undulations, like a babe in his cradle. Am I not gentle? But hark—the wind is rising. What do you say to my voice now? Do you see my foaming lips? Do you feel the rocks tremble as my huge billows crash against them? Is not my anger terrible as I dash your argosy? No, not anger;

deaf, blind, unheeding indifference, that is all. I change not. I look not at you, vain man, and your frail transitory concerns, save in momentary glimpses.

" 'Ye whose thoughts are of eternity, come dwell at my side.* Continents and islands grow old, and waste and disappear. Look on me. "Time writes no wrinkle" on my forehead. Listen to me. All tongues are spoken on my shores, but I have only one language; the winds taught me their vowels, the crags and the sands schooled me in my rough or smooth consonants. Have you a grief that gnaws at your heart strings?

---

* In one of his shorter philosophical essays, "Civilization and Its Discontents," [5] written at the age of seventy, Freud refers to the comment of a friend on a former essay, "The Future of an Illusion," published a few years earlier. There Freud has regarded religion and thoughts concerning eternity as an illusion. This friend, while agreeing with the opinion concerning religion, regrets that Freud had failed to take into consideration the real source of religiosity. The latter is a feeling which we can assume is felt by millions of people —a feeling of eternity, a feeling as of something uncircumscribed, limitless, something Oceanic.

After a long discussion of the origin of this "Oceanic feeling" Freud, at the end of the essay, apparently agrees in stating: "I can imagine that the Oceanic feeling could become connected with religion later on. That feeling of oneness with the universe, which is its ideational content, sounds very like a first attempt at the consolation of religion, like another way taken by the ego of denying the dangers it sees threatening it in the external world."

It seems likely that the longing for the Ocean described above depends upon Kirkwood's search unconsciously for consolation in face of the danger associated with falling and pain and the atmospheric impressions which accompanied it and which were repeated so often in later years. The solace to be found in religion and in thoughts of eternity has been previously considered in the case of *The Guardian Angel.*

Come with it to my shore. There, if anywhere, you will forget your private and short-lived woe for my voice speaks to the infinite and the eternal in your consciousness.'

"To him who loves the pages of human history, who lives in the study of time and its accidents rather than in the deeper emotions, in abstract speculation and spiritual contemplation, the RIVER addresses itself as his natural companion.

"'Come live with me. I am active, cheerful, communicative, a natural talker and story teller. I am not noisy, like the ocean, except occasionally when I am rudely interrupted. I am not a dangerous friend, like the ocean; my nature is harmless, and the storms that strew the beaches with wrecks cast no ruins upon my flowery borders. Trust yourself to me, and I will carry you far on your journey, if we are travelling to the same point. You will find it hard to be miserable in my company; I drain you of ill-conditioned thoughts as I carry away the refuse of your dwelling and its grounds.' *

---

* The river is often symbolic of urination, generally of the masculine stream. The lake is more apt to be symbolic of female urination—making a puddle or a lake. The unconscious association of water (urination) with birth can be gathered from the following amusing little incident in the nursery reported by a patient.

He had two boys aged six and four and in the nursery parlance the penis had been the "rivers" and urination "making a river." His wife was expecting an addition to the family. As the nurse who had taken care of the two boys was now to care for the newcomer and the boys were to have a new nurse, the mother thought it best to prepare them for it. So she told them that "mother was going to have a baby." The youngest boy immediately became curious and challenged her—"Where do you keep it now?" "Mother keeps it in her, close to her heart," she replied somewhat sanctimoniously. "And how does it get out?" snapped the boy. She became greatly embarrassed but before she could think of an answer satisfactory

"But to him whom the ocean chills and crushes with its sullen indifference, and the river disturbs with its never-pausing and never-ending story, the silent LAKE shall be a place of rest for his soul.

" 'Vex not yourself with thoughts too vast for your limited faculties,' it says: 'yield not yourself to the babble of running stream. Come to me when the morning sun blazes across my bosom like a golden baldric; come to me in the still midnight, when I hold the inverted firmament like a cup brimming with jewels. Do you know the charm of melancholy? Where will you find a sympathy like mine in your hours of sadness? It is true that my waters are renewed from one season to another; but are your features the same, absolutely the same, from year to year? We both change, but we know each other through all changes.'

"I have had strange experiences and sad thoughts in the course of a life not very long. Oftentimes the temptation has come over me with dangerous urgency to try a change of existence. Ocean was there, all ready, asking no questions, answering none.

"Shall I seek a deeper slumber at the bottom of the lake I love than I have ever found when drifting idly over its surface? No, again. I do not want the sweet, clear waters to know me in the disgrace of nature, when life, the faithful body servant, has ceased caring for me.

"If I must ask the all-subduing element to lead me out of my prison, it shall be the busy, not unfriendly, river.

---

to her the boy relieved her of the necessity by saying, "Oh, I know, it comes out with your rivers."

In the above essay it is likely that symbolically the ocean would represent the eternal forces against which man battles; the river, his birth into these forces, and the lake, a haven (the waters around him before birth) to which he unconsciously hopes to return.

"But Ocean and River and Lake have certain relations to the periods of human life which they who are choosing their places of abode should consider. Let the child play upon the seashore. The wide horizon gives his imagination room to grow in, untrammelled. The mighty ocean is not too huge to symbolize the aspirations and ambitions of the yet untried soul of the adolescent.

"The time will come when his indefinite mental horizon has found a solid limit, which shuts his prospect in narrower bounds than he would have thought could content him in the years of undefined possibilities. Then he will find the river a more natural intimate than the ocean.

"It is individual, but it means well to you, bids you good-morning with its coming waves, and good-evening with those which are leaving. A river, by choice, to live by in middle age.

"In hours of melancholy reflection, in those last years of life which have little left but tender memories, the still companionship of the lake commends itself to the wearied spirit. The loneliness of contemplative old age finds its natural home in the near neighborhood of one of these tranquil basins." *

---

* The symbolism of water is frequent and important in mythology, dreams, and the ideology of childhood, especially in connection with the birth phantasy. Greek philosophy begins, as was pointed out by Rank, with Thales's statement that water is the origin and womb of all things. In this formula the conception of the individual origin of Man in the mother is extended to a universal law.[6] Sometimes the heroic figure is not born through the uterine waters but is found in or on the water, as were Moses and Noah.

In the determination of neuroses, Rank overrated the experience of being born and the importance of the waters of the amniotic fluid which accompany birth. He subsequently proposed the theory that the neuroses were reproductions of and reactions to the trauma of birth. The theory lacked adequate clinical proof and is generally regarded as not valid.

Miss Vincent pondered long upon this paper. She was thinking very seriously of studying medicine and had begun reading with Dr. Butts, to whom she carried the essay.

Whatever faults there were in this essay, there was nothing suggesting insanity of the writer. The references to suicide were of a purely speculative nature.

Months passed and the enigma remained unsolved. In the meantime Maurice had received a visit from the young student at the University whom he had rescued and with the student also came one of the teachers, a native of Italy. After they left, the instructor asked many questions.

"I feel satisfied," the instructor said, "that I have met that young man a number of years ago. Of course he has altered in appearance a good deal; but there is a look about him of apprehension. I think it is the way a man would look that was followed by a spirit or ghost. He must have been fifteen or sixteen years old when I saw him and the time was about ten years ago."

We must put this scrap of evidence with the other scraps. It is like a piece of a dissected map; it means almost nothing by itself, but when we find the pieces it joins with we may discover a very important meaning in it.* The fact that the

---

Aside from its general importance in the process of birth, water is often symbolically associated with cleanliness and absolution. People wish to wash away their sins, and "cleanliness is next to Godliness." The compulsion to wash one's hands nearly always is associated unconsciously with the need to be rid of some dirty, guilt-laden activity which is usually hidden and of a sexual nature.

* In each of the psychiatric novels Holmes has adopted a deductive method of arriving at his conclusions similar to that later popularized by Dr. Conan Doyle in Sherlock Holmes. In an abridgment such as this it has not been possible to retain the minutiae of which Holmes's physicians took advantage in attempting to solve the mystery of conduct which each novel graphically portrays.

Italian teacher thought he had seen Maurice before was made
the most of, turned over and over like a cake, until it was
thoroughly done on both sides and all through.

Lurida talked about it with her friend, Miss Tower, for here
was one more fact to help along. The two young ladies remained intimate friends and were the natural complements of
each other. Every word they spoke betrayed the difference;
the sharp tones of Lurida's head voice, penetrative, aggressive,
sometimes irritating, revealed the corresponding traits of
mental and moral character; the quiet, conversational con-
tralto of Euthymia was the index of a nature restful and sympathetic. All the freedom of movement which Euthymia,
"The Wonder," showed in her bodily exercises Lurida, "The
Terror," manifested in the world of thought.

When Lurida took up the first book on Physiology which
Dr. Butts handed her, it seemed to him that, if she opened at
any place, her mind drank its meaning up, as a moist sponge
absorbs water.

"I want to know about this terrible machinery of life and
death we are all tangled in," she told Dr. Butts. "Besides I
want to know everything."

The doctor smiled. She had reached that stage of education in which the vast domain of the unknown opens its
illimitable expanse. We must never know the extent of darkness until it is partially illuminated.

"When I talk about my ignorance, I don't measure myself
with schoolgirls, doctor. You must talk to me as if I were a
man, a grown man, if you mean to teach me anything. I want
to study up the nervous system. I am of nervous temperament
myself, and perhaps that is the reason." *

*   *   *

* Most people would agree that masculine and feminine types of
thinking are readily distinguishable. The distinction finds popular
expression in such phrases as "he talks like an old woman," or she

Lurida was in an excited condition, reading in various books bearing on medicine and antipathies.

"I have been reading about the nervous system," said she to Euthymia one day, "but I did not know how the centres of energy are played upon by all sorts of influences, external and internal. I believe I could solve the riddle of Mr. Kirkwood, if he only would stay here long enough.

"I believe there are unexplained facts in the region of sympathies and antipathies which will repay study with a deeper insight into the mysteries of life than we have dreamed of hitherto.* I often wonder whether there are not heart

---

has "the mind of a man." To the latter class Lurida would belong. Such a woman usually finds great difficulty in psychosexual adaptation, for the intellectual interest is of a type which interferes with the development of feminine characteristics. The disharmony between the "masculine mind" and the feminine body predisposes to a schism in the personality. Clashes occur between the intellectual drive, unconsciously appreciated as manly, and the demands of society for contribution to strictly feminine fields of activity and endeavor. The conflict may lead to attempts at repression of the alien type of thinking and this mechanism in extreme cases may produce the feeling of not being oneself, estrangement, unreality and depersonalization.[7]

* So far as I know this is the first plea by any physician for the investigation of the mystifying paradoxes of normal human conduct through the study of the neuroses. Later the essential structure of the extensive psychoanalytic theory was built up by Freud through the clinical observation of neurotic conditions in patients whose infantile impressions and reactions he carefully studied. However, not all of Freud's theories were based upon observations actually made on patients. His ingenuous exploration of the origin of paranoia and theory of its mechanism (projected unconscious homosexuality), for instance, grew out of the analysis of the writings of an insane judge, and the "Analysis of an Infantile Neurosis" depended entirely upon the reports of the parents of a five-year-old whom Freud saw only once in consultation.

waves and soul waves as well as 'brain waves,' which some
have already recognized." *

Euthymia wondered to hear this young woman talking in
the language of science like an adept. The truth is, Lurida
was one of those persons who never are young and who, by
way of compensation, will never be old. They are found in
both sexes. Just such exceptional individuals as this young
woman are met with from time to time in families where
intelligence has been cumulative for two or three generations.

One day Lurida was in the doctor's study having just
brought back a thick volume on Insanity, one of Bucknill and
Tuke's, which she had devoured as if it had been a pamphlet.**

---

* Whether or not the expression "brain wave" was in common use
in Holmes's time, except in telepathy to indicate the possibility of
thought transference, I have not been able to learn. Its use as a
scientific term in neurology and psychiatry is recent. In 1929 Hans
Berger introduced the electro-encephalogram, a method for regis-
tering brain waves. He demonstrated the existence of normal brain
rhythms of two types, "alpha" brain waves which are large and slow
and "beta" waves which are shorter and faster, which can be recorded on a graph. Increasing experimentation with the electro-
encephalogram has shown marked variation in these brain waves
(especially the alpha waves) in conditions such as epileptic convulsions and brain tumors.

** In all English-speaking lands, the name of Tuke is synonymous
with reform in the care of the mentally ill. York Retreat in England was established by William Tuke, a Quaker, in 1792, at about
the same time that Pinel began similar improvements in the treatment of the insane in France. Dr. Samuel Tuke, grandson of William, continued the work and his son, Dr. Daniel Hack Tuke
(1827–95) became a leading English psychiatrist of his day. With
J. C. Bucknill he wrote an important work on mental disease, A
Manual of Psychological Medicine (1858).

Dorothea Dix (1802–87), whose life was largely devoted to the

"What is the first book you would put in a student's hands, doctor?" she asked. "Not that certainly," he said. "It will put all sorts of notions into your head."

"I should like to know what kind of a condition insanity is. I don't believe they were ever very bright, those insane people. Are not most of us just a little crazy, doctor? It seems to me I never saw but one girl, Euthymia, who was free from every hint of craziness. What a doctor she would make!"

"Well, what does she say to it?"

"She thinks that now and then women may be fitted for it by nature but not many."

"I am disposed to agree that you will often spoil a good nurse to make a poor doctor. I am for giving women every chance for a good education, and if they think medicine is one of their proper callings to let them try it. The trouble is that they are so impressible and imaginative that they are at the mercy of all sorts of fancy systems. Charlatanism always hobbles on two crutches, the tattle of women and the certificates of clergymen, and I am afraid that half the women doctors will be too much under those influences."

"But what is the first book a medical student ought to read?"

"What do you say to my taking the subject before the Society? Most people listen readily to anything doctors tell them about their calling."

"I wish you would, doctor, I want Euthymia to hear it."

*   *   *

betterment of conditions in the prisons and insane asylums of America, received her inspiration from the Tukes and York Retreat. Miss Dix barely missed securing Federal care of the mentally ill in America, when the Senate in 1854, passed a bill making provision for the indigent insane. The bill was vetoed by President Franklin Pierce.

Dr. Butts' Paper, Read before the Pansophian Society.

"Next to the interest we take in all that relates to our immortal souls is that which we feel for our mortal bodies. I am afraid my very first statement may be open to criticism. The care of the body is the first thought with a great many. People send for the physician first and not until he gives them up do they commonly call in the clergyman. Even the minister himself is not so very different from other people. We must not blame him if he is not always impatient to exchange a world of ever-changing sources of excitement for that which tradition has delivered to us as one eminently deficient in the stimulus of variety. Besides, these bodily frames, even when worn and disfigured by long years of service, hang about our consciousness like old garments. They are used to us and we are used to them and to all the accidents of our lives—the house we dwell in, the living people round us.

"There is a familiar story about one of the greatest of English physicians, Thomas Sydenham. When a student asked him what books he should read, the great doctor told him 'Don Quixote.' But Sydenham has recorded his medical experience and he surely would not have published them if he had not thought they would be better reading for the medical student than the story of Cervantes. No remedy is good, it was said of old, unless applied at the right time in the right way.

"But if you ask me what reading I would commend to the medical student of a philosophical habit of mind, you may be surprised to hear me say it would be 'Rasselas.' The fortieth and the following four chapters of 'Rasselas' will teach you modesty and caution in the pursuit of the most deceptive of all practical branches of knowledge. Faith will come later when you learn how much medical science and art have actually achieved for the relief of mankind and how great are the promises it holds out of still larger triumphs over the enemies of human health and happiness.*

"The Terror" in her enthusiasm for solving the Kirkwood mystery finally discovered a case in an old Italian medical journal of a young man who reacted with certain neurotic antipathies, including color, after the bite of a tarantula. She believed this to be an actual description of Kirkwood's illness and triumphantly reported her solution to Dr. Butts. Holmes uses this incident for the following general comments upon medical literature.

"There is a great deal in medical books which it is unbecoming to bring before the general public, a great deal to repel, to alarm, to excite unwholesome curiosity. It is not the men whose duties have made them familiar with this class of subjects who are most likely to offend by scenes and descriptions which belong to the physician's private library. Goldsmith and even Smollett, both having practised medicine, could not by any possibility have outraged all the natural feelings of delicacy and decency as Swift and Zola have outraged them.

"Without handling doubtful subjects, there are many curious medical experiences which have interest for every one as extreme illustrations of ordinary conditions with which all are acquainted. No one can study the now familiar history of clairvoyance profitably who has not learned something of the

---

* The psychiatrist even more than the ordinary physician should be acquainted with human conduct as observed and described by inspired writers, poets, and artists. Thus the noted neurologist, Professor C. L. Dana, in his introductory lecture in the course on neurology at the Cornell University Medical School used to say: "The textbooks for this course will be three: Conan Doyle's *Sherlock Holmes*, William Thackeray's *Vanity Fair*, and C. L. Dana's *Textbook on Neurology*." And then he added with a whimsical smile, "You need not bother about the last but be sure to read the first two."

vagaries of hysteria. No one can read understandingly the life of Cowper and Carlyle without having some idea of the influence of dyspepsia upon the disposition and intellect."

*   *   *

Dr. Butts knew too much to interrupt Lurida as she spoke excitedly and positively of her discovery. But he had been an angler and knew a yielding rod and an easy-running reel.

"These accounts from Baglivi in Italy are interesting," said the doctor, "but I am cautious about stories a hundred years old. A very pretty prima facie case; yet I do not know that Mr. Kirkwood has any aversion to color. I am curious about the young man, but I have found that eggs hatch just as well if you let them alone in the nest as if you take them out and shake them every day."

Again the doctor felt it his duty to guard Lurida against indiscretions into which her theory of the equality, almost the identity, of the sexes might betray her. Too much of the woman in a daughter of our race leads her to forget danger— too little prompts her to defy it. Fortunately this last class of women are not quite so likely to be perilously seductive as their more emphatically feminine sisters.*

---

* Holmes repeatedly refers to vital differences between the sexes. He apparently appreciated that a certain degree of bisexuality exists in most people. Some of Holmes's contemporaries regarded him as "fussy." Perhaps for this reason he insisted upon the desirability that each sex develop fully its own biologic characteristics.

In the literary group which Holmes dominated with all the force of a realist was the sharp-witted, overeducated, rather generally disliked Margaret Fuller. When she was born her mother had prayed that "she would have Timothy's [her father's] mind." Holmes had known her since childhood. Margaret Fuller, whose life strivings were strongly determined by an envy of man's intellectual achieve-

Dr. Butts had watched the development of Lurida's intelligence from its precocious nursery life and had seen Euthymia grow up, every year more attractive. He knew that if anything was to be done with his self-willed young scholar, it would be more easily effected through Euthymia than by direct advice. So one day his chaise stopped at Euthymia's home. Once, during that friendly talk, she blushed a little as she said, "I thought Mr. Kirkwood's face a remarkable one, but he looked very pale as he passed us."

"What color was your mantle?" asked the doctor.

"A black mantle on a white dress. Lurida believes Mr. Kirkwood's illness depends on a combination of colors. Her head is full of tarantulas."

"Believe it, Euthymia, it is a great deal easier to get into a false position than to get out of it."

"I know. But she is full of all sorts of devices which are liable to be misconstrued. You remember how she won us the boatrace?"

"The classical story of Atalanta, like that of Eve," commented Dr. Butts, "as illustrating the weakness of woman which provoked her to make trial of the powers of resistance in the other sex."

*　　*　　*

Young women are much given to writing letters to persons whom they know only indirectly. They are the spontaneous outflow of young hearts and undoubtedly give great relief to solitary persons who must have some idealized reflec-

---

ment, might well have served as a pattern for Lurida. Said Holmes, when as a boy he was a schoolmate of Margaret, "She has a neck like a swan's—but from certain angles it might be said to resemble a snake's." [8]

tion of themselves yet know not where to look, since Protestantism has taken away the crucifix and the Madonna.

Such is a letter to Kirkwood written by Lurida which she asked Euthymia to read.

My dear Sir,—

You will doubtless be surprised at a letter from me for there is a feeling that it is unbecoming in one of my sex to address one of your own with whom she is unacquainted. This I am by no means disposed to concede. If one human being has anything which deserves being communicated, I see no occasion for bringing in the question of sex. I do not think the homo sum of Terence can be claimed for the male sex as its private property.

You may ask me why I address you. It is because I was deeply impressed by the paper on Ocean, River, and Lake, partly because I recognized some of the feelings as my own.

My brother, you are lonely; take me into your confidence. I long to know what influence has cast its shadow over your existence. I can bear to be considered unfeminine, but I cannot endure to think of myself as inhuman.

Lurida Vincent

As Euthymia finished this letter, her feelings found expression in an old phrase of her grandmother's, "Well, I never." She would have liked to tear it into pieces.

*   *   *

There is nothing like the pillow for an oracle. There is no voice like that which breaks the silence of the stagnant hours of the night with its sudden suggestions and luminous counsels.* When Euthymia awoke in the morning, her course of

* In psychoanalytic practice the interpretation of dreams is regarded as the most important means of revealing to the patient his unconscious desires. In the dream we usually find the disguised ex-

action was clear before her as if it had been dictated by her
guardian angel. She sought out Lurida and told her in tones
of deep anxiety.

"I have read your letter, my dear. It does you great credit
as an expression of the truest human feelings, but your desire
for knowledge is the ferment under them perhaps more than
you know. Will you go with me to the doctor's and let him
read it?—but it must not be sent to Mr. Kirkwood."

Lurida's cheeks flushed and whitened more than once. She
respected Euthymia's intelligence too much to take offense
at her advice, but she could not give up her intentions merely
from the fear of consequences.

At noon the two maidens rang at the doctor's door. The
servant said he had had a hasty summons to Mr. Kirkwood.

The physician found Maurice just regaining his heat after a
severe chill and knew too well what this meant. The autumnal fevers to which our country towns are subject, in the
place of those "agues," or intermittents so largely prevalent
in the South and West, were already beginning.

Paolo would fain have taken sole charge of his master but the
doctor insisted that he must have a nurse. At the mention of
the word "nurse" Paolo exclaimed in a thoroughly frightened
way,

"No woman. I stay by him day and night but don' let no
woman come near him—if you do, he die."

The doctor explained that he intended to send a man who

---

pression of a repressed wish. Some investigators of the dream work
think that problems may become clarified by unconscious mentation during sleep or that the dream is a reflection of unconscious
mentation but does not necessarily reveal definite wishes, merely
indicating in which direction action upon a given problem is likely
to move or should move (Alphonse Maeder). In this sense the
dream may become somewhat prophetic of a person's subsequent
acts.

was used to taking care of sick people. And so Maurice was to play the leading part in that drama called typhoid fever, with its familiar incidents, its emotional alternations, and its denouement, sometimes tragic, oftener happy.

At no time did the typhoid fever become immediately threatening but the physician knew its uncertainties only too well. The most natural interpretation which the common observer would put upon one of these autumnal maladies would be that some noxious combustible element had found its way into the system which must be burned to ashes before the heat which pervades the whole body can subside.*

For the most part Maurice's intellect was unclouded. Although he spoke only a few words, the doctor felt sure that something was oppressing him. One day he whispered to Dr. Butts:

"I commit the secret of my life to your charge. My whole story is told in a paper in that desk. If I die, let the story be known; it will show that I was—human—and save my memory from reproach." **

---

* This widespread, dread autumnal malady has, along with diphtheria in the winter and cholera infantum during the long summer months, practically vanished from the picture of disease today. Their conquest represents the great triumphs which the auxiliary medical sciences, such as biology and chemistry, that Holmes championed so vigorously, have brought to medicine.

** Some psychiatrists are inclined to attribute the improvement observed in depressed and schizoid persons after intense shocks produced by insulin, metrazol, electricity, and the like, to a death threat. The patient is for a very short time near death or momentarily dead. Such a threat of death possibly mobilizes the patient's energy and at the same time makes it free for its rearrangement and redistribution. This fluid energy can then be employed in weakening or changing the direction of fixed currents of thought which have previously sustained the patient's abnormal mental trends.

A single tear stole down his hollow cheek. The doctor turned his head away for his own eyes were full. Presently Maurice's eyes closed but the doctor saw a tranquil look on his features which added encouragement to his hopes. He took the paper from the desk and opened it.

"I am an American by birth, but a large part of my life has been passed in foreign lands. My father was a man of education and fortune; my mother an accomplished and amiable woman. I was their first and only child. My mother died while I was yet an infant and if I remember her at all it is as a vision, more like a glimpse of a prenatal existence than as a part of my earthly life. At the death of my mother I was left in the charge of the old nurse and I became absolutely dependent on her, who had for me all the love of a mother. I had been told that I was a smiling infant, with nothing to indicate any peculiar nervous susceptibility—not afraid of strangers.

"I was still a babe when the event happened which changed my whole future. I cannot relate it even now without a sense of terror. I must force myself to recall the circumstances as told me and vaguely remembered, for I am not willing that my exceptional life should pass away unexplained, unvindicated. My nature is a kind one but I have lived apart, as if my heart were filled with hatred. If there are any readers who look without pity upon those who show by their averted eyes that they dread companionship and long for solitude, I pray them to stop at this point. They will not believe my story, nor enter into my feelings. But if there are any to whom all that is human is of interest, who have felt in their own consciousness some stirrings of invincible attraction to one individual and equally invincible repugnances to another, who know by their own experience that elective affinities have their necessary counterpart and as it were their polar opposites, let them read with unquestioning faith this story of a blighted life.*

"My cousin, Laura, a girl of seventeen, was considered beautiful. In my second summer she visited my father who but recently had become a widower. Laura was full of vivacity, impulsive, thoughtless occasionally, as it is not strange that a young girl of her age should be. It was a beautiful summer day when she saw me for the first time. My nurse had me in her arms, walking back and forward on a balcony with a low railing, upon which opened the windows of the second story of my father's house. While the nurse was carrying me, Laura came suddenly upon the balcony, grasped me from the nurse's arms, began tossing me after the fashion of young girls who have been so lately playing with dolls. The abrupt seizure frightened me; I sprang from her arms in my terror and fell over the railing of the balcony. I should probably enough have been killed on the spot but for the fact that a low thornbush grew just beneath the balcony, into which I fell and thus had the violence of the shock broken. But the thorns tore my tender flesh and I bear to this day marks of those wounds.

"That dreadful experience is burned deep into my memory. The sudden apparition of the girl; the sense of being torn away from the protecting arms around me; the frantic effort to escape; the shriek that accompanied my fall through what must have seemed unmeasurable space; the cruel lacerations

---

* Notwithstanding the great increase in knowledge concerning human motivations and mental mechanisms and the spread of this knowledge through psychiatry and its popularization in the cinema and fiction, very few physicians or laymen are ready today to accept this view of uncontrollable impulse. This opposition is due largely to a reluctance on the part of us all to acknowledge that we, too, are susceptible to similar irrationalities and a wish to condemn in others what we cannot master in ourselves.

of the rending thorns,—all these fearful impressions blended in one paralyzing terror.

"When I was taken up I was perfectly white and the physicians said that no pulse was perceptible. After a time consciousness returned; the wounds, though painful, were none of them dangerous, and the most alarming effects passed away. My dear nurse and my father believed that no permanent evil would result. Laura was deeply distressed to feel that her thoughtlessness had been the cause of so grave an accident. As soon as I had somewhat recovered she came to see me, very anxious to make me forget the alarm she had caused me. I was sitting up in my bed, bandaged but not in any pain, and to all appearance in a perfectly natural state. As Laura came near me I shrieked, put my hand upon my heart as if I had been stabbed and fell over unconscious. It was much the same state as that in which I was found immediately after my fall.

"The cause of this appalling seizure was but too obvious. The approach of the young girl and the dread that she was about to lay her hand upon me had called up the same train of effects which the moment of terror had already occasioned. The old nurse saw this in a moment. 'Go, go,' she cried to Laura, 'go, or the child will die.'

"After Laura had gone I lay senseless and cold as marble, for some time. The doctor soon came and by the use of smart rubbing and stimulants the arrested circulation was again set in motion. The doctor thought that after a few days I should recover from this morbid sensibility and receive my cousin as other infants receive pleasant-looking young persons. The old nurse shook her head. 'The girl will be the death of the child,' she said, 'if she comes near him.' *

---

* The sequence of circumstances and incidents which follow correspond to those which an analyst hears daily from patients whose

"Once more the experiment was tried, cautiously, but it was too evident that a chain of nervous disturbances had been set up which repeated itself. I never saw my cousin Laura after this last trial.

"If the effect of the nervous shock had stopped there, it would have been a misfortune but hardly a calamity. The world is wide, and a cousin or two more or less can hardly be considered an essential of existence. I often heard Laura's name mentioned but never by any one who was acquainted with all the circumstances for it was noticed that I changed color.

"Alas, this was not all. While I was suffering from the effects of my fall among the thorns, strangers and friends were all alike excluded from my nursery, with one exception, that my old grandmother came in now and then. With her it seems that I was somewhat timid, following her with rather anxious eyes, as if not quite certain whether or not she was dangerous. But one day, when I was far advanced towards recovery, my father brought in a young lady, a relative of his. She was, as I have been told, a very handsome girl, of about the same age as Laura, but bearing no personal resemblance to her. The same sudden changes began to show themselves before she had reached my bedside and I was in a state of deadly collapse.

"Some time passed before any recurrence of these terrifying seizures. A little girl of six years was allowed to come into the nursery one day and bring me some flowers. I took them from her hand but turned away and shut my eyes. There was

___

neuroses he is attempting to unravel. In clinical practice the initial scene here so vividly described, might never come to light but might be reconstructed from many facts the patient remembered. At the end the psychiatrist often has an involved story which rivals the drama of fiction.

no seizure but a certain dread which it might be hoped that time would overcome.

"The daughter of a neighbor, the prettiest girl of the village was anxious to see me and as I was so nearly well it was determined that she should pay me a visit. I had previously always delighted in seeing her. I was sleeping when she entered the nursery and came and took a seat at my side in perfect silence. Presently I became restless and a moment later I opened my eyes and saw her stooping over me. I again became so like death that it had well-nigh been mistaken for it.

"The dangerous experiment was not intentionally tried again, but chance brought about more than one renewal until it became fully recognized that I was the unhappy subject of a mortal dread of woman, not absolutely of the human female, for I had no fear of any old, wrinkled face and had become accustomed to the occasional meeting of a little girl or two, whom I nevertheless regarded with a certain ill-defined feeling that there was danger in their presence. I was sent to a boys' school so that during the first ten or twelve years I had rarely an occasion to be reminded of my idiosyncrasy.

"How shall I describe the conflicts of the dreamy, bewildering, dreadful years of adolescence. Visions of loveliness haunted me sleeping and waking. Sometimes a graceful girlish figure would so draw my eyes towards it that I was ready to forget all my fears and find myself at her side, like other youths, then I—I—under the curse of one blighting moment, looked on hopeless. Sometimes the tone of a sweet voice stirred within me all the instincts that make the morning of life beautiful to adolescence.

"I reasoned with myself:

"Why should I not have outgrown that idle apprehension which had been the nightmare of my earlier years? Why should not the rising tide of life have drowned out the feeble growths that infested the shallows of childhood? How many children there are who tremble at being left alone in the dark, but who, a few years later, will brave all the ghosts of a haunted chamber. Why should I any longer be the slave of a fancy that has grown into a half-insane habit of mind? *

---

* Most children are subject to transient fears of one kind or another, such as fear of darkness, of water, of solitude or of separation from accustomed environment. They "outgrow" them about the age of six or seven when they grasp that the threat against which the fears protect are really not as dangerous as they felt. A phobia is generally associated with anxiety and develops concerning situations which the person appreciates are not fraught with real danger.

True phobias may occur in young children and rarely disappear spontaneously. Children and adults often attempt to overcome such phobias by forcing themselves to brave the thing they fear without understanding why they fear it or what the thing feared may unconsciously symbolize. It is rare that such a phobia can be dissipated by forcing oneself or being forced by others. Occasionally in the course of the treatment of a neurosis the physician may ask a patient to expose himself to some specific situation he fears, not that he will be cured by this, but that his reactions at that time may reveal the sources of his latent anxiety.

A physician, aged fifty, who consulted me because of a compulsion to agree with opinions which he did not approve, related the following experience. As a boy of ten, when most of his companions began to learn to dive, he developed a great fear associated with anxiety when he attempted to dive. To overcome this phobia he forced himself to dive again and again. Each time the anxiety returned and each time he became more determined to conquer it. He became an expert diver and swimmer, so good, in fact, that he captained the water polo team when in college but the phobia persisted unchanged.

When he had reached forty-five he was riding across the Arizona

"Why did I not brave the risk of meeting squarely some one of those maidens whose far-off smile at once attracted and agitated me? It is enough to say here that the 'nervous disturbance' which the presence of a woman in the flower of her age produced in my system was a sense of impending death, sudden, overwhelming, unconquerable. It was a reversed action of the nervous centres,—the opposite of that which flushes the lover's cheek and hurries his bounding pulses as he comes into the presence of the object of his passion.

"At this period of my life my father determined to try the effect of travel upon my bodily and mental condition. I say bodily as well as mental, for I was too slender for my height and subject to some nervous symptoms. That the mind was

---

waste lands with two guides when they came to an arroya about six feet deep which cut across the trail. The three riders halted their horses at the brink of the cut and stood there undecided how they should continue. Suddenly the old fear and compulsion seized my patient. He kicked his spurs into the horse's flank and jumped him (made him dive) down the bank into the river bed. Fortunately he landed without mishap.

The two guides sought an easier way down the side of the arroya some distance beyond and when they rejoined the doctor, scolded him angrily for his folly in defying danger and risking his life. Following this incident where he drew upon himself the disapproval of more experienced men (older hands, father surrogates) for his need to plunge, the fear of diving decreased markedly. What had happened may be formulated as follows: Father types had told him positively—"Sonny, you're a fool. You can't overcome your desire to stay near your mother by forcing yourself to plunge. It is unnecessary and futile. Real men don't act that way. Look for more reasonable ways, such as we have shown you." Now at forty-five the Doctor had reached a stage of maturity where the vehement suggestions of the well-intentioned guides could have some effect.

largely concerned in these there was no doubt, but the mutual interactions of mind and body are often too complex to admit of satisfactory analysis. Each is in part cause and each also in part effect.*

---

* Just at the present time a marked increase in the interest in this problem of the interrelationship of mind and body, especially in hospital cases, is apparent under the important sounding name of psychosomatic medicine. This may be attributed to certain fairly constant correlations which the cumulated psychoanalytic studies have demonstrated to exist between repressed aggression and such definite diseases as gastric ulcer, mucous colitis, hypertension, and others.

The reasons why a specific organ should be affected by such emotional conflicts remain very much in the dark. One theory leans to the idea that the organ affected is biologically weak and therefore becomes diseased by a generalized body tension which eventually settles upon the site of weakness. Another theory is that the function of the organ, such as the stomach or the lungs, has a particular psychological value to the patient because of some quality with which it has become invested. For instance, a stomach-ache may be something for which a child has been punished repeatedly because he has eaten forbidden foods such as candy, whereas a cold or cough is something for which he is not responsible and he therefore may be coddled when it does occur. A feeling of guilt may eventually center about the sinning stomach or, if the desire for sympathy is predominant, the child may become "sensitive to colds."

Sometimes the form of physical conversion seems to depend upon an identification process. The dissatisfaction with a current situation may be expressed in symptoms of a disease from which a parent suffered—such as heart trouble—or which happens to be momentarily fashionable—as appendicitis forty years ago or "sinus trouble" and "allergy" today.

An amusing little incident will illustrate by analogy this mechanism of identification and its use at an early age for the advantage of the individual. One of my friends is a busy general practitioner,

"We passed some years in Italy where I was placed in a school conducted by priests. There I had opportunity of seeing the influences under which young Catholics, destined for the priesthood, are led to separate themselves from the sex associated in their minds with the most subtle dangers to which the human soul can be exposed. I became in some degree reconciled by seeing around me so many who were self-devoted to celibacy. The thought sometimes occurred to me whether I should not find the only natural solution in taking upon me the vows which settle the whole question.

"But impressed as I was with the excellence of many of the young members of the Roman Church, my early training rendered it impossible for me to accept the credentials which it offered me. My instructor had to set me down as a case of 'invincible ignorance.' This was the loop-hole through which he crept out of the prison-house of his creed and was enabled to look upon me without feeling absolute despair.

"I have said that accident exposed me at times to the influence which I had such reasons for dreading. Here is one example vividly impressed upon my memory. A young friend whose acquaintance I had made in Rome asked me one day to come to his home. I had been but a short time in his library when a vague sense of uneasiness came over me. I could feel my heart stirring irregularly, as if it were some frightened creature caged in my breast. There was nothing

---

also doing much obstetrics, in a suburban community. His irregularity at meals is a frequent source of contention between him and his wife. One day their five-year-old daughter Mary was playing in the yard when her mother called her to lunch. Mary did not come. After a few minutes the call was repeated, again without result. Finally the mother called sharply, "Mary, come in to lunch this instant." Replied Mary, "I'm very busy. I'm playing confinement and I won't be home to lunch."

that I could see to account for it. A door was partly open, but not so that I could see into the next room. The feeling grew upon me of some influence which was paralyzing my circulation. I begged my friend to open a window. As he did so, the door swung in the draught, and I saw a blooming young woman—it was my friend's sister, who had been sitting with a book in her hand, and who rose at the opening of the door. Something had warned me of the presence of a woman, that occult and potent aura of individuality, call it personal magnetism, spiritual effluence, or reduce it to a simpler expression if you will; it had warned me of the nearness of the dread attraction which allured at a distance and revealed itself with the terrors of the Lorelei if approached too recklessly. A sign from her brother caused her to withdraw at once but not before I had experienced the feeling as if about to fall in a fainting fit.*

"Nothing in life is so strange or exceptional as it seems to those who have not made a study of its mysteries. I have never known just such a case as my own, and yet I cannot doubt that there have been many like it. Let my reader

---

* From the description of these attacks one could possibly classify them as epileptoid. The genesis of fainting attacks in trauma has been studied by Kardiner [10] who maintains that "in certain neuroses, as the result of a trauma which injured either psychic or somatic portions of the body-ego, a series of purely inhibitory or contractile phenomena appear." One of these contractile phenomena is the epileptoid attack and in it the ego periodically attempts to rebind the originally "archaic destructive energies" by a return to the birth situation. Clinical evidence all favors the assumption that the unconscious reactivation of psychic trauma, psychic conflict, or even mental phantom formation, predisposes to the production of fainting or epileptoid reactions.

suspend his judgment until he has read the paper of the
Royal Academy of Biological Sciences, to which I will refer
later. In this paper the mechanism of the series of nervous
derangements to which I have been subject is explained in
language not hard to understand. Such a change of polarity
in the nervous centres is only a permanent form and an extreme degree of an emotional disturbance which, as a temporary and comparatively unimportant personal accident, is
so frequent that not a few must have had more or less serious experience of it in their own private history.

"It must not be supposed that my imagination dealt with
me as I am now dealing with the reader. I was full of strange
fancies and wild superstitions. One of my Catholic friends
gave me a silver medal which had been blessed by the Pope,
and which I was to wear next to my body. I was told that this
would turn black after a time, in virtue of a power which it
possessed of drawing out original sin. I wore the medal faithfully and watched it carefully. It became tarnished and after
a time darkened, but it wrought no change in my condition.*

"There was an old gypsy who had the reputation of fore-
telling the death of Cavour, so I was persuaded to let her try
her black art upon my future. I shall never forget the strange,
wild look of the wrinkled hag, as she took my hand and
studied its lines and fixed her wicked eyes on my young coun-

---

* A procedure very likely having its inspiration from this notion
was still used in 1908 by Dr. C. L. Dana, under whom it was my
privilege of serving in Bellevue Hospital. On at least two occasions
a large, old bronze Roman medallion was chilled ice cold or heated.
It was then strapped to an hysterically paralyzed arm of a patient
with the solemn assurance that it would cure him but without, I
may add, any greater therapeutic effect than in the case of the
blessed medal mentioned above; this patient, also, lacked faith.

tenance. She shook her head and muttered some words, which as nearly as I could get them would be in English like these:

Fair lady cast a spell on thee,
Fair lady's hand shall set thee free.

"Strange as it may seem these words of a withered old creature whose palm had to be crossed with silver to bring forth her oracular response have always clung to my memory as if they were destined to fulfillment. My affliction disposed me to believe the incredible with reference to all that relates to it. With trembling fears, with mingled belief and doubt, wherever I have found myself I have sought with longing yet half-averted eyes for the 'elect lady' who was to lift the curse.

"Sometimes I have been led to the hope that I had found the object of my superstitious belief. It was always on the water * that the phantom of my hope appeared before my bewildered vision.

"Again it happened on the Tiber. I was floating with the stream in the little boat in which I passed many long hours of reverie when I saw another boat with a boy and a young girl in it. The boy had let one of his oars slip and was hopelessly rowing round and round. I could not refuse my assistance. I picked up the oar and brought my skiff alongside of the boat. The young girl thanked me in the exquisite music of the language which 'sounds as if it should be writ on satin.'

"She was a type of Italian beauty, a nocturne in flesh and

---

* Kirkwood's fantasies and dreams are symbolic of rebirth. Before or during his attacks, he "was floating in the little boat in reverie"; he had "died more than once and been resuscitated"; "wanted the dreamy stillness of a tranquil sheet of water"; and it was "always in the water that the phantom of my hope appeared."

blood, but it was her voice which captivated me. An hour later I was found lying insensible on the floor of my boat, almost pulseless.

"What prospect have I of ever being rid of this deep-seated infirmity? I have had of late strange premonitions, to which, if I were superstitious, I could not help giving heed. But though I am not superstitious, I have a right to be imaginative, and my imagination will hold to those words of the old zingara. I have had both waking and sleeping visions within these last months which have taken possession of me and filled my life with new thoughts. Sometimes on the bosom of the lake, sometimes in the woods in a distant glimpse, once in a nearer glance, which left me pale and tremulous, yet was followed by a swift reaction, so that my cheeks flushed and my pulse bounded, I have seen her who —how do I dare to tell it so that my own eyes can read it?—I cannot help believing is to be my deliverer.

"I have been warned by experts that it would be at the imminent risk of my existence if I should expose myself to the repetition of my former experiences, that any emotion is liable to arrest the movements of life: terror, joy, good news or bad news. I had already died once, as Sir Charles Napier said of himself; yes, more than once, died and been resuscitated. The next time, I might very probably fail to get my return ticket after my visit to Hades.

"What had I to live for if the great primal instinct which strives to make whole the half life of manhood is suppressed, crushed out of existence? I am alone save for my faithful servant through whom I seem to hold to the human race as it were by a single filament. My father, who was my dearest and best friend, died three years ago and left me my own master, with the means of living as might best please my fancy. This season shall decide my fate. One more experiment and I shall find myself restored to my fellow beings or to a sphere where all our mortal infirmities are past.*

"I have passed through different stages of feeling from infancy to manhood. At first it was blind instinct about which I had no thought, living like other infants the life of impressions without language to connect them in series. In my boyhood I began to be deeply conscious of the infirmity and in youth began that conflict of emotions and impulses with the antagonistic influences of which I have spoken, a conflict which has never ceased but to which I have necessarily become to a certain degree accustomed, and against which I have learned to guard myself. You, young man, at least will understand me. Does not your heart throb, in the presence of budding womanhood as if it 'were ready to crack' with its own excess of strain? What if instead of throbbing it should

---

* Confessional histories and interpretations of this type find their way into the record files of every psychiatrist. Often they describe the patient's difficulties with the sensitivity, subtle understanding, and clarity of one who has lived with those difficulties for a long time and has painfully learned their significance and variations.

These confessional writings often have the effect of relieving the mind of burdensome thoughts. Secret diaries serve much the same purpose in their recording of weaknesses, unexpressed loves, unapproved ambitions, guilts, and hatreds. The code diaries of sly Samuel Pepys and shrewd William Byrd of Virginia (who every day "said his prayers and had good health, good thoughts and good humor") must have afforded considerable solace to these two amiable reprobates.

I am inclined to think that Kirkwood's document was written by some patient whom Holmes had treated early in his practice and that he had actually observed a cure of some condition similar to this through a sudden shock. In this story, "shock" is almost synonymous with "fair woman": "Fair lady set a spell on thee, Fair lady's hand shall set thee free."

falter, flutter, and stop as if never to beat again? You, young woman, who with ready belief and tender sympathy will look upon these pages, know what it is when your breast heaves with uncontrollable emotion and the grip of the bodice seems unendurable as the embrace of the 'Iron Virgin' of the Inquisition. Think what it would be if the grasp were tightened so that no breath of air could enter your panting chest.

"I have reached the time of life which, I have ventured to hope, might be the limit of my sentence. Martyrs have gone singing to their flaming shrouds but never a man could hold his breath long enough to kill himself; he must have rope or water, or some mechanical help, or nature will make him draw in a breath of air though he knew the salvation of the human race would be forfeited by that one gasp.

"There are many shy natures which will recognize tendencies in themselves in the direction of my unhappy susceptibility. Others, to whom such weakness seems inconceivable, will find their scepticism shaken by the Report drawn up for the Royal Academy. I am but a bird of passage that lights on the boughs of different nationalities. I belong to no flock; I build no nest; today I am here, tomorrow on the wing."

Of course the case of Maurice Kirkwood is an exceptional one, but if the reader has reached middle life let him look back over his acquaintances and see if he cannot recall more than one, who, for some reason, shunned young women as if because of a deadly fear.

Maurice, with a philosophical equanimity to his fate, lived chiefly by himself, as the easiest mode. He had learned to look upon himself very much as he would upon an intimate, not himself—upon a different personality. A young man will naturally be ashamed of his shyness for it is something which others believe, and perhaps he himself thinks, he might overcome. Kirkwood had accepted the effects of his first terror as

he would have losing his sight or hearing. Nature was peremp-
tory with him, saying in language that had no double meaning: "If you violate the condition by which you hold the gift
of existence I slay you on the spot." *

He was not insensible because he looked upon himself with
the coolness of an enforced philosophy. He bore his burden
manfully, for he lived in hope, and the thought of throwing his
illness off with his life, he rejected as unworthy of his manhood. How he had speculated about it is plain enough from
the paper, "Ocean, River, and Lake." **

*　　*　　*

---

* The scientific study of the neuroses had received little attention
from psychiatrists in 1885. Some of the foremost failed to appreciate that a persistent compulsion or phobia is entirely beyond the
control of the patient and that often his only method of handling
it is to adjust his habits of life to it. For instance, a patient with a
fear of crossing a wide street might take a bus crossing such an
avenue although he would have to go a mile out of his way to get it.

Since the time of Freud, because more attention had been directed to the neuroses, they have been presumed to be on the increase. Whatever increase appears to exist is probably due to the
fact that people now are willing to acknowledge the existence of
phobias without fear of being considered on the borderline of insanity and that they no longer think it a disgrace to seek psychiatric
treatment. The apparent greater frequency of neurotic disorders is
often attributed to the complexity of modern social and environmental influences but is also due to the fact that patients no longer
find it advantageous to conceal them.

** Often it is said that people who threaten suicide never carry out
the threat. This idea is possibly based on the fact that many of
those who do commit suicide have given no indication to their
associates that they had such an intention in mind. They are usu-

I would now submit the paper promised by Kirkwood describing a case similar to his own: namely, a report to the Royal Academy of the Biological Sciences.

"The case will arrest the attention of those who have learned the great fact that Nature often throws the strongest light upon her laws by the apparent exceptions and anomalies. Today we meet with surprising facts, which a century or two ago would have been handled by the clergy and the courts, but now are calmly judged by the best light of our knowledge of the laws of life. It must be owned that there are stories, full of evidence in their support, which, notwithstanding, leave us sceptical in spite of all the testimony. In this category many will be disposed to place the case to which we apply the term Gynophobia.

"The heart is the centre of every living movement in the higher animals, furnishing the needful supplies to all parts of the system. If its action is diminished, faintness is the immediate consequence; if it is arrested, loss of consciousness; if its action is not soon restored, death, of which fainting plants the white flag, remains in possession.

"How closely the heart is under the influence of the emotions we need not go to science to learn, for all literature is overflowing with evidence. Scripture is full of it. Especially is the heart associated with the passion of love.

"Love has many languages, but the heart talks through all

---

ally people who felt driven to suicide because no other course was open to them. On the other hand, the person who threatens suicide is in doubt; he feels forced in that direction against a strong desire to live. By his threat he effectually says, "See my plight. I need help and need it urgently—so urgently that if I do not get it, I will be compelled to give up the struggle." When a patient mentions or implies thoughts of self-destruction, the psychiatrist, therefore, always notes it as an issue which he dare not ignore.

of them whether its hurried action is seen, or heard, or felt. This saying was not meant to be taken literally, but it has its literal truth. Many a lover has found his heart 'sink within him' and leave him weak as a child.

"One who faints is dead if he does not 'come to,' and nothing is more likely than that too susceptible lovers have actually gone off in this way. The mechanism of the heart's actions becomes an interesting subject, therefore, capable of intense emotions. Between it and the brain there is the closest relation. The brain is the seat of ideas, emotions, volition. It is the great telegraphic station with which many lesser centres of nerve cells are in close relation.

"There are two among the special groups of these nerve cells which produce directly opposite effects. One acts as the spur, the other as the bridle. According as one or the other predominates, the action of the heart will be stimulated or restrained.

"The centre of inhibition plays a terrible part in the history of cowardice and of successful love. No man can be brave without blood to sustain his courage, any more than he can think, as the German naturalist says, not absurdly, without phosphorus. The fainting lover must recover his circulation, or his lady will lend him her smelling-salts and take a gallant with blood in his cheeks.

"In well-known cases of deadly antipathy the most frequent cause has been the depressing influence of the centre of inhibition. A single impression, in a very early period of atmospheric existence—perhaps, indirectly, before that period, as was said to have happened in the case of James the First of England—may establish a communication between this centre and the heart which will remain open ever afterwards. How does a footpath across a field establish itself? Its curves are arbitrary, and what we call accidental, but one after another follows it as if he were guided by a chart on which it was laid down. So it is with this dangerous transit between the centre of inhibition and the great organ of life. If once the path is opened by the track of some profound impression, that same impression, or a similar one, is likely to find the old footmarks and follow them. Habit only makes the path easier to traverse.

"We do not doubt that there have been similar cases, and that in some rare instances sudden death has been the consequence of seizures like that of the subject of this Report. The case most like it is that of Colonel Townsend. He could by a voluntary effort suspend the action of his heart for a considerable period, during which he lay like one dead, pulseless, and without motion. After a time the circulation returned, and he does not seem to have been the worse for his seemingly dangerous experiment. But in his case it was by an act of the will that the heart's action was suspended. In the case before us it is an involuntary impulse which arrests the cardiac movements.*

---

* At the beginning of this century when psychoanalysis presented a more effective way of allowing the patient to deal with the unconscious, interest in hypnosis as a therapeutic agent began to wane in this country.

Many vaudeville performances had among their acts hypnotists who would demonstrate this phenomenon, nearly always using professional subjects who were scattered among the audience. I had an opportunity to examine and study one of these men who had been repeatedly hypnotized. He claimed that he, in common with other repeatedly hypnotized persons, would frequently lose his identity and involuntarily become amnestic for his own personality. His frequent indulgence in autohypnosis had led him to develop a phenomenon similar to that described above, namely, a voluntary control of the cardiovascular system. He could extend one of his arms,

"The subject of this paper is now more than twenty years old. It might have been hoped that the changes of adolescence would have effected a transformation. On the contrary, the whole force of this instinct throws itself on the centre of inhibition, instead of quickening the heart-beats.

"Is it probable that time and circumstances will alter a habit of interactions long established? We are disposed to think that there is a chance. If once the nervous impression which falls on the centre of inhibition can be made to change its course, it will probably keep to its natural channel ever afterwards. And this will, it is most likely, be effected by some unexpected impression. The nervous current then might be changed about as easily as the reversal of the poles in a magnet. But he cannot throw himself into the water just at the right moment and accident may effect the cure which art seems incompetent to perform.

"It is hard to determine the wisest course to be pursued. The question is not unlike that which arises in certain cases of dislocation of the bones of the neck. Shall the unfortunate sufferer go all his days with his face turned around or shall an attempt be made to replace the dislocated bones which may cause instant death. The patient must be consulted as

---

which had the normal tint of flesh supplied with blood, slap it with the other hand, and command the extended arm to become rigid. He would then say, "Follow me," and as he stroked the extended arm with his fingers one could observe the fingers, the hand, and forearm become a deathly white. He had apparently stopped the flow of blood, although he probably did not reverse the current. The upper arm in turn became somewhat bluish red. After he had kept the blood stream at this level in the upper arm for a few minutes he would stroke his lower arm downward and say, "Follow me," and the blood would return to the finger tips, restoring normal color.

·

to whether he will take the chance but the practitioner may be unwilling to risk it. Each case must be judged on its own special grounds.* We cannot think that this man is doomed but we fear we must trust to as energetic a shock to displace the malady as that which brought it into existence."

* * *

Dr. Butts believed that his patient would recover from his typhoid fever and began thinking deeply of what he could do for him after that. He was not a male gossip nor a match-making go-between but he could not help thinking what a pity it was that Euthymia and Maurice could not come together, and began speculating as to the possibility of the personal presence of an individual making itself perceived by some channel other than one of the five senses.

Among many other thoughts which came up was one which involved the suffering of multitudes of youthful persons who die without telling their secret: how many young men have a fear of woman, as woman, and in consequence of which sex attraction is completely neutralized. Love is the

---

* Often the psychiatrist faces similar dilemmas. Many cases exist in which a distressing situation has developed because of a conflict in a dependent adult who consciously wishes to be free and yet remain immature and retain the indulgences and support of childhood. If the psychiatrist should succeed in liberating the patient, the financial support of a dominating parent might be withdrawn because the latter does not wish to lose his power over his child. The patient, untrained, unaccustomed to work for a livelihood, would be unable to exist if thrown on his own resources. The decision in such a situation would be to temporize and compromise rather than to attempt an immediate cure, in the hope that a gradual change may occur in either the parent or child or both, or in the external situation.

master key, he went on thinking, that opens the gates of happiness, hatred, jealousy and, most easily of all, the gate of fear.

The illness had left Maurice in a state of profound prostration so that the doctor waited for the right moment to mention the manuscript he had entrusted to him.

"I wish some additional facts about your history," the doctor said one day. "What led you to Arrowhead?"

"Certainly," Maurice answered. "I was tired of the sullen indifference of the ocean and the babbling egotism of the river. I wanted the dreamy stillness of a tranquil sheet of water that would leave me to my thoughts. The season has gone by too swiftly since my dream has become a vision."

The doctor was sitting with three fingers on Maurice's pulse and, as he spoke these last words, noticed the pulse fluttered.

The next day his patient was well enough to enter once more into conversation.

"You said something yesterday about a dream which had become a vision," said the doctor, with his fingers on his patient's wrist. He felt the artery leap, stop, then begin again. The heart had felt the pull of the bridle but the spur had roused it to swift reaction.

"I will tell you: You remember the boat race? I watched it through an opera-glass and saw one face which drew me away from all the rest, that of the young lady who pulled bow oar. Since that day I have had many distant glimpses of her and once I met her so squarely that the deadly sensation came over me."

"You are not the first young man who has been fascinated, almost at a glance, by Euthymia Tower."

The doctor gave him a full account of the young lady, her character, her accomplishments. When the doctor left Maurice said to himself, "I will speak with her if it costs me my life."

* * *

Euthymia had had admirers enough, but she had fairly frightened more than one rash youth disposed to be too sentimental, so that people doubted whether she would ever be married. The ideals of young women cost them great disappointments but often save them from those lifelong companionships which accident is constantly trying to force upon them in spite of their obvious unfitness. Beneath Euthymia's abstractions was a capacity of loving which might have been inferred from the expression of her features, the tones of her voice, all of which were full of the language which belongs to susceptible natures. How many women never say to themselves that they were born to love until all at once the discovery opens upon them, as the sense that he was born a painter is said to have dawned suddenly upon Correggio.

If Maurice had been suffering from some contagious malady Euthymia would have risked her life to help him without a thought that there was any wonderful heroism. Lurida might have been capable of the same sacrifice, but it would be after reasoning with herself as to the obligations which her sense of human duties laid upon her.

* * *

One morning Dr. Butts found Maurice worse. Later in the day, however, the nurse, a trustworthy man enough in the main, finding his patient in a tranquil sleep left his bedside for a little fresh air.

Maurice fell into a dream which began quietly but, in the course of the sudden transitions which dreams are in the habit of undergoing, he became successively anxious, distressed, terrified. His earlier and later experiences came up before him, fragmentary, incoherent, chaotic even, but vivid as reality. He was at the bottom of a coal mine in one of those long, narrow galleries, or rather worm-holes, in which human beings pass a large part of their lives, like so many larvae boring their way into the beams and rafters of some old building. How close the air was in the stifling passage through which he was crawling. The scene changed, and he was climbing a slippery sheet of ice with desperate effort, his foot on the floor of a shallow niche, his hold an icicle ready to snap in an instant, an abyss below him waiting for his foot to slip or the icicle to break.* How thin the air seemed —how desperately hard to breathe. He was thinking of Mont Blanc, it may be and the fearfully rarefied atmosphere which he remembered well as one of the great trials in his mountain ascents. No, it was not Mont Blanc—it was Hecla that he was climbing. The smoke of the burning mountain was wrapping itself around him; he was choking with its dense fumes; he heard the flames roaring around him, felt the hot lava beneath his feet, uttered a faint cry and awoke.

The room was full of smoke. He was in the smothering

---

* Most analysts would interpret this dream as a birth fantasy, possibly of birth per rectum, which is quite a common infantile concept. The confusion between Hecla and Mont Blanc would usually be considered as symbolic of the contrast between the warmth of the mother's body and the colder outer world. People who repeatedly have dreams of this nature are those who have strong dissatisfaction with life and hope for better luck the next time through return to the womb and rebirth. In the resuscitation of Maurice, which followed a few minutes after the dream, the description contains many expressions—the rush of air, the thorns of the cradle, etc.—which might be applied to the experience of a child during birth. Indeed he was "borne" (symbolically re-born) "back into the arms of a woman as easily as if he had been a babe."

oven which his chamber had become. He tried to call for help and made a desperate effort to sit up in bed but the effort was too much for him. He felt that his hour had come—the fate of many a martyr, to be first strangled and then burned. But death had not the terror that it has for most young persons. The closed vista of memory opened, and past and present were pictured in a single instant of clear vision. He felt the impotent spasm—the rush of air—the thorns of the lacerating cradle into which he was precipitated. One after another those paralyzing seizures, which had been like deadening blows on the naked heart, seemed to repeat themselves. The vision of the "inward eye" was so intensified in this moment of peril that an instant was like an hour of common existence. The rush of unwonted emotion floods, the undeveloped pictures of vanished years stored away in the memory and the vast panorama of a lifetime in one swift instant came out as vividly as if it were again the present. Then all at once rose the vague hopes which he had cherished of late. The passionate desire for life came over him—not the dread of death.

What happened? One of the lazy natives had thrown a burning stump in at an open window and it fell among the straw of an old mattress. The blaze was fierce and swift.

The attendant, returning to the house, rushed to make his way to Maurice's room and save him. Every man, woman, and child within reach of a human voice came from their houses, and two young women, in boating dresses of decidedly Bloomerish aspect, suddenly joined the throng. A few hurried words told them the fearful story. They looked each other in the face for one swift moment.

Poor Lurida forgot all her theories and sank fainting to the ground. But Euthymia was not to be held back. Taking a handkerchief from her neck, she dipped it in a pail of water

and bound it about her head. Then she took several deep
breaths of air and as a willing martyr, if martyr she was to be
and not a saviour, passed within the veil that hid the sufferer.

It seems as if we were doing great wrong to the scene in
omitting the description of circumstances and individual feelings that passed through the minds of the awe-struck company gathered about the scene of danger. That is an impos-
sibility, for consciousness is a surface; narrative is a line.

Maurice had given himself up. "Oh, for a breath of air—
too late," he gasped.

"Not too late." The soft voice reached his obscured consciousness as if it had come down to him from heaven, and
he found himself rolled in a blanket and in the arms of—a
woman. Out into the open air he was borne as easily as if
he had been a babe.

This was the scene upon which the doctor appeared. As
the fresh breeze passed over the face of the rescued patient,
his eyes opened wide and his consciousness returned in almost
supernatural lucidity. Euthymia had sat down upon a bank
with his head resting on her bosom. Through his awakening senses stole the murmurs of the living cradle which rocked
him with the wave-like movements of respiration, the double
beat of the heart which throbbed close to his ear. Every instinct and every reviving pulse told him in language like a
revelation from another world that it was life and not death
which a woman's embrace had brought him.

The doctor said: "Hold him just so, Euthymia. I will say
when he is ready to be moved."

*   *   *

It was perfectly clear to Dr. Butts that if Maurice could
see the young woman to whom he owed his life and experience the revolution in his nervous system which would

be the beginning of a new existence, it would be of far more value than all of the drugs in the pharmacopoeia. He told this to Euthymia and explained the matter to her parents, urging them that she be allowed to visit Maurice.

The first of her visits to the sick man presented a scene not unlike the picture on the title page of the old edition of Galen. The doctor was perhaps the most agitated of the little group. He took his seat by the bedside and held the patient's pulse. As Euthymia entered it fluttered for an instant as if with a faint memory of its old habit, then throbbed full and strong. Euthymia's task was a delicate one but she knew how to disguise its difficulty.

"Here is a flower I have brought you, Mr. Kirkwood," she said, and handed him a white chrysanthemum. He took it and before she knew it he took her hand into his own. It was with him as with the dying whose eyes may light up but rarely shed a tear.

The river which has found a new channel widens and deepens it; it lets the old water course fill up and never returns to its forsaken bed. The ill which a fair woman had wrought a fairer woman had abolished.

"You must come every day," the doctor said.

One day she found Maurice beginning to walk about the room. She was startled. She had thought of herself as a kind of nurse but the young man could hardly be said to need nurses any longer.

The change which had taken place in the vital currents of Maurice's system was as solid a fact as the change in a magnetic needle when the boreal becomes the austral pole. It was well, perhaps, that this change took place while he was enfeebled by the wasting effects of long illness.*

---

* Years before the introduction of fever therapy in the treatment of mental disorders through malaria or artificially induced heat,

"You look so much better today, Mr. Kirkwood," she said. "that I think I had better not play Sister of Charity any longer. The next time I hope you will call on me."

Presently Maurice spoke:

"No, you must never leave me. To you I owe it that I am living and with you I live henceforth, if I am to live at all."

The further course of the story is told in two letters from which we may quote briefly. The first is from Lurida to her friend Euthymia, now Mrs. Maurice Kirkwood, on a honeymoon trip abroad.

My dearest Euthymia,

You have told me all about yourself and your happiness and now I want to tell you about myself and what is going on in our little place. I have given up the idea of becoming a doctor. I have studied mathematics so much that I have grown fond of certainties and medicine deals chiefly in probabilities. I want knowledge pure and simple.—I do not fancy having it mixed.

---

it had been noticed that many abnormal mental conditions were temporarily improved during or after the fever accompanying a severe general infection such as pneumonia or erysipelas.

The exact mechanisms responsible for the mental and emotional improvement which follows infective fevers, high temperatures artificially induced in the body by electric heat, or modern shock therapy which produces convulsions, have not been definitely determined. Possibly the improvement is due to the fact that the patient has been exposed to an actual threat of death and that in face of this threat he abandons mental symptoms which protected him from other, inner, threats and challenges. However, most observers today agree, as Holmes intimated, that patients seem more acutely sensitive to impressions received immediately after a fever or a shock. Thus most psychotherapists now recommend that, for permanent results, the convulsive shock treatments should be followed by intensive psychotherapy, particularly in the case of persons with schizoid or neurotic tendencies.

I don't say that I wouldn't marry a physician—I could teach him a good deal about headaches and backaches and all sorts of nervous revolutions as Dr. Butts says the French women call their tantrums. On the whole I don't think I want to be married at all. I don't like the male animal very well. They are all tyrants,—almost all,—so far as our sex is concerned and I often think we could get on better without men.*

You want to know all about dear Dr. Butts. They say he has just been offered a professorship in one of the great medical colleges. I told him he ought to stay in Arrowhead Village. There are plenty of men that can get into a Professor's chair and talk like Solomons to a class of wondering pupils: but once get a really good doctor in a place, a man who knows all about

---

* In the two preceding stories we have called attention to Holmes's appreciation of the role of homosexuality in the formation of character traits. (See notes page 42 and 84.) In the relationship between Lurida and Euthymia he comes definitely into the open in revealing his acquaintance with the inversion—quite a daring thing, especially in New England at a time when the discussion of sex was a forbidden topic. Necessarily he felt the need to veil his allusions to Lurida's perverse tendencies which quite exceeded the common school-girl crush.

At a previous point in the story Lurida had remarked to Euthymia, " 'It is a shame that you will not let your exquisitely molded form be portrayed in marble,' . . . She [Lurida] was startled to see what an effect her proposal had produced, for Euthymia was not only blushing but there was a flame in her eyes which she had hardly ever seen before.' " Dr. James C. Wood [11] commenting on this passage says, "Few modern authors have so delicately and subtly referred to an age old perversion." Even today mention of the homosexual impulse is usually considered quite improper, so that the book *The Well of Loneliness* and the moving picture *Girls in Uniform* were considered something of a sensation when they appeared about 1930.

everybody, whether they have this tendency or that tendency—such a man as that, I say, is not to be replaced like a missing piece of a Springfield musket or a Waltham watch. Well, Dr. Butts is not going to leave us. . . .

Always your love,
Lurida.

The second letter, from Dr. Butts to his wife, was written after the Kirkwoods' return from Europe and some time after the birth of their son.

MY BELOVED WIFE,—

This letter will tell you much news.

Lurida Vincent is engaged to a clergyman with a mathematical turn. The story is that he put a difficult problem into a mathematical journal and Lurida presented such a neat solution that the young man fell in love with her on the strength of it.

Summer visitors have arrived and Euthymia and her husband gave a grand party the other evening. Now comes the chief event of that evening. I went early by special invitation and Maurice took me into his library.

"I have something of great importance," he said, "to say to you. My cousin Laura is staying with a friend in the next town to this. You know that we have never met since the almost fatal experience of my early years but I have determined to defy the strength of that deadly chain of associations and have begged her to come this evening. I wish you to be present.

"There is another reason why I wish you to be here. My boy is not far from the age at which I received my disorganizing shock. I mean to have little Maurice brought into the presence of Laura and see if he betrays any peculiar sensitiveness. It seemed to me not impossible that he might inherit some tendency and I wanted you to be at hand if any sign of danger should declare itself. For myself I have no fear. I have been born again in my susceptibilities and am in certain respects a new man."

Imagine with what interest I looked forward to this experiment.

"My cousin Laura," whispered Maurice to me, and went forward to meet her—one of those women so thoroughly constituted that they cannot help being handsome at every period of life. Both looked pale at first but Maurice soon recovered his usual color.

The child was brought down in his night clothes, wide awake, wondering apparently at the noise.

"See if he will go to that lady," said his father. Both of us held our breath as Laura stretched her arms. The child looked for an instant searchingly, but fearlessly, at her welcoming smile and met her embrace as if he had known her all his days.

The mortal antipathy had died out of the soul and the blood of Maurice Kirkwood.

Comments

As has been indicated in the introductory remarks (see p. 200), Holmes expected that *A Mortal Antipathy* would appear preposterous to most people, physicians included. But, in fact, while it received very little approval, it did not evoke the type of criticism he anticipated. In a letter to Mr. Alexander Ireland, dated April 5, 1886, Holmes wrote: "I was a little afraid that it would be scouted as altogether beyond the bounds of credibility: and so I shored it up with scientific evidence of one kind and another. Oddly enough whatever fault has been found with it not one of its critics has accused it of improbability."

As a rule neuroses do not disappear spontaneously, but it is possible for long-standing compulsions, phobias, and disturbing character traits to be greatly improved or permanently cured as a result of psychiatric treatment. Often, the parents of a neurotic child hope that the mere passing of time will of itself remove the child's pathological fears and outbursts—as, indeed, is sometimes the case. Many adult patients cherish a similar hope that even a well-formed neurosis of long duration will vanish completely; this is particularly true if and when favorable external conditions temporarily alleviate the tantalizing compulsions and terrifying fears. The patient uses this complacent, if wistful, attitude to shield his sensitivity concerning the abnormality; at all costs, he must protect his secret illness from exposure. The attempt at concealment arises because he somehow recognizes that his difficulties are connected with a sense of guilt and personal responsibility. The parents of the child, or the adult patient, of this type are apt to postpone seeking psychiatric advice until some really incapacitating, threatening, or otherwise alarming situation has developed.

In the psychoanalysis of a neurotic phobia of the kind here presented, the infantile trauma held responsible for Kirkwood's antipathy would surely be accredited an important causative role, but it would not be held solely accountable for the existence or the persistence of the phobia. Great attention would be paid to the force of repression—in this case, perhaps, Kirkwood's repressed hostility against his father because of the son's inability to free himself from dependency upon the father. Weight would also be given to the absence of the continuing influence of mother love. This might possibly have produced an overattachment to the father which the patient began to resent as he grew older. All these factors combined might well prevent a young man from achieving a satisfactory growth to normal relations with women.

Practically every person afflicted with a mental disorder is disturbed with regard to its direct transmissibility to his offspring. The ending of this story would be in accord with the best present-day knowledge concerning the inheritance of neuroses. A neurosis is regarded as a compromise reaction between the demands of the ego, continuously reinforced by primitive drives, and the ideals established for that ego. The ideals—Freud's superego—are environmental and cultural, and, therefore vary enormously not only in different families and communities but at different periods in the lifetime of a single individual.

The strength of primitive urges may be hereditary, but we do not know this definitely. Likewise, there may be an innate predisposition to anxieties; and there may be a tendency to react too submissively to restrictions imposed by the national culture and also, apparently, to standards of living prescribed by the immediate social group. Nevertheless, a full-fledged neurosis, as such, cannot be inherited. There may not even be a real predisposition in this direction; but, obviously, a child watching for patterns by which he can meet external situations may adopt compromise reactions if he is taught them from day to day by persons responsible for his upbringing and whom he unconsciously imitates and by whom he may be punished for nonconformity.

It is an old, old formula which Holmes has invoked for the relief of the emotional difficulties of two principal characters, Myrtle Hazard and Maurice Kirkwood—namely, success in falling in love. Contrariwise, the failure of young Langdon to respond to the love offered by the sensitive, groping Elsie Venner is made responsible for her death.

In this respect Holmes's conceptions are quite in harmony with the aims of psychoanalytic therapy. This attempts to investigate the misdirection or stagnation of primary instinctive drives, of early but strong unconscious fixations on specific love objects, of crippling, unconscious inhibitions fostered by early admonitions. And it does so by means of a procedure based upon scientific principles. It employs this method in the effort to set the individual free from inhibitory influence and to permit him to progress to full emotional maturity, and to experience mature love for a person of the opposite sex. Here again the philosophy and therapy of Holmes and Freud meet at a common point, for the latter has also said: "We must . . . love in order that we may not fall ill, and must fall ill if in consequence of frustration we cannot love." [12]

When a child has been starved for love he may react in several ways, two of which are quite common. He may become shy, uncommunicative, sullen, and unsocial, or he may go through life always seeking for some genuine manifestation of the love which he has missed. Thus, a patient, aged forty-eight, married, the father of three children, who came under treatment for severe gastrointestinal disturbances, related the following circumstance. From earliest childhood he felt that both his parents had discriminated against him in favor of an older, more aggressive, demanding, and attractive brother. At the age of forty-one, when his mother was on her deathbed, she mentioned that there had been four men in her life—her father, her husband, her brother, and the patient, whom she mentioned by name. She omitted the name of the older brother whom he hated and feared. At once the patient had felt an intense relief; here was a sign for which he had been looking since childhood, namely, that he was loved not merely as much as, but more than, his brother. At the time of the interview he was living in the hope that his very old father would say on his deathbed that he, too, had always loved this son better than the brother.

The value of giving love and the need for receiving it is the essence of that gentle philosophy which for nearly two thousand years has been the guide for the Christian faith: "Love thy neighbor as thyself." Equally clear was this precept to the exceptionally sensitive, half-mad Coleridge, the sublime somnambulist, who wrote much of his best poetry from the lucid depths of states bordering on the unconscious:

> He prayeth best who loveth best
> All things both great and small.

The story of psychiatry, however, is only amplified by such clear flashes from the mentally disturbed genius, from the loves and despondencies, the hates and despairs of the Poes, the Coleridges, the de Maupassants, the Van Goghs, or from the bitterness of the Nietzsches.[13] Psychiatry has learned much through the appreciation and exposition, by rare men like these, of what happens in the profundity of the minds of all men. But psychiatry does not take its cues only from exceptional minds in its search for the motivations, the meanings, and the truths which are common to all of us and which may help us comprehend the extreme mental deviations.

So much concerning psychiatry has appeared of late in popular and semiscientific literature, in the drama and in motion pictures, that many people have been led to infer that psychiatric treatment may be expected to perform miracles. In most psychiatric conditions, however, such quick cures are the exception. Even with the best methods administered by the most skilled physicians, treatment is apt to be a long process.

The compromise reactions which take the form of neurotic thoughts or acts are the result of long-standing and incompatible strivings, often unconscious, between what we are and what we would like nobly to be; what we have and would greedily like to possess; what we do and how we would ideally like to act. These conflicts may appear in myriad guises. They occur many times during the day in any person who is subject to the impositions laid on him by the culture of which he is a part or the one to which he is at the time exposed. They become neurotic only when the individual vacillates so continuously that he can make no decision, or becomes so obsessed with the impulse to repeat over and over again apparently purposeless acts or thoughts that he cannot pursue his work effectively. In actuality these devices represent a compromise protecting him from desires he feels he should not have and at the same time permitting him to indulge in something forbidden which he unconsciously desires.

In 1910, when Jung felt he could no longer support Freud's theory of the role played by the instinctual sex urges in causing neuroses, he postulated a clash between the individual's realistic strivings and a collective unconscious existent in us all. From that time up to the very present, many psychiatrists have attempted to place the origin of these clashes at various levels of consciousness. In each instance the physician has relied essentially upon Freud's fundamental concepts and procedures. Generally it is a matter of emphasis on or denial of one aspect or another of the elemental drives of hunger or sex, or on conflicts attributed to varied cultural developments. However, there are very few ideals in any culture which do not involve the abnegation or at least the attenuation of lusts of various kinds, and the evaluation and redirection of such drives become essential to the readaptation of individuals suffering from frustrations brought about by the suppressions demanded in group living.

In making the readaptation, confidence in the physician is an important factor, and I would again refer to the phenomenon of transference already frequently mentioned in the notes. It exists in every doctor-patient relationship—at times to such a degree that the same pills given by Dr. A. and by Dr. B. to the same patient for the same ailment will be effective in the case of Dr. A. and fail with Dr. B. This element which we may call faith is observed with especial frequency in neurotic patients. The physician should understand the nature of the patient's trust in him, or lack of it (the so-called transference situation), which psychoanalysts have studied exhaustively. Great caution and skill are needed in handling the emotional response with which the floundering patient invests his physician. In psychiatric treatment, dependency is permitted, at times even encouraged, in the hope that after temporary support the patient will liberate himself from his need and develop the capacity to become substantially independent of artificial aid. In some patients the reassurance does not come from an active emotional attachment to the physician (an attachment which is closely akin to love) but from a shallow, demanding dependence such as a child exhibits toward its parents.

The specific time at which the patient is made to realize the meaning of the loves and hates which he finds reflected in the physician is extremely important in effecting rehabilitation. If realization comes too abruptly—that is, before the patient is quite ready to receive it—his uncertainty, his vacillations, and his panic may only be increased and may cause him to cling the more frantically to his pillar of safety.

"Never lie to an insane man, Doctor, he knows when you are not telling the truth," a wildly excited patient struggling in a continuous, sedative, tepid bath once said to me. It is a warning which every doctor of the mentally ill might well take to heart. So it is that, from the habits, mannerisms, and utterings, the demands and the refusals, the silences and the protestations of all people, even the lowliest in the mental scale, as well as those of the desperately sick with manias or distressingly split in their thoughts (schizophrenia) that psychiatry seeks to understand the conduct of the mentally ill and to heal their sickness. Furthermore, the study of such intensely disordered minds has thrown much light upon the habits and foibles, the prejudices and strivings of people whom we regard as normal. The understanding thus gained should in turn lead to a recognition of causes and to a greater tolerance and forbearance for character weaknesses now regarded as criminal, and to a hope for improving the relationship of each to all. Holmes was among the first American physicians to plead for greater latitude in criminal procedures. He drew many parallels between abnormal conduct arising from the functional incapacities caused by injury to the skull and abnormal conduct arising from the unseen scars caused by a psychic trauma. Rose Alexander [14] has called my attention to an article in which she notes that, in the Venner family, insanity appears in one member, Elsie, and criminality in another, her cousin Richard.

The most recent of these man-created threats is the atomic bomb with its realistic menace of world destruction. This has again emphasized the necessity for man's understanding of himself and his motives so that in the end he may not totally destroy himself.

Perhaps from the descriptions of mentally distraught figures such as Holmes has presented in these novels, and from the interpretations and light which the work of psychiatrists from Pinel to Freud have cast on human vagaries, the reader will have gathered that mental disorders are particularly important for their sociological effect upon the individual and the whole community. It seems not unlikely that in the near future a family psychiatrist may take the place of the fast-vanishing family physician to act as a counsellor and guide in the problems of education and social adaptation which inevitably arise within the family unit.

One of the great achievements of American psychiatrists is that they were among the first to diminish the emphasis on the diagnosis of mental diseases. The label which is placed on the patient is often of little matter, especially to him. Psychiatry today centers its interest more intensely on the care and restoration of the mentally ill person and on the social implications of psychiatric discoveries as they affect family relations, criminology, penology, pedagogy, and communal health. Psychiatrists, particularly in the United States, have carried this knowledge surely and swiftly into the practical aspects of interpersonal relationships as they appear in the home, the school, the courts, and in the general hospitals, especially the out-patient clinics, where opportunities for service appear almost limitless. For psychiatric principles may be applied to an endless variety of social situations, in health as in disease, whenever the latter affects either the body or the mind or, as is so often the case, disturbs both.

It is hoped that the reader has also inferred that, in addition to this humane comprehension of man's frailties, effective scientific methods have been developed for the cure of psychiatric illness. Psychoanalysis is only one of these methods, but it has been mentioned so frequently in these notes because it is particularly adapted to the interpretation and treatment of the type of disorders presented nearly one hundred years ago by Holmes.

Along with or supplementary to many other psychiatric methods —reëducation, persuasion, suggestion, occupational therapy, convulsive shock therapy, and so on—psychoanalysis is used to treat the specific mental disorders of the individual. But aside from the cure of patients, the psychiatric approach offers real hope for the prevention and amelioration of many of the cultural woes which society has made for itself.

BIBLIOGRAPHICAL REFERENCES

Introduction

1. O. W. Holmes, *Medical Essays, 1842–1882* (Boston: Houghton Mifflin, 1892).
2. E. Warren, *Some Account of the Letheon* (Boston: Dutton and Wentworth, 1847).
3. E. F. Dakin, *Mrs. Eddy* (New York: Scribner, 1929), p. 58.
4. P. R. Lehrman, "Freud's Contribution to Science," *Hebrew Medical Journal*, I (1940), p. 176.
5. Boston: Houghton Mifflin, 1892; Chapter VIII.
6. New York: Dutton, 1937.
7. J. Breuer and S. Freud, *Studies in Hysteria* (New York: Nervous and Mental Disease Publishing Co., 1936).
8. Holmes, *Pages from an Old Volume of Life.*
9. *Ibid.*

Elsie Venner

1. Sandor Rado, "Natural Science in the Light of Psychoanalysis," *Psychoanalytic Quarterly*, I (1932), 700.
2. Phyllis Greenacre, "Predisposition to Anxiety," *Psychoanalytic Quarterly*, X (1941), p. 93.
3. Burton Hendrick, *Bulwark of the Republic* (Boston: Little, Brown & Co., 1937, p. 426.
4. Francis Biddle, *Mr. Justice Holmes* (New York: Scribner, 1942).
5. S. Freud, *Neue Folge der Vorlesungen* (*Gesamt-ausgabe*, Vol. XII), p. 182.
6. J. B. Rhine and others, *Extra-sensory Perception* (New York: Holt, 1940).
7. John T. Morse, Jr., *Life and Letters of Oliver Wendell Holmes* (Boston: Houghton Mifflin, 1896), I, 259–62.
8. From W. Hertz, *Der Werwolf* (1862), p. 73. Quoted by Ernest

Jones, *Nightmare, Witches, and Devils* (New York: Norton, 1931), p. 141.
9. C. P. Oberndorf, "Sublimation in Occupational Therapy," *Occupational Therapy and Rehabilitation*, XI, No. 3, November, 1932.
10. C. P. Oberndorf, "Co-conscious Mentation," *Psychoanalytic Quarterly*, X, January, 1941.
11. A. A. Brill, "The Concept of Psychic Suicide," *International Journal of Psychoanalysis*, XX (1939).

The Guardian Angel

1. Leland E. Hinsie, *The Psychiatric Dictionary* (New York: Oxford University Press, 1940), p. 105.
2. Smiley Blanton and Norman V. Peale, *Faith Is the Answer* (New York: Abingdon-Cokesbury Press, 1940).
3. C. P. Oberndorf, "Reaction to Personal Names," *Psychoanalytic Review*, V (1918), No. 1.
4. Frederick H. Allen, *Psychotherapy with Children* (New York: Norton, 1943), p. 305.
5. W. S. Kennedy, *Oliver Wendell Holmes* (Boston: Cassino, 1883), p. 175.
6. Richardson Wright, *Forgotten Ladies* (Philadelphia: Lippincott, 1928), p. 94.
7. C. P. Oberndorf, "Depersonalization in Relation to Erotization of Thought," *International Journal of Psychoanalysis*, XV, Parts II and III, April–July, 1934.
8. A. A. Brill, "Alcohol and the Individual," *New York Medical Journal*, May 6, 1919.

A Mortal Antipathy

1. John T. Morse, *Life and Letters of Oliver Wendell Holmes*, p. 266.
2. S. Freud, *Collected Papers* (London: Institute of Psychoanalysis, 1924–25), Vol. I.

3. Otto Sperling, "Appersonation and Eccentricity," *International Journal of Psychoanalysis*, XVIII (1937), p. 90.
4. C. P. Oberndorf, "The Psychogenic Factors in Asthma," *New York State Journal of Medicine*, XXXV, No. 2, Jan. 15, 1935.
5. S. Freud, *Civilization and Its Discontents* (New York: Cape and Smith, 1921). Translated by Joan Riviere.
6. Otto Rank, *The Trauma of Birth* (New York: Harcourt, Brace, 1929).
7. C. P. Oberndorf, "Depersonalization in Relation to Erotization of Thought," *International Journal of Psychoanalysis*, XV, Parts II and III, April- July, 1934.
8. Helen E. Marshall, *Dorothea Dix* (Chapel Hill: University of North Carolina Press, 1937), p. 158.
9. M. B. Stern, *The Life of Margaret Fuller* (New York: Viking Press, 1942), p. 15.
10. A. Kardiner, "The Bio-analysis of the Epileptic Reaction," *Psychoanalytic Quarterly*, I (1932), pp. 478–79.
11. James C. Wood, "In Retrospection," *Bulletin of the Academy of Medicine of Cleveland*, December, 1943.
12. S. Freud, *Collected Papers* (London: Institute of Psychoanalsis, 1924–25), IV, 42.
13. Karl Menninger, *Love and Hate* (New York: Harcourt, Brace, 1942).
14. "Oliver Wendell Holmes—Psychiatrist," *New York Medical Record*, October, 1939.

INDEX TO INTRODUCTION AND NOTES

Abolition, Holmes and, 29
Abolitionists, vicarious self-liberation, 7
Acting, as release, 186
Adolescence, 138, 148 f.
Affect, 15; release through verbal catharsis, 82 f.; release of in analysis, 165
Agoraphobia, case of, 139
Alcoholism, as escape, 174
Allen, Frederick H., 128, 260
Allergies, 207 f.
Ambivalence, 75, 78
Amnesia, following shock, 184 f.
"Analysis of an Infantile Neurosis" (Freud), 217
Anesthesia, 3
Antipathy, 104
Anxiety, 73 ff.; Freud's view of, 22
Appersonation, 205 ff.
Association of ideas, 8; Holmes's understanding of the mechanism of, 10 f.
Asylums, 41 f.
Authority, dependence upon, 177 f., 247

Berger, Hans, 218
Bergson, Henri, 121
Berthelot, Marcelin, 9
Biddle, Francis, 259
Birth fantasy, 250; see also Rebirth
Birth trauma, 21 f., 214
Bisexuality, 17, 42, 222; see also masculine and feminine traits
Blanton, Smiley, and Norman V. Peale, 260
Blushing, 87
Body, overinvestment of emotion in chronic illness, 168 f.
Body and mind, conversion symptoms, 93 f.; interrelationship, 234
Borderline states, 90, 130
Braid, James, 4
Brain wave, 218

Breuer, Joseph, 8, 161 f.
Brill, A. A., 111, 174, 260
Brooks, Van Wyck, on Holmes's "Mechanism in Thought and Morals," 7
Bucknill, J. C., 218
Byrd, William, code diary, 240

Calvinism, Holmes vs. repressive influence of, 4-5, 18, 30, 153; demoniacal obsession in, 157 f.
Cardiovascular control, in autohypnosis, 245 f.
Catatonia, 95; refusal of food in, 100 f.
Catharsis, verbal, therapeutic use of, 82 f.; mental, 162
Censor, role of, 8
Charcot, Jean-Martin, 3, 17
Children, delinquent, and neglect, 71 f.
Children, emotional effect of disrupted homes, 34; conscience in, 47; rejected, 75; discipline, 126 ff.; phobias in, 232 f.
Christian Science, 4, 114 f.
Chronic illness, overinvestment of body with emotion in, 168 f.
Clairvoyance, 34 f.
Clergyman, 120; in the novels, Holmes's father the prototype for, 30
Common sense, 195
Complex, "hidden," 65 f.
Compulsion neuroses, 242; guilt as symptom in, 163; washing, 215
Confessional writings, 240
Conscience, 47 f.
Conscription, for the armed forces, 192
Conversion symptom, 93 f.
Coolidge, Calvin, 190
Counter-transference, 160, 162 f.; see also Transference

Crime, definitions of responsibility for, 64; Holmes *re*, 263

Dana, C. L., 221, 237
Danger, 73 f.
Death, grief vs. depression in bereavement by, 78; wish for, 111
Death threat, in shock therapy, 226, 254
Dementia precox, 70, 90; catatonia in, 95; first description of, 149; terror and, 209
Demoniacal obsession, 157 f.
Dependence, infantile, desire to retain, 66 f.; on authority, 177 f., conflict caused by, 247
Depersonalization, 146 f.; in clash of masculine and feminine traits, 217
Depravity, total, Holmes vs. idea of, 20
Determinism, in Holmes's novels, 17 f.
Determinism, psychic, *see* Psychic determinism
Discipline, 126 ff.
Disease, modern triumphs over, 226
Displacement, 181
Dissociation, 25, 117
Dix, Dorothea, 218 f.
"Double consciousness," 85 f., 116 f.
"Dream and Occultism" (Freud), 35
Dreams, and unconscious thought, 8; problems solved in, 11; Holmes on, 11-12; meaning of, in a case of chronic anxiety, 73 ff.; interpretation of, 224 f.

Eddy, Mary Baker, 4, 259
Ego, 153; enlarged in appersonation, 206 f.
Elan vital, 121
Elliottson, John, 159
Elsie Venner, 20-111; critical reception, 14; love affect in, 15; prenatal influence, 16; introductory comment, 20-23; type of mental disorder, 23; homosexual components, 42; conclusions, 109-11
Emmanuel Movement, 116
Emotions, repression of, 8, 52 f.; repressed, release through catharsis,

82 f., 162; overinvestment of body with, 168 f.
Emperor Jones (O'Neill), 113
Epileptoid reactions, 236
Extrasensory perception, 35

Faith cure, 4; and belief in the miraculous, 114; use of medallions in, 237
Faith Is the Answer (Blanton and Peale), 116
Family, quarreling and sibling rivalry, 44; discipline, 127; attitude toward analysis of a member, 165 f.; homosexuality in parent-child relationship, 170; murder impulse, 172 f.
Fear, morbid, theme of *A Mortal Antipathy*, 17, 200, 202, 204; death from, 209
Feeblemindedness, 90
Ferenczi, Sandor, work on hypnosis, 159
Fever therapy, 253 f.
Fitz, Reginald, 194
Food, refusal of, 100 f., 110 f.; idiosyncrasies, 207 f.
Freud, Sigmund, 259; student at Salpêtrière, 4; and Holmes, parallelisms between, 6-13; use of term "unconscious," 8; re indestructibility of infantile thought and impressions, 8, 208; hostility of physicians toward, 13; first lectures in America, 18 f.; re telepathy, 35; and Mesmer, 60 f.; re masculine and feminine traits, 77; libido, 121; superego, 135; id, 153, 187; work on hysteria, 161 f.; on reanalysis of analysts, 163; three categories of the mind, 187; on neuroses, 202, 217; on "Oceanic feeling," 211
"Frozen mind," 95, 109 ff.
Fuller, Margaret, 222 f.

Gall, François, 60
General practitioner, *see* Physician
Germans, 26; dependence on authority, 66
Girls, adolescence, 138
Greenacre, Phyllis, on anxiety, 22, 259
Grief, vs. melancholia, 78
Guardian Angel, The, 112-99; heredi-

tary influences, 16 f.; theme, 112 f., 197 ff.; infantile shock in, 131; homosexual parent-child relationship, 170; *Guardian* dream symbolism, 180

Guilt, feeling of, 130; Holmes re, 8 f.; religious conflict and, 93; in compulsion neurosis, 163

Hall, Stanley, 18
Hallucinations, 149
Harvard Dental School, 2
Hawthorne, Nathaniel, *The House of the Seven Gables*, 18
Hendrick, Burton, on Chief Justice Holmes, 29, 259
Heredity, and personal responsibility, 16 f., 20; and determinism of mental illness, 22 f.; multiple personality and, 112 ff.; ancestral influences, 113
Hertz, W., 58, 259
"Hidden" complex, 65 f.
Hinsie, Leland E., 260
Hitler, unconscious identification with, 25
Holmes, Abiel, 4-5; in Holmes's novels, 30
Holmes, Oliver Wendell, background, 1, 4-5; professional career, 1 ff.; "On the Contagiousness of Puerperal Fever," 2, 194; vs. Calvinism, 4-5, 18, 30, 153; talents and character, 6; poetry, 6; and Freud, parallelisms between, 6-13; "Mechanism in Thought and Morals," 7 ff., 13; use of word "unconscious," 8; as a clinical psychiatrist, 13-19; as novelist: 13 ff., the doctors in his novels, 14 f., similarities in characters and plots, 15 ff., determinism the common theme, 17 f., names of characters, 123; reception of his theories, 19; a New England "Brahmin," 20, 29; ahead of his time, 194; incident of the hall clock, 200; use of deductive method, 215; plea for study of neuroses, 217; references to vital differences between the sexes, 222; on Margaret Fuller, 223; use of love as cure, 257 f.

Holmes, Oliver Wendell (Chief Justice), 29; and his father, 29 f.
Homosexuality, 42; in *Elsie Venner*, 84; in *The Guardian Angel*, 84 f.; obsessive, as compulsion neurosis, 90; unconscious, and depersonalization, 146 f.; parental-filial, 170; projected, unconscious, 217
Hospital, lack of provision for spiritual needs, 108
Hostility, family, 44; of the world toward man, theory of, 121; punishment, and formation of, 130; unconscious: in bereavement, 78, and allergies, 207 f.; repressed, in *A Mortal Antipathy*, 256 f.
Hypnosis, 3 f., 17, 60 f.; treatment by, 159 ff., 185, 245
Hysteria, 259; in *A Mortal Antipathy*, 17; hypnotic treatment of, 159 f.; work of Breuer and Freud, 161 f.

Id, stage of primitive impulses, 153, 187
Identification, 25 f., 84, 125, 138, 147; in treatment by hypnosis, 159; in stage roles, 186; in interrelationship of mind and body, 234 f.
Illness, as punishment, 114 f., 163; chronic: overinvestment of body with emotion in, 168 f.
Impulse, uncontrollable, 228
Incest, 77; *see also* Oedipus complex
Indulgence to excess, as escape, 174
Infantile impressions, indestructibility of, 8, 21, 131, 208; phobias caused by, 201 f., 208; in *A Mortal Antipathy*, 256 f.; *see also* Primal scene
Inferiority, constitutional psychopathic, in borderline states, 90
Insanity, defensive role of, 139
Interpretation of Dreams (Freud), 22
Isolation, patient and family, in mental disorders, 37; of rejected children, 75

James, William, 19; use of term "unconscious cerebration," 8
Jones, Ernest, on Werewolves, 58 f., 259

Jung, Carl, collective unconscious, 113, 125
Juvenile delinquency, 71 f.

Kardiner, Abram, 236, 261
Kennedy, W. S., 260
Kraepelin, Emil, 70, 149

Lake, symbolism of, 212 f.
Language, expression of mental and physical counterparts, 93; as symbol of thought, 190
Lehrman, P. R., 259
Letheon, 3, 259
Libido, 121
Lourdes, 115
Love, element in the novels, 15 f.; need for giving and receiving, 44, 98, 109 ff., 160 f.; excessive, of child for parent, and conscience, 47; "frozen mind" caused by denial of, 109 ff.; success in, as cure for emotional disorders, 257 f.

Maeder, Alphonse, 225
Manhattan State Hospital, 65 f.
Manic-depressive psychosis, 70, 90; terror in, 209
Manual of Psychological Medicine (Tuke and Bucknill), 218
Marital relations, disparity in aging as cause of unhappiness in, 168
Marshall, Helen E., 261
Masculine and feminine traits, 77, 216 f.; inheritance of, 113, 144; Holmes re, 222
Masturbation, 98; and sense of guilt, 171 f.
Mather, Cotton, 173
Melancholia, 70, 78; conscience and, 48
Menninger, Karl, 261
Mental disorders, heredity and, 22 f.; modern treatment of, 41 f.; need for medically regulated public residence, 42; early treatment, 60 f., 218 f.; borderline states, 90; defensive role of, 139; old theory of demoniacal obsession, 157 f.; fever therapy, 253 f.; popular ideas re inheritance of, 256; see also De-

mentia precox; Manic-depressive psychosis
Mesmer, Franz Anton, 3-4, 60 f.
Mind, Freud's categories of, 187
Mind and body, *see* Body and mind
Miracle, need for belief in, 114
Mitchell, S. Weir, 54; rest cure, 156
Morse, John T., Jr., 200 f., 259, 260
Mortal Antipathy, A., 200-261; theme, 17 f.; study of compulsion type of fear, 17, 200, 202, 204; introductory comment, 200-202; primal scene, 131 f., 229 f.; rebirth symbolism, 238, 250; shock therapy, 240
Morton, William T. G., 3
Multiple personality, 8, 112 f., 116-17, 144 f., 198
Murder, unconscious impulse toward, 73 ff.; impulse in suicide, 172 f.

Name, personal, effect of, 123
Nazarene Movement, 116
Neuroses, solution of, 199; Freud's theory of, 202, 208, 217; scientific study of, 242; course of, 256
——compulsion, 163, 215, 242
New England, cultural background, 3, 18, 20, 29, 135; suicide in, 173
New Thought Movement, 116

Oberndorf, C. P., "Co-conscious Mentation," 260; "Depersonalization in Relation to Erotization of Thought," 260, 261; "The Psychogenic Factors in Asthma," 261; "Reaction to Personal Names," 260; "Sublimation in Occupational Therapy," 260
Obsession, demoniacal, 157 f.
Obsessional neuroses, *see* Compulsion neuroses
Occupational therapy, 82
Ocean, symbolism of, 211
Oedipus Complex, 30, 186
O'Neill, Eugene, *Emperor Jones*, 113
"On Mechanism in Thought and Morals," (Holmes), 7 ff., 13, 194
"On the Contagiousness of Puerperal Fever" (Holmes), 2, 194

Orphan, 112; psychic handicaps, 22
Overcompensation, 181

Patient, individual needs of, in treatment, 102; spiritual needs, 108; the "will to get well," 111; idea of illness as result of sin, 114 f., 163; illness as means to a desired goal, 139; relation with physician, 160 ff.
Peale, Norman V., 260
Pepys, Samuel, 240
Personality, integration of, 125; disintegrated, unconscious forces and, 130; Freud's study of, 153; see also Multiple personality
Phantom guardian, 112, 133, 135
Phobia, in A Mortal Antipathy, 200 ff.; in children, 232 f.
Physician, need for "intuitive" gifts, 5 f.; in the novels, 14 f., 52 f.; the small-town general practitioner, 36 f., 40; as psychiatrist, 55
Pinel, Philippe, 218
Poe, Edgar Allan, 74 f.
Prenatal influences, re snake venom in Elsie Venner, 21 f.
Primal scene, 21, 201 f., 229 f.
Primitive impulses, 187
Prince, Morton, 19
Private schools, 34
Psychiatrists, and literature, 221; American, 258; see also Patient; Psychiatry; Transference
Psychiatry, in Holme's time, 5-6; release of repressed emotions, 52 f.; need for women physicians, 138; function and method of, 257 f.
Psychic determinism, 20 ff.
"Psychic dualism," 86
Psychic phenomena, 34 f.
Psychic trauma, eleptoid reactions in, 236
Psychoanalysis, important pillars of, noted by Holmes, 8 ff.; study of individual patients' needs in treatment by, 102 f.; for personality and character defects, 130; problem of transference in, 163, 165; timing of suggestions in, 170, 177 f., 198;

use of the unconscious to interpret patient to himself, 180
Psycho-dramatics, 187
Puerperal fever, 2, 194
Punishment, unconscious force of forgotten incidents in, 130
Putnam, James Jackson, introduces Freud to America, 18

Quakers, 68 f.
Quimby, Phineas, 4, 115, 159

Rado, Sandor, 259
Rage, 181
Rank, Otto, 22; re birth trauma, 214, 261
Rebirth, symbolism in A Mortal Antipathy, 238, 250; fantasy, in The Guardian Angel, 149, 151, 153
Rejection, emotional effect of, 75
Religion, guilt and, 93; healing powers of, 114 ff.; consolation in, 211; prohibitions sanctioned by, 197 f.
Religion and science, see Science and religion
Religious cults, emotional outlet via, 4
Repressed desires, in dreams, 224 f.
Repression, 83; effect on children, 114; of emotion, 8, 52 f.
Responsibility, desire to avoid, 66 f.
Rest cure, 156
Rhine, J. B., 35, 259
River, as symbol, 131, 212
Roman Catholic Church, Lourdes, 115
Rousseau, Jean Jacques, 60

Sampson, Deborah, 141, 144
Schizoid, voluntary isolation a symptom of, 37
Schizophrenia, see Dementia precox
Science and religion, conflict of, 114; and concept of demoniacal obsession, 157
Self-love, arising from love denied, 98
Self-Murder, 172
Semmelweis, Ignaz Philipp, 2
Sex, Holmes's avoidance of direct reference to, 42; drives, 261
Shock, and resultant amnesia, 184 f.
—— therapy, 201; as death threat,

Shock (*Continued*)
226, 254; in *A Mortal Antipathy*, 240
Sibling rivalry, 44
Sin, patient's idea of illness as result of, 114 f., 163
Snake, symbolism, 21 f., 54, 58
Snake venom, medical uses of, 59
Social adjustment, discipline as factor in, 127
Sperling, Otto, 261
Spiritualism, 34 f.
Stammering, 83
State, the, and the child, 128
Stern, M. B., 261
Sublimation, 183
Suicide, viewed as crime, 61; "psychic," 111; in *The Guardian Angel*, 131; among adolescents, 171; murder impulse in, 172 f.; in New England, 173; threat vs. performance, 242 f.
Superego, 153, 259; as "guardian angel," 135
"Suppressed desires," release of, through masquerade, 186 f.
Symptoms, protective function of, 139

Telepathy, 34 f.; Freud vs., 35
Theory and practice, contradiction between, 68 f.
Thought, and expression, 51; unconscious mentation, 61; co-conscious mentation, 86
Thought transference, 34 f.
Timing, of suggestions, importance of, 170, 177 f., 198
Totalitarianism, 127 f.
Transference, 115, 159 ff.; counter-transference, 160, 162 f.; problem of, in analysis, 160 ff., 163, 165
"Transference cures," 103, 115
Transvestitism, 144 f.
Traumatic neurosis, 202
Tuke, William, 218

"Unconscious cerebration," 8
Unconscious, Holmes's concept of, 8 ff.; and effects of punishment, 130; psychoanalytic means of interpreting patient to himself, 180; *see also* Association of ideas
Unconscious, vs. conscious, in dissociation, 25; collective, 113, 125; ancestral influences on, 113 f.
Unconscious forces, 130
Unconscious mentation, *see* Thought

Visions, 149
Voltaire, François M., 60

Washing, compulsion of sexual nature, 215
Water, symbolism of: 214 f., purification, 115, 215, birth, 140 f., rebirth, 151, 238, 250
Werewolf, 58 f.
Wharton, Edith, *Ethan Frome*, 18
Will, breaking the child's, 126 f.
Will, freedom of the, 8
Witchcraft, persecution for, 173
Woehler, Friedrich, 9
Women, masculine traits in, 77, 141, 142, 217, 222; psychiatrists, 138; fear of, 200, 202
Wright, Richardson, 260

York Retreat, 218

DATE DUE

GAYLORD   PRINTED IN U.S.A.